KINDLE EDITION

PUBLISHE
J. H. G. FOSS on A

'The Portal of Re
Copyright 2000 Jonathan H

NILLIMANDOR

PECHENGA

Pik Seduva

VEGAS
Nathro
Dixnar
Mirama
Malbro
OREBRO   IXNAY   Mu River   Goldhind
                                       Wastes
Axeblade Mountains   Claw Clan
                                       Lands
Kolopu   LEAD HILLS

LUXOR
JOPPA

JUGLIA

TOMSK
Duloma
Gnarlwold
STYKE   EASK   LODZ   NOROB
TIMU   Bedmarca   FOREST
                        TYNGZ

Plumlow
ENTTLAND
BELLAVIA   Glamis   VANT
TULLIS
                Werfret

LUNARIA

THE GREAT FOREST

TYRA
                FOONA
The Forest River LYSANDER   CHE

GIJON
            THE SAVAGE LANDS

ERTIA
(North   USAK
Nogland)
                                   FERRON

The Southern Nog
     Nations

FIARKA

The Portal of Returning

Book 1

Chapter One - The Beach

It began with a light. No. It began with a smell, a thought of a smell. A sleepy reminder of childish memories of the sea. A smell of salt, and sand, warmth and light. I was lying on warm sand, on a beach. My eyes were shut and I could remember nothing.
Who I was, and what I was, it had seemed to slip my mind. I must have been someone, I realised that, I wasn't born here, lying on the sand, but the memory was too dim, a life lived by another, as distant as a star reflected in a well. Maybe there had been a woman, a house, a job, all the things you would expect in a man. It felt of very little consequence.

My eyes opened, and then were dazzled shut. I rose, and slowly focused on a gently moving blue horizon. I looked around, and found myself, apparently lying on a beach on some bright tropical shore.
The sand was a brilliant white, the sea was a light azure blue. Looking up I saw an almost unbelievably blue sky, without a single cloud in it to mar its perfection. A large ripe sun threw down its warmth onto my shoulders. Behind me was a green wall of vegetation, its dark depths speaking of ancient vine covered temples. I looked down in bemusement at the warm sand that sifted through the toes of my bare feet.
I tried to recollect what I could have been doing to have arrived at such a place. Had I been at sea, and been shipwrecked? For all I knew, I had been plucked from my bed and deposited here by some unknown hand. As a wave of panic hit me, I considered the possibility that I was dreaming. I looked around, the sea, the sand, the dark green leaves of god knew what sort of plants, seemed to me almost too real in the warmth of the sunlight. The smell of the seaweed, the sensation of the breeze on my face, and the sound of the waves gently breaking on some distant unseen rocks, could not be confused with illusion. It was all too sharp and in focus, there was no doubt in my mind at all. A dream can be mistaken for reality, but reality can never be mistaken for a dream.
It dawned on me, that whatever had happened, I at least had no recollection of it. It embarrasses me now to think of the confused self-pity I felt for myself then, before I had any inkling of what fate had in store for me. I had no more idea of what to do than a new-born baby, but I do remember my first few actions involved running up and down as stark terror began to grip me, and an awful lot of screaming and yelling for help. It started with pacing up and down, putting my hands to my mouth or eyes, and muttering half incoherent sentences, trying to spring a memory from

my foggy mind. Like many people, when left all alone I will start talking to myself, and I found my mutterings getting louder and louder until all sense was drowned out by my fast developing fear.

There was only so much shouting I could sustain, however, a fact, which had nothing to do with my lack of desire to do so. As it began to grow dark, the fear I had been feeling began to grow, and as the sky grew redder, I still had no idea who I was or how I had got here.

The stars began to come out, and a large moon illuminated the beach, almost as if it were day. The magnificence of the sky drew my attention and at last I began to return to myself. The stars were incredible, a great heavenly display of light and wonder. I was sure I had never seen anything like it in my life, these strange constellations, alien to me, and yet speaking to me, a peaceful whisper.

My next thoughts were that surely I must have died, and that I was experiencing the afterlife. Contemplating this I drifted off to sleep.

I awoke, in the cool morning, and as my mind reconstructed and remembered, I leant towards more rational explanations. A shipwreck, of course. I noticed for the first time, that I was only wearing shorts and a white T-shirt. This added weight to the argument. Perhaps I had been on a holiday cruise ship, or on a private yacht? I must have amnesia, which prevented my recollecting anything about how I had come to be a castaway, I reasoned.

I paced out a stretch of the beach, as I tried to recall any memories of what had happened to me. I found that while my mind wandered, my feet decided their own direction, and when I had once again come to my senses, I guessed that I had walked along several miles of the brilliantly white sandy beach. I turned to look at the prints that I had left, as the gentle tide began to wash them away. I was lost in a deep reverie, I could have been anywhere, and I felt that these prints were those of another man. Surely it wasn't me, walking here and leaving temporary marks on this strange foreign shore? It was an overwhelming experience, not exactly panic, but almost as if I was adrift from my own body. I certainly didn't feel part of it any longer. I felt, for a moment, that I was drifting away completely, but suddenly my attention was grabbed by an object appearing around the jut of a rocky promontory. It was an ancient sailing vessel, like a galley or trireme, in full sail, and with oars rising up and down in the surf. In a moment I was shouting out as loudly as my raw throat would allow, and waving my hands to attract the attention of the craft. I saw dark figures move around the deck, and they seemed to study me, they did not appear to be in any great hurry to attempt a rescue. Presently a boat was lowered and two of the dark figures clambered into it and began to row towards the shore.

As they grew closer, I saw that one of them was rowing, and that the other was sat in the stern of the boat. They surely must be very tall men, I thought, at least seven feet each. They got closer still, and doubts began to enter my head. I could not see the rower's face, as he had his back to me, but the passenger seemed to be wearing a Halloween mask of some kind. A sort of boar's face mask, with tusks, and red malevolent eyes, with coarse brown hair tufting out from underneath his hat.

I took a few steps back.

Suddenly I realized I had no more time for speculation, these two beast men were on the beach and advancing purposefully towards me. They were wearing leather breeches and long blue coats, one of them had a three cornered hat on, and the other wore a simple bandanna. They were huge creatures, broad shouldered and powerful in appearance, but the most striking feature was their animal like faces, which marked them out so obviously as something other than human. Without speculating further, I fled for the tree line, driven on by panic.

Not looking behind me, I could hear that the two creatures were pursuing, and I could make out their grunts and cackles, as they called out to each other. I fled headlong between the roots of the tall trees, with little care as to what I was blundering into. I fell several times, but scrambled up instantly, and accelerated back to as fast as I could go. I could still hear them crashing through the undergrowth, and glancing back, caught a glimpse of one of them, a huge dark figure silhouetted in the light of the sun filtering through the trees. It was then I received a stunning blow to the head, and I had enough sense in me only to perceive I had run right into a branch. I looked down at my feet, they appeared to be a long way off, and I wondered why I couldn't get them to move. As I began to lose consciousness, I felt the beasts lay their hands on me, with no more concern than a man might have picking up a rabbit.

There were three beds in this room, but there were only two people currently within. The door was shut, so they had been talking in privacy. None of the beds were occupied, the starched sheets had been left undisturbed. It was a hospital ward, a familiar place. Pale green walls, with nothing to decorate them but medical paraphernalia and a strong smell of disinfectant and simple efficient furniture.

A man sat on a chair in one corner of the room, and a woman wearing a doctor's coat stood beside the window. The man was dressed in ill fitting jeans; two sizes too big, and held up with a leather belt. On his body he wore a T-shirt with a print on it of Daffy Duck. He was tall and thin, possibly in his late twenties, although his face was aged by two or three weeks growth of stubble. He had a very distant look on his haggard features. The woman was obviously a doctor, from her white coat, with a stethoscope thrust into one of the pockets, and the large round glasses that somewhat spoiled her pretty face. Her whole demeanour spoke of a medical profession, from the way she stood, and the look of concerned interest she affected. This one was probably in her early thirties, although she was dressed to look older, in a plain white blouse and grey skirt.

The sun had come out briefly, in between the clouds, and sifting through the blinds, it cut the room into neat little slices.

Dr. Lock looked down at the pen she had been clutching, unaware that she had been holding it. She put it down on the windowsill.

'That's quite a ... yes'

The speaker's eyes glanced nervously away from the doctor.

'What a way to break a three week silence.'

Dr. Lock appeared lost in thought for a moment or two, then casting off the spell of the speakers words, she remembered that she was a neuro-oncologist, and had a duty to perform.

'Do you remember who you are?'

No answer.

'Do you remember how you got here?'

Again the speaker didn't respond.

'What should I call you?'

The speaker shrugged, and then after a pause said, 'The nurses have been calling me Yarn.'

'Ah yes, they do have a taste for irony,' Lock replied. 'Still you'll surprise them all, now that you've found your tongue.'

Yarn didn't answer.

'OK,' said Lock, looking at some papers, which she had pulled from a pink folder.

'I'll run over some things for you. You were admitted to the Royal, in a state of severe confusion. Amnesia, delusions, hallucinations. You were able to verbalise, but mostly incoherently. X-ray showed no trauma of any kind, and the consultant at the Royal.. ah.. Dr. Heart referred you here, to the Weston for an MRI. You're due for your scan tomorrow.'

Yarn, who had been looking intently at the doctor, shifted his gaze to the floor.

Dr. Lock took this moment to review the things that had just happened. Yarn had been sat in the chair when she had arrived, and had started speaking as soon as she had approached the window. His voice was captivating. Strong, dynamic, and fascinating, a sombre baritone, the voice of a natural storyteller, it almost talked straight to the ancestral part of her that had listened to spoken tales for thousands of years before the invention of television. She had been lured right into the story from the first sentence, and had totally forgotten who she was, or where she was from the very first second. For all she knew or cared, she was eight again, being read 'Lord of the Rings' by her father, prior to bedtime. She had been there with him on the beach, and it had taken her a second or two to return to this room.

Yarn broke the silence and said, 'Scanning for what?'

Dr. Lock ahemed, telling herself, I am the doctor, he is the patient, try and remember that Heather, your not a little girl anymore, and said, 'A brain tumour, but I should stress that this is just to rule out the possibility.'

'And if there was one, will you cut it out?'

8

'That would depend on the type of tumour.'
'Would you do it?'
'I'm a consultant, not a surgeon. Mr. Hood is our resident neuro surgeon.'
'Ah,' Yarn sighed.
'But I'll pop in to see you tomorrow, after the scan.'
Yarn remained silent.
Dr. Lock talked for a bit longer, but she gradually realized that her patient wasn't paying any attention, and that she was wasting her breath. It looked like he had drifted away to whatever world it was he had just come from. Wordlessly Dr. Lock left the room.

Chapter Two - The Galley

I'm sorry if I caught you by surprise at our last meeting. I have written and re-written the beginning of this tale in my head many times and I know it all off by heart now. Tales and stories, these things have become my closest companions and my best assets. I am a story teller. Later I was to become many other things, but my first calling was telling tales, to earn my keep and entertain my friends.

So, to continue.

I was on the galley.

If I ever need to make money, I might publish a book called 'Two months to a flatter stomach: A Galley slave's diet', or 'Physical fitness with whips and chains.' The time I spent chained to that infernal oar, day after endless day, was shear misery, but, like Ben-Hur, I gained weight and muscle, and became fitter than I had ever been in my entire life. My captors, the Nog, had big appetites, and fed us on their ample leavings, so we were not starved. Punishment beatings and indiscriminate floggings were always close at hand, but it's funny how one adapts, and rearranges ones priorities. The first few days I thought I must surely die, such was my misery and despair. After my capture I had been chained to an oar in the bowels of the galley, between two other misfortunates. The hairy barbarian on my left never once grunted at me, but the smaller man on my right was happy to have someone to talk to, even if we didn't understand each other. I slumped into a pit of fear and confusion, and might well have died through apathy, had I been willing to let go of my basic human desire for survival. But after a while, maybe a period of a few weeks, and it was the strangest feeling, the things that I was worrying about - Where was I? How did I get here? Why me? - gave way to more basic problems, such as - What is the best position to sit on the bench to avoid sores? Will I get a bone in my slops? What are the best ways of avoiding being whipped? What are the pro's and con's of various techniques of rowing?

I could tell you a great deal about living your life chained to a wooden bench. How, for instance, the only thing that seems to occupy your mind is how sore your bottom is, what was the best position to sleep in, and most importantly, what method to use to alleviate the pain of a bad whipping.

I eventually devised the best method that worked for me. If we were rowing, I would row a hundred strokes, sitting forward, on my left buttock, then sit back, for the next one hundred. Then I would go forward again, this time onto my right buttock, and then finally, sit back again, on the same buttock. If we weren't rowing, then I tended to spend as much time as I could crouching, slightly off the bench, and flexing my leg muscles, to encourage circulation, and prevent getting deep vein thrombosis. It was amazing how much time I spend devoted to thinking about such subjects. At night, and during unsupervised moments, my right hand companion and I would talk. His name was Apic, and he was from Tullis, which is a town on the coast of Bellavia. This information was as meaningless to me then, as it is to you now. I am ashamed to say that he mastered English a lot faster than I learned Bellavian. He had been a galley slave for nearly a year after being captured by Noggish Pirates.

Apic was an odd sort of fellow, and had an excitable way of talking. Whatever the subject was, it always seemed to be of the greatest importance to him. If his hands were not chained down to the oar, I'm sure he would be gesturing wildly every time he had cause to open his mouth. He was very skinny, and I suspected that he would have been positively wraith like had it not been for the enforced weight training we had to endure each day. He was a picky eater as well, and I suspected he gave some of his food to a pet rat in the scuppers, or some other hairy article. As soon as we could comprehend each other, we talked about every subject under the sun, including our captors.

The Nog were splendid fellows, half man, half beast, who made their living raiding and enslaving other cultures. They were brutal and cruel, in an even-handed sort of way. Like a racist that hates everyone, they were at least not hypocrites. The best thing that I could say about them was that they were really in touch with themselves. They were who they were, and what they were, and anyone who didn't like it, well; they usually met a violent death on the end of a long pointy stick. At best.

They spoke their own guttural language, which Apic had also learned, made unique by the fact that no word ever stretched to more than one syllable. We quickly identified the main characters.

There was the captain, Tup, the largest out of all of them, who had more of a noble air. He never dirtied his paws with beating slaves. He left that to Ack, the chief slave wrangler, who was never far away, to punish crimes real and imagined, and to throw overboard those that were sick, or not pulling their weight.

The first time I witnessed a drowning I was horrified, but much to my dismay now, I grew accustomed to it. Perhaps it was for the best, for those poor fellows. Better a quick release, than to sit in your own dysentery and disease for a week, slowly being whipped to death.

Next up was Zort, the ships shaman and political advisor. He generally wasn't seen much, but he was the main focus of gossip amongst the slaves, especially his dark rituals that occasionally demanded human sacrifice. There were many more of them, but they all looked the same. Big, ugly and stupid was how they bred them in Nogland.

There was about fifty of them and about two hundred of us, separated into two decks. We were in the lower deck, which meant no sunburn, but more disease. I was a miserable wretch, and may well have gone mad, but for having Apic to talk to.

Apic didn't believe me, that I came from a country called Scotland, or all the other things I told him, about machines that could fly, and ships that could power themselves. He informed me that I was a sorcerer from beyond the Norob Forest, and wouldn't be persuaded otherwise.

I couldn't tell him my name, because I couldn't remember it, but he named me 'Shiv - Pollo', which I later learnt meant 'Mad One', something that he found highly amusing.

In our misery we were constantly cracking jokes, and inventing stupid stories, usually about our masters.

One particular favourite was a complicated tale I had woven involving all I could remember from an Australian soap opera, but working in some of the nog sailors, usually with violent consequences. It kept our minds active, and the more ludicrous the stories became, the better I felt. It was a struggle to make up some new nonsense each day and Apic had a huge appetite for it, but then I suppose I did have a captive audience. I think it was as early as then that I began to develop my talent as a story teller, adapting and re-inventing stories from the events and media of my previous existence. I began to wonder if it had all been real, or maybe I was just a slave that had been whipped so much he had gone insane and had begun to delude about a make believe world. Thus we spent out time.

One day, about three months into my voyage, Zort came out onto our deck and walked down its length. Resplendent in his blood red robes, decorated in black and silver runes, and carrying a large studded staff, he cut a superior figure above the average nog. He was glancing left and right as he walked along the central gangway, fixing people with first one beady eye, then the other.

'What the devil does he want?' Apic asked in his excellent English.

'Maybe he wants to give you a big kiss on the bottom.'

Apic, who was no match for my cultured wit, started to giggle silently.

'No, it is you he wishes to kiss on the bottom, Shiv,' he countered.

'I fear not, Apic, I overheard him talking to Tup, he said, I wish to kiss Apic's bottom as it is so round, and like a dessert peach.'

Apic could speak no longer as he was trying to control his laughter.

We quickly stopped our banter as Zort came closer.

'Shit, here he comes,' I muttered.

He looked up the row in front of us, then stepping forward and looking straight at me, struck his staff on the deck.

I glanced guiltily at Apic.

Zort motioned to a nameless nog minion and said, 'Bog nut app' (Unchain this one.)

I began to protest, thinking I surely must about to be punished, or used as a religious offering.

'Master, I have done nothing!' I said in Bellavian

'Silence scum!' he replied in the noggish, very loudly.

The nog minion dragged me off, with Zort, to the prow of the ship and to behind a bulkhead that served as Zort's quarters.

He talked to the minion in noggish, none of which I followed, but it offered me a chance to look around.

Everything you might expect to be in a barbaric shaman's travelling itinerary was here. Totems, fetishes, feathers and bones were very much the order of the day. There was a gently smoking hookah, and a sort of sofa made from hide. I gulped as I noticed it had several tattoos on it, indicating what sort of skin it was likely made from.

Presently the minion left, and Zort sat down and drew on his pipe. He examined me, with his beady animal eyes, his goat like pupils contracting in the gloom. He then blew out a great cloud of smoke that engulfed me like a vampiric mist.

'I hear you tell many strange tales,' he uttered in Bellavian, his speech several octaves below that of the deepest human voice.

Getting over my surprise at a nog intelligent enough to speak another language, I replied, 'I don't know what you mean master.'

'Where are you from?'

'Scotland?' I hazarded, then quickly, 'Master... I mean, Scotland, master.'

'I know not of this place. Tell me of the machine that flies, and the device for seeing far off places.'

I stuttered for a second, then realizing I'd better come up with something quickly.

I replied, 'Ah yes, master, in my land we might travel in the machine that flies. It can go faster than the speed at which my words travel to your ears. And we have devices that can see far off things, and the pictures travel at the speed your eyes can see me...'

Zort seemed to contemplate this. Again he drew on his pipe and puffed out a colossal cloud of smoke. The room was quickly filling from floor to ceiling in its white narcotic haze as he said,

'They call you Mad One.'

'Yes master,' I admitted.

He lent forward, although I was standing and he was seated we were still at eye level and fixed we with his penetrating gaze.

'Tell me of the device which may destroy a city in a single moment.'

Oh god, I thought, my stupid stories had just landed me in a huge pile of trouble.

'I... uh...that is...' I said. 'The device that may destroy a city is very big, and shaped like a whale. It takes the smallest thing in the world, so small that you cannot see it, and so small that you cannot get smaller. It takes this and cuts it in half. The gods dislike this, and in the area of the cutting an... a... ', I didn't know the word for explosion, but the noggish word for fire was "crik".

'A crik so big, it consumes everything, master.'

Zort lent back again, then said, 'And you can make such a device?'

I froze, 'Ah...ah...that is...'

I couldn't decide whether to lie, or tell the truth, not knowing which answer was more likely to get me killed.

'Enough,' growled Zort, 'You are a mad man, you may go.'

'Yes master,' I bowed and got ready to leave.

'And report to Ack for a beating before you go back to your place.'
'Yes, master.'
I scuttled off, breathing a sigh of relief and went to find Ack. My head was reeling a little from whatever nasty substance Zort had been smoking, but I found the slave wrangler quite easily. He wasn't busy, as for some reason known only to the nogs, the galley was currently stationary. He was standing in the waist of the ship, tying a knot in a length of rope, his favourite implement for hitting people with.
'Master,' I said. 'I am to have a very mild beating.'
Ack grunted, 'Speak. Nog. Dog.'
I sighed, ' Bic Pot Flek Zort Atc.' (Please beat me, Zort's orders)
Ack grunted again, then said, 'Zort, ahhh.... Come, Tup.'
I was certainly going round the houses today, I thought, as Ack quickly marched me to the captain's cabin. This was situated at the stern of the ship, so we had to promenade the whole deck to get to it. I certainly picked up some odd looks from my fellow slaves, and Apic gave me a weak smile as I drifted past him. Ack's knock was acknowledged and I was pushed inside, tripping slightly as I entered the dark cabin, lit only from the stern windows.
Tup, was standing at one of the windows, dressed in a formal blue officer's coat, black boots and britches. He wore a starched white collar, and the hairy pelt of his neck tufted out of it at odd angles. His white fangs shone from the dark shadow of his bestial face. He reminded me slightly of those novelty paintings that you get of dogs dressed as humans engaged in games of billiards or cards.
Again I was left while the two nogs spoke away, none of which I followed. Ack left and I was alone with Tup in his spartan cabin, wondering what on earth fate could have in store for me now.
However, what was said, and the events which followed, must, I fear, wait for another occasion.

Rain began to hit the glass of the window, waking Lock from the revere she had been in.
'Ah... right... Yarn, thank you,' she said and paused. She took a moment to readjust herself to the real world and collect her thoughts.
Even after this though, she still had difficulty breaking the silence that the conclusion of Yarns last part of the tale had left.
She obviously had something to say, but seemed to be wondering the best way to say it and whether it would be fully understood or not.
Eventually she ventured, 'I'm sorry, I have some very bad news for you. The scans show a large tumour in your left frontal lobe. Here, see for yourself.'
She stepped over to the light box and switched it on. Next she took the black and white scans from a folder and clipped them on.

'It's quite large, as you can see, and we would like your permission to operate. The radiographer believes you have a tumour type called a pilocytic astrocytoma. I know that won't mean anything to you yet, but all you need to know at this stage is that the course of treatment recommended for this type is surgery.'

Dr. Lock paused to let all that sink in.

'We think, a biopsy is appropriate in your case, which will give us...'

'No operation,' interrupted Yarn.

'Yes, I know this must be very upsetting, but I can...'

'No operation.'

Dr. Lock blanked for a second, and then said, 'Well, radiotherapy is also an option; however I must inform you, that without an operation, you might not live longer than nine months. I'm really sorry to have to say this, but...'

'Radiotherapy,' said Yarn. 'Radiotherapy, yes.'

'Right, I'll book you into the mould room as soon as possible,' Lock paused then said, ' One of the possible symptoms of a brain tumour is hallucinations, have you been experiencing these occurrences regularly?'

'I'm not hallucinating, I'm telling you the truth,' replied Yarn with a shrug and a smile.

'Yes, I expect they can appear very real. Have you been suffering from anything else? Headaches? Seizures?'

'No,' said Yarn, almost apologetically.

Lock smiled and said, 'Well, I'll send Sara by later, she's our Clinical Nurse Specialist, I hope you won't mind a check up and a chat with her.'

No response.

'I'll drop by tomorrow then.'

As she walked out the room, she thought sheesh, I've seen a lot of odd behaviour in people with brain tumours, but nothing like this.

Next day on the South Corridor.

'Hey Heather!'

Dr. Lock turned to greet Sara Brown, the Neuro-Oncologist CNS, who was clutching a large pile of red patient notes. Sara appeared to be a slim, good-humoured woman in her early forties. She was dressed in a smart brown suit. The only indication that she was a nurse was the badge on her lapel that said so.

'Hi!'

'I didn't get a word out of your man there,' she said in her deep Welsh brogue. 'He did all the tests, the ten metre walk, the nine hole peg test. Wouldn't do the WDRT (William's Delayed Recall Test). He wouldn't say anything!'

'That's odd, every time I see him, he never shuts up. He tells me part of this really weird story.'

'Oh,' Sara replied, slightly hurt. 'I never got a thing out of him. He must like you!'

'Must do!' laughed Lock.

'Got to dash, anyway, late for clinic, see you later!'

Sara walked sprightly off down the corridor, her high heels clicking on the black and white lino.

Dr. Lock shook her head and walked off in the opposite direction, up the ramp to DCN.(*Dept. of Clinical Neuroscience.), where she was to have a meeting with Mr. Hood.

Chapter Three - Usak

One of the few pleasures that could be gained from life on the noggish ship, and they were few and far between, on that brutish violent disease ridden hulk, was to be on the deck, to smell the pure clean sea air, and to catch a glimpse of the rolling blue waves, like a vast blanket, reflecting the sun. The weather outside seemed to be as balmy as always. I could hear the distant sound of seagulls which made me realise that we may be close to a shore. I reflected on what my chances would be if I was to take a leap out of the open window. Slim, probably.

It was a time before the captain said anything, and I took the opportunity to continue gazing longingly out of the stern windows. The view out of the window was the most interesting feature in the cabin. There were several pieces of purely utilitarian furniture, and a large table with a few scrolls on it, but nothing that spoke in any way of the character of the beast that dwelled here.
Tup stood at the other end of the cabin, in grim contemplation.
Eventually he turned, looked down at me and said, 'You speak Bellavian?'
'Yes master.' I said and bowed. I was used to showing respect to these beasts, as the only way to avoid a beating.
'Soon we will be in battle human. A great sea battle against rebel tribes. It is a bitter thing, to be fighting one's kin.'
I was surprised to hear a nog speak so well.
'Master?'
'We go to join Clak's fleet. Then on to the port of Usak, to meet and fight the usurper's navy.'
My mind was racing, why was I being told all this?
'Word as reached me that Zort was seen with you...ach! Curse it!'
Suddenly the huge nog stepped towards me and punched me to the floor. I landed in a heap, my head ringing.
'Zort is not a follower of the old ways. He is Jube's man, and Clak's eyes on this vessel. My fathers would curse the day I was sired, if they knew how much power that pack of dogs have over the clans.'
As my ears stopped ringing, I began to piece bits of information together. Little snippets from overheard noggish conversations and information Apic had given me. The rebellion I knew nothing about, but I knew that there was a power struggle between the clan lords and the shaman, a sort of church and state thing.
'Tell me what he said to you?' he hissed as he towered over me.
'I... he asked me about my lands, master.'
'Is that all?'
'I swear, I told him about the magic we have in my lands, but he thought I was mad.'
Tup gave a hoarse laugh.

'Well, can your magic save us? We go to meet the usurper, and his fleet is mightier than ours. In two weeks we are all fated to die. The lands to the south threaten to engulf us, and all the chiefs can think about is petty politics!'

Tup paced the room in agitation. He looked down at me again, and I thought, by the look in his eye, that he was going to kill me, but he opened the cabin door and said to Ack, who was standing outside, 'Nut app tak nag.' (Take this one back.)

'So what was that all about?' asked Apic, as we pulled at our oars, the ship maintaining a steady cruising speed.

'I know not, but we have an informer in our midst.'

Apic sighed, then said, 'Let us speak English then.'

'OK,' I nodded in reply.

'I bet Zort is pissing in his pants,' he said after I'd told him what had happened, 'He must know about this suicidal attack and will try anything to prevent it.'

'Why attack such a stronger opposing force, if you know you are going to lose?'

Apic considered this, 'Well, from what I know of noggish politics, I wouldn't be surprised if the shaman have whipped the clans into some sort of religious fervour, and convinced them that their dark gods will protect them, the battle will be won. However, I bet that it's more to do with the shaman wanting the battle to be lost, so they can pin the blame on the clan chiefs involved, get rid of them, and gain more power. This usurper character must be the leader of the south nog tribes, we are part of the north nog fleet, as you are no doubt aware. I presume we are going to teach him a lesson at Usak, or so if would at first appear. In actual fact it is all a political ploy, mark my words.'

'Wow, you're good. How did you figure all that out?'

'All I do is sit at this bloody oar all day don't I? Well, at least when I'm drowning, I'll know all these hairy bastards are drowning with me.'

'Oh that,' I said, 'I could tell them how to win this battle easily. I just need to know how to turn it to my advantage.'

Apic turned to me in interest, and was about to speak, but I said, 'Keep pulling on that bloody oar. There's three of us here you know, and me and Bluto are doing all the work!'

Bluto was the name I had given to our silent oar mate. He never once gave us a look of recognition, or uttered a word of any kind, not even when he was whipped. His great bearded bulk sat hunched over the oar twenty-four hours a day, and gave no indication that whoever it was that lived there resembled anything human. I had developed a sort of affection for him though. In circumstances like these I had the greatest respect for anyone who wasn't hitting me.

'Oh, ok,' spat Apic, and applied himself more manfully to the oar, 'How?'

18

'Shh... I'm thinking... there must be a way to out smart these idiots. They go to the toilet where they're standing for christsake. They have tusks! They are just a bunch of angry animals.'

Apic began to snigger, but quickly shut up when a nog glanced sternly at us and cracked the whip over our backs.

'Yes, thank you,' I hissed under my breath.

We rowed well into the night, and soon everyone was grumbling about missing our evening slops. Eventually the buckets came round, but I was still no closer to finding a solution to my dilemma.

'What's this?' I said, examining a bone suspiciously.

'Don't worry. They only start eating slaves when the pigs run out.'

I chewed on the bone thoughtfully, 'And have they?'

Apic shrugged.

'You sleep now!' bellowed one of the nogs and our fellow slaves began to stretch out on the benches. I lay down in my favourite spot next to the stowed oars. Like everyone else, I was asleep as soon as my head was down, we had never been called on to row as far or as hard before, and several of the weaker slaves had already expired and been thrown over the side. I had no intention of joining them for the want of sleep.

The next morning, out of the oar hatch we could see the shoreline, and about a dozen other galleys. The starboard slaves reported numerous vessels on the other side. The deck was awash with gossip, even with the constant whipping to try and silence it.

'It's all happening,' I muttered. 'Fun, eh, Bluto?'

The big barbarian, as ever, said nothing.

Apic was glued to the oar hatch.

'By the prophet's beard, I have never seen so many noggish galleys,' he then turned to me and said, 'Have you had your idea yet?'

'No, I'm just going to wing it.'

Then and there I decided it was time to risk an all or nothing attempt on saving my skin. I looked up and shouted to the nearest nog, 'Take me to Tup!'

The nog advanced, whip raised.

'Don't beat this one! Tup not like!' I yelped.

The nog grunted in disgust, and looked over to Ack, who nodded.

Quickly I was unchained and frog marched to Tup's cabin. A couple of the other slaves wolf-whistled at me, I had fast gained a reputation as the captain's pet. When we entered the cabin, Tup was resting on a sofa, a scroll in his hands and a deep frown wrinkling his brow.

Getting up he growled, ' This had better be good slave.'

I summoned up my courage and said, 'The god's have granted me wisdom, I can tell you how to defeat the usurper's fleet, but you must release me and my companions first.'

Tup stood up and growled, 'What if I beat it out of you?'

I cowered behind a chest.

'But master! I am to die in two days anyway by your account, and besides the gods have instructed me!'

Tup towered over me, his huge paw raised.

'And besides,' I said, talking quickly 'What is the life of a couple of slaves to you? For the chance to win a famous victory, and to make your fathers proud?'

Tup lowered his hand and considered.

'All I ask is to be put ashore, and I will tell you.'

'Tell me now!' he bellowed.

'The gods have instructed! The gods have instructed!' was all I could say as I cowered and waited for the blow.

'I care not for your diseased gods! Tell me now!' and he grabbed me by the throat, 'Or by the ten gods of Nog, I will squeeze the life out of you right now!'

'All right,' I gurgled in terror, my feet dangling far from the deck, 'Put me down and I will tell you.'

Once my feet were back on the ground I began.

'You have forty ships here, so I suppose the usurper has about eighty ships. If they are like these ones, they are all built of wood. His are all in port. Don't wait for him to leave port to engage in battle, but instead send out a picket to watch from a distance. Wait for a favourable wind, set fire to five of your galleys and sail them into the harbour. The wind will carry the fire onto his galleys and burn them all.'

Tup sat for a full minute. I waited and watched as all the possibilities of this plan crossed his bestial face.

He cried something in noggish, then said,

'Good! A devious ploy! And a famous victory! I must discuss it with Clak at once! Ack get rid of this dog!'

'But!' I protested as I was dragged from the cabin. I had the strongest feeling that my lot wasn't due to improve any time soon.

The acrid smoke stung my eyes, but I could just make out the black sails of Chow the usurper's fleet, anchored in Usak harbour. It was a very large natural basin, with a small town situated on the west bank. As we got closer I saw that the whole area in front of the town was full of vessels, loading supplies and slaves. The vessels were all made of wood, as were all of the jetties and cranes. In fact the whole town was made of timber, and forests grew on the hills surrounding it. Everything natural and everything manufactured had a distinct woody quality about it. The place was a tinderbox.

I strained at the chains, but it was no good.

'Tell me again, how we ended up in this mess,' groaned Apic.

'You know why,' I cursed. 'Tup's sense of irony. He liked the plan all right, and to ensure success, and grant favour from their gods, they've chained us to the leading fire ship.'

The fire was all over the ship now, and although we weren't ablaze yet, it was getting very hot.

'Yes, but why are me and Bluto here? Because we are your bench mates?' queried Apic.

'Yes, and well, because I mentioned you both, but I was only trying to save you!'

'Well that's just great!' Apic cried in sarcasm, something he had learned from me.

I began to cough, 'We're getting closer.'

Through the smoke and flames I could see tall noggish figures on the black galley decks, beginning to panic as it dawned on them what was about to happen.

All three of us were chained to the single, central mast of the galley. I felt something tighten under my arm.

'What was that?' I asked trying to look round.

'Is that you Bluto? Are you trying to break the chains?'

The chains tightened again. My manacles began to dig into my wrists.

'Go on son! You can do it!' I cried. Apic began to scream encouragement as well. I heard the barbarian let out a grunt.

The manacle on my left hand was digging in so much the pain was excruciating. I was screaming, and so was Apic, when suddenly something went ping, and my left arm was released.

'The other one Bluto!' Apic cried looking at the manacles. Bluto began to muscle up to the mast again.

'No wait!' I cried in desperation. 'Step over me, you idiots, we are all chained together!'

I leapt underneath Bluto's arm.

After a brief struggle we were all free of the mast.

I was chained to Apic, and he was chained to Bluto.

'Right, over the...ack!' I yelped as Bluto ran to the rail, dragging Apic and me with him.

And then it was all water, and smoke, and confusion and near drowning. Somehow we made it to a jetty, and with difficulty clambered up onto it and ran along its length to the shore. Luckily the nogs were all on board their ships well away from were we had disembarked. We crossed the dockyard and were soon pelting down a muddy street. The streets were narrow and dirty, with discarded fish guts and worse making the mud treacherously slippery.

I noticed that the houses were human sized as we fled past them, and they even had the figures of human villagers lurking within them.

We ran on further, as fast as the mud and the fact that we were all chained together would allow. By now, everyone, humans and nogs were in the streets, either running to, or from the fire. Three runaway slaves didn't seem to be cause for much comment and no one seemed keen to attempt our recapture.

Panting and gasping we ran up a flight of stone steps, which seemed to go on forever, and out onto a sort of square. The fire must have really taken hold, as the smoke wasn't thinning out at all as we ascended the steps. Somewhere nearby someone was ringing a temple bell. Black sooty smoke obscured everything, but the square seemed to be deserted except for the occasional shadowy form flitting through the murk. So far, in our bid for freedom, Apic had been having the worst time of it, as he was chained between Bluto and me.

'Look! look!' I yelled, trying to drag them towards a building I had just spotted.

'What? You're wrenching my arm out of its socket!' protested Apic.

I pointed at the building. It had an anvil outside it.

There was a nasty looking man inside, but before he could say anything, Bluto had bludgeoned him unconscious. The small room was full of blacksmith's tools.

'The pliers! Here, I'll do you first!'

Lots of cursing and small bloody wounds on the wrists ensued before we were all unchained and free.

'At last!' cried Apic. 'Dam those chains. I've worn them for a year and a half!'

'Look,' I said, panting, with my hands on my knees and looking at Bluto, 'He's smiling! Bluto is smiling.'

And indeed he was, the big man, practically the size of a nog was smiling so wide we could see all his large white teeth. He burst into a huge baritone laugh, and soon we were all laughing like maniacs.

Dr. Lock had been picking a strand of cotton from the cuff of her cardigan. She looked up as she realized that Yarn had stopped talking.

'Then what?'

Yarn gave her a quick smile, then looked down nervously, 'That can wait until next time.'

Dr. Lock tapped her pen on her teeth for a second then said, 'I take it Bluto wasn't the big guys name?'

'No, his real name was Carab.'

'Usak then, humans and nogs living side by side?'

'Yes, we didn't spend much time there, but apparently such places are common in that area. The humans are dark and swarthy and mix with the nogs.'

'I see,' Dr. Lock paused then said, 'I scheduled another visit from Sara, she's a good councillor, why don't you speak to her? She would be very interested to hear all this.'

Yarn sat with his hands underneath him, and looked at the floor.

'Listen, why make it hard on yourself? Having a brain tumour is a very traumatic life changing experience. I'm going to prescribe a course of steroids for you, that may help with the... um... delusions.'

Yarn sighed, and Dr. Lock clucked her tongue anxiously for a second.

'Ok, I'll be back on Tuesday, I will see you then, and think about what I said.'

As she headed for the door, Yarn said, 'The tumour is not what you think. I know what it is, and I can deal with it myself. No drugs.'

'If you don't want to be here, you can discharge yourself!' Lock said sharply, instantly regretting her tone.

Yarn seemed not to notice, smiled and said, 'But I haven't finished my story yet!'

Chapter Four - The Great Forest

We left Usak as discreetly as possible, which wasn't difficult, considering the chaos we had caused there. The land around the small port was deeply forested. Besides the clothes we were standing in, Apic had stolen a dagger from the blacksmiths, and Bluto had taken a large mallet. I had salvaged a long black cloak and a metal tipped staff.

As we entered cautiously into the gloomy forest we discussed what our next course of action should be.

'What now, Shiv?'

'Who made me leader? And my name isn't Shiv!'

We paused as we leapt across a small stream.

'What is your name then?' queried Apic.

'It's...' I stumbled, 'I don't know...'

Apic looked at me as I scratched my head in bemusement. I shook myself and changed the subject, 'What about you Bluto? What's your real name?'

Bluto, who had been about three paces behind us, came forward and said, 'Carab.'

'He speaks!' gasped Apic.

'Carab, son of Carris, thane of Vegas.'

'A toff, no less,' I laughed.

Apic tugged at my cloak, 'Vegas I have heard of that place. It is in the cold lands far to the north of Bellavia,' then in a whisper. 'It is an evil place full of ghouls and demons.'

'Really?' I replied, then addressing Carab. 'What's it like in Vegas?'

'It is a great kingdom, peopled with strong serfs and mighty warriors. My father owns ten thousand thralls, and is the greatest warrior in the kingdom.'

I scratched my stubbly chin in thought, by this time we had all stopped walking.

'Where is Vegas from here?' I asked Carab.

'I know not.'

'Hmm... Well looking at you, let me guess, Vegas has short summers and long winters, the landscape is mountainous, with great U-shaped valleys, many with glaciers in them. Erm... feudalistic farming... probably very war like. In any event, north of this place.'

Carab looked at me in surprise, 'That is correct!'

'You are indeed a sorcerer!' proclaimed Apic in obvious satisfaction, and quite happy to bask in my reflected glory.

'A geographer more like,' I paused deep in thought, then said, 'OK, the people down in Usak look like,' in English, '"Mediterraneans", and the weather is really hot here. The trees are all small, like acacias and olive trees. What lies north of here?'

They both shrugged.

As sailors we had all learnt to recognise the equivalent of the North Star in this region, and we had been heading west from the port. We all looked north in a speculative fashion.

'Well I don't know about you guys...' then a thought hit me, 'Apic, describe the climate of Bellavia.'

'Ah,' tears practically welling up in his eyes, 'Bellavia is a land of rolling pastures and rich summer harvests, the winters are sometimes harsh, but...'

'So Bellavia is north of here too! That settles it, let's go!'

So we headed north, for several days, eating whatever we could find, olives, dates, figs and the like. My stomach was constantly rumbling from the rich diet, but my bowels were the least of my worries.

I tried not to think about what was happening to me, and when ever I started to, I tried to stop. Since the immediate day to day terror of death on the galley had been taken away, I was beginning to risk thinking in wider terms, mainly about what had happened to me, why I was here, and what it would take for me to somehow get home. I was also worried about why I couldn't remember my own name, or any specific details about my life prior to my mysterious appearance on that unnamed shore. I could remember everything about my previous world very well, but only in general terms. I could remember things like television, computer games, Christmas and teapots, but nothing personal, like family, friends and what I had done for a living. Sometimes I felt like weeping, and I would go away from the others. Carab never talked unless directly addressed, but Apic and I kept up a steady stream of constant chatter, partly to keep our minds off our troubles and partly because we both like the sound of our own voices. Through it all I got to know quite a lot about Bellavia. It sounded like the equivalent of a northern European medieval kingdom. It was constantly at war with its neighbours, and if you weren't a soldier, you were a peasant or a monk. It was probably a really dull place. Its capital city was Staturos, but Apic didn't know much about the place as he had spent most of his life in the port of Tullis on the west coast of Bellavia, and he would get all misty eyed when asked to describe it. It was a very busy place, by his account, and quite different from inland Bellavia. A hundred cultures met and traded here, and as a result it had a freedom about it that nowhere else in the world had, apart from some of the island kingdoms. Its streets were narrow, and the buildings tall, like Usak, but the streets were kept clean by the strict rules of the town council. There was a saying, that if you couldn't buy something in Tullis, you couldn't buy it anywhere. It thrived on trade, and the guildmasters of the town allowed the citizens every freedom, as long as it didn't conflict with their solemn, enshrined purpose of making money. As a result, the town was prosperous, and anyone with money could spend it all in any of the hundred taverns and brothels that littered Tullis like raisins in a particularly fruity fruitcake. It sounded a great place, and I agreed with Apic, that we would visit it at our earliest convenience.

That night we camped out in a thicket of olive trees, Carab, who turned out to be a real boy scout had just returned from gathering firewood. I was busily explaining some of the finer points of modern living to Apic.

'I don't know, they sort of bake them I think, but that's potato crisps. I prefer the, I don't know the word for it, .. um wheat ones. In English, "cheesy puffs", mm... nice!'

'I don't understand,' sighed Apic.

'It's not proper food. You don't have a word for it. In English its "snack". They are for eating in between your regular meals. I'd kill for some right now. Or a bloody cup of coffee, or a cigarette for gods sake!'

'Your speaking English again,' said Apic in English.

'Do you have herbs that can be put into little bowls and burnt?' Apic watched my hand gestures intently. 'Then you suck the tube at the top? But in my land, we roll the leaves in paper and suck the tip. No? The nogs used hookahs, they were smoking something.'

'I know not. Why would anyone want to breathe in smoke? Why not use the fire?' Apic gestured at the camp fire, in confusion.

'It has to be special leaves,' I sighed and was silent. I put my head in my hands.

Sensing my sadness, Apic said, 'Chocolate sounds nice though.'

'Too right!' I exclaimed, looking up again. 'You'd like chocolate, right enough. My stomach can't stand all this healthy food! It wants Cadburys, Monster Munch and Coca-Cola!'

'Your land sounds like it is full of lazy, fat merchants,' grumbled Carab, joining in the conversation. 'If Vegas ever battled you, there would be rich pickings.'

Both Apic and me gave him a 'who rattled your cage' look.

'No Carab, my land has weapons. Even me, with one of these weapons could kill a hundred warriors in ten seconds.'

Carab snorted in derision, and said, 'Wizards and witches are burned in my land.'

Since our freedom, Carab had shaved off his beard, and tied back his hair. He couldn't have been more than twenty-five years old, and was ruggedly handsome, if you happened to like that sort of thing. He was a confirmed sceptic, and when he could be bothered listening to us, cast scorn on all my claims.

Apic, however, swallowed up every word. Several times I had been tempted to tell him a whole load of nonsense, about giant flying space worms or somesuch.

'See how this dog mocks you, great sorcerer!' accused Apic. 'Cast a spell on him, so that he may feel your might!'

'Hmm... I've been thinking about that.'

Carab smiled and popped an olive from the collection in his hand into his mouth.

'I preferred you when you never talked,' I said.

Apic looked at me in anticipation.

'I don't know! I wish there were something I could dazzle you with, but I can't think of anything.'

Apic sighed and glanced at Carab who shrugged and laughed.

'Forget it,' I said. 'If I had a cigarette lighter I'd blow your minds though.'

The next day found us again tramping through the murky woods. A damp mist descended and the temperature dropped. The vegetation seemed to be changing also, from small bush-like olive and fig trees to taller gnarled oaks, elms and beach trees. We all felt a strong oppression on us, like a presence was watching from the mists. The conversation dried up, and we pushed on in silence, anxious to clear this forbidding area.

I spotted something up ahead and cautiously approached it.

'Yuck!' I grimaced. It was some sort of totem, made of three skulls and bloody feathers, staked out in a natural clearing in the woods. Some of the skulls were human, but most of them seemed to be smaller, like children's, but more animal like. Chimps or monkeys, possibly.

'The blood's quite fresh,' said Apic nervously, pointing to the red ichor dripping from the feathers.

Carab silently surveyed the trees around us, then quickly crouched down and examined the ground.

'Goblins.' he hissed.

'Huh?' I asked.

Carab quickly moved forward into the mists.

'Hey!'

Carab broke into a run, and Apic and I had to gallop dangerously in-between the trees to keep up with him. As I caught up with Carab I gasped, 'Why are we running?'

'Shh!' Carab silenced me.

We ran on for about ten minutes, which felt forever to my poor stiff legs, then suddenly Carab halted and crouched down again. Apic flopped to the ground in an exhausted heap and I anxiously looked round.

'Well?' I gasped.

'That was a goblin totem. There must be a cave near by.'

'And we want to find this why?' I queried.

'Because then we can avoid … ak!'

An arrow thudded into the tree right beside Carab, and then almost simultaneously one whizzed past my ear. I heard Apic yelp.

'Shit!' I cried, as we all broke into another run.

We all headed in the same direction but we weren't waiting around for each other.

Suddenly I fell over a dark huddled figure, and we both went sprawling onto the forest floor. I got up in a flash and swung my staff onto the small things back with all my might. It shrieked in pain, so I hit it several more times then ran off after the others.

As I ran I collected up the broken images of what had just happened into my head. It had been a small figure, no more than five feet tall, and dressed in dark rags and leather. It had been wearing a ragged cloak, and I think it had been clutching a rusty dagger, which had been dropped, when I had run it over. It also had had a small bow, which had snapped in half with a sound like a gunshot when I had struck it on the back. I had caught a glimpse of its face, which was slightly reminiscent of that of a nog, except that it was far smaller and hairless. The complexion of its skin had been a dirty green colour, and the blood that had oozed from its bleeding mouth had been a dark red.

I could hear the other two ahead of me, and as I ran on the ground rose sharply upwards and the mists began to thin. I nearly knocked Apic over as I blundered into him. Nervously I looked back and could see the fog shrouded valley sprawled out before us.

'Wow...' then I looked up and said, 'Hey! I got one, did you see me? I totally got him!'

Apic laughed grimly, 'Only by accident.'

Carab patted me on the shoulder, 'My grandmother could kill a goblin in a fair fight, but they rarely fight fair. Luckily for you I know their ways. I often hunted the Claw Clan with my father in Vegas.'

'Uh-huh,' I said, gasping for breath, 'Will they follow us?'

'I know not. Probably. From a distance, to revenge the two that I killed, the one Apic got, and your lucky blow.'

'Oh right,' I said flatly. 'Apic your arm...'

'An arrow grazed me,' Apic said, feeling the blood on the arm of his tunic with a shrug.

Later that night, as we once again camped in a murky forest glade, I pressed Carab for as much information as I could get on the subject of goblins. He wasn't a very amiable tutor, but he soon realised the only way to get me to shut up was to tell me what I wanted to know, as he was too tired to get up and walk across to hit me.

I took in everything he said. Goblins rarely formed civilizations, and generally went in for packs or tribes of a few hundred, and would make war on any neighbouring tribes, or anyone who strayed into their territory. They kept away from the other races, in the wilder parts of the world, and lived in caves if they could find them, or burrows if they couldn't. They rarely made anything worthwhile, like tools or weapons, preferring to steal them from the other races. There were areas of Vegas, such as the Lead Hills, and the Goldhind Wastes that were infested with them and the largest of the tribes was the Claw Clan. Members of this tribe were generally a little larger and more cunning than your average goblin, and presented more of a challenge to a goblin hunter than these 'southern runts', as Carab described them. However, they excelled in underhand tricks and were masters in laying traps for unsuspecting travellers. Carab's own uncle had died in a goblin pit trap, which had been made deadly by the addition of sharp wooden stakes in its bottom. As a species, they were a blight on the lands, and there wasn't a country in the whole of the world that didn't have a serious goblin problem. They were much more insidious than nogs. People died at the hands of nogs in battle, if you were killed by a goblin, usually he was miles away in his cave cackling with glee, while you die slowly and painfully, impaled to a tree.

It was quite possible for nogs and goblins to interbreed, and repulsive as the idea sounded, they could also breed with humans. There was actually small populations of nog-human half-casts, descended from, I presumed, unfortunate human women raped by noggish raiders. I found it hard to imagine a human male raping a noggish wench, however hard up he was. In any event, these poor half-breeds were called gorts, and were universally shunned. All this aside, goblins were our main problem now, and I prodded Carab back onto the point. Goblins were the scourge of the forests, and travellers who strayed from the paths and roads that crossed these great areas, would find that it wasn't long before they found a goblin trap, or even worse a band of foragers. Goblins preferred not to engage in combat with the larger species, but would do so, if they had weight of numbers, or if there was a great advantage to be won. They were cowards all, and would run away at the first sign of trouble. They were good trackers though, which was another reason to be wary of them, we would have to set a watch for tonight, and for each night hereafter. Carab refused to say anymore, but volunteered to take the first watch.

I agreed, as I had grown tired, and the need for sleep was overwhelming me.

Over the next few days, we skirted through many goblin territories, but with Carab in charge we got on fine. The tribes in these parts tended to set vicious traps everywhere for unwary travellers, as Carab had predicted and he always stopped to point them out for us, and to show how to spot and disarm them. Pit fall traps, spring traps, traps that catapulted a spike at you, traps that caught you by the legs, all designed to administer a slow, nasty death. If it had not been for Carab, Apic and I would have been dead a hundred times over.

Other concerns included the fact that we were all close to starvation. We ate what we found, but it wasn't much, and we daren't spend time hunting, although the occasionally unfortunate boar or deer, which had stumbled into a goblin trap, provided some welcome, if slightly gamey meat.

Only once did we run into some more of the creatures, but they ran off as soon as they saw us. They were short, between four and five feet, dressed in skins and rags, similar to the one I had killed. As they scuttled off, they snarled at each other in a strangled language that sounded a bit like noggish.

The worst aspect of our journey was at night. As there were three of us, there had to be a first watch, a middle watch and a last watch. First watch was ok, as you just had to stay awake for a while, until the summer sun had all but gone, and then wake the middle watch. The last watch was the next in preference, as it was simply a case of having to rise a few hours before the others, and potter around in the gloomy dawn twilight until it was time to break camp. By far the worst watch, and I used to dread it coming around to me again, was the middle watch, when it was pitch black underneath the canopy of the forest. What made it even worse was the little sleep you were getting was broken in two. You got a couple of hours in the late evening, then a couple of hours in the early morning, and it made the exhausting day ahead even more unbearable. At Carabs insistence, the fire had to be large, as goblins feared the flames, and fuel would have to be gathered all through the night. And in the darkness of the woods, each second was filled with terror, and each noise in the impenetrable gloom outside the light given off by the fire was a goblin waiting for the opportunity to slip a dagger between your ribs. If I were on middle watch I would gather a pile of wood before hand and threaten the others to touch it on the pain of death so that I would have it ready for me. I also considered actually sleeping on the pile, to keep them off it, but after we had talked it through we decided we should always have a middle watch pile, and no one was to touch it, whoever's turn it was that night. There was never enough though, and you always had to gather more to keep it going.

One night, at about the same time as it happened every night, I ran out of wood. It was a real dilemma, trying to keep as much wood as possible to prevent it running out, and keeping the fire as banked as possible so that the darkness didn't creep in any closer. I got up and staggered off into the dark and looked for broken branches as my eyes began to adjust to the lack of light.

One of the little green bastards leapt right out at me, in an attempt to knock me over, a sharp little dagger clenched in one of its claws. I was taken totally by surprise, and adrenaline instantly began to surge through me. I managed to keep my feet, and staggered back carrying its full weight, as it practically tried to clamber onto my shoulders. I saw its arm go up, and I had just enough time to block its dagger as it brought it down in a scything motion, but I felt the blade graze my chin, and blood began to flow down my neck. Then, just as quickly as it had landed on me, it was off and into the trees. I spun round and ran back to the fire, shouting at the others to wake up, and as they began to arise, I picked up brands from the fire and started tossing them into the undergrowth.

Carab saw the blood on me and seemed to instantly understand the situation. There was a chattering from somewhere in the undergrowth then half a dozen arrows flew into the campsite. Goblins are notoriously bad shots, however, and the only one that came close, Carab easily batted to one side with the flat of his hand. Just as we were wondering what to do next, they rushed us with there daggers drawn, maybe a dozen or so of them, making a dreadful din with some sort of screeching battle cry. Carab charged right into the middle of them, swinging his mallet wildly with both his hands. He knocked one of them off its feet, and this had the effect of scattering the other attackers. I lashed out at one with my staff, but missed as it flew past me. I could see Apic lunging at two of them with his dagger out of the corner of my eye, but I had problems enough all of a sudden, as a small group of them attempted to rush me, and I fended their knives off with swings from my staff. One of the raiders totally misjudged a strike with its dagger and left itself wide open. Seeing the opportunity I swung the staff up under its chin, breaking its neck and sending it crumpling to the ground. The other two, seeing this, made a run for it, and I chased after them, leaping over the body of their fallen comrade. I ran past Carab who was killing off one of the creatures by kicking it in the head while he fended of his remaining foes with his mallet. I stuck my staff out and tripped one of the ones I was chasing, sending it flying into a tree.

Just then I heard Carab shout, 'Shiv, behind you!', and I turned just in time to hit another one as it tried to stab me. I knocked it to the ground, and finished it off with a blow to the head as it fell. I noticed that this one was smaller than the others, an adolescent or a female, but I didn't spare it another thought. I looked up, and stepping over its body ran back to the fire, looking for more enemies. My blood was up now, and I would have happily fought some more, but it was all over. It could have only lasted a minute from beginning to end, and I joined Apic by the fire where he had killed two of them. We grinned at each other like mad men.

There was no sign of Carab, but he emerged from the darkness, with a small cut on his arm, long before we had thought about starting to worry about him.

Since it all appeared to have ended we stoked up the fire, and eventually Carab said, 'Good work, I think we got eight of them all told. They won't be back tonight.'

'Why would they attack in a frontal assault like that?'

'I know not,' replied Carab. 'Perhaps they got confused after they tried to ambush you, or they thought we were an easier prey. It matters not, you can get some sleep now.'

But Apic and I were much too excited and we spent the rest of the night talking about the encounter, like two football supporters going over a particularly exciting match, with many a,

'Did you see it when I...' and

'What about when it...' until we finally grew so tired we fell asleep were we sat.

One afternoon we were walking through the seemingly endless forest as usual. We had grown used to this sort of life by now, and while neither Apic nor I could be called woodsmen yet, we had come a long way for ignorant sailors. We could spot the simpler, less cunningly concealed goblin traps, and we both had keenly developed our abilities to find food. We had found that there wasn't much in the forest that you couldn't eat if you were hungry enough and we were constantly hungry. It didn't help that all we ever talked about was food. All day it was a ceaseless exchange of stories, all varying slightly on the theme of 'great meals I have had', and we were practically driving each other to distraction.

We were making our way cautiously through the forest on another warm day then, making the usual conversation, when a piercing scream sounded through the trees. This was an unheard of event for us, so far the only screams we had been expecting to hear had been our own. What we had just heard sounded distinctly female and had a certain 'damsel in distress' quality about it.

Carab ran off to where it had come from, with me and Apic following, muttering behind.

'Big chief Carab to the rescue,' I quipped.

Apic smirked and replied, 'With trousers that size, he is invulnerable.'

That was the start of a long running joke between Apic and I about the size of Carab's trousers, something that I will endeavour to never mention again.

I had enough time to see Carab kick a goblin off another larger figure, with a hefty boot to the rear. The goblin literally sailed through the air with the force of the blow, and the other prone figure quickly got up and bolted for the bushes, screaming in a very feminine way.

Carab followed her.

We discovered them in a small thicket. the feminine figure was struggling against Carab, who was trying to hold her still. The cowl of her cloak fell down, revealing a young pretty face, and suddenly her eyes met with Carabs.

Electricity flowed.

'Carab's made a friend, look.'

'Perhaps we could eat her,' whispered Apic.

I gave him a withering look.

There was silence for a moment.

'Who was she?' asked Dr. Lock.

'That is for next time.'

Then the tape stopped. Dr. Lock picked it up.

'What do you make of that?' she asked.

Dr. Barage, who had been holding his hands in a steeple, put them on the desk. He and Dr. Lock were sitting in his cluttered office. Dr. Barage was short gentleman, no more than five foot five, and in his forties, with a short crop of greying hair. He wore a small oval pair of glasses, which gave him a slightly owlish look. A very cheeky owl.

'He's brilliant, a natural story teller, I wish I could be present at one of his recitals. His voice is very commanding.'

Dr. Lock smiled and said, 'I'm not talking about his narration abilities, Ian, what do you make of him clinically?'

'Ach,' sighed Dr. Barage, 'Who cares? He's a nut right? He's got a year at best. If he wants to just sit there and tell stories, that's his prerogative. Plus with nowhere to go he's just taking up space in the wards.'

Dr. Lock placed the index finger of her right hand to her temple, then laughed.

'Jeez, you nearly had me then! I must be losing it!'

Dr. Barage laughed, 'Yeah sorry, bad joke, but listen, as his assigned psychiatric doctor, I say, if his condition isn't deteriorating, don't force any unwanted treatment on him.'

'That's your professional opinion?'

'Sure, why not?' laughed Dr. Barage.

Heather looked at her watch and stood up.

'And Heather,' said Dr. Barage standing up also, 'Can I get a recording of your next interview? I want to know what happens next, it's annoying it's only you he talks to!'

'Aye, no problem Ian, catch you at the x-ray meeting.'

Dr. Barage waved her out his office as his phone began to ring.

Chapter Five - Che

The girl tried to grab her muddy cloak around herself. She was bloody and bruised and had twigs tangled up in her hair. Her complexion was very dark, like that of an Italian, or someone from southern France. She was very pretty, with big round brown eyes, and a slightly twisted mouth, that was currently clenched tightly closed. Carab had trapped her in a small thicket of bushes, and after we had arrived, he slowly let go of her arms, but remained kneeling by her side. She made no other move to try and escape, and eyed us suspiciously.
'She's Enttish,' said Apic
'How do you know?' I asked.
'She looks Enttish.'
'Ah,' I nodded stupidly.
'Her clothing looks rich,' I said pointing at her.
'I speak Bellavian!' she said sharply, making Carab stand up. 'Don't speak about me like I'm not here!'
'Steady on, we just saved your life!' I protested. 'Well, he did anyway,' I finished gesturing at Carab.
'Well, I thank you very much,' this entirely directed at Carab who was smiling like a dumb ox.
'He's a dark horse!' I laughed in English.' Six months at sea, and he never says a word, the moment he sets foot on shore, he's picking up chicks!'
'What language is that?' she said in confusion, 'Stop speaking it!'
'Sorry,' I said, this time in Bellavian, and nudging Apic, to stop him from smirking. 'What's your name?'
'I...' she started, then said, 'I'm Princess Adea of Enttland, my father will pay you a great reward for my safe return.'
'Oh right,' I nodded, suspecting she was lying, 'Well, Princess Adea of Enttland, meet Prince Carab of Vegas, I'm Lord Flat Eric of Levi, and this is the second Earl of Pantaloons.'
Apic managed to keep a straight face.
'It's a pleasure to meet such...'
'What happened to you?' I interrupted.
'I was travelling with my retinue to Ferron, but myself and a few others left the main group and strayed from the forest path. We had been lost for days, when the goblins attacked, I ran, it was awful. I fear everyone else is dead.'
I was about to say something else, when Carab seemed to come to his senses and said, 'Talk later. We must leave now, before they come back. Come!'

Later that night, we camped inside a ravine beside a gurgling stream. As usual we had gathered up a large amount of firewood, and cooked what meagre supplies we had. Some cured meat, a small variety of root vegetables seasoned with some herbs found by the stream. Fruit and berries to follow, with just a small dollop of some honey Apic had bravely acquired for us a few days ago. Princess Adea had obviously not eaten anything in several days, so we let her finish off the rest of the meat. Apic sat close to the fire, licking honey from his fingers, and Carab was close by examining the ground, probably looking for tracks or something. I had been reclining vacantly against a large tree root, enjoying the feeling of food inside my stomach for the first time that day. There was still some daylight left, so I got up and went over to Adea, who was sat on a rock a little way off from the camp.

'Let me look at your leg.'

Adea started and replied, 'It would be unbefitting of a lady of my...'

'Yeah, yeah, look, you've been limping, and there's blood on your dress. It needs looking at, and besides you're holding us up.'

Adea gave me a scowl, 'You are no kind of doctor, I'm sure!'

'I know more than you might think young lady, and I am the best you are going to get out here in Mirkwood.'

She looked at me in confusion, but eventually sighed and carefully began to hitch up her skirts.

'There's no need for you two to be present!' she scathed at Apic and Carab who were suddenly both standing nearby, slack jawed. 'Go about your business!'

They coughed guiltily and went to attend to the fire.

'God's teeth, how many skirts do you have on?' I asked as she pulled up her various slips and petticoats.

She gave me a look with daggers in it.

The wound was all stuck to her stocking, just above the knee. She complained bitterly as I cut it away with Apic's dagger to reveal the bloody wound underneath. Once I had cleaned it with water from the ravine, I was a lot happier. It was a nasty cut, but nothing serious, and would be fine as long as it didn't get infected.

'It's not too bad, not too deep. We can use one of your petticoats as a bandage.'

She protested, but I wouldn't hear a word of it.

'Do you want me to call Carab, to come and hold you down?'

That silenced her.

Once I had finished she sat down by the fire and aimed nails and rocks at me with her eyes.

Apic and I carried on our usual conversation about food we would like to eat, half in Bellavian, and half in English. The conversation soon turned to our new companion, however.

'I doubt she is a princess, my friend.' said Apic.

'Why so?'

'Her dress is that of a noble, but not a princess, not even for travelling. More like a lady in waiting. That, I could believe.'

'Hmm...It doesn't really matter anyway. She may not be the only deceiver around here.'

Apic looked surprised, 'You suspect Carab?'
'No, you, you great kidney stone, you're no ordinary Bellavian peasant. You know too much!'
'Ahh...' sighed Apic.
'Don't try and deny it. Just how did you come to be on a noggish galley?'
'Ahh, I was going to tell you, but, you know...'
'Come on, spill the beans.'
'The beans? Oh right, the truth. The truth is, I was a thief, I'm not even from Bellavia, but I lived there a long time. I came to Tullis when I was just sixteen and I lived there from then on. I fell in with a bad bunch, who trained me to be a thief and a housebreaker. If only I had listened to Nymella! I wasn't very good, I didn't like violence, and I never liked the idea of killing someone for the sake of money. I robbed a house one night, and a servant spotted me, just as I had gathered up the valuables in the downstairs rooms. I had been informed the house was empty, so I was not wearing my mask. Despite this I spared his life, but the ungrateful swine identified me in front of a magistrate. I was tried and sentenced to death, commuted to life in slavery. It's a little known fact that Bellavia has a slave trade with the southern kingdoms. I know not from what port, the south somewhere, but from there I was shipped to north Nog and sold. I ended up as one of the thousands of human galley slaves of the north nog fleet. The rest you know. You are not angry, Shiv?'
I smiled at Apic knowingly, 'No, course not.'

I had been trying to build up a map in my head of the lands I was in, pieced together from what Apic and Carab could tell me. I overlapped it with a map of Europe.
If I assumed that Usak was the equivalent of southern France, say, and we had gone about two hundred miles due north, to say Lyon, if we were headed for Bellavia which sounded like south England, or Holland, then we had another five hundred miles ahead of us, at a very rough guess. I had questioned Adea until she was utterly fed up with me. Enttland was east of Bellavia, and they shared a border. It was land locked, and had terrible relations with all the kingdoms around it, especially to the south and east. There was a country of savage madmen to the south, who periodically raided the southern regions of Enttland, coming down from the mountains in marauding bands in the middle of the night. Vegas sounded like it could be placed around Oslo, or further north, I got a bit vague here, Carab wasn't much help, but Vegas was at least seven hundred miles away, probably a lot more, which was a very depressing distance. Bellavia could be reached overland, but Vegas might not be. Travelling north would get us there, or to Enttland. According to Adea there was an ancient road that led all the way to Ferron, which I would place around Italy. If we kept going north, eventually we would hit it, the road that is, as it ran south-east to north-west, for most of its length. If we followed it west, we would eventually find Che, a town, which marked the boundary between the

'civilized' lands to the north and the savage lands to the south. Adea had passed through Che, and it sounded like a place where we might hitch a lift with a trade caravan travelling north.

Apic watched me as I drew maps in the dirt.

'What is this place?' he said pointing at my sketchy map of Europe.

'It's my land. I'm using it as a gauge for distance.'

'How?'

'I'm judging mainly by the differences in climate.'

'I see,' said Apic, clearly not.

I sighed and looked up. 'It makes no bloody difference though. I'm still no closer to home.'

'If we can get her highness back to her father, at least we'll get some food and some clean clothes,' said Apic.

I laughed. 'That would be enough to start with, my friend!'

It was with a certain amount of satisfaction that I stepped out of the forest and onto the ancient highway. Three days had passed, and we had reached it just as I had predicted.

'And that way leads to Che!' I proclaimed.

We all stood about with our hands on our hips.

'Yes, well done, oh wondrous sorcerer,' said Adea, who had been listening to a lot of my conversations with Apic, and was at home with the concept of sarcasm. 'If only we had one of your flying machines, we would be home by now.'

Carab looked around and said, 'I do not know this land, but this road is not much used.'

He was right. Most of it was packed earth, with the occasional cobblestone sticking through. It led into the trees each way, snaking into the forest, which was mainly made up of tall conifers.

'Not this bit of it,' said Adea, in her usual condescending way. 'But it is a busy road from Che to Werfen in Enttland.'

'I can see it from here!' cried Apic who had moved along the road a little.

'Don't be silly, Enttland is hundreds of…'

'No, Che!' he yelled, pointing.

Sure enough, down the road, through the trees we could see a distant town.

'Come on then!' I cried. 'Civilisation beckons.'

As we approached the gates of the town, some rough looking characters wearing armour and black livery drew their swords and quickly surrounded us.

In a flurry of confused blows and bustling about, they detained us, despite our cries, and we were frog marched through the gates and into the town. There were many more guards here, all with the same steely expression and the same armour and black livery. I didn't get much of a chance to get an impression of Che as I was moved along quickly by the guards, but what I did see was sturdy looking stone buildings with red slate roofs. Over the rooftops I saw a tall clock tower, slated in red tiles like all the other buildings, and somewhere nearby there must have been a river, as I could hear the sound of flowing water. The citizens appeared to be a tough looking lot, and wore woollen robes, with sword belts holding them around the waist. They all seemed to be armed in some way, and most of them shared the same dark skin and black hair. I locked gaze with a particularly stony faced looking individual and had to glance away from his commanding stare. I suddenly felt self-conscious about my appearance. Unshaven and dressed little better than a beggar, I must have looked like some sort of dangerously insane vagabond. Apic and Carab were little better, being dressed in the same rags they had worn on the galley. Only Adea was semi-presentable, although her fine clothes were now very travel stained. I looked around again. We were being shepherded into a windowless construction that was built right into the town walls. I was separated from the others and marched down some steps and into a long dark corridor. At the end, a cell door hung open, and I was pushed towards it.

'Get in there!' one of them shouted, and gave me a shove in the back. 'What is this?' I wailed, but it did no good, and the door slamming behind me, plunging the cell into complete darkness.

At least I was warm and dry, I reflected. Weeks out in the elements, wandering lost in an unfriendly forest, had made me swear never to take up camping if I ever reached civilization. I paced out the cell, it was no bigger than six feet by four feet. I could just about lie in it diagonally. It was full of straw, which smelled suspiciously unpleasant, but I wasn't bothered, I was fast asleep in no time.

After a time I woke up, and it took me a while to recollect were I was, then remembering, I rolled over and with nothing more pressing to do I prepared for my second doze.

Just as I was snuggling in, thinking... ah, peace, no goblins chasing me, no nogs whipping me, just darkness and warm straw, the door opened and my eyes adjusted to the light. Two armoured figures reached in and grabbed me.

'Just one more hour lads?' I pleaded, but it fell on deaf ears.

I was escorted down the gloomy corridor to another gloomy corridor, and thence to a larger well lit cell. There was a bench, which a guard pointed to, and on which I sat down, but little else. The guards left, shutting the door behind them, leaving me to my thoughts.

Enough time went by for me to think that I had been forgotten about. I considered knocking on the door and saying, 'Excuse me', but that seemed silly, so I stretched out on the bench and tried to sleep again.

I woke up quickly as two men entered the room. One was broad, wore a thick black beard and was dressed in a chain mail shirt and tabard. He looked like a guard captain or something. The other had a pudding bowl haircut I would associate with a religious zealot. He wore black robes, and had a simpering and yet aloof manner of someone who has a position of power but whom everyone hates.

Without any ceremony the captain said,

'Where did you come from? Who sent you?', and grabbed me by the shirt.

'Now, my lord, softly...' simpered the other.

Oh god, I thought, it's the old, good peasant, bad peasant routine.

I stuttered, trying to think of something to say.

'Right', said the captain, releasing me. 'One question at a time, who are you?'

'I...I'm not to sure, my friends call me Shiv, but that's not my real name.'

'You don't know your own name?' demanded the captain.

'Possibly brainwashed by noggish spies,' confided the zealot in the captain's ear.

'No I'm not,' I cried. 'I hate the nogs! Really I do!'

'Why did you come to Che then?'

'We were going north,' then to fill the silence, 'I don't know, me, Apic and Carab escaped from a noggish galley and were trying to get to safety.'

'Convenient story, that,' mused the zealot.

'It's the truth.'

'Curse it!' cried the captain, 'I hate this, those dammed noggish shaman, turning our own people against us. You could be a spy and not even know it lad!'

I shrugged, 'Well, there's no hope for me then, just put me back in my cell and I'll be fine.'

'No, you shall be dealt with in the usual way that we deal with spies,' said the zealot ominously.

'No,' countered the captain. 'Due process must be served.'

Whatever the zealot was about to say in reply to that was suddenly caught short by an explosion that rocked the cell and plaster falling from the ceiling.

'Sabotage!' cried the captain. 'Another incendiary. Come on, just put this one with the others, we have more important matters to attend to.'

And with that they left me, and another guard stepped in and took me to another larger cell, with about a dozen people in it. This must be the main holding area, I thought, by now an expert in all forms of prison cell. Apic and Carab were there.

'Where's Adea?' I asked.

They both shrugged. I turned to look at the other prisoners. They looked like a miserable lot.

'Hey,' I addressed one at random. 'What's the story with this place? What's going on?'

He gave me a long look and said, 'Che's going to go any day now...' and was silent.

Another man, smaller and brighter looking approached me and said,

'What my friend means to say is that Che, our fair jewel of the south, will soon fall to the hands of the nog. The highway is closed, and noggish spies have been setting fires for months. There is to be no help from the north, so we stand or fall alone.'

'Oh.'

'Yes indeed, I am a scholar of history and have studied this at great length. It in many ways resembles the ancient battles of Carmalle and Cito, back in the days when honour really meant something... ahem, yes. The noggish warlords banished parts of their tribes to north Nogland, what was once Ertia. The usurper overthrew the shah of Nogland, and now the north nogs consider themselves to be the only true nogs left. A huge war rages, and the northern nogs are being pushed ever further north. Unfortunately we are in the way.'

'But the south nogs were in Usak, which is north of Nogland.'

'Ah yes,' agreed the friendly scholar. 'An ancient noggish strong hold, the most northerly hold the nogs once had. Usak was always true to the shah, and was at one point open to all nogs, whether they be of the north or south faction, but all that changed when, as I said the usurper deposed the shah ...'

Another explosion rocked the cell, and more dust settled on us. We all looked up and then at each other anxiously. The speaker gulped and continued,

'Indeed, recent rumour has it that the north nogs won a great victory and wrestled Usak back from the hands of the usurper, and driven on by their conquering lust, will soon be at the very gates, a huge horde of them.'

I glanced guiltily at Apic and Carab. In unspoken agreement we decided to keep our involvement in that little episode to ourselves.

'Everyone suspicious is being rounded up. The noggish shamans like to capture humans and turn them to their own devices, apparently using some sort of...'

A section of wall suddenly gave way and collapsed towards us in a deafening rush of noise, mortar and bricks. We all tried to run for cover, but there was nowhere to go, and everyone to a man got crushed under the rubble. I had enough time to see a brutal noggish head poke itself through the huge hole in the wall before I lost consciousness.

Dr. Lock looked up.

'I've still got a free half hour. Don't leave it hanging like that.'

Yarn smiled and said, 'Classic story telling technique, leave a cliff-hanger at the end. It makes the listeners come back for more.'

'Well, you'd better have it prepared for tomorrow, because that's when you'll be seeing me next.'

Yarn raised an eyebrow, and she continued,

'I think the sooner you get to the end of this story, the sooner you'll be willing to listen to reason about a course of therapy.'

'However you wish it,' replied Yarn. 'But what if the story never ends?'
Dr. Lock considered this, then said, 'And will it?'
'Oh yes,' replied Yarn, 'Remember this is all true, and eventually my story will catch up with me in this room, telling you this.'
'Good. Then maybe the story will be about you taking a course of radiotherapy and feeling better?'
'I doubt it, but hope springs eternal, eh doctor?'
They then found that they had been smiling, and they both looked down at the same time.
'So what exactly happened in the mould room? Sally said you got the mould done fine, but when they showed you the simulator you would not have anything to do with it.'
'It's complicated.'
'Hmm, well, there's nothing that can be done until you have a go in the simulator.'
'Yes, I know, but not just yet.'
'If you're worried about hair loss, or sickness, why not talk to Sara?'
'It's nothing like that, I'm sorry,' apologised Yarn. 'All this talking has made me sleepy, so I will see you tomorrow?'
'Yes'
'I'll look forward to it.'

Chapter Six - The fall of Che

I realise to you I sound like a delusional mad man, and that my stories are the rantings of some one who is very ill. I am ill. I must be, because I feel so confused. The thing in my head is trying hard to make me forget, and it is very important that I don't. There are certain things that I must hold onto, and certain things that I must recall to memory or all is lost. Everything hinges on this, me telling this story, and sorting the truth out from the confusion the thing in my head is trying to trick me with. I have forgotten so much already, but as I talk to you, the words form in my mind as if they have a life of their own. I know what you think of me, but we can agree on something at least. There is something in my head, and today I'm going to tell you about how it got there.

Today I will tell an important part of the story. If I am lucky I can put a name to something that needs to be named. Names are important, with names you can often control the thing that is named. That is a universal law of magic. But magic is another thing, for another day! Sorry, I am getting ahead of myself, and it is very dangerous for me to give too much away right now.

To continue then, I could hear Carab calling to me from very far away, and gradually I awoke to find myself cradled in his arms like a baby.
'All right, all right, I'm awake.' I said, 'Where's Apic?'
Carabs face was ashen as he pointed at Apic's crumpled body nearby. He wasn't moving and his left arm was bent in a way that it shouldn't.
'Aw... crap...' I moaned and pulled myself over to him. He was still alive, but unconscious. I looked around. All the other prisoners had disappeared, except for one, who was clearly dead from a fractured skull.
'Apic?'
'He awoke, Shiv, but clutched his arm, and fell unconscious again.'
'Oh. Right. Um. Aww... Dam, it's a break, and a nasty one too. He needs a splint, and jeez, someone's going to have to reset it, the bones sticking out through the skin.'
Carab looked at me like a forlorn dog.
'Ok, right. I'll do it,' I said.
As quickly as I could I held open the wound and popped the broken bone back under the skin. I could feel the two ends grate together, which made me wince in discomfort.
Suddenly Apic sat up, and let out a terrific blood-curdling cry, then slipped back, thankfully, into a stupor.
'Carab,' I said. 'Go get some wood for a splint, and something to use as bandages. I'll hold the wound shut until you get back.'

After a brief struggle with the writhing Apic, we rigged a splint on his arm, and slung it up onto his chest. We pulled him up between us and dragged him outside into the street. It was raining fairly hard, but I could still make out several fires. There was a fair bit of rubble around, and many bodies, most of which were human, but some, I noted with grim satisfaction were noggish.

I was at a loss as to what to do when suddenly we saw our friend the scholar, picking his way through some rubble.

'Over here!' he cried. 'Everyone is heading for the north orchards on the other side of the river. Come quick before they destroy the bridge!'

We jogged in his direction as fast as we could. Keeping to the side streets we avoided the noggish soldiers, who seemed more intent on looting than killing. The soldiers seemed to be of a different set than the sailors we were familiar with. The noggish love for heraldry was very obvious in the uniforms their soldiers wore. They were dressed in bright red tabards with gold piping over the chest and shoulders, underneath were worn tight starched shirts with stiff collars. On their legs they wore coarse looking baggy trousers, tucked into black leather boots. They all wore a black symbol of a dragon on their tabards and were armed either with long dangerous looking sabres or twelve-foot pikes.

We joined a few more people heading in the same direction. It was getting darker now, and that combined with the rain, aided our escape.

The scholar disappeared around a corner, and as we turned it also, we saw the bridge.

It was flat and made of wood, and crossed a fast flowing river. There had obviously been a pitched battle here, as bodies lay everywhere, but the nogs must have been driven off, as only some tough looking human soldiers remained. There were several at the head of the bridge, ushering civilians across it. As I crossed I noticed several more soldiers pouring barrels of pitch onto the wooden planks.

'They mean to burn it!' I gasped at Carab, who nodded.

We reached the opposite bank, and joined a group of people milling around in the orchard. The orchard itself was neatly laid out in rows of fruit trees, and I could see small groups of people gathered underneath the low branches. The moans of the wounded could be heard all around us, which had a very unnerving effect in the gloomy night drizzle. I gently put Apic down, and placed my cloak across his body to protect him from the rain.

Carab disappeared into the trees, but was quickly back.

'Adea is not here, we must go back,' he stated simply and taking a discarded sword, ran back towards the bridge.

My cries of, 'But you hardly know her!' and 'Have you checked over here properly?' went unheeded and I raced to catch up with him.

As we carefully skirted around a wall, keeping as low as we could, on the other side of the river, I said,

'She could be anywhere Carab.'

'She is back at the prison, Shiv, and you know it.'

I gritted my teeth, and held the stout stick I had found as a weapon in the orchard more firmly.

We skirted around the burning buildings and bands of noggish raiders. Through the mist and drizzle, the occasional scream could be heard.

We had a sudden and brutal clash with two nogs, both of which Carab slew with his sword in a business like manner. The only contribution I made was to club one as he went down.

It was a disjointed and terrifying experience, our journey to the prison, intense emotion every second, inter-spaced with moments of running away from things. But we probably got there a lot sooner than it felt like, and before I knew it, we had breached the gates and were inside the prison.

Crouching and panting for breath, we loped up the steps to the main hall in bounds of three. Sounds of a violent struggle came from within.

Down a hallway, and then down some steps to the cells we ran. In the next corridor we saw a human prisoner fighting a guard who was on his knees with blood covering his face. The prisoner broke past us and ran up the stairs.

'Where is the girl?' said Carab, addressing the stunned guard.

He shakily pointed down the corridor. I grabbed the keys from his belt as we went past him.

There was only one cell door that hadn't been forced open, and if she was in this corridor, then she must have been held within. I barged Carab out of the way, and I went towards the lock with the keys.

More sounds of violence came from above, spurring me on, as I fumbled with the keys, trying them one by one. Eventually I hit upon the right one, and the door gave a click as it unlocked.

'At last!' gasped Carab as I finally got the door open.

'Adea?' we both whispered into the darkness, and suddenly she flew out, and fell stumbling into our arms.

With no time for explanations, Carab grabbed her and we raced up the stairs, leaping over the now unconscious guard.

The doors to the main hall were currently the location of a bloody battle. A group of desperate guards and soldiers had been beaten back by a superior nog force. They were surrounded and had no chance of winning, but they seemed to be selling their lives dearly. Many lay dead already. We dove into an open doorway and into a sort of shuttered antechamber.

Carab pulled a thick curtain from the rear wall revealing a high window. With a few grunts we levered and boosted each other out, and into a dark alley.

Desperately we crept to its entrance and onto a larger street. I looked round the corner and seeing it clear, as far as I could tell in the mist, I ran forward, the others close behind me.

This proved to be an unwise course of action, as something truly monstrous suddenly loomed out of the mist dwarfing even the nog warriors that stood around it.

I skidded to a stop and Carab bumped into me, knocking me to my knees. The nogs all turned to face us, and I froze in terror. The vast back of the giant figure rippled with muscle as it turned, and revealed its long face, like a horse's skull, but with more teeth, and a malevolent red gaze. The demon, or whatever it was, was well over ten feet tall, its broad shoulders nearly touching the tall buildings on either side. Rain ran in rivers down its bare musclebound chest and its hairy goat like legs. On its head it had two huge horns, each at least four feet long, curved out from the front of its face at a dangerous looking angle, extending past its long skull snout. Its skin was a dark red colour, it wore no clothing, but shaggy hair covered most of its lower body and fore arms. Each finger on each hand terminated in a claw the size of a carving knife, and its hooves struck sparks on the cobbles as it shifted its weight. It was something from a nightmare, truly. I could feel my stomach turning to water.

It turned its head to one side to fix one of it's eyes on us. I heard Carab gulp.

Adea let out a terrified gasp.

Carab whispered, 'There are nog behind us as well...'

I couldn't tear my eyes away from the beast's horrible glare. It moved its head again, this time fixing me with its other eye, and let out a low snickering rumble, which made the nogs standing around it, all back off a step.

One of the nogs, obviously a shaman, he was wearing the same red robes that Zort had worn, stepped in front of the horror, and shouted, 'My master, kill them!' to the demon, and then he named it. A name I cannot recall now.

I tried to say something, but it came out as, 'Eep.'

The demon beast took a few steps towards me and said something in some strange abyssal tongue. It stopped, as if confused, then spoke again, something that sounded like a question. The part of me that wasn't currently soiling itself in terror picked up on the fact that this awful being was puzzled by whatever it saw when it looked at me. It reached out a clawed hand for me and as the first of its talons closed on my head there was a sudden blazing light that made me close my eyes and fall into a crouch.

After that it all went blank.

I woke up underneath my cloak lying next to Apic. Groggily I moved myself up onto my elbows. I had a splitting headache.

'What happened?' I asked sensibly.

'Look,' someone said, and then Carab and Adea were crouched beside me.

'Are you ok?' another voice said, it sounded like it came from the bottom of a well.

I put my hand to my forehead. There was a bandage around it.

'I dunno...' I looked around, we were under a tree in the orchard, it was still raining, but we were quite dry sheltered as we were. I had no idea what sort of time of day it was.

'If you can walk, we can't hang around here, I will tell you what happened on the way,' said Carab.

I sluggishly got up, and felt dizzy, but Apic supported me as he also stood up.

'The walking wounded,' he noted.

In the event, it was Adea that told me what had happened, as she was much more willing to talk, Carab not being the most articulate of fellows. 'You were sucked towards the... thing... by the light, then I couldn't see much, but I felt Carab drag me back. Then there was a great inrush of air, and all the mist was sucked in towards where you and the thing were. Smoke poured out of the ground, and when it cleared, there was just you and the shaman standing there. All the other nogs had run off. The shaman, well, the nog in the cloak anyway, was turning round and round, he seemed to be confused and beside himself with anger. The beast demon thing was no where to be seen. The shaman then looked at you, and hit you on the head with his staff and ran off. He said something as he did that, but I didn't understand it. You fell to the ground, and we went and got you. Carab carried you back to the bridge, which they were about to set fire to, but we got across just before they did. Ah... that's about it, you were unconscious for about eight hours.'

'Bloody hell,' I said, and put my hand to my head again. 'What was that all about?'

'It proves you are a powerful sorcerer,' chipped in Apic. 'As if there was any doubt anyway.'

This aimed at Carab.

As we walked on, I felt my headache begin to clear, but I could still feel something there. That shaman must have fetched me a right crack, assuming that was all that had happened to me.

'So you think this is what caused the tumour?' asked Dr. Lock, when she realised that Yarn had stopped talking.

'Well, the evidence would suggest so.'

They were in the day room, which was strangely quiet. The rain was off, but the sun wasn't out. A usual dull Scottish day. Yarn was sitting in an armchair, his head lent back on the chair. They were the only ones in the room.

'What happened to the demon?' she asked.

'Search me.'

The doctor considered this, and took her glasses off and rubbed her eyes. 'What would it been like, if I'd told you that you didn't have a tumour, that you had had a stroke or something? Would the story be different?'

'Please doctor, don't try and catch me out, I'm telling it, as the events happened.'

'OK then, well, do you want me to come visit you again tomorrow?'

'That would be lovely.'

There was a pause, as if Dr. Lock waited for Yarn to say something else, then she said,

'What's the matter, are you in pain? My god, you have gone white!'
'No, no, I'm ok. Today has been a good day. I have remembered something important, I cannot tell you any more than that at the moment, please leave me, I am sorry to be so rude.'

Dr. Lock reached over and switched off the dictaphone. They were in Dr. Barage's office again. It was in the usual state. Papers and folders everywhere, he had the sort of filling system that drove secretaries to the edge of distraction.
'Brilliant,' said Dr. Barage. 'It better than one of those audio books, can I take it home for the kids?'
'Ian,' scathed Dr. Lock.
'What, you don't believe him? I believe every word. You can't just make that sort of stuff up off the cuff.'
'Ian, say something sensible please, for a change.'
Dr. Barage laughed and said, 'Ok then, well, it may be that his story is being influenced by his diagnosis, but I would steer well clear of trying to lay a trap for him, it would be totally unethical to tell him something erroneous, just to see how it effected the story. You could get sued. Let him get on with it, whether he is on treatment or not, he's still a patient and deserves the best we can do for him.'
'Yes,' agreed Dr. Lock.
'I can tell you have got a special interest in him, so just continue to look in on him at the end of each day, that's what I'd do. As long as his condition doesn't deteriorate, then we are doing fine. But, please keep coming to me with the tapes, I'm hooked! I love all this sub-Tolkien stuff! Did you write down any of the earlier sessions that you didn't record?'
'I've started to.'
'Well, send me a copy in the internal mail will you?'
'Yes, Ian', said Dr. Lock, in a drawn out sarcastic way, 'We wouldn't want you to miss out.'
Dr. Lock got up to leave.
'Hey, are you going to that guys leaving do?' Ian asked.
'The guy in the centre, yes.' she nodded.
'See you tonight then!'

Chapter Seven - Foona

I kept Apic amused by teaching him English swear words for a while, and even though his face was ashen and grey, he managed a smile or two.

'No, bugger means, well, it means when two men, you know, who do it to each others bottoms.'

'Get off!'

'No, surely it must happen here too!'

Apic gave me an arch look. Carab, who was walking beside us, muttered. 'What sort of deprived land do you come from?'

'I don't do it!' I protested. 'Just some people, and anyway, it's the word that's important.'

We were all wet, tired and depressed. There was me, Apic, Carab, and Adea, the scholar, whose name was Mollo, and a few other refugees. Mollo was an interesting sort of fellow. Short, maybe about forty-five, balding and sporting a straggly beard. He was very talkative, nervously so, being burned out of your own town must be a pretty stressful experience I supposed. He had a very animated face, and waved his arms around a lot as he talked.

Oh, and there was Nadia, which I thought was a girl's name, to be honest, who was the unfriendly zealot from the prison.

We had been separated from the main body of refugees when a gang of goblins had attacked from the trees. I ran off, closely followed by my friends and later we'd found Nadia quivering under a bush. This whole section of the forest was crawling with the little green bastards, but Carab and I had become very adept at spotting them, and their nasty little traps.

'Anyway, this is the best one, you'll like it!' I continued.

'OK, I'm ready,' nodded Apic.

'Fuck!' I cursed.

Carab nodded in approval.

'This is a good word. Like a blow or a strike. I don't speak your language but I can guess what it means.'

'Fuck,' said Apic. 'Fuck.'

'Good eh?' I smiled. 'Here are the derivatives. Fucking, Fucker, Fucked.'

Apic laughed like a child with a new toy, he was a natural with languages.

'My fucking arm is fucked. It's so fucking sore that I want to cut the fucker off!'

He stumbled on ahead, effing and blinding with every step. I shared a look with Carab.

Adea mouthed the word, but decided to remain silent, and gave me a scowl instead.

'What is that you and Apic are always speaking anyway?' she asked.

Carab cut in before I could speak and said, 'Pay no attention, it is a dirty language.'

Later that day we came across a small inn on the path. It had a tall wooden stockade fence all around it, but the gate was open, and the place seemed to be deserted. After a quick look round for danger, it wasn't long before we entered the main hall. It was like everyone had vanished. There were even a few half-empty tankards on one of the long tables.

'Have a look round for food and beer,' I ordered.

To poor travel-worn refugees this place, humble as it was, was a small piece of heaven. The larder was still mostly full, and there were three barrels of the local brew in the cellar, as well as countless racks of wine.

'They must have buggered off, when they heard Che had fallen,' remarked Apic, the consummate swear-monger, as he tucked into a big plate of potatoes and beef stew. Everyone else was doing the same.

'Yes, a god send,' replied Mollo, whipping grease from his chin.

'Shiv brings us luck,' winked Apic. 'We were galley slaves until he got us out.'

I coughed, 'Oh yes, I'm the luckiest man alive. Do you know were I come from, you can adjust the temperature of a room by the flick of a switch. You can get hot water whenever you want it - there are no goblins for a start, and definitely no nogs.'

Carab raised his eyes to the ceiling. He's off again.

Adea joined in the conversation. She had been delicately nibbling on a cutlet.

'Excuse my ignorance, but I seem to remember, in one of your previous lectures, that you said not everyone lives like that in your land.'

I sighed, 'Not everyone, but I did, and I wasn't a noble, like you my lady, just a regular free-man.'

'No bondsmen?' asked the scholar.

'Slavery is abhorrent to us, no man is a slave, and our monarchy has no real power. The people run the country, in a parliament.'

'What a foolish notion.'

The others had gathered around now. Sensing I now had an audience, I stood up and took a large swallow from my tankard.

'Not as foolish as all that, when you consider the alternative. Feudalism has long since been replaced by other concepts of rule. Good, like Democracy, Congress, Parliament, and darker concepts, such as Communism and Fascism. Let me tell you about a great war, which was fought against the tyranny of evil in my land. There once was a man called Adolf Hitler…'

I treated them to the extent of my O grade knowledge of the Second World War well into the night, and after D-Day and Adolf and Eva's suicide in the bunker, and the story had ended, a peaceful calm descended in the inn, and people shared looks of satisfaction.

'That was a good story Shiv, did you make it up yourself?' asked Mollo

'It's true!'

Carab pulled his lower eyelid down, in a gesture that meant, 'tall tales'.

'Well, suit yourselves, I was just saying.'

'True or not, friend Shiv,' said Mollo. 'It was a good story.'

'Yeah, gosh, it must be pretty late though.'

I was getting sleepy, and I noticed that some of the others were settling down for the night. I suddenly realised how much beer I had drunk to keep my throat well lubricated for my tale and as I contemplated whether or not I should have any more I fell asleep at the table.

Someone poking me in the ribs with a sword rudely awakened me. Grumbling in displeasure I looked up at a figure dressed in green leather armour, and a picture of a tree embroidered on his tabard. Glancing around, I could see that the inn was full of these men, all dressed the same way, and that they were waking up my friends in a similar manner.

'Oh shit,' I said.

We were all herded out of the inn and into the courtyard, the guards joking and laughing to themselves about another load of birds for the king's pot. There was a wagon waiting outside into which we were placed, and the sturdy door locked behind us. The walls of the wagon were simple bars, so we could see out, and the wind and the rain could get in. The driver geed up the wagon horses and we rattled off onto the road. One of the guards, who was riding along beside the prison cart told us,

'Looting one of the royal hostels of Foona is a capital offence, my boyos. You lot are to be taken to Lysander to stand trial.'

'We are refugees,' I protested. 'Che has fallen to the nog you know.'

'Well,' he replied good-humouredly. 'As to that I don't know, but you can certainly tell that to King Real.'

'Oh,' was all I could manage to reply.

The guard then spurred his horse on, muttering, 'I doubt it will make any difference though.'

The journey took about three days. As we got closer to Lysander, the wagon got fuller and fuller, with other refugees and general ne'er do wells, until we were all standing uncomfortably cheek by jowl. We didn't talk much, as the guards would take a very dim view of idle chatter from the wagon, and would rattle their swords in their scabbards at the first word. It was a cold uncomfortable journey and I was glad when it was over. The others were equally glum, especially Adea, who disliked intensely the arrangements for ablutions, which consisted of a small hole in the floor of the cart. As the only female captive, apart from the last day, when we were joined by what looked like two prostitutes, she insisted that Apic, Carab and I turned away from her and acted as a shield from the prying eyes of the other prisoners. As hardy veterans of the noggish galleys, none of us menfolk had any notions of nicety whatsoever. Still, tempting as it may have been to make jokes at Adea's expense, we refrained from doing so, as she could usually give as good as she got, and it was a delicate subject after all, although Apic and I did occasionally exchange an amused glance.

'So much for being lucky,' grumbled Adea.

For some reason I was alone in a cell with her, I didn't know where the others were.

'Well at least we are seeing a bit of the world.'

Adea shot me a pained look, 'All we seem to see is the inside of jail cells. Do you know how long it's been since I had a bath?'

I rubbed my head where the scar was.

'And don't pick that, it won't heal otherwise,' she scolded.

I growled and slapped my hand down by my side.

'Tell me about Enttland then.'

Adea sighed then seemed to accept this topic of conversation, 'It's very nice. Sheltered by hills, which makes it warm. It has rich pastureland and pretty little villages in the valleys. I've told you all this,' she sighed. 'I miss it very much.'

'Admit it. You're not a princess are you?'

Adea's mouth became a thin line.

'I'm not telling you, you might tell Carab.'

'Oh right. Here we are in a prison cell, god knows where, probably about to be executed for looting and you're worried about what your boyfriend might think about you?'

'Well, Apic's a thief, and your a, I don't even know what you are...'

'Thanks.' then I laughed. 'I'm Lord Flat Eric of Levi, didn't I tell you?'

'Carab is so good and kind. I don't want him to think I'm a lair.'

'Well, I won't pry. How's your leg?'

'Fine.'

Just as she said that, the cell door was unbolted and in stepped one of the guards. I was becoming an expert on guards, as well as prison cells. This one was grinning, always a bad sign.

'Well, the princess and the magician. It's your lucky day. King Real wants to deal with you personally.'

As we were ushered along a gallery, and down diverse corridors, and eventually to a chamber that opened onto what I presumed was the throne room, Adea was whispering to me,

'Let me do the talking, I've moved in noble circles, I know what to say,' and 'I'm sure King Real will be a reasonable man.'

I nodded and said nothing. We were motioned to stop, so we did. The guards rested on their pikes, and looking over their shoulders I could see into what looked like a large throne room.

We were in the doorway of a side corridor, so I couldn't see the entire hall, but we could see the actual throne from where we were and the people who stood around it. From what I did see, the room was lavishly decorated with wall hangings and trophies. There was fine seasoned looking furniture against all the walls displaying objects d'art and curios. The throne itself was made of rich mahogany, inlaid with gold and jewels, and stood on a slightly raised stone dais.

A man, who I presumed was King Real, lounged on the throne in an arrogant pose. He was a swarthy looking fellow, with very pale skin and dark hair. Two elderly gentlemen dressed in black robes and skullcaps stood either side of the throne. They could have been twins.

Light filtered in from tall arched windows that lined the length of the hall, cutting the room into alternate sections of light and dark. There was a smell of incense, and the smoke from burners that I couldn't see, but must have been nearby, drifted in and out of the patches of light, giving the room a further feeling of richness if further were needed.

Armoured royal guards stood in rows down the hall, and although I couldn't see, I suspected there was a lot more around than the ones within my field of vision. They didn't wear the green livery of the road wardens, but chain mail and black tabards emblazoned with an eagle, the crest of the royal guard. The four that escorted us wore the same livery, and were so tall I had to stand on tiptoes to see what was going on.

King Real was concluding some court business. There was a slick of some sort of black red substance on the floor in front of the throne.

'Bring forth the next plaintiff!' decreed the king.

A man crept forward, and approached bowing.

'Ah… your majesty.'

'Well?' smirked the king.

'I…' stammered the man, tugging on his grey beard. 'I represent the tanners and weavers guild your majesty. I, that is, me and my fellow guild members are concerned at the recent rise in taxes... that is…'

'You dislike the taxes? Hah! A guildmaster who dislikes taxes!'

The guards laughed nervously, as did the two men who stood behind the throne, chamberlains I presumed.

'And, I'm sorry you majesty, ever since Burgher Amis was executed it has been almost impossible to employ descent pickers. Many people are leaving the guilds. You can't hire a decent bledlow for love nor money these days.'

'Oh for gods sake!' cried the king. 'Shut up! I hate this! Moan, moan, moan. It's all I ever hear.'

The guildmaster bowed and grovelled.

'Tell me, Master Stemple, Amis was your brother-in-law wasn't he?'

'Yes, your majesty,' gulped the guildmaster.

'And where is your sister now?'

'The Stone Lock.'

That was the name of the large prison, close to the palace. I knew that, because that was where we had first gone to, before being taken to the palace. The Stone Lock was a squat dark building, and looked exactly like the sort of place where hundreds had died, and hundreds were suffering.

'Good. And your niece?'

'The Lock too, your majesty.'

The king laughed and motioned to one of the guards.

'No she's not.'

The guard brought forward a frightened looking girl of about thirteen. Stemple's facial expression was a visage of horror. I craned my neck past the guard's shoulder and chewed on one of my fingers.

One of the men behind the throne whispered in the king's ear.

'Dam you, Clyis, I will not! He's had his fun, and now I'll have mine!'

The man called Clyis took a step back.

'Please you majesty!' cried Stemple

'Don't you dare address me directly!' screeched the king.

I put my hand to my mouth, and looked at Adea. She had gone very pale, neither of us could guess at what awful things were going to happen next.

The king motioned for the girl to be brought closer to him, and he said, 'What is your name child?'

The girl glanced at her devastated uncle then said, 'Helena.'

'Take this, Helena.' he said, taking his dagger from his belt, 'If you can kill your uncle, I will let your mother go.'

The poor girl stood there motionless.

'Do it!' shouted the king, and pushed the girl towards her uncle. I took an involuntary step forward, but was pushed back by one of the guards next to me.

Crying, the girl approached her uncle.

'Come here darling,' sobbed the guildmaster.

'And you shut up!' cried the king. 'Come on Helena, be a sport, you don't have to kill him, even, just maim him a little, to show how much you love your dear sweet mama.'

Helena raised the dagger, and Stemple whispered something to her, which may have been,

'Please just do it.'

But Helena suddenly turned on her heal, and rushed at the king, screaming, with the dagger held high above her head. A guard stepped in and cut her down, and her momentum carried her into the king's lap.

Stemple leapt up and rushed towards them, but he too was cut down by a guard, and more blood splashed onto the flagstones.

The king held the dying girl, and said,

'What is it about you people? You never do the right thing. You never learn obedience,' and he let her body fall to the floor.

'Get this mess out of here!' he shouted to the guards, and the bodies were dragged out of a side door, leaving streaky trails of blood on the stone floor.

'Next!' shouted the king happily, whipping blood from his gown with a cloth.

Adea and I were pushed reluctantly forward, into the presence of the mad monarch.

'What a day,' sighed the king. 'I wish mother was here to enjoy it. Ah yes, the princess and the sorcerer, that's right isn't it?'

'Yes, your majesty,' I said and bowed.

'Well, it's nice to see that someone today has remembered their manners. Are you going to make any assassination attempts?'

'Certainly not, your majesty,' I said, but thought, not today anyway you vicious bastard.

Adea remained silent.

'What do you make of all this, sorcerer?' asked the king.

I considered, then said, 'People will do almost anything if pushed far enough, your majesty.'

'Yes,' laughed the king. 'I can see we understand each other. Why are you before me?'

'We were in one of your hostels, it was deserted, but we were desperate, as we had just escaped from the fall of Che…'

'Yes, yes, yes, so what sort of magician are you?'

'I'm not really a magician, you majesty, I simply tell stories…'

The king looked around, clearly getting a bit bored now.

'Oh well, no magic tricks.' Then something occurred to him, and he smiled, 'Well, master non-magician, your crime wasn't very serious, and I have decided to be merciful. Ever since mother died, there has been a lot more use for the torture chamber. And the old goat that used to run it, what happened to him?'

One of the chamberlains whispered in the king's ear.

'Oh yes, that's right, I had him killed. Well, you can replace him, how does the post of court torturer grab you?'

The king leant forward on his throne, to watch my reaction.

'That is very kind of you, your majesty.'

Disappointed at my lack of reaction the king waved me away.

'Very well, take him down to the torture chamber.'

'And the princess, your majesty?' asked one of the guards.

'Oh,' replied the king. 'Take her back to the Lock, until she decides to be more interesting.'

I tried to smile reassuringly at Adea, as I was dragged off, but she seemed to have retreated into herself.

As I was taken from the throne room, I heard the king shout, 'Bring in the ambassador!'

I was taken towards an archway on the other side of the hall, and suddenly it was filled by a seven-foot figure. I reeled back in surprise, as the nog advanced past me and into the throne room. I had just got a glance at his bestial face, but had I just nearly bumped into Tup?

'Gosh, what happened after that?' asked Kirsten.

'I dunno, that's the end of the tape,' replied Mark.

The ECNO, or the Edinburgh Centre for Neuro Oncology, was the office where Sara was situated, on the South Corridor of the Weston General, and where Mark and Kirsten worked. It wasn't typical of hospital offices in that it was quite new, and as a result the furniture and computers were fairly modern. It was typical however, in that the curved pine desks were covered in papers, paper clips, pens, post-its, dirty coffee mugs, staplers, staple removers and a hundred other objects that are the common detritus of modern working life.

Dr. Mark White was a dark, bearded man. The fact that his father was Iraqi made him look somewhat like a terrorist, a fact that his friend Gavin, the recently departed IT student, and another office clown, had pointed out. In his early twenties, he had been at the centre for a year, the office's official statistician, and unofficial wise guy. Kirsten Smith was a student on a work placement in the centre for three months. She had the pretty round face of a girl just out of her teens, dark hair and eyes.

'Where did you get this?' Kirsten continued.

'From Barage, he got it from Heather. You remember that weird patient Sara was telling us about. That's him!'

'Oh wow! I know him, I've seen him. He's quite good looking in a distant sort of way. It's such a shame. He must be less than thirty.'

'Uh-huh, we were all talking about it last night at Gavin's leaving do. Ian brought it up, and Heather was really embarrassed. I got Ian to make me a copy of the tape. I'm going to have to let Gavin hear it, he loves all that sort of stuff.'

'Mark! It's private. I think it's really sweet, Heather is the only one he talks to, and here we are listening to their private conversations. Hey, do you think she's got the hots for him? She is single isn't she?'

'She has *definitely* got the hots for him! You should have seen Ian and Gavin taking the piss out of her. I was laughing so hard I spilt my beer into the sweet and sour chicken. You should have heard her going on about him, like they were married or something,' Mark laughed.

'You're terrible!'

'Not as bad as Gavin, she got so angry with him, she poked him in the eye!'

'No! Really?'

'Yeah!' exclaimed Mark. 'Gavin was crouched down, laughing and holding his eye, and Heather was standing there like, I just poked you in the eye, how do you like that?'

'Oh my god!'

'It was so funny, you should have been there, they were all plastered!'

Mark moved his chair over to his computer, and proceeded to log into his e-mail.

'So, is Heather going to see him today?'

'She goes to see him every day.'

'I think that's so sweet, but it's such a shame.'

Mark pulled a face.

Chapter Eight - King Real's court

My first day as King Real's court torturer went better than I expected. The ever-present guards all visibly relaxed once we were out of the general vicinity of the king, one of them even struck up a short conversation with me.

'Court torturer, that's a good post. You're lucky.'

'What happened to the last one?'

'The king had him roasted alive, for letting the Bellavian ambassador die too soon.'

'Shit.'

My apprentice quietly showed me around the gloomy torture chamber. It was a low ceilinged room and filled with a wide variety of implements and devices for hurting people in imaginative ways. It was like a set from a hammer house of horror film. My apprentice's name wasn't Igor and much to my disappointment, he had neither a big hunched back or one great bulging eye. In truth he was a lad of about fourteen and his name was Viol. He had a strange sort of innocence about him that I found a little disturbing. His sweet, if somewhat grubby face looked up at me as I followed him around the torture chamber and showed me the various tools of the trade. This poor unfortunate child had probably seen things that people of any age should never see, and appeared to be deeply traumatised. There was something in the way he walked, and the slow way that he talked that spoke of an emptiness within him.

His voice was monotone as he named all the devices on a low bench.

'Thumbscrews…scrappers... pincers… noggish nipple clamps.'

I looked into an alcove.

'Oh my god! There's an old geezer in here!' I said, describing what looked like a bag of bones in an over sized parrot's cage.

'That's old Roy, he's been here years. He doesn't say much.'

'God's sake.' I cried as I unlocked the chain holding the door closed using the bundle of keys I had been given. 'Let's get him out of this!'

'Come on Roy,' sighed the boy. 'Time for your punishment.'

The old man grumbled and flopped out of the cage.

'What first master? The rack?' asked Voil.

'For heaven's sake no! Get a blanket round him and get him out of sight.'

Voil shrugged and led the geriatric off.

There were many side chambers, one of which had a bath of acid to dissolve bodies in, and another had some sort of chute for dropping bones and rubbish down. There was also a chamber with a large treadmill in it which was connected to a fly-wheel. This in turn could be used to power a couple of the more unpleasant devices of torture. The largest sub-chamber was the living quarters for Viol and me. He had kept them quite tidy. There was a small fireplace with a couple of old chairs beside it, making the place cosier, if a torture chamber could ever be such a thing. There was even a picture on the wall that Viol may have got from the top of a box of biscuits or something and had placed above his bed. It was a crude etching of a young lad walking with a dog over a pleasant cornfield on a sunny day. I found this pathetic little picture very hard to look at without getting a knot of anger in my stomach.

'Put him by the fire, give him something to eat,' I ordered Voil.

Old Roy was oblivious to it all, but seemed quite happy to be out his cage and for once not being prodded with something uncomfortable.

There were no windows down here in the bowels of the castle, but it felt like evening when our next guests arrived, escorted by some of the ever present guards, tough looking characters in the ubiquitous black livery with the golden eagle.

'Nothing specific, just to be tortured to death,' reported the sergeant as our guests were pushed into the chamber.

It was Apic and Carab. They were in chains, but I soon had them off on one of the anvils.

'You're the torturer?' gasped Apic in disbelief.

'Yep. First day on the job.'

Apic was well and truly gob-smacked, '*How*?'

'The king took a shine to me.'

Carab rubbed his red wrists.

'I hate chains,' he grumbled.

I started to bind up Apic's arm again. I had some bandages, sometimes a torturer had to prevent a client from bleeding to death too quickly, and I used these to re-splint Apic's arm. If it didn't set properly it would never be right. I tutted and fussed, and quite annoyed Apic, until eventually Carab rubbed his chin and asked,

'Where's Adea?'

'It's always Adea, Adea, Adea with you,' I grumbled as I did one of the ties on Apic's arm, 'I swear she gets into trouble just so that you can come and rescue her. I don't know, she and I got separated in the throne room, but I think she may have been taken back to the Stone Lock.'

Apic swore as I tightened the last of his bandages.

'Guess who else is here?' I asked, leaving him to nurse his arm and looking up at Carab.

'Who?'

'Tup.'

They both looked at me. 'Tup?' said Apic, 'Tup as in Captain Tup, the nog?'

'The same. All nine feet of him. He's some sort of ambassador, must be cutting a deal with King Real.'

'Fucking hell.'

'Who's that?' grunted Carab, pointing his chin at Voil, who was standing in the entrance to the living chamber.

'My apprentice Voil, he's ok...'

Voil bolted back behind the doorway. I escorted my friends into the living area, and closed the door.

'We should be ok in here for a while.'

Apic sighed and fell onto a pallet and was soon asleep. Carab looked around. I settled into one of the seats by the fire and Carab remained standing.

'You sure make friends quickly,' he said nodding at the old man.

'That's Roy, a permanent resident, and before you say it, I know we have to find Adea.'

'Yes.'

'But it's no good rushing out into the corridor and getting killed off by the guards. We need some sort of plan.'

Carab crossed his arms and scowled at me.

'And anyway, she might turn up down here sooner or later.'

Voil knocked over something in the back of the room.

'Hey you! Stay where I can see you,' I growled at him.

Voil grudgingly came a little closer.

'Pretty weird, huh?' I asked him. 'But you don't expect me to torture my friends do you?'

'No, master.'

'And it's not like…oh sod it. Look at him Carab, totally desensitised. You used to see it on the news back home on the faces of famine victims.'

Carab clambered up onto the lip of the chute and I spooled in the rope that was attached to his waist.

'Well?' I asked.

'Some sort of charnel pit. There is a door. I could open it with some of the tools up here.'

'Where's the torch?'

'I left it down there.'

'Ok, I'll take a look.'

'Suit yourself, it stinks though.'

It did indeed stink, the smell of old bones and rotting flesh was very unpleasant. The chute was very long, and curved around a bit. I guessed it must lead out of the castle completely and somewhere into the surrounding area. The chute terminated in a large round chamber, with a vast pile of bones in its centre. From where I was I could climb down from the chute quite easily and clamber awkwardly down the scree slope of old bones. It really did smell something dreadful, and I held my nose as I crossed the chamber to the wrought iron door, gasping for breath. I had a bag of tools slung over my shoulder, and the door in the pit soon gave way from the force of a crowbar. I pushed the door open as cautiously as I could, but it was the entrance to a crypt, and necessarily had to make a great sighing creak as I pushed, enough to wake the dead. I stepped out into what appeared to be a dark and gloomy graveyard, headstones spread out like a grim reapers harvest all around me. It was night time and a gibbous moon hung over the graves. I looked up. The brooding castle towered above me. Behind the cemetery gates the town lights shone brightly. It looked like the sort of place that sits at the foot of a mountain that has a castle full of vampires on it. Tall dark buildings and twisted smoking chimneys were much in evidence, silhouetted against the night sky. Excellent, an escape route, I mused. Much as I wished I didn't have to, I climbed back up the chute.

'You can take him,' I said, pointing at the snoring body of Apic, 'Get into town and try to infiltrate the Stone Lock and find Adea. Find an inn, and come back and tell me were it is, so if Adea turns up here, we can meet you there.'

'Yes,' agreed Carab. 'A good plan.'

'I'll leave the rope, so you can get back up if need be, but don't skulk around the graveyard too much, that's my only way out.'

Carab woke Apic, and soon they were off.

A few days later, and no sign of Adea, although we did get another visitor. A young fellow was dragged in, and roughly thrown onto the paved floor.

'Find out all he knows about the rebellion. The king must be informed,' stated the surly guard sergeant, and shrugged.

I was wearing my blood stained leather apron to look the part, so nodded and smiled, 'No problem, leave it to me.'

I waited until the guards had left, their hollow steps echoing up the corridor and up onto the iron stairs that eventually led to the cellars of the castle. Whoever had designed the castle had decided to keep the torture chamber as far away as possible from where decent people were eating and sleeping, probably much to the disgust of the present King Real.

That suited me fine though, and I had sent Voil into the cellars and lower regions of the kitchens to get me supplies. Wine, decent food, blood and guts from the butcher's bins, and other things I thought I might need. I also sent him to the smith to get me certain pieces of metal that I needed for a plan that I had germinating in my mind.

I did a little bit of sneaking around myself, but couldn't get past the guards at the top of the cellar steps. Voil had more freedom and appeared to be fairly trustworthy, but he had not seen Adea anywhere.

Our young victim stood up, rattling the chains that had him hunched up under their weight. He looked quite dangerous, lean, muscular, and had the air of a cornered animal.

I looked at Voil, and he looked at me.

'Oh right, hello, what's your name?' I tried.

The young man frowned up at me.

'You'll get nothing out of me,' he growled.

I sighed, and rubbed my stubbly chin with my left hand.

'If I unchain you, you'll probably try to kill me and the kid and make your escape.'

The fellow looked at me like I'd asked a trick question.

'So I'm not going to unchain you just yet.'

The prisoner grunted at this remark.

'I think I'll just put you in here for the time being, if you don't mind,' I said, gesturing at one of the cells, 'You should be ok, Viol will bring you some food shortly.'

'This is the torture chamber isn't it?' asked the young prisoner in confusion.

'That's right, but it's your lucky day, we use more modern methods now, wait until you've tasted some of Viols cooking!'

Luckily for me, Carab showed up the next day, clambering all the way back up the chute again and we unchained the prisoner under close supervision. He limbered up his sore arms, and accepted some breakfast.

'Why aren't you torturing me?' he asked.

We spent several hours trying to convince him it wasn't some sort of trap, and eventually we agreed to send him down the chute with Carab, in return for just enough information for me to fake some sort of confession.

Carab escorted him off the premises in the usual manner, and returned to tell us what he had learnt.

'Well, Shiv,' he said. 'His name is Ena. He is connected to a secret society who is strongly opposed to the tyrannical king. There are a few hundred of them in the town, although they are not very organised.'

'Good, do they have any plans?'

'No.'

'Well, see if you can meet with them, try and organise something, if you can persuade them to storm the Stone Lock, then that would be a good way of getting to Adea, if she is in there.'

Carab considered this.

'Yes Shiv. What about you?'

'If I get any more like him, I'll send them down to you. In the meantime, I've got a little plan of my own that might help things along a bit in this hole of a kingdom.'

'What are you planning?'

'I'll let you know, it may be nothing yet, but I have developed a very strong dislike for that King Real.'

The next night, we got a royal visitor. We knew in advance he was on his way, as the sergeant very kindly tipped us off, without having to be bribed as well, which was unexpected. So we had time to prepare, and when the king arrived he had a good view of me and Voil, mopping blood from the floor, and cleaning bits of skin and bone from the instruments. There was a long streak of blood leading to the acid bath, which bubbled away, merrily eating at the pig carcass I had just deposited in it.

'I hope he had something interesting to say, before he died,' said the king, addressing me as he stepped into the chamber.

'He sung like a nightingale, your majesty.'

'Good, I'm glad to see you are taking to your work so well.'

'Thank you your majesty.'

'And what did he have to sing about?'

'Your majesty, I am sad to report, there is a plot to kill you. The young man didn't know who, but he says there is someone very close to you, who is, at this very second, planning an attempt on your life.'

At that moment I was standing less than three feet from him.

'Hah! Just as I expected!'

'Yes your majesty, even now they are plotting to kill you, they have some nefarious scheme for your untimely demise.'

The king spun round in anxiety, as if the assassin was at that very moment right behind him, then locked his gaze on me again.

'I have always known this would happen, ever since I had to get rid of mother!'

'Yes your majesty, I advise you to trust no one.'

'Yes, yes,' said the king as his emotion reached a feverish pitch. 'Yes, I will go and discuss it with Clyis at once,' and he stalked out the chamber.

'And remember your majesty, it could be anyone!' I said as he left.

I hoped I hadn't over played my hand, although he'd lapped it all up, as if that was exactly what he wanted to hear. I just hoped that I wouldn't be flooded by too many members of the palace staff whose only crime was having excited his paranoia by looking at him funny.

During this period, the wound on my head healed up, leaving a small bald patch on the front of my head that I hoped would grow over with hair again, given time. The headaches I had been getting as a result of the blow didn't abate at all though. Sometimes they would go on for agonising hours, and I would either have to busy myself with some work or task, or go and lie down. If I slept I was often plagued by disturbing dreams that I couldn't recollect upon waking. Even when I wasn't being bothered by the wound, it itched and tickled constantly. It was like having an itch on the inside of my skull that I couldn't get to, to scratch. After a while I started to ignore the sensation, although, like a toothache or the knowledge that you had to do something unpleasant within the next few days, it was constantly there in the background.

Most of the time, life down in the dungeons was pretty dull. The King had grown bored of his occasional visits, and moved on to other distractions. According to the sergeant, he was inventing new ways of butchering dissenters from the outer provinces of the kingdom. As I'd expected we got a lot more business, but we sneaked them down the chute, and into hideouts that Ena and Carab were arranging. About half of our customers were entirely innocent of any ideas of rebellion, but they were willing converts by the time we'd finished with them.

Adea had been located in the Stone Lock and I gathered from the occasional reports Apic sent, the rebels had instantly warmed to the idea of storming the prison and Carab was preparing a daring plan for the release of the princess.

I busied myself with my own projects. I was planning a regicide, and I had the tools to do it.

The main chamber had a forge and two anvils for making the implements of pain, and many tools for turning and manipulating metal. This was the part of the job Viol liked the most, he certainly didn't mind the change in pace of his career. Anyway, not to keep you in suspense any longer, I had decided to make a revolver.

This was very difficult, even with my knowledge of firearms, but we did have gunpowder, which I had Viol pilfering from the royal fireworks supply in the cellar. Viol was a wonder, once I had described and drawn what I was trying to make, there was no stopping him. I could see in his eyes that he had already thoroughly understood the concept, and had an image of the object in his mind, which he had made his life's mission to conceive in reality with powder and metal.

It was to be a 5 ½ inch barrel, .45 calibre, single action revolver. Viol found some walnut to make the stock from. If you know anything about revolvers this was a three screw model and there was no transfer bar, no safety, and no half-cock. I had only a vague idea of where this knowledge was coming from, perhaps in my previous life I had been involved in their manufacture, or perhaps I'd been a real gun nut, I don't know, but for whatever reason it was all there in my head.

Some of the hardest parts to create were the slide to frame fitting mechanism, then fitting the match barrel, and the barrel chambering. The workings of the trigger mechanism were a major topic of frenzied discussion between me and Viol the budding young gunsmith, I freely admit that the loading lever case was all his work.

But the hardest thing to get right was the rifling on the barrel itself. After a few abortive attempts we soon discovered that we would need a tough alloy for the interior of the barrel. Of course to make that though we would need tools tougher than the metal we were working on. All would have been lost but for the discovery of some fairly well made and powerful lathes in one of the many chambers beneath the castle. How they had come to be there or what function they had served we had no idea, but I managed to convince two of the guards to drag it down to my chamber on the pretence that it would make an ideal torture device, which I suppose it would have done. The drive shaft we hooked up to the treadmill and fly-wheel, and a good hard run by either me or Voil would give us enough power to machine the barrel for a short time.

I will stop talking about such technical matters now. We dedicated ourselves to the task nearly twenty-four hours a day, sleeping and eating but rarely. It was such a difficult undertaking, that if it hadn't been for the boy, I would have probably given up. Each time we sorted one problem, it seemed to create three more new ones, and it would be back to the lathe.

When we finally got the trigger mechanism working properly, we had to completely redesign the match barrel. That sort of thing seemed to happen every day.

And then we tested it. I did it from a distance, by pulling on a bit of string, from the next room.
I wasn't foolish enough to test the entire assembly, this was simply to gauge how much powder to put in the bullets. We made an identical barrel, and a simple cocking hammer to strike the caps of the bullets with, set up on a metal tripod and pointing prudently at the room's rear wall.
The gun blew up, and imbedded some of itself in the stonework of the ceiling.
'Bugger me,' I exclaimed, brushing white dust from my hair.
Viol went over to examine the wreckage.
'Perhaps less powder, master?'

We tried again the next day, we had nothing but time. After a few more failed attempts, we hit on a mixture of powder that finally worked as I'd hoped it would. The gun was complete, and we were gleefully satisfied with our accomplishment, but it hadn't been as easy as it had been in 'A Yank at the Court of King Arthur'. We manufactured quite a few bullets as well, all hand made by Viol, who insisted on turning them out in their dozens.
The look on Viol's face made it all worth it. The sense of achievement he felt seemed to have lifted a great weight from him. He was especially proud of the revolving mechanism activated by the cocking hammer, which had been created all to his design.
And my god it worked all right, it could punch a bullet through a piece of wood an inch thick. The noise of us testing it didn't even bother the guards, strange goings on in the castles lower strata seemed to be practically an expected phenomena.
I wrote a message to send to Apic, to put the next part of my plan into action, but events started to overtake me, when the attempt to storm the Stone Lock failed.

The throne room was littered with even more bodies than usual. I recognised some of the faces as those of people who had passed through the torture chamber. Armoured guards stood about everywhere, and I could hear shouting coming from somewhere else close by.
'There he is!' screeched the king as I rounded the corner with my armed escort.
To my dismay, Carab, Apic and Adea were nearby too, in amongst a group of dishevelled revolutionaries. They were being covered by eagle-crested guards with their swords drawn.
Carab had blood flowing down his left arm and dripping from his fingers.
Even worse than that, Tup could be seen looming in the shadows.
I gulped, then stumbled and was prodded by one of the guards behind me.

'Well, if it isn't my court torturer!' cried the king. 'Perhaps you'd care to explain something to me?'

'Certainly your majesty,' I replied, trying to stop my voice from quivering.

'Perhaps you'd care to explain how it is that all the rebels and insurgents I have sent to you, to be done to death, come to be here, attacking the royal goals and invading the castle!'

'I can explain that your majesty,' I tried to say as evenly as I could. 'I have been letting them all go instead of torturing them.'

'Well,' paused the king. 'I admire your honesty. I wonder what I should do with you?'

'Let me and my friends go.'

'Insolence!' shrieked the king, 'Don't dare address the king like that! Guard, give me your sword, I will cut him down right now!'

The king grabbed a sword from a nearby guard and advanced toward me. I drew the revolver from my belt and pointed it at him.

That confused him.

'What's that?'

I was at a loss what to do. When I had pictured this moment in my head, something I had done a hundred times while below in the torture chamber, I had thought I'd just stand there and shoot, as simply as saying it, but I was having trouble gearing myself up to do the deed.

'Um… It's a magical device and I'll use it to kill you, if you take one step closer.'

The king giggled and looked around.

'Oh! A magic wand no less! Tup, have you heard of such a thing?'

Tup stepped forward, he didn't appear to recognise me, perhaps we all looked the same to him, or perhaps he wasn't letting on.

'No, your majesty,' he growled in his low, heavily accented baritone.

'Perhaps, you can shed some light on the subject, hero of Usak?'

'I am as in the dark as you are, your majesty.'

The king suddenly stepped forward and swung his sword at me, and before I knew what I was doing I'd pulled the trigger and shot him in the chest. The thunderclap of the gunshot silenced everyone in the hall, and a cloud of powder smoke swept up into the rafters.

Instinctively I turned round and looked at the guards behind me. One of them backed off, and the other advanced towards me with his pike. I shot him as well, and he went down in a groaning pool of blood.

'Oh man,' I whispered.

I heard a commotion behind me, and saw Tup crashing across the floor towards me like a steam train. I shot him, which didn't seem to do much, so I shot him again, and by the time he got to me, he was on his knees, which put me at about eye level with him.

'Do I recognise you?' he gasped.

'Yes,' I said, and stepped away from him as he fell to the floor.

'Anyone else?' I shouted. The guards didn't appear to know what to do. A chamberlain crouched behind the throne said, 'Please leave!'

'Certainly. Come on,' I said to my friends, who didn't need telling twice, and we all rushed out into the courtyard leaving the blood smattered throne room behind us.

There was part of DCN, on the top floor, called the penthouse, which had recently had a small patient area added to it. There was a small balcony, which gave an excellent view of the castle, Carlton Hill, and beyond that, Arthur's Seat. It was here that they had been sitting. The bad weather had finally broken, and the sun was out in all its glory, hogging a clear blue sky all to itself.

As the weather got better, the patients were drawn towards the sunnier parts of the hospital, coming out onto the balconies in their dressing gowns and blinking in the sunlight as if it were something new to them. While the larger balcony below had several tired looking cancer sufferers enjoying the rare weather on it, the penthouse balcony was deserted expect for the storyteller and his audience. Thin wisps of cigarette smoke drifted up from below.

They sat on those red plastic chairs that are ubiquitous in hospitals and schools. Dr. Lock was rocking back and forth gently knocking against the balcony railing, her feet propped up on a large plant pot.

Yarn stood up, and went to the rail to gaze out across the city.

Dr. Lock glanced at her watch, 'Good grief, it's after nine, no wonder my stomach has been rumbling.'

Yarn laughed, 'I had to speak up, to be heard over it.'

'Well,' replied the doctor. 'I take it you got out of Foona ok, or you wouldn't be here to talk about it.'

'You seem more cheerful today, you looked a bit poorly yesterday,' said Yarn changing the subject.

'I was hung over,' admitted Dr. Lock.

'Ah, did you have an exciting night?'

'You could say that.'

Yarn laughed and said, 'Well, that might explain it then!'

Heather's face took on an irritated expression as smoke rolled up from the balcony below. She stood up and leant over the hand rail.

'Nigel, put that bloody fag out!'

'Sorry Doctor,' came the petulant reply from below.

Chapter Nine - The Temple

'Yes, these are interesting times,' said Mollo the scholar, and threw another branch onto the fire.

'Curse it all, Che has fallen, my house is in ashes, King Valos is in exile, my life is in ruins,' said the other. I presumed it was Nadia.

These two were camped out in the woods, all by themselves, sharing a decent sized fire, and eating from a meagre supply of rations.

I stepped into the light of the fire, and they both stood up.

'Shiv!' cried Mollo. 'You're alive!'

'Yes, thank you, although I am not as glad as you.'

'What's wrong?' he asked.

Apic piped up, 'He is sad because he had to kill a man, but if you want my opinion, I think he did the world a favour,' as he stepped into the circle.

'Ah, and Apic also, why what happened?'

'He killed King Real.'

'My gods, a regicide!' Mollo shook his head. Nadia was still silent.

'Hey, what are you looking at?' said Apic, addressing Nadia in his best Robert De Niro.

'Nothing,' muttered Nadia, and turned away.

'And the others?' asked Mollo.

'On their way to Enttland together by ship, we're going to meet them there. Apic and me decided to walk. There's a temple around here that Viol told me about which I want to visit.'

 Mollo looked at me quizzically.

'Viol, my apprentice. Now probably setting himself up as the master gunsmith of Foona.'

'Well, I would be glad to accompany you, now that I am a vagrant,' said Mollo.

'And what about you, laughing boy?' I asked Nadia.

'Nothing, I want nothing.'

Apic and I sat down by the fire, and searched through our own supplies for something to eat. It had been a long trek up here into the high forests, five miles north of the Foonish border, and we were very tired and hungry. As we ate, we talked about our recent adventures.

We had left Lysander, the bleak capital of Foona, like children quietly leaving a ruined room before their parents turned up. Smoke poured out from the castle and from the Stone Lock further across the river. We walked for nearly twenty hours before reaching an inn on the road to Tullis, exhausted and numb. I was anxious about leaving Viol behind, but I supposed he could probably look after himself. At the inn, we decided to split up. Carab and Adea had no other desire than to get to Enttland as quickly as possible, and according to the landlord, the quickest way was to get on a barge to the coast, then book passage on a coastal trader which would take them all the way up the Gylefen River, right into the heart of

Enttland. I had enough money to give them and the next night they were off. I was very sad to see them go, and Carab's eyelids fluttered a little as I shook his hand in farewell, which for him was an embarrassingly overstated display of emotion.

Adea would never give me the time of day, but I had secretly always thought that she had a soft spot for Apic and me. I'm not always right, but this time I was, and she shed a tear on my shoulder as we hugged prior to their departure. She even had a smile for Apic, a creature she had previously treated as if he had just crawled out of a noggish latrine.

Apic and I would continue overland, try to reach Tullis on foot, and make a short detour to the temple that had piqued my curiosity. The soldiers at the border had no idea of the disasters befalling their kingdom, and were quite happy to let two villainous looking characters leave. We waited a few days on the other side of the border, to see if anyone we knew was going to pass through, and an escapee from the storming of the Stone Lock mentioned seeing an odd couple of jailbirds on the road, an owl and a crow.

As we sat round the flickering firelight, and the cool night closed in, Mollo filled in the rest of the story.

He and Nadia had been sharing a cell with some other vagrants and refugees from Che, and felt as if they had been pretty much forgotten about. Mollo was no stranger to incarceration, after spending six months in a cell in his home town. Indeed, he had known several of the others in the cell. Nadia, needless to say, was not in favour, and received several beatings from frustrated fellow inmates, as he had been responsible for jailing them in Che.

They had just started to settle in, when the Stone Lock was stormed, and the place was overrun with the revolting populace of Lysander. It was a night of blood and smoke. They watched the first attack from a window in the cell, and Mollo shouted down reports to the others, such as,

'There goes another guard.'

'The kitchens are on fire,' and

'My god, the guards are cutting them down like wheat.'

After the first attack failed, the remaining guards went from cell to cell, killing off prisoners whom they thought might cause trouble, or with whom they had old scores to settle. Three were killed in Mollo's cell.

Later on that day, after I had killed the king, the town descended into anarchy, and the guards all left the Stone Lock and headed off into the streets to go and try and defend their homes. Soon, rebellious citizens went into the prison to release the unfortunates inside.

Mollo and Nadia joined the general exodus from the city, and had decided to travel north, in the hope that they might meet up with me and my companions.

Apic and I had certainly become a lot more rugged in our outlook in life. If our time on the nog galley hadn't toughened us up, our subsequent adventures on shore certainly had. Being involved in the siege of Che and the brutality of King Real's regime had dulled our feelings a bit, and I was beginning to wonder if I'd ever feel remotely human again.

Things had gotten out of control, and I needed some time to get my head together. I had sent Carab and Adea on ahead by sea partly for this reason. They would reach Enttland well before us, and I saw the little jaunt to the temple as a way of taking my mind off things.

The temple lay on the road from here to Tullis, and the highway was reputedly very safe. Although that might change now that Foona was leaderless and likely to be facing a rough time. But like a failed relationship, I planned to put all that behind me.

The road was very quiet. I had money, funds I had acquired during my stay in the castle, and we all had plenty of food. Mollo made a great travelling companion and I pumped him for knowledge on all the subjects that he knew anything about. It was mainly ancient history, and about as relevant as the stories of the Hellenistic period of Greece would be to a lost tourist in London, but it was still interesting stuff.

But he also knew a lot about the state of the world at present, and the current threat of the noggish nations to the south. Mollo predicted the northern 'true nogs', would hold off the southern clans for maybe a year, before finally being crushed, and then nothing would be holding them back from the human kingdoms. By reputation the southern nogs were a lot more violent and xenophobic than their northern cousins, who had been softened, if such a concept was possible, by decades of contact with humans. Tup's presence in King Real's court showed that the northern nogs were looking for possible allies. My understanding of the local geography increased by a hundred fold as well, and I could draw a map of all the kingdoms west of the Norob Forest with great confidence after one of his long fireside lectures.

The kingdom we were passing through was called Tyra, and didn't seem to have any sort of structure at all. Mollo explained to me that it was just another forest province that had never amounted to very much. The road we were on lead us through small villages and past coaching inns, and after what we'd been through it felt like the pinnacle of civilisation. The locals would stare at us stupidly, but refugees from Che and Foona were becoming more and more common, so we didn't excite much comment, which was just the way I wanted it. I'd had enough of excitement and adventure.

But, the best, the absolute best, was sleeping in proper beds again! After months of sleeping on either the forest floor, or in a cold dungeon, it was heaven sent. A few days into Tyra and we were more or less guaranteed an inn every fifteen to twenty miles. To be able to get inside at night, have some food, and a nice soft bed to sleep in, it's difficult to describe to someone who hasn't been deprived of it for as long as we had.

The first night, the other two couldn't sleep for the sighs of Apic and me.

'Oh yes!'
'By all the gods! I have ascended!'
'Oh my god, yes!'
'Yes!'
Mollo gasped and said, 'Gentleman, some decorum please!'

Each inn we stayed in was much the same as the last, full of locals from the surrounding area, mainly trappers and woodsmen and travellers from Foona and Bellavia. Again, on the first night, half to remind myself of who I was, and half to entertain Mollo and Apic I started telling stories about my homeland. This began to draw a crowd, until everyone in the room was listening. After I'd finished, all the listeners said,
'Nonsense,' and 'What tall tales, a talking mouse with a castle for children, for all love!'
But I found myself a little bit richer, as many low denomination coins were pressed approvingly onto the table.
That set a precedent, and each night we earned our keep by selling my wild tales. I found myself warming to my role, and was soon adapting stories that I knew, by far better storytellers than me. Dickens, Tolstoy, Victor Hugo, George Lucas, and Steven Spielberg, could always be relied on for good material, or perhaps I would steal from some mini-series nonsense or anything at all I remembered from television. Nobody here would know I was a plagiarist would they? And the audience absolutely lapped it up. There was a strong story telling tradition here already as you could imagine in a pre-industrial society, but they had no idea about sarcasm, witty one-liners, and utterly no concept of timing. The cultural diverseness between me and these people was immense, and I sensed the irony in the fact that the greatest gift I had to give them was things I'd learnt from watching Father Ted and Frasier.
As I got into my stride after a week or two, I could eventually, with practice, hold the whole room's attention in the palm of my hand. They would hang on my every word, and each sentence was worth gold to them. I learned to modulate my voice, to have a rich deep tone for narration, and to breathe life into each of the characters I was representing by giving each of them a different voice.
I could imagine that each story I told would be re-told again and again in houses and taverns in an ever-increasing radius from each inn I travelled to. Sometimes one of my stories would catch up with me, and I would hear a different version of it being told to a merchant by a traveller stood at the fireside as he dried off his boots.
And I loved it. I'd never been any sort of showman, but I would start out talking to Apic and Mollo, and soon the crowd would form. And Apic, bless him, if he saw me flagging, would prompt me with,
'Tell us of the man who was made of metal, and was sent to kill the princess of the past?' or

'Tell us the tale of the friends who defeated the evil empire, in the war of the stars?' and I would be off and away.

It was the nearest I'd come to being at peace since landing on the beach. I was hard as nails, tough as old boots, and had been through the mill and survived. Here I was, telling simple folk about stuff that the people I used to know would find boring, and getting paid for it. All I cared about was where my next meal was coming from and where my bed was. I could remember a time, when things like jobs and mortgages were important, but that all seemed to be some sort of mental trick I'd played on myself. Surely if someone wasn't whipping you, and you had a full belly and a bed, that was happiness enough?

Where was I? Ah yes, the temple. It had been something Viol had told me about, after I'd bored him with my fireside stories, back at the torture chamber. My tale had been about how tall the buildings were in the cities of my lands, and he had then told me of a temple or some sort of strange structure, which was tall and had many windows, and had doors at the front that went round and round.

It seemed impossible, but to me that sounded like an office building.

To get to it, we had to turn off the main road and head off into the deep wood. As I'd mentioned, Mollo was a good travelling companion, but Nadia was not.

With Carab, and his large trousers gone, Nadia became the butt of the jokes of Apic and I.

Why he tagged along with us was a complete mystery to me, and perhaps in hindsight we shouldn't have been so nasty to him, but when you've been brutalised as much as we'd been your social niceties tend to be all but non-existent.

In any event, we spent a lot of time gently annoying the poor fellow, and trying to draw out information so that we could turn it into jokes that we could then use against him. Real playground stuff.

He did ask for it though.

'Nadia? You're religious aren't you?'

No answer, he continued walking.

'Come on Nadia, play along, I'm just talking.'

Nadia new that if he didn't say anything, I would start prodding him in the back with my staff, or stick it in the small of his knee, to make him involuntarily bend down, so he said,

'I am religious, in that I was the advisor on religious matters to King Valos in Che.'

'Religious matters, aha, did that involve burning people at the stake?'

'No. Shut up. I have had enough of your lies.'

Apic and I both went, 'Eeeew!' and clutched imaginary handbags.

'Burning people is wrong, you do know that Nadia?' I said, picking up my pace a little to keep up with him as he tried to get some distance between us.

Apic shot me another amused glance, 'Not if they are heretics,' he joked.
'Ah yes, heretics, or suspected nog spies.'
'Shut up demon!' cried Nadia.
'Oh dear, he's seen through my act!' I mocked.
'If I had you within my power again, I'd have you both burnt at the stake...'
That was such a classic, that I burst into laughter.
'A rise! I got a rise out of him!'
Apic was laughing too, but Mollo said, 'Gentlemen, please, we are off the main road now, and it is foolish to draw attention to ourselves with this revelry.'
'Right,' I said, calming down. I gave Nadia a friendly punch on the arm and he shot me a look like a flaming torch setting light to a bundle of faggots.
'Look!' cried Mollo, who was walking ahead. 'The temple!'

And there it was, a great big crumbling ruin, overgrown with moss and ivy vines, but still recognisable. It looked like a big high street department store had been up rooted from some city centre and plonked down right here in the forest. A flight of birds flew from its roof and into the woods.
'Amazing.' I said. 'Truly amazing. It looks like Jenners.'
I took my revolver from my belt and started to load bullets into it. The others looked at it in reverence. The weapon one used to kill kings.
'Let's take a look.'
The others followed me nervously forward.

The doors had once been revolving, but had long since been destroyed. The entrance hall must have been some sort of perfumery. It was overgrown, but there were still displays and stands. I picked up a bottle and squirted it. It smelled nice. Apic picked up another one and did the same and laughed.
'Wow,' I said.
'Do you recognise this temple?' asked Apic.
'It's from my lands.'
'How did it get here?'
'The same way I did, maybe, I don't know.'
I moved through the hall, and headed up some stairs. The next hall was far larger, and much more impressive. There were two balconies looking down on us, and a glass domed roof, high above, filtered light onto the floor. The goods for sale here looked in quite good condition.
'One man might not be missed, but a whole building? Buildings don't just disappear!' I exclaimed.
'They did when that man Adolf Hitler was around, did not whole cities disappear?' asked Mollo.
'They were destroyed, not disappeared, but yes, that's a good theory, but that would mean that something very nasty happened to me before....'
'Yes,' replied Mollo, 'best not to dwell on it.'

I tried on a waxed barbour jacket, which fitted me rather well, and picked up a golfing umbrella and opened it up. It was still in good condition. I went over to a hat stand, and started trying on hats. Then I noticed a display of backpacks and went over to choose a good one.

I lost sight of the others, but I suspected Apic had found the lingerie section, from the strange gurgling noises I could hear him making. I picked a large pack, and started looking for useful stuff to put in it. There were some fire lighters and a small gas stove, so I took them. There was an ice pick, and several Swiss army knives in the display, so I took then as well. I tried to think of what other stuff I might find useful. This place had a distinctly British feel about it, so I imagined the only gun in this place was the one in my belt. I went over to a derelict lift on the other side of the hall and studied the sign at its side. It had been a long time since I'd read anything written in English, and I almost burst into tears, when I started to read a language that had been long dead to me.

'Toys and Gifts .. Basement,' I read with wonder.

'Foodhall … Second Floor, Seasonal Shop, Bridal Room, China and Crockery. Gentleman's Toilets.'

'What's this?' said Mollo, who had followed me and had an object in his hand.

'That is a toaster.'

Mollo pondered this.

'Hmm...' I said. 'Third Floor… Tools and Electrical Goods.'

'You can read that?' said Mollo and gestured.

'It's my language.'

We took the stairs up to the third floor and I looked around for things to stuff into my pack. I took a few things, then thought, some books on engineering and physics might be useful. As I pondered this, there was suddenly a shriek, then a booming guttural voice, which said something like,

'Arse.'

There were a few more cries and shrieks and then the booming voice demanded,

'Who dares defile the sacred objects of the temple? We'll have no trouble here!'

I rushed back down the stairs and onto the balcony and looked down to see Apic, who was dressed in a tartan mac, and wearing a big pink hat. He was brandishing a shooting stick at something I couldn't see as it was directly underneath me. I leant over the balcony.

It was big and green.

It had to crouch to get out from under the balcony and then straightened up. I could see it had a black pelt of hair on its back that flowed over its hunched shoulders. The monster's gangly muscular arms reached nearly to the floor and terminated in huge fists the size of barrels. I could have stepped onto the top of its head, which was the size of a table, from where

I was, if I had any desire to, and flicked its ears, which were the size and shape of canvas bags.

'A troll,' gasped Mollo, who had reached my side. 'And a big one.'

'Run for it Apic!' I shouted.

The troll looked round and up at me, so I shot it in the eye.

'Arse!' it bellowed, and slapped its huge hand to its face, 'Arse, that hurts!' It lashed out with its other hand, but Mollo and me were already vacating the area.

'I'll grind you to mush, for that!' bellowed the troll, shaking socks and handkerchiefs from their racks. 'Don't worry, you'll not get far!'

Mollo and I sheltered in a doorway and considered our options. We could have easily gotten out one of the back doors, if they hadn't been blocked off with piles of bricks, so it appeared that we had no choice but to cross the hall where the troll was. The troll turned, and walked towards us, and we backed off into the rear rooms. Ground Floor, Menswear. I shot it two more times, but they only aggravated it like bee stings. Little gouts of green blood squirted out of each bullet hole.

'Arse! I'll kill you!'

'Up the stairs!' I shouted to Mollo, who had been stunned by the shots. This was another set of steps, and we rushed up them, all the way to the sixth floor, which had offices in it. I looked out of a window. There was Apic and Nadia standing a good distance away from the building and looking up at it. I could hear the troll ascending the stairs, but it must have been quite a squeeze, as I could hear it cursing below us.

I picked up an office chair and heaved it out of one of the larger windows. There was a small ledge, which I stepped out onto. It was a long way down. I looked around, seeking a means of escape, but there was none from here.

I rushed into another office, which must have been a director's at some point as it was all done out in mahogany panelling. I picked up another chair and broke another window. We were so high up, even the trees were below us.

Then I started to use my brains.

There was another door in the office. I opened it and found a set of steps going down. The staff stairs. I rushed down them, closely followed by the gasping Mollo. We got to the ground floor, but all the exits from the landing were blocked off. The only way to go was further down. It sounded like the troll was at the top of the flight of stairs we had just come down and it was forcing it's way down the narrow stairwell.

'For god's sake,' I cursed, and leapt down the stairs to the basement. They terminated in a bolted door. I looked up and to my horror saw a big hairy arm snaking around the corner, the crate sized hand grabbing and clutching like a man trying to get at a coin down the back of a bed.

We burst through the door and rushed down the corridor. The walls were all cold grey stone and dripping with water. It was so dark down here that I grabbed a torch from my pack and switched it on. Thankfully it worked first time.

There was a big blue object at the end of the gloomy corridor, right next to a steel shutter. I skirted round the object, and saw that it was a delivery van. I doubted if I could get it started so I rushed over to the shutter and tried to lift it. There was a padlock looped around an iron ring on the floor. 'Bastard!' I cursed.

I stood up and shone the torch around.

'Hah,' I laughed, when I saw a key hanging on a hook in the door frame.

'Shiv!' cried Mollo, 'It's coming down the corridor!'

'Right,' I grabbed the key and unlocked the rusty padlock. I then heaved up the shutter and the daylight that streamed in was blinding.

'Run!' and we fled down the steep hillside, cartwheeling our arms to try and keep our balance. The troll grunted, picked up the van and heaved it at us.

'Look out!' I yelled, as it went whistling over our heads and crashed into a tree.

'And don't come back!' roared the troll.

We caught up with the other two, and made tracks to put as much distance as possible between us and the temple before nightfall. We made camp in a place we chose only because we were so exhausted we couldn't go any further.

We talked a little in whispers about the temple and the troll.

'So, that place was from your world? This is the temple you worship at?' asked Apic

'No,' I said. 'Well, sort of I suppose. It was a shop.'

'A shop?'

'Yes, a very big one.'

'Amazing, all these things you have been telling us must be true,' said Mollo.

'Yes, but there is only one thing bothering me.'

'What's that, Shiv?' asked Apic.

'This,' I said and pulled the big pink hat Apic was wearing off his head and threw it into the fire.

Dr. Lock snorted in laughter, then said, 'Oh', when she realised the story was over for that night.

'At least I didn't leave it hanging this time,' said Yarn, looking at the doctor and smiling.

Their gaze met for a second, and they both looked down. This is ridiculous, thought Dr. Lock, I'm falling for a man with nine months to live, and who believes in trolls and goblins.

Yarn stood up and stretched his legs, and looked out across the city again. This seemed to be his favourite place, up here on the small balcony of the penthouse. Heather doubted if he had any feelings for her, she doubted if he even knew where he was. He was attractive in a skinny sort of way, she admitted, but the whole idea was so ridiculous, she decided not to think about it anymore. She was getting her feelings of pity for this man confused with something else, and his stories were sucking her into a realm of fantasy and imagination she had never encountered, and wasn't equipped to deal with. And having analysed the situation with her highly trained intellect, she put the situation into a pigeon hole labelled, 'Just one of those things', and did her best to forget about it.

Yarn sighed and rubbed his head.

'Are you ok?' asked Dr. Lock

'I'm fine thank you. It's just that my headaches are coming back.'

'Oh dear, do you feel anything else?'

Yarn was about to say something else, but smiled instead,

'No, I'm fine, Doctor', and he emphasised 'Doctor'

'Sorry, I forgot, I'm not supposed to be your doctor.'

'That's right, you are not my doctor, you are my audience.'

Chapter Ten - Tullis

The headaches I had been getting, finally started to fade away. I was still missing a lot of hair, but it was getting less noticeable, and it wasn't as if I cared much about my appearance anyway.

I could feel whatever it was in my head, like an unwelcome guest. It was lodged somewhere at the front, and it didn't cause me any pain, but it irritated like a piece of meat caught between the teeth.

Even that sensation was beginning to dull, and with it the constant worry of, what the hell had it been that that nog demon had implanted in my head? It wasn't the demon itself was it? After all, it had disappeared when whatever it was that happened, happened. I found it was best not to dwell on it.

Apart from that, things were looking up. The stuff we'd salvaged from the temple, and the money I was earning as a storyteller bought us tickets on the coach all the way to Tullis. I had no desire to spend any money on a ticket for Nadia, but bizarrely he paid for his own, out of his on secret funds, just so he could still travel with us.

All four of us sat on the roof of the coach as it rattled along the rutted highway.

'What's with you Nadia? We take the piss all day and yet you still want to travel with us?' I pried.

'Leave me alone.'

'I wonder which one of us he is in love with?' jested Apic.

Nadia gritted his teeth. I could see he was in no mood to be teased today. I doubted if I prodded him all day with my umbrella he still wouldn't be any sport, so I changed the subject.

'I wonder how Carab and Adea are doing?'

'They will be in Werfen by now. They've probably already got married!'

'Yeah! He'll not get much happiness from that shrew though,' I laughed.

Mollo was dozing, but I saw a smile play across his lips.

I sighed, 'It's almost gotten boring now that we're out of immediate danger. It was odd seeing the temple. Another lost thing from my world. I wonder if there are any more like me here?'

'Let us pray it is not so, Shiv,' replied Apic, rolling his eyes to the heavens.

'Bless you, Apic! Maybe I will be able to take you back to my lands, if I ever figure out how to, and you will make as equally a big impression.'

'Fuck, I hope not.'

We chatted about inconsequential things after that, and in fact the rest of the journey to Tullis was equally uneventful. Just a pleasant and relaxing coach journey, and a warm inn to stay in each night. It was my idea of heaven.

About four days from the temple we arrived in Tullis. It was quite odd to be out of the forest at first, which had been ever present since we'd landed at Usak. Just as I was getting over the shock of seeing open fields and bare grassy hills, the coach rolled into a more urban area, and we were suddenly in a bustling medieval port.

'Well, this is your town. Where to first, Apic?'

'Ahhh!' he replied, and rubbed his hands together in a mock evil vampire pose, then jumped down from the coach.

We had paid in advance and so we just picked up our luggage, hopped off the coach, and followed Apic into the thronged streets. The town was very much as Apic had described it to me and I was quite impressed, I seemed to remember being in Carcassonne in France, and it reminded me a bit of that. Narrow winding streets, with all sorts of wares being advertised for sale, and throngs of people all trying to barge past each other. It wasn't even as dirty as I thought a medieval town should reasonably be, although it was certainly smellier than any Scottish city I had ever been in, with the possible exception of Glasgow.

Apic led us directly to a tall house, with lanterns hanging outside and heavy green shutters on the windows. The door was open, and he walked in and gestured for us to follow him.

'Apic!' someone cried, and suddenly he was engulfed in a large woman. Several more women, of varying sizes, came into the hall and started clucking.

'How did you get here? We thought you must be dead for sure,' asked the big woman.

'Thanks to my friend here, Shiv.'

To my horror, the woman engulfed me in a hug.

'That's quite all right, Mrs.. ah?'

'I'm sorry,' said the woman, disengaging herself from me.

'These are my other companions, Mollo and Nadia,' continued Apic. The woman nodded and smiled at them, then said, 'My name is Nymella, this is my house, these are my girls,' and she made a grand sweeping gesture.

'House? Girls? Is this some sort of…?'

'Now, Shiv,' said Apic, 'It would be impolite of you to enquire too deeply. Come, we are all in need of a hot bath and something to drink perhaps?'

The large rustic building on Port Row, was to all intents and purposes, a house of ill repute. Nymella was an old, old friend of Apic's, and it wasn't because he had been a regular patron, he assured me. This wasn't your typical dock side knocking shop, in fact it was more of a hide out and storage place for thieves and villains like Apic, which used the 'legitimate' front of a brothel as cover. The girls were left to their own devices. Nymella was an imposing figure, but had a heart of gold, Apic declared, and they were not forced into doing anything that they didn't want to. This sounded a bit unlikely to me, but I took everything Apic told me at face value. I didn't see that I was in any position to judge while the madam of the house was feeding and clothing me for free. Nymella and Apic went way back, he informed me, to when she was a common streetwalker and Apic used to talk to her coming to and from his midnight excursions. He had done her so many favours in the past that the house was always open to him.

Bathed and fed, with mugs of wine in our hands, and dressed in white robes, Apic and I sat on the balcony of the house, which gave an excellent view of the square and the harbour behind it.

'This is the life, eh, Shiv?' said Apic.

'Yes, indeed. And you're a dark horse and no mistake. A thief and a pimp.'

'Not at all, Nymella is a very old friend, nothing more.'

Impulsively Apic took my shoulder and said, 'And to think we could so easily have died on that cursed galley, and that...' but he had trouble getting the rest of it out.

'Easy tiger,' I said in slight concern.

Apic sniffed it back, and although I wasn't embarrassed exactly, because I knew exactly how he felt, I was glad there wasn't going to be an emotional scene. Apic and I shared a glance, and a lot of meaning was passed in that brief second. What we said to each other in that second was this.

We have been to hell and back together, and you have always been there for me, I value you as my best friend, and although I want to tell you all this, we are both far too hard bitten for all that mushy stuff, and besides why should I when you know it already?

Perhaps my experiences had made me a trifle sexist, I don't know, but I find it hard to think that many women would understand this. To have a strong emotional attachment to someone, and not have the urge to talk about your feelings. In actuality, to avoid doing so, to get satisfaction from things left unspoken. In any event, the moment passed, and by way of changing the subject, I said,

'Where are the other two?'

'Mollo has gone to bed, and Nadia is skulking around somewhere. I don't think he feels comfortable in this place.'

'I'll bet he doesn't! I'm surprised his cassock didn't catch fire as soon as he set foot in the doorway!' I said and we both laughed.

'Well, I think I might turn in too, this sunset is amazing, but I'm very tired.'

'Of coarse, Shiv my friend, and which girl would you like sent to your room?'

I considered the question for a second then said, 'The tall, dark haired one?'

Well it would have been rude not to!

As you can imagine, I had no great desire to leave that house on Port Row in Tullis, but we had made an arrangement to meet Carab and Adea, so we had to make our move eventually. Nymella had provided us with simple suits of clean clothing for our journey. It certainly made a change from being dressed in rags. I wore my good warm barbour jacket, and carried my backpack, draped with a wolf hide, to cover its modern alien appearance that might have attracted unwanted attention. I also had a new staff which I used to walk with, when I wasn't swaggering with my umbrella at my side, and I had recently bought a sword which I usually kept in a linen scabbard in my pack. Apic wore a black cloak, and had bought a short sword from somewhere, which he wore at his belt. He carried a large satchel for his supplies, and a bag for a simple two-man canvas tent. We had horses as well, that Apic had 'acquired' from somewhere. A gentle chestnut mare for me and an evil, malcontent black beast for Apic, called Bessy. We were well prepared, and with the horses just recently acquired had no reason to delay our journey any longer.

Mollo elected to stay in Tullis, which caused a bit of a scene with Nadia. As we were preparing to leave, I caught up with him, and before I started to talk to him, Apic gave me a look, which meant, make it quick.

'Nadia, listen, we got you back to civilisation, which is more than you could have expected from us, I doubt if you like our company any more than we like yours, so why don't we go our separate ways?'

Nadia was silent for a moment, then looking me in the eyes, he said, 'You don't know it, but there is a demon within you, and sometime soon it is going to try and get out. I wish to be at hand when it does, so that I may destroy it.'

'Ok,' I said slowly. 'I'm not going to pretend I don't know what your talking about, because some pretty weird stuff happened back in Che, but just you let me worry about what may or may not be in my head.'

Nadia seemed to be getting redder.

'You ignorant oaf! I have studied at the University of Delloma, and I read demonology for three years. I have spent twenty years as a Monk of the Many Hammers, and I know a case of demonic possession when I see it!'

'Belt up Nadia!' I shouted back. 'I don't want you following us around any more, and that's that, ok!', and to emphasis the point, I gave him a push. 'Come on, lets go Apic.'

We went downstairs and said farewell to everyone else, and saddled up the horses. Nymella was very sad to see us go, and hugged Apic for so long, that I feared he might asphyxiate. Eventually I persuaded her to let him go, and waving our good byes we rode off down Port Row and out onto the main street, Nymella crying to us, 'Shiv, just you keep on looking after him, or you'll have me to answer to!'

As we left the town, that morning and began to enter the surrounding pastures, I looked back to see a familiar black figure following us on foot. 'What are you going to do, Shiv?'

'Hmm.. if I had any sense I'd kill him before he gets a mob of his hammer monks together and causes me some grief. But he can't out run horses, so let's go.'

We cantered off, along the road, which followed a wide sluggish river, for several hours, until Nadia was many miles behind us.

'What troubles you, Shiv?' asked Apic

We had been travelling for several days, but this evening we had misjudged the distance to the next inn, and had been forced to make camp on the banks of the river. I had been gazing off into the fire.

'Oh, lots of things. My back is getting stiff at the thought of sleeping on the ground again.'

'Mine also. I am sure you miss your tall girl too.'

'Pff... yes. I'm sure I used to have a woman back in my lands, but I can't remember.'

Apic couldn't find an answer to that, so I said, 'Never mind, best not to dwell, is there any point in setting a watch tonight?'

'Not really,' replied Apic, who slept like a cat, 'We should be safe enough on the royal highway.'

As it turned out, he was wrong.

Ever since Che, the troublesome dreams I had been getting had gotten worse. I even had names for them. There was, 'Chained to an oar for all eternity' and then there was, 'Charge of a hundred angry nogs' and my personally least favourite, 'Killing - blood, guts and gun smoke.'

Almost every night bought some sort of horror with it and I could almost guarantee at some stage I would wake up in a cold sweat.

Apic was lucky, it was almost as if he was born to this sort of life. He'd probably been having madcap adventures long before I had come along. The thing in my head would gnaw away at me, and although I didn't feel like it was driving me insane, I could see it as an event that might happen in the future. Something to look forward to then.

Tonight was no exception, and I was awake when the dark figure stole into our camp. I thought it might be Nadia, but I lay motionless except for moving my hand slowly to my belt where my revolver was. I wondered if Apic was awake as well, but if he was he gave no indication.

The figure moved over towards the horses, which were both standing quietly beside a tree. I watched as he then started to untie the rope that was around my chestnut mare's neck.

I leapt up and said, 'That's enough, get away from my horse.'

There was a flash of steel and a zing, as he drew his sword. The voice that came afterwards had something odd about it.

'Don't interfere with me, or you may have cause to regret it!'

I slowly stepped back, and said, 'I don't want to hurt you.'

I looked down to check my staff was still at my feet.

'Likewise stranger, but I have great need of this horse.'

I was in two minds what to do next, but my bloody-mindedness got the better of me.

'Flaming cheek! Just get away from my bloody horse right now, or it will not go well for you.'

'Very well, defend yourself!' cried the figure and came at me with his sword.

Now, the thing about owning the only revolver in the world is that you can't wave it at someone and shout, 'Get back, or I'll shoot!', and expect them to know what the hell your talking about. As a deterrent it was next to useless, and I had realised even before I had made it, it was a case of shoot first, explain the principles behind ballistics later. I had no desire to gun down some poor sod in cold blood, but it was a well-known fact to myself and my friends that I was at best a very indifferent swordsman. In any event, my instinct for self-preservation was too great and I drew the gun and fired.

Three things happened at once, my assailant went flying backwards, the horses tried to bolt, and Apic woke up.

'Oh no!' I cried and leant down over the prone figure.

He was wearing a bandanna over his face and I pulled it down. By the light of the dying fire I saw that my victim had been a young woman.

'Oh no!' I repeated.

'The revolver, you used it! My gods, what a noise! I can smell it! That noise!'

'Stop babbling man, help me!'

We found where the bullet had hit her, just directly above the heart.

'Wait!' I gasped in disbelief as I pulled back her tunic, 'No blood!'

Apic took something out of her shirt, it appeared to be a very thick pocket book of some kind. With a big hole in it.

'Incredible,' said Apic.

'Thank god', I said, 'If I'd killed her…'

Well, I don't know, I would have probably thrown the gun in the river, and myself after it.

She awoke, and coughed and spluttered. Apic had fetched some water from the river and thrown it on her face.

'Hello,' I said.

She made to try and get up, but I pointed her sword at her and she wisely decided to remain still.

'What happened? Did a horse kick me?'

'Sort of.'

'My book…'

'Here,' I said, and threw it at her, 'It was lucky for you had it where you did.'

'It's an old duellists trick,' she muttered. 'Against rapier thrusts.'

Apic nodded and went, 'Ahh…'

'What do you intend to do with me?' she asked.

I studied her closely. With her hat off, I could see her long red hair, tied into a knot, which was working its way loose. She was quite pretty, in a freckly sort of way.

'I know not. Probably let you go.'

'Oh,' that had obviously surprised her.

'What do you think, Apic?'

'You caught her, Shiv, it is up to you.'

'Oh well, if it's up to me, I'll just get an explanation and let her is on her way. I don't know much about horse thieves, but I doubt if she is typical of the profession. So what's your story?'

She looked at me glumly. I expected her to make up some nonsense to keep me happy, about a starving granny or something. I didn't really care what she was going to say I was just glad I hadn't killed her. But what she actually said came as a bit of a shock.

'Oh please, you can't leave it there. It's so obviously a plot device to keep me hooked!' protested Dr. Lock. 'You know I'll be back tomorrow anyway, there is no need to use a lure!'

Yarn smiled self consciously, 'I'm sorry, even as it is, I've gone on a bit longer than I meant to.'

Dr. Lock stood up and stretched her arms out. The sun was setting over Edinburgh. It was going to be a very mild night. The distant noise of the city drifted across to them on a gentle summer breeze.

'What a lovely evening,' remarked Dr. Lock, 'I've totally lost track of time', then, 'My God!' as she looked at her watch.

'Sorry, see what I mean?'

'Well I take it you'll eventually meet up with Carab and Adea in Enttland?'

'In Glamis, in Enttland, yes.'

Dr. Lock considered this,

'Good, I like those two, I'd hoped you hadn't dropped them.'

'Dr. Lock, how many times do I have to remind you that this is a true story? All these people really exist.'

'Yes, Yarn,' she smiled at him, 'but you're logical enough, you know I'll never believe it unless I have proof.'

Yarn laughed.

'Well,' she said and shrugged.

'I can prove it easily enough, but I don't think you're ready for it yet.'

Dr. Lock hid a smile behind her hand, 'How can you prove it?'

'Well, things began to change for me when I reached Enttland. The girl had a small hand in it. Up until then I was only called a sorcerer. Later, I was to become one.'

'Sounds intriguing.'

'Yes,' said Yarn, then he slapped the arms of the chair he was sitting on and stood up. 'And it can wait until tomorrow. Go home!'

The next day, Dr. Lock met with Dr. Barage in his office.

'Dr. Hood is interested in your boy, he had a look at his scans yesterday,' said Dr. Barage as Heather entered the room.

'Oh really,' she replied.

'Yes, he was wondering why we hadn't recommend a biopsy.'

'Uh-huh,' said Dr. Lock as she sat down opposite the untidy desk. 'What did you say?'

'I said that it would be unwise, because we might release a demon into the operating theatre. We don't want some sort of devil running around DCN, the Weston is in the papers enough without that sort of thing.'

Heather snorted in laughter, 'I doubt if he saw the funny side in that.'

'No, Tiger Hood isn't known for his sense of humour. He seemed to think that he would be able to waver the patient consent form, given that this is an exceptional circumstance. Diminished responsibility and all that.'

'Well, that's your department, Ian, he can't operate without your say so.'

'That's what I said. I thought I might talk to you about it, seeing as you know him better than anyone.'

Dr. Lock went over to the cooler and poured herself a cup of water. She seemed unwilling to say anything.

'So what do you think?' pressed Dr. Barage.

'It's tricky. He's quite lucid, and very intelligent. Apart from the hallucinations, flights of fancy or whatever you want to call them. He was quite explicit about his desire not to be operated on.'

Barage considered this then answered, 'Yes, but Tiger argued that the patient is being his own worst enemy. A debulking of the tumour could easily extend his life by six months, and it could well clear up the hallucinations. Yarn would probably thank us for it afterwards. It could also help his amnesia.'

'So he wants a resection, not a biopsy?'

'Prior to another scan, yes.'

Heather took a sip from her cup and shrugged her shoulders, 'I would have to say no, from what I know of the patient, I think he would be very upset if we forced a procedure on him. The story he is telling is leading up to something. I have a feeling it could all be over in less than a fortnight, perhaps he would be more receptive then.'

'Yes,' pondered Barage. 'It's a tricky one all right. Perhaps you should talk to Hood about it, you know what he's like when he gets an interest in something, he never lets it lie.'

Heather sighed and rubbed her shoulder.

'I'll go and see him after clinic.'

End of Part 1.

Part 2

Chapter Eleven - Mallonax

'Behold, the tower of my master,' declared Temina, as we stopped out horses to view the edifice.

The tower of Mallonax stood brooding over the landscape, a gigantic finger of rock pushing out from the hills and scattered wooded valleys. We could see it from our vantage point on the rise of a grassy outcrop, and it struck me as being of a fine size, and that we still had a fair distance to travel before we reached its foot. It was hard to judge, but I estimated the tower to be over a hundred feet tall. It was wide and sturdy looking, with the only windows up above the third floor. There seemed to be a dome-like structure on the roof.

Temina, the slight, red headed girl had been our guide and travelling companion for the last few weeks. We had bought her a horse out of our own funds, and had set a quick pace along the highway to Werfen, and had reached the border to Enttland sometime the day before. This area was hardly populated at all, and the last few nights we had been forced to camp out again, much to our annoyance. The landscape had changed little from that of Tullis, although it did get a little warmer. The road we followed slowly wound through the gently rolling grassy hills occasionally covered with ancient forests of oak, beech and pine. The land between the hills was invariably marshy, and at night a mist would settle in these hollows and chill us to our bones. In the distance to the south we could see a hazy range of tall mountains, brooding over the landscape like thinly veiled threats. Most of the hills looked like they had never seen cultivation, the villages we passed through were very small, and widely distributed.

Temina told us that this area of Ent, Glamis, was all like this. It wasn't until you travelled further east towards the heartland of Enttland that you would be able to ride for miles through fields and plantations.

I had taken us several weeks to reach the tower, but I was determined to call at it, before going to Werfen. After what Temina had told us, it seemed like a good idea to give her master a visit. When asked to give an explanation for her actions, which lead to her narrow escape with death, this is what she told us.

She had been raised from a small child by her master Mallonax, who was the greatest wizard in Glamis, and possibly of all Enttland. She had no aptitude towards magic, but served her master in every way that she could. Often he would need ingredients for spells, and magical items delivered from far afield. She had travelled many times to Tullis to pick up shipments for her master that had come from as far away as the island kingdoms, and the dark mysterious continents that lay beyond them. On her last expedition, the shipment had not come in, and the vessel that was carrying the cargo had been reported to have been captured or sunk by noggish pirates. Temina confided in us that she was very upset at this news, and had gotten wildly drunk in a tavern in Tullis in her grief and accidentally started a fight with a rake from Staturos. The argument had started when she had seen him roughly handle a serving girl and had stepped in to prevent further sinfulness, an imposition that the young rake had greatly resented.

I got the impression that Temina had read one too many of the pocket romance pamphlets that were so common in Tullis. These things were devoured by the literate in the area, and told daring stories of highwaymen and duellists.

The rake had no more idea that he was quarrelling with a woman that I had had, as Temina had years of experience in the art of passing herself off as a man. They had stepped outside the tavern to settle it like gentlemen and Temina had run him through like a sack of straw.

Needless to say, she saw this as an appropriate moment to leave town, but not having the opportunity to hire a horse for the return journey, and in a very desperate rush to put as much distance between her and any charges that might come up against her regarding illegal duelling within the city limits, she had fled on foot.

She kept away from the coaching inns and hostelries for fear of arrest, and moved at night, wrapped in her huge black cloak and surviving by her wits. The sight of two travellers foolishly sleeping at the side of the road had put temptation in her way, and she had decided to try her hand at horse theft.

I was impressed at her story, and I suggested that in return for introducing me to her master, I would forgo handing her over to the road wardens, a deal that she happily agreed to.

We eventually reached the base of the tower, and it was even more imposing standing directly below it. There appeared to be no door, but there were obviously windows high above us.

'I shall intone the magical command of opening,' said Temina, and started to chant in a language I couldn't understand.

She soon stopped, then stood and waited. Both Apic and I looked at her expectantly.

'Ahem, there seems to be a... I will intone the magical command of opening again.'

The second attempt yielded no more result than the first.

Apic looked at me and raised one eyebrow. I smiled slightly.

Temina put her hands on her waist petulantly and sighed.

She then looked up at the windows and shouted, 'Mallonax! Mallonax!'

A shadowy figure appeared at one of the lower windows and looked down, 'What?' it cried back.

'The door is broken again, throw down the ladder!'

We were soon inside, and were ushered into a cosy chamber, with hangings and tapestries on the walls and a glowing fire throwing out red light from one corner. It was a very cluttered space, with tables and chairs piled high with papers and scrolls, and various strange looking implements. There wasn't a stuffed crocodile hanging from the ceiling, but it would have felt right at home.

Mallonax appeared to be a man of declining years, and receding hairline. I was a bit disappointed that he didn't have a long flowing white beard, although he did have a lot of white stubble, which probably had more to do with laziness than intended effect. He wore a blue shirt, gathered at the waist with a large embroidered woollen belt. On his legs he wore black linen trousers, hanging loose at his shins, his feet tucked into what looked like carpet slippers.

Temina introduced us, and we sat down on comfy chairs by the fire.

'Where's Dombaba?' asked Temina.

'I was in the middle of repairing him when you arrived. Could you be a dear and fetch us something to drink?'

Temina grunted and getting out of her chair as if it physically pained her, went over to the wooden staircase and ascended to another level.

When she was out of earshot, the elderly gent muttered, 'Lovely girl, but still a long way to go.'

Then seeming to collect himself, he addressed us, 'So what brings two such fine fellows to such an out of the way place as this?'

I lent forward and put on my friendliest smile.

'Well, we caught Temina trying to steal our horses, and in return for not turning her over to the road wardens, she agreed to take us to her master, and that you might be in more of a position to offer us an explanation.'

Mallonax put his hand to his eyes in a gesture of despair. 'Ah, the errand that she was on was of great importance to me, but I certainly didn't instruct her to become a horse thief. You won't get any officer of the law to ride out here I'm afraid, they all avoid this area.'

'That's ok,' I said to allay any concerns he might have about me pressing charges, 'I have forgotten the whole incident. I only wished to meet you out of my own curiosity.'

Mallonax looked over to the corner of the room where Apic was lurking. 'Please, sir, for your own safety, I implore you not to touch that object!'

Apic put down the odd looking contraption he had been holding like it had suddenly become scolding hot, then went over to look at one of the tapestries. He's probably wondering how much it would fetch in Tullis market, I thought.

'Well then,' continued Mallonax. 'It is always a pleasure to receive guests. But is there a particular reason that you wanted to come all this way out to see me?'

I was about to say something, when Temina arrived, bearing a tray laden with mugs and plates.

'Ah thank you dear,' said the old man, as she laid down the tray on a nearby table.

He handed me a mug and said, 'Here, try this, it is an acquired taste, but I assure you, it is excellent for restoring the humours.'

I took the mug from him and looked at the hot black liquid contained within. I sniffed it.

'Holy shit! It's coffee!' I looked at the tray, there was a small bowl of honey, and a jug of milk.

'You know of this substance?' asked the wizard in disbelief as I busily poured in some milk.

'Know it? I used to live off it!'

'But that's impossible, if you knew were I got it from, you would... ah, but perhaps you are having a jest with me?'

'Not at all, where I come from we call it coffee. It's ground from beans, then you add hot water to it. If you drink enough of it, it will keep you awake all night. I know this stuff alright.' And to prove it I took a mighty swig, and managed to scorch the roof of my mouth, 'Hot, hot, hot', I gurgled in pleasure.

I had finished half my mug when I said, 'So were on earth did you get it?'

'I am completely taken aback,' replied Mallonax, 'You have confounded me, sir, and I must gather my thoughts. You surely must be a wizard of some sort? Do you have a well?'

'I don't know what you're talking about,' I answered.

Both Apic and Temina had been listening in on our conversation.

'Master,' implored Temina, 'This may be a trick...'

'Nonsense child,' then addressing me. 'Where did you drink this... *kofee*?'

'Back at home, it is grown in warmer countries than mine and exported to my land. Just about everyone drinks it.'

'Great gods of Ent!' cried the wizard.

Mallonax's well wasn't a well in the traditional sense. It was housed in the highest room in the tower, and was situated lying vertically on the north facing wall. It did have water in it though, which was a bit disconcerting. Around it lay many barrels and sacks, crates, metal objects, wooden objects and about a hundred other things that I couldn't even describe. In front of the well was a large wooden contraption, which looked like a crane. It was on a small railway, and was forested with levers and switches. There was a great big brake handle, which applied a large metal pad to one of the crane wheels. The crane itself looked like some sort of industrial sized fishing rod. A fishing rod for catching whales. The reel was the size of a base drum, and it had seemingly miles of strong looking rope on it.

Attached to the business end was a large net. The rails curved right up onto the wall and ran either side of the well, so that if need be, the crane could be positioned right above it, like a great big spider suspended from the wall.

'Crikey,' I said, as I looked round to take it all in.

'This is my well. I inherited this tower from my great master, Kettering, and the well was here long before he was. The coffee is one of many things that I have fished out of it. Three large sacks of it arrived about a year ago. After reading through my old masters notes, I established that it was a drink of some kind, something to be offered to guests.'

'Bloody hell,' I said, pointing. 'You use that. To fish in that. And you pull out… things?'

'Essentially yes. Sometimes you might not get anything for weeks though.'

I picked up a familiar looking object from a crate and examined it.

'Ah, perhaps you could help me with that, I cannot decipher its function.'

'It is called a "walking man", you use it to carry music around with you. The batteries must be dead. Hey, Apic, do me a favour and go and fetch my pack?'

Apic nodded and rushed off downstairs.

'For carrying music around, that is interesting.'

'Although you might not describe this as music,' I said as I popped open the cover and looked at the tape.

Apic was soon back with my rucksack, and I rummaged around in it for a bit, and found what I was looking for in a side pocket.

'Batteries! Salvaged from the temple!'

I took the old ones out of the Walkman, then tore open the cardboard packet of the new ones. I put the headphones on and pressed play.

The wave of memories and nostalgia that hit me was almost overpowering, as the music played, Chemical Brothers, Block Rocking Beats. I listened to it for a bit, but it was too much, I stopped the tape and handed the device to Mallonax.

He placed the headphones to his ears like someone putting a rattlesnake round their neck and hit the play button. His face took on a look of horror, and he quickly took them off.

'That was music?'

'A kind of music, my favourite kind, as I seem to remember.'

Apic tried on the headphones, then quickly ripped them off, and danced around flapping at his ears as if he was being plagued by a swarm of flies.

'Tell me,' I asked. 'Has anything living ever come from that well?'

'No, but dead bodies have.'

Apic and I were invited to stay the night and we duly accepted. The old man retired to bed early, so we helped ourselves to his brandy decanter. I also found a stash of cigars, and I introduced Apic to the pleasures of smoking. Like most beginners he started off by coughing a lot, but after a few minutes he was puffing away like a good'un and enjoying himself tremendously.

'I must say, Shiv, when I am with you, every days seems to bring a new experience,' he remarked.

'Just you wait until tomorrow, we're going fishing!'

After a pleasant breakfast of eggs and rabbit pie (I was later to learn why rabbit was such a popular dish at the tower), we went back up to the well chamber to try our luck. Mallonax was already there and waiting for us, and wearing a leather apron he was oiling the joints and pulleys of the crane.

'Ah good, there you are at last! I trust you had a good breakfast?'

'Excellent thank you.'

'Good, well, if you gentlemen would be as good as to stand here,' said Mallonax, gesturing at the levers on the side of the crane. 'And pull the switches as I call them out, we can get things moving.'

After much shouting, grunting and cursing we manoeuvred the crane right up to the wall, and extended the arm out so that it entered the water in the vertical well.

'Now the black switch, if you please Apic.'

Apic nodded and quickly pulled down the switch. The reel was released and a series of weights started to fall, and humming and whirring the line played out into the murkiness of the well.

'What now?' I asked.

Mallonax climbed down from the platform he had been standing on and said, 'And now, we play the waiting game.'

I shrugged and waited for a minute or two. Then spotting a colourful box nearby amongst all the crates and sacks I said. 'Sod that, it's boring. Let's play Hungry Hungry Hippos instead.'

We had some lunch taken up by a grumbling Temina.

'What's that?' I said, looking dubiously at the dishes of dark brown stew.

'Hasenpfeffer,' she replied curtly.

'More rabbit? We had rabbit for breakfast,' muttered Apic.

'Well, if you want to take a turn in the kitchen, be my guest!' cried Temina huffily.

'Ok,' grinned Apic. 'Wait until you try some of Nymella's recipes, there isn't much going on up here anyway.'

They wandered off to the stairs bickering together about cooking and cuisine.

It wasn't until late in the evening that we hooked something. I had been having a great time raking through the piles of junk that had been collected over the years on other fishing expeditions and that lay around in huge stacks and piles in the large well chamber.

There were many things that I couldn't identify, but there was much that I could. A carburettor, a mousetrap, an alarm clock, a box of twenty-four pairs of tights, a wing mirror, several pieces from a television, a plastic toy samurai sword, a pair of handcuffs rimmed with pink fur, a mini FM radio, a world war one German helmet, a complete set of pokemon cards, several compact discs, but nothing I had any desire to listen to, a beer glass, a human skull made into an ash tray, a weather vane, loads of coins, some of them British, I counted out five pounds twenty-three in loose change, a wallet belonging to someone from Russia, a Stanley knife, a gold fish bowl, a crash helmet, a pair of jeans.

Suddenly I was awakened from the nostalgia trip that an ageing copy of the Fortean Times had awakened in me by a crashing and grinding sound. I looked up from the crater I had created in the piles of junk as the crane lurched up onto the wall, squealing and complaining almost to the point of deafening me.

'We have got something!' cried Mallonax, as he climbed up onto the wooden platform by the crane with a bucket of water.

I rushed up to join him and help pour water onto the smoking reel. Line was playing out at such a terrific rate, the reel was in danger of catching fire.

Then the reel stopped, and Mallonax applied the break. Everything went quiet, and I suddenly felt I was in a scene from Jaws.

'Now what?' I whispered.

'Pull that switch,' said the wizard pointing to a lever beside my leg. I pulled it and some gears ground into life, and the line was slowly drawn in. After a couple of minutes, the reel stopped, and there was a terrible metallic grinding sound as the crane arm began to bend and buckle. Mallonax released a lever, and played out some more line.

'Is it always like this?' I asked.

'Only if we get something big.'

I considered this, turned to him and said, 'Is it likely to be, you know.. scary?'

Mallonax turned to me and said, 'Define scary.'

Just as he said this there was a sudden blinding light and a great deluge of water sprayed out of the well, and soaked us to the skin. We both ducked down and tried not to be swept off the platform by the torrent. I gasped and gagged for breath, and grabbed the old man as he lost his grip on the railing.

Just then the water subsided and the reel went loose, Mallonax quickly pressed another lever and the line began to wind in again.

'Are you sure we want what ever it is that's on the other end?' I said, but he ignored me.

I tried to get a look at the large bulky object in the net as it was drawn from the well. It was a vast white square metal thing.

'Oh god,' I said. 'All that for a bloody gas cooker!'

Apic had grown bored and had gone for a ride in the countryside with Temina. The last few days I had spent in deep conversation with Mallonax. I told him all about my lands, and we agreed that about ten percent of everything that was caught on a fishing expedition was something that I could recognise, including kitchen appliances. I now had an agenda, and I was sure that there was some way that this old man could get me home. It didn't turn out to be as easy as that though. He knew of a spell that could possibly get me back to my home, but it had never been cast in his lifetime to his knowledge, and would take years for me to become proficient enough a sorcerer to even begin to think about casting. It was a spell of returning, and the person who intended to use the spell had to be the one to cast it. Mallonax dragged out some dusty old tomes from his library, and showed me some pictures of a portal and a grim faced wizard standing in a pentagram, his hands raised high above his head, calling down lightening from the surrounding mountains.

'Looks great,' I commented.

Mallonax nodded, 'That is the mighty wizard Yeates, from times of old. When he stepped into the portal of returning he was never seen again. '

I was despondent about all this, but I at least now had a glimmer of hope. I asked Mallonax if he could train me in the mystical arts, and he readily accepted me as his apprentice.

We also discussed what had happened to me in Che. While Mallonax could offer me nothing definite, he did know a little about the noggish demons. He knew that there were ten of them, and that it was forbidden to say their names. Magical entities in general did not like 'anomalous material', as he put it, it disrupted their power, even the awkward and heavy gas cooker we had caught earlier would give a wizard or shaman a headache. It was not meant to be here, it went against the weave of this realm.

A deity, or any other mystical being would have trouble trying to use any of its powers on it.

Perhaps in some way I had interfered with the noggish demon as it had tried to destroy us, or whatever it had tried to do, and a sort of short circuit had occurred, and things had all gone a bit wrong. Mallonax knew it was very unwise to cast spells on material that came from the well, the results could be highly unpredictable. He felt sure he remembered Kettering telling him of a djinn being trapped for all eternity inside a bottle or a lamp, perhaps something similar had happened. I also knew of stories like that, but it didn't help me much. Mallonax even went as far as to examine the scar on my head, but he could offer no more advice. He said that in his opinion it was highly unlikely I had a demon in my head, more likely it had been banished back to its own plane of existence, and that it was all best left well alone. In that, I agreed with him.

The next day I was introduced to Dombaba, Mallonax's servant. He was lying on a table in several bits. If you have ever seen an artists wooden posing model then you have seen what Dombaba looked like, except for the fact he was over six feet tall. His constituent parts seemed to have been turned from wood. His hands were fine examples of craftsmanship, and looked very functional, but the designer had spent no time on the feet and face. The feet had no toes, and there was no face at all, his head was a featureless oval ball. Currently he was in six bits, arms, legs, head and torso.

'Dombaba is an automaton,' explained Mallonax. 'Entirely my own work, although I had some basic plans from my old master. He is infused with a magic energy, which gives him life.'

'Why is he in pieces?'

'I was seeking a method of giving him a voice, but it was a lot harder than I at first imagined. Now I am having enough trouble just trying to reassemble him.'

I gave the old man a hand for the rest of the day, and although I wasn't of much use, I gave lots of encouragement, as I was very eager to see Dombaba alive.

Eventually he was assembled and rigged up to a vertical frame like a metal-spring bed, and hooked up to a bunch of tubes and wires. Mallonax pulled a switch, and a nasty green substance flowed down the tubes from vats in the ceiling and into the automaton.

Dombaba jerked and convulsed against the restraints, in such an alarming way, I started to have doubts of what we were up to. Shelly like thoughts about foolish scientists tampering with forces beyond their control, that sort of thing. But soon he was calm, and Mallonax signalled me to help unrestrained the now limp Dombaba.

A concerned Mallonax looked up at him, 'How do you feel?'

The automaton shook his head, and rapped his fist against his temple.

'How many fingers, Dombaba?' and he held up three fingers in front of Dombaba's face.

Dombaba also held up three fingers. How did he see? I wondered. Dombaba stood up groggily and shook his head, then put it in his hands. It was quite scary, he must have weighed well over four hundred pounds.

'Now, now Dom, you should be ok in a while. Once you've got your bearings, you can go and take over from Temina in the kitchen.'

The automaton seemed to sag in resignation as Mallonax spoke these words.

The next day I went down to the kitchen to see him at work. I found Dombaba fascinating, he was a very docile fellow, and had a very gentle manner about him. He was a reasonable cook, but seemed unable to kill any live animals, and this task was done by Temina. He understood Bellavian and Enttish, but wasn't exactly communicative. I got the feeling that he was content with his life of drudgery, but perhaps deep inside his wooden heart somewhere he dreamt of doing something else, something more meaningful? Maybe he dreamt of being a tree, Apic had once remarked wryly.

As the days progressed into weeks I got into a sort of routine. Apic soon grew bored of the quiet life in the tower, and went off to Werfen to meet Adea and Carab, riding off on his bad tempered mare, Bessy. I would wake early and have my breakfast with Dombaba before the others rose, and have silly little conversations with him, trying to get him talk about himself. I tried to teach him a simple sign language, but he wasn't very quick. After that I would go to the library and read, study and compile notes. I would eat lunch in the library and in the evening I would receive tutorials from Mallonax or study by myself in front of the fire in the living chamber, the room that we had been in on our first night in the tower. Occasionally we would spend a day at the well, and about once a month Temina would go to the nearest village for supplies.

Mallonax's tower had five main levels. The lowest level was given over to stables and other areas for keeping livestock. The next was a storage area for supplies and there were many rooms piled with miscellaneous junk down there. The third level was the main living area, where the sitting room, kitchen and bedrooms were. The fourth floor was where the library was situated, with many more rooms for experimentation and storage of magical and thaumalogical equipment. The top floor was mostly taken up by the sun room, the dome of which protruded out onto the roof, where Mallonax had several telescopes. Between the fourth and fifth level was a small mezzanine level, where Temina had her quarters. I rarely had reason to go there, and I often wondered what her rooms actually looked like. She always kept the door locked, so I laughed to myself that a tough cookie like Temmy probably had a secret supply of teddy bears and other stuffed animals, all laid out on a big pink bedspread.

One early evening I was sat out studying on the balcony of the sun room, and looking out over the grasslands when I spotted three riders descending down the ridge into the valley.
I was already at the base of the tower by the time they had arrived.
'Shiv!' cried Carab.
'Carab! And Adea!' I returned in delight and wrestled him from the saddle and we tussled on the ground like children.
'Haha! Get off me you mad man!' he laughed.
I stood up and embraced Adea, who had dismounted.
'You are looking well Shiv,' she said and smiled.
'Come in, come in, and you Apic, you rogue, and have something to eat and drink! Gods, it's good to see you again!'
So, we had a very pleasant evening catching up with each other, I told them of all our adventures since leaving Foona. They had already heard it all from Apic, but they nodded and listened to me indulgently. I told them of the temple, and Tullis, of our upset with Nadia, and introduced them to our resident highwaywoman, Temina.
Carab shook her hand warmly enough, but I detected a little bit of tension as the two strong willed women met for the first time. I think Apic noticed it too, because he gave me a brief knowing look.
They in turn told me of their adventures. Their journey down the Forest River by barge from Lysander had been uneventful and they had arrived in Gijon on the Diamond Sea refreshed. Gijon is a real den of thieves by all

accounts and they had a small amount of difficulty getting passage to the Gylefen River. I wondered how much bloodshed constituted 'a small amount of difficulty' in Carab's books. They eventually got a berth on a coastal trader, the 'Sweetheart' that would luckily take them all the way to Werfen, and they had little doubt that the hold was full of contraband. However, it did mean that the captain of the ship new all the quiet coves and inlets on the way so that they not only avoided the revenue clippers, but noggish pirates as well. They only had one encounter with pirates, who they engaged at close quarters. The nog boarded, and it was touch and go for a while until the forward thinking captain of the Sweetheart tossed a huge grenade into the hold of the pirate ship, blowing it to smithereens. After that it was a simple case of shooting the desperate nog from the rigging with crossbows. Carab had been heavily involved in the battle, and smiled as he tallied up how many he had killed.

The journey up the Gylefen River was safe, and apart from interesting midnight flights from police vessels, uneventful. The whole voyage only took two and a half weeks and at long last Adea was joyfully reunited with her family. As it turned out, she wasn't a princess after all, which I have to admit, wasn't much of a shock, but she was a member of one of the finest families in the city.

We spent all of that night talking and catching up, and ate a fine meal prepared by Dombaba and I introduced them to the pleasures of coffee, brandy and cigars.

The next night saw everyone gathered around the fireplace in Mallonax's large cluttered living chamber, digesting the excellent roast duck and rabbit pies that Dombaba had prepared.

I was in my, by now customary, seat in the shadows of a corner near the fire. Apic sat opposite, nearer the fire in his over stuffed armchair. Mallonax as always sat by the table in the centre of the room, facing sideways towards the hearth, drinking wine and water. Temina also had a favourite place, curled up on a sheepskin rug right by the fire, her head held up by her arm, and a glass of wine getting warm beside her. As guests, Adea and Carab had the best seats, on the long comfortable sofa.

Apic and I blew smoke up at the ceiling, and I swilled the brandy around in the bottom of my glass.

'I really must compliment you on your hospitality again Mallonax. I imagine you didn't expect to be imposed on so much when you accepted Shiv as your apprentice,' said Adea.

'Not at all,' smiled the old man, 'You are most welcome guests. The place has been so quiet in recent years, eh, Temina?'

Temina grunted.

Carab crossed his booted legs and sighed, which made me laugh.

'This is a long way from Usak, Carab,' I said.

'I was just thinking that,' he replied.

There was a pause then Adea said, 'How are the studies going then Shiv?'

Temina suddenly leapt up and left the room, saying, 'I will go and help Dombaba bring up the desserts.'

When she had left and I could hear her boots on the stairs, I turned to Mallonax and said, 'What's wrong with her?'

Mallonax sighed and said, 'I know not. Well, no I do. She is upset that I took you as my apprentice and not her I think. It is not her fault, but she has no gift for magic, and besides; I never imagined taking her on as an apprentice. I suppose she had just hoped that as I advanced in years, and with no one to pass on my knowledge to that...' he left the sentence unfinished and shrugged.

'Poor Temina,' said Apic thoughtfully.

Carab suddenly laughed, 'You a wizard Shiv! I just can't imagine it.'

I looked at him archly and said, 'And why is that?'

'I don't know, I always see you as... I don't know. A charlatan.'

I laughed.

Apic gasped, 'Call forth a bolt of lightning to strike him down right now for such blasphemy!'

'How many times do I have to tell you Apic, I can't actually cast any spells yet!'

'I know, I was only joking,' he replied and burst into laughter.

We all started laughing then. We had come a long way since Apic had naively believed that I was a mighty sorcerer.

'I admit, Carab it seems odd to me as well. Still here we all are,' I said.

We were all quite drunk, and laughter was coming easily. Mallonax smiled and rubbed his eyes, perhaps feeling the effects of even watered down wine.

'A charlatan?' said Adea, 'I shan't mention what I thought of you when we first met, Shiv!'

We were all still laughing and joking when Temina and Dombaba came in with trays laden with honeyed fruits. Temina slammed her tray down on the table and cried, 'I hope you are having a great time at our expense. Some of us have been here a lot longer than you. Here are your desserts for all the good they may do you.'

She stormed from the room leaving us in stunned silence. Mallonax got up to pursue her, and nearly fell off his chair.

'That's ok Mal,' said Apic gallantly, also getting up. 'I'll go.'

After that, the party mood left us and we drifted off to bed.

Carab and Adea could only stay for five days, and although I was very sad to see them leave, I was happy to get back to my studies. Carab was not yet ready to travel north to Vegas, it was approaching winter anyway, and the best time to make the passage was late spring, but he seemed to have found things in Werfen to keep himself busy. Adea had returned to her place in the palace, and had caused a great sensation on her return, especially as her rescuer was considered such a handsome young man by the ladies of court. I agreed to come and visit them as soon as my studies permitted, but in truth it was quite a while before I saw either of them again.

Dr. Lock stood with her elbows resting on the railings of the balcony. She looked distractedly down at the cigarette butt filled plant pot at her feet.
'A magician then?' she said and smiled.
'Too right, you had better watch out, or I'll turn you into a frog!' exclaimed Yarn, wiggling his fingers.
'So you can really do magic tricks then?' said Dr. Lock turning round to lean with her back to the rail and facing Yarn.
'Well, yes. I prefer to call the process "casting spells" rather than magic tricks.'
'Go on then.'
'That's the thing, I'm scared to. As Mallonax said, spells cast on gas cookers in his world could have dangerous and unpredictable results. After many hours of study and discussion with my master we worked out what might happen if a mage was to cast a spell in a world that had never seen magic.'
'What?'
'Well, one of three things. One,' replied Yarn counting them off on his fingers. 'The spell will work. Two, it won't work, or three...'
'And three?' prompted Dr Lock, after Yarn stopped in thought.
'And three ; the resulting displaced energies will cause a thaumatic chain reaction that will implode the universe into a super-dense black hole and shrink all matter and time to a point of singularity. '
'Ah. I think I understand,' nodded Dr. Lock sombrely, then said, 'Listen, have you thought any more about surgery?'
Yarn scowled and looked down, 'You know how I feel about that.'

Dr. Lock didn't leave the hospital until half past nine, and as usual she walked out to the car park through out patients main reception. She spotted Mr. Hood walking into the reception area, and quickly glanced round for somewhere to hide or run.
'Ah, Heather!' called Mr. Hood, waving at her. 'I'd like a word, if possible.'
Dr. Lock sighed and replied, 'Sure, Terry,' here he comes, she thought, Terry the Tiger.
'About your patient on Ward 33,' he smiled and looked down at her through his thick glasses.
'Yes?'
'I take it you have read his notes?' Heather gritted her teeth as he talked. 'The man is in need of surgery.'
'It is still the law in this country to get the patients consent before operating on them.'
'Ah yes, I was talking to Ian about that.'
Heather glanced over to the reception desk were a foreign girl was talking to the receptionist.

'Heather?'

'Yes, Terry, I know, I know, but the simple fact of the matter is that in my opinion the patient is lucid enough to make his own decisions. And by the time you get it past a board of inquiry, he'll be dead anyway, so you may as well drop it.'

Mr. Hood stretched up to his full height and ponderously looked down at Dr. Lock.

'Now Heather, there is no need to take that tone.'

Heather was distracted by the girl at reception again, she had a very strong French accent. She appeared to be looking for someone, but was being a bit vague about his name.

'Heather!' exclaimed the surgeon. 'I know what people say about me, I can't help that people find my height intimidating, or my manner, a trifle... shall we say abrupt.'

Heather began to tune Hood out, the receptionist was being very unhelpful.

'Heather. Please pay attention!'

'Huh?' said Heather glancing round, and suddenly realising just how hairy Hood's ears were, 'Oh, sorry Tiger, I mean Terry, it's late, I should be getting home.'

'Very well, Heather, I will see you tomorrow,' said Hood, although he continued to stand in her way.

Tearing herself away from Tiger Hood's hirsute ears she looked back round at the reception desk, but the girl had gone.

Chapter Twelve - A year of study

I think in total I spent nearly a year studying with Mallonax. We were rarely alone though. Temina was often sent on errands, and like the assassin in the night that she dreamed she was, she would drift in and out of our lives like a beautiful stranger. Apic was often about the place, except for a period of about six months when he went off to Tullis to settle some of his affairs. Adea didn't visit again after the first, but she did send some very long and excellently written letters. Carab spent most of his time riding around Enttland, and getting involved in local politics encouraging the idea of spending more money on defence and trying to convince people of the noggish danger to the south. He seemed to be delaying returning to Vegas for some reason. The world didn't stand still during my apprenticeship, and the noggish threat grew to be a bigger menace on a daily basis. Carab popped in every now and again to see how I was getting on, and it was odd, to see him coming out of his shell so much, and becoming much more talkative. I think he was finally beginning to throw off and forget some of the dreadful things he had experienced on the galley, and his truer self was beginning to be revealed. He never mentioned Adea, which lead me to suspect that he may have fallen in love with her.

In any case, I was much too busy with my studies. Although all I wanted was to learn how to get home, Mallonax insisted that was the last step on a long journey, and that I had to learn the simplest of spells first. I had an advantage over other apprentices he had had. I was pretty sure I had studied for an engineering or electrical degree in my past, and the process of learning and applying knowledge was ingrained within me. After the first few months, a delighted Mallonax confided in me that I was learning at about five times the expected rate.

The first steps in my apprenticeship were to learn and understand the basic principles of magic, and its use and manipulation. Put in simple terms it is the distortion of reality using the power of the mind. The human mind cannot achieve this by itself, instead magic users learn techniques for harnessing an universal energy, which goes by many names, but which I generally called 'mana'. I quickly learned how to channel mana towards me, by visualising strands of thousands of threads stretching out from around my body. Depending on the power and experience of any given magic user, the individual would be able to channel lesser or greater quantities.

A pupil starts at the lowest level, or 'bach', and as he gains more experience he gains the ability to channel more mana, and progresses onto higher bachs where he could learn more powerful spells.

It took a while to understand the concepts of channelling mana, and controlling it. But this and the study of the history of magic, ingredients, reagents, the usage of staves, pentagrams, rituals, chants, runes, gestures, secret writings, potions, powders, the manufacture of magical artefacts and weapons, were all that I thought about day in and day out. Although it was mostly book learning I never got bored, I was fascinated.

One day, a month or two into my studies, I was continuing with my lessons as always, in a world of my own, mixing spell ingredients with a pestle and mortar for one of the more complicated summoning spells. It would be a long time before I could cast such a spell, but as Mallonax was constantly pointing out to me, it was better to learn such things first. I don't think anyone realised I was in the sun room. I wasn't in the usual experimentation chambers as there wasn't enough ventilation. The fumes from the compound I was working on were very unpleasant, and I preferred it up here where I could fling the big balcony windows open and get a good breeze.
I heard footsteps on the corridor, then some voices, 'Hello Apic.' said a female voice, and therefore I deduced belonging to Temina.
'Hello Temina,' came the reply
'Where is your master?' she asked.
'My master, I have no master!' he cried indignantly.
'Yes you do! Shiv, your master!'
'He isn't my master!' Apic snorted.
'Well, what is he then?' asked Temina, genuinely puzzled.
'My friend. We go back a long way. I told you all about that, oars, whips, nogs, all that business, remember?'
'Yes, but… oh well, my mistake, I apologise, I just thought that…'
'Hmm,' laughed Apic. 'Well, now you know. I am as free a man as any other.'
They began to walk away, so I wasn't treated to the rest of the conversation, and I had a little smile to myself as I continued about my work.

It was many months before Mallonax trusted me to cast an actual spell, but after constant nagging on my part he was persuaded to push my training forward a bit. The first spells I learned were mere cantrips, very simple things, and to me now, laughably easy to cast, but I remember how nervous I was. We were sat at one of the experiment tables in the main laboratory, where I was to cast my first ever spell.
'Right Shiv,' Mallonax explained to me. 'This is simple. Or it should be. You have already studied the spell you are to try and cast today in Toaden's Thaumic Primer.'
'Oh, which one?' I replied.
'Magical Flame. A very old spell. As I said. It is a simple spell, a good one to get started on. First, as always you must empty your mind.'
I tried to relax, and not let my nervousness control me. I employed the method of meditation that Mallonax had taught me and pictured a blank slate, waiting to be written on.

'Good, I can see by that stupid expression on your face, that your mind is empty. A task I'm sure you found very easy.'

I sneered at his jibe, but maintained my concentration.

'Take the sulphur then,' he said, indicating the small pellet on the table by my elbow. I had not noticed it before, and picked it up and help it in the palm of my right hand.

'Muster you mana.'

I breathed out, and concentrated every effort into channelling my supplies of mana towards my hand and focusing it on the pellet.

'Not all of it you idiot, just a little, it will only take a little.'

I glanced up at him, and then back at the pellet. I re-focused, and began concentrating again. Sweat began to bead on my brow.

'No, no, no,' said Mallonax. 'Don't force it, feel it.'

I rolled my eyes at him. Keeping the mana force I held within me in my grasp was hard enough, without trying to siphon off a portion of it into my hand. It was like trying to grab at greased eels. Then I recalled something from my youth. What Mallonax had said, 'Don't force it. Feel it.' had triggered a memory in my head. Of long lazy afternoons spent in amusement arcades and in front of the Playstation. I remembered how I had excelled at these games, especially the scrolling shoot-em-ups, the utterly unrealistic games were you flew along in a powered up space ship, or P-51 aircraft or whatever, destroying wave after wave of enemies. By some secret universal agreement, all of these games had to have a series of harder and harder 'end of level bosses' as they were called, who shot hundreds of, usually, small round red missiles at you. The air around you would get so thick with them that it was only possible to survive by navigating a single small path of safety by predicting were a space in the fire pattern would be, rather like trying to run along a very busy crowded pavement. I found that I eventually got so good at these games that my level of expertise was almost legendary, and my friends would gather around whatever game I happened to be addicted to, and watch in slack jawed amazement. I would get so good at these games, that it became natural, I no longer had to think about what I was doing, by pure instinct and reflex my mind and fingers found the way. In a blinding flash of insight I saw mana as something like that. Something that never stayed still, that always has to be manipulated and juggled, never forced, just nudged into the space where you wanted it.

A smile crept across my face, and Mallonax clapped his hands, 'Now you're getting it!'

I nodded in excitement.

'Now intone the magical words, Shiv,' he ordered.

'Murisyfg Alinjyt Prtinbvt,' I said.

For the first split second I thought nothing was going to happen, then like petrol thrown onto a barbecue the pellet ignited. After the initial flash I was left with a small flame burning in the palm of my hand.

'Very well done Shiv! Now that will burn until you dispel it.'

I released the breath that I hadn't released I had been holding and gasped, 'Wait until I show the others this!' and leapt up from the table and rushed off downstairs, leaving Mallonax to smile and shrug to himself.

'Yes, well. I am impressed,' said Apic in an unimpressed way. 'It's very good.'
I held the flame still in my hand, it burnt with the intensity of a candle.
'Apic you moron. Don't you see, I called it up from my very own magical powers.'
'Yes I know,' he replied. 'It's just. I don't know. I expected something a bit more… amazing.'
'Oh well then!' I cried.
Temina who had been peering at the flame critically said, 'Hmm, I suppose it is ok, for a first effort. Hadn't you put it out now, before you set fire to yourself? It has been three hours now, isn't your arm tired?'
Then they both laughed at me.
'Sod the both of you then!' I sulked. 'I'm going to my room!'

From there on in I learned a new spell roughly at the rate of one a week. Next I learned a spell to make foreign languages comprehensible for a short period. This was another comparatively easy spell to learn. After that I learned a spell to magically lock doors and chests. As summer turned into autumn I learned one of my favourite and most useful spells, Kyle's Magical Umbrella, a spell to protect you from getting wet in the rain. The last cantrip I learned that season was a spell to produce a small creature from a hat or a sleeve. It doesn't take much to figure out how this trick can be done using slight of hand, by simply having the rabbit slung in bag at the side of a table, or up the sleeve, but this was different. This spell gave me real problems, in fact I had real problems with all the summoning spells. Where did the rabbit really come from? I cast the spell, waved my hands about, and suddenly there was a white rabbit squirming down my sleeve! By that time I could channel enough mana resources to cast that spell about twelve times a day, so soon the place was overrun with rabbits and doves. Incidentally this was the reason for the high proportion of rabbit and pigeon in our diet. Even Mallonax was uncertain as to whether the animals were simply created then and there by mystical forces or whether they were pulled from some dimension populated solely by white rabbits. Eventually I put off worrying about these thaumalogical debates to continue my studies in spell craft.

During my apprenticeship, as well as applying myself to my studies every day, my relationship with Dombaba continued to grow, if you could call it a relationship. I found his company fascinating, and would often torment him as he busied about his endless chores. We learned sign language together, from books taken from the library and eventually had a vocabulary of several thousand words. I would greet him every morning in the kitchen, then we would ask each other how we did, and we would both reply that we did very well thank you. Then I would ask him what he planned to do today, and he would reply that he would go and water the tea plantation, or feed the goats, or clean the fourth floor landing today, or whatever. Dombaba was a very good carpenter, I suppose it made sense seeing as he was made of wood, and I asked him to help me carve a chess set and some evenings we would whittle away together by the fireplace in the kitchen, enjoying each others company in complete silence. Mallonax took to the game easily, but I got the most pleasure from playing with Dombaba. He would look at the pieces so seriously. Ok, I realise he had no face on his blank wooden head, but it looked like he was serious. He wasn't a very good player, but he took to the game so much, that I said that he should keep the set for himself. At first he refused, but I insisted, and eventually he took it.

Later, that winter, I was to really apply myself and learn more advanced and dangerous spells. The first was a spell to cast a fireball from your hand to your enemy, one of the most useful I ever learnt. The next month I learned a spell that enabled you to fly small distances. That was a bit scary, floating off the ground and slowly making a circuit of the tower. Despite my terror, I managed to do three circuits of the sun room before drifting back to the balcony. Now this really did impress Apic and Temina, who stood on the balcony practically clutching each other in trepidation as I ghosted around with nothing but fresh air under me for forty metres, and an expression on my face that you might expect to see on a tight-rope walker.

As the nights drew in, I had even more time to learn spells, and Mallonax was amazed at my dedication and the speed at which I learned. In my final month I really got to grips with some powerful magic and advanced to the second bach, something that would have usually taken three years.
I was now ready to leave Mallonax, and go in search of the things I would need for my greatest spell, and possibly the thing that would enable me to reach home.
The form of magic that had been taught to me, often required the caster to use a series of complicated hand gestures and chants, and often in conjunction with a regent, for example, the pebble required to create a magical bridge, or the sulphur pellet needed for Magical Flame.
The spell I wished to cast now, 'Kettering's Portal of Returning (untested)', required me to find a specific spot, and be there at a specific time. The spell could only be cast from inside a magical circle, which had been bathed in darkness and star light for five solid days. No daylight must fall on it, and it must be outside. That had me puzzled, as there was no known spell powerful enough to blot out the sun for five days, the ancient wizards must have had some method to do this. Mallonax claimed that back in the old days they simply had been that powerful, and could stop the heavens in their progression whenever they wished.

It might take me several more years to prepare for this spell, and even then, there was no guarantee that it would work. However, I was no longer the pretend sorcerer of a year ago, I was about a hundred times more deadly, and I felt like a martial arts black belt who was looking for any sort of fight to test his abilities on. Physically I had mellowed a little though, my galley slave physique had sadly gone, and although not yet podgy, I was only a few cakes away.

It was a sad fareway that I said to Mallonax and Dombaba. Mallonax, although often cantankerous and a little bit too fond of the bottle had become a very close friend. After we had got know each other, in the first few months, all pretence of formality dropped between us. We had practised our humours on each other constantly. To me he was the doddering old imbecile, and to him, I was the ignorant youth with only the sense that he, Mallonax, had managed to beat into me. I had been his apprentice, and he had never let me forget it, and as such, no more important than a pot plant. We had something in common, in that we were both utter slovens, and often roamed about the tower wearing nothing but our undergarments and slippers, eating some random piece of food grabbed from the kitchen, usually in the middle of the night. If it hadn't been for Dombaba, our never complaining servant, we would both probably have contracted horrible diseases associated with domestic uncleanliness.

'Farewell, Mallonax,' I said, as I looked down at them both from the saddle of Chestnut. We were all stood at the base of the tower. It was a sunny summer's morning, 'The tower will be tidier now that it is minus one slob.'
'Too true,' replied Mallonax, and nodded.
'Perhaps it is as well you never gave Dom a voice. He may have had something to say about our messy behaviour.'
Dombaba nodded and rapped his skull with his fist. That meant, Yes, I think so.
Mallonax and I looked at each other and smiled for a moment, then Dombaba gave Mallonax's robe a tug.
'Oh yes, Dom,' said the wizard. 'Well, give it to him then.'
Dombaba brought forth a small case from his satchel, and came forward sheepishly and offered it up to me.
'What's this?' I asked as I opened it. It was a miniature chess set, exquisitely carved from mahogany for the black pieces and pine for the white.
My eyes twinkled a little, as I said, 'Dombaba, I am touched beyond words.'
Dombaba made a few signs. It is for travelling. I hope you like it.
'I do Dombaba, I do.'
Mallonax cleared his throat, 'We shall both miss you Shiv.'
'I will miss you both very much. If I make it back to my home, and I can figure out a way of contacting you, I will do so.'
'Good. Take care, my friend.'

We clasped hands one last time, and as I rode off I called back, 'Look after each other!' and they waved back.

I decided to go to Werfen and meet with Carab, and then discuss with my old friends what my next course of action should be. Apic was not around, I'm sure he had told me were he was going, but I couldn't quite remember where, I had been so preoccupied with study of late. I think he had begun to find my company a little distant. I left word with Mallonax where I was headed, so he could catch me up if he wanted, if he happened to put in an appearance.

'That was sweet,' said Heather, taking her glasses off and rubbing her eyes.
'He was a character,' replied Yarn.
As usual they were sat out on the balcony of the penthouse. It was another warm clear night.
'So this is the truth behind your secret magical powers then.'
'Now you know everything. I have no more secrets,' said Yarn and smiled.
'You mentioned a tea plantation? What was that all about?'
'Oh yes, that was one of my own plans. I planted them from seeds that came from the well. They took very well to the soil around the tower. Soon we were always taking tea.'
'I'm more of a coffee person myself.'
The conversation took on a light bantering humorous tone.
'You don't take tea?'
'I don't care for tea.'
'You don't care for tea?'
'I'm afraid not.'
'Oh,' said Yarn, as if totally miffed. 'Doesn't take tea. Doesn't care for it she says.'
Heather laughed and pointed at the three dirty mugs on the floor by Yarn's chair, 'I can see you take tea anyway.'
'I know,' he replied. 'I've got to admit, I used to take coffee, but then I found that I preferred to take tea.'
'It must have been because you where growing it yourself.'
Yarn clicked his fingers and pointed at her, 'That's probably it.'
Heather looked at her watch, and said, 'Well, I can stick the kettle on, if you fancy one last brew before I go.'
'Now you're talking.'

Dr. Lock took the one o'clock taxi from the Weston to the Royal Infirmary to see Dr. Heart to talk more about the circumstances of Yarns admission, but he wasn't very helpful. Just that the police brought him in to be checked over, after he had been found.
'I do remember that was an odd week though,' mused the elderly Dr. Heart. 'A body builder type came in, never seen injuries like it... hmm...'

'Oh really?' replied Heather, sipping her coffee with Dr. Heart in the canteen.

'Oh yes, I remember,' laughed the good doctor. 'A big fellow, huge lacerations, on his chest you know, and shoulders, like he'd been mauled by a tiger, according to the police he came in the same night. It's a miracle really. Still up there, on ward twenty-seven. But I'm afraid, I was very... very drunk at the time!'

Heather spluttered her coffee, then said, 'Oh I see, the Fast Show, do you know, you look a lot like him!'

'That's what my grandson says!'

Heather went up to see the fellow on Ward 27, not really knowing what to expect. In the event he was fast asleep and the ward sister snottily informed her that he was not to be disturbed, as he had a tendon operation the next day. As Dr. Lock left the ward and opened the swing door, she bumped into another woman coming the other way, and they both smiled and said 'Sorry,' to each other. The small woman bowed at her, she was wearing a headscarf and a large black coat, and entered the ward.

It wasn't until she was back in the car park she realised it had been the small French girl she had seen at the reception desk back at the Weston.

Chapter Thirteen - Werfen

The highways of Enttland are well kept, and very pleasant to ride upon. It is a land of rolling hills, with always the far off purple shadows of mountains to the east. The road to Werfen ran east, and the mountains would be my constant companions all the way to the city. The land I was riding through was very sparsely populated, it had a wild quality, the dark hills brightly decorated with heather and gorse.

I had ridden through a village, a small collection of houses by the side of the road really, an outpost on the way to Bellavia. As I began to ride out of the other side of the hamlet and up out of the valley, a figure on a dark horse came galloping up. I recognised the horse before I did the rider. It was Apic's dark mare, an evil tempered beast, prone to biting, but made distinguishable by the white blaze on her forehead. I presumed then that the slight figure, muffled from the summer dust, was none other than the horse's master.

'Hail, Apic. What news?'

It wasn't Apic however, the figure removed her muffler and took off her three cornered hat to wipe the sweat from her brow.

'Apic will be along presently,' she said.

'Ah, you wish to ride with me aways?' I said and smiled, I always put on a bit of a dandy highwayman act with Temina whenever I spoke to her.

'If you will permit me, my lord. Are you leaving Glamis so soon?' she said tartly.

I pulled my mare back a little to prevent her being nipped by Temina's evil steed.

'My studies are done, I have become a journeyman now, and I have one great task to perform.'

We began to ride along side by side.

'Yes, Mal sent me word of that. He did not tell you that I was to accompany you?'

'No he did not,' and I felt sure he would have if that had been his intention, but I kept this observation to myself.

'It must have slipped his mind, he is getting old after all.'

'Quite.'

Later that afternoon, standing like a robber at a crossroads, there was Apic, himself, on a horse I did not recognise.

'That is a fell beast,' I said. 'Even more malcontent looking than Bessy here, and a good three hands taller.'

'She is of a more even temperament. I thought Temina should have Bessy after her horse died last year. I won enough money playing cards around here to buy this horse from a grain dealer in Tullis. She is the daughter of Old Bones, who was my father's.'

'Oh yes,' I nodded, I seemed to be getting more information than usual from Apic. I wondered if something was going on.

'And what brings you out here on such a fine day?' I asked innocently.
'I was merely taking the air, I have lodgings here abouts. And what are you about today, it is strange to see you so far from the tower.'
'It will be further yet, I am bound for Werfen.'
'Well, well, Shiv, on the road again. In that case I had better accompany you, without me around anything might happen.'
I wondered why we were talking in such a gentlemanly fashion, and realised it might all be for Temina's benefit.
'Certainly, friend Apic, I would not have it any other way.'
Apic joined us on the highway, and although I tried to engage him in some of the friendly banter as we used to do on our travels, I got the impression he was preoccupied with other matters.
Two chance encounters on the highway, I thought, and had a little smile to myself.

The majority of the roads and highways of Enttland are very safe. This area was not overly troubled by bandits or goblins. Once we were on the main highway, which headed west to east along the backbone of the country running parallel to the great Gylefen River, it was pretty much plain sailing. Every so often we would pass another band of travellers on the road and bid then good day, or perhaps we might spot a vessel on the river to our north and exchange a friendly wave. Every twenty or so miles on the main highway there is a royal hostel, which while a trifle more expensive than the privately run inns, were excellently provisioned. It was one of my favourite journeys, that fortnight through the gently rolling hills of the shires of Enttland. Me on Chestnut, that quiet, pleasant natured beast, Temina on Satan's own stead, Blackhearted Bessy, and Apic on the long legged hunter, Old Bones' Daughter. It reminded me of... what? It reminded me of something anyway. I had never learnt how to ride in these lands, so I assumed I had learnt previous to my displacement. The rides were great, the scenery marvellous, the land peaceful, and after a long mile-eating trek we had good stables for the horses and good food and lodgings for us. All three of us were quite heavy drinkers as well, and would set about getting reasonably drunk each night in a purposeful manner. The ride out in the morning in the cool breeze would insure any hangover cobwebs were blown away.

The only encounter we had of any note was a run in with a patrol of mounted road wardens. They were hunting for highwaymen, and stopped us at a crossroads for questioning. There were five of them, one of whom was obviously their leader. He was dressed in green leathers and had long white hair across his shoulders and a spiky white beard. Across his back was slung a scabbard that held a massive two-handed sword. He squinted at me in the sunlight.
'Hail travellers, where did you come from and where are you bound?' he asked.

'We come from Mallonax's tower and are bound for Werfen,' I replied, I didn't see it as any great secret.

'If you will allow the impoliteness of self introduction, I am constable Yarrow, can I ask you for your names?' the constable looked at us shrewdly.

'Shiv,' I said.

'Apic,' said Apic.

Temina remained silent, and I turned to look at her. She was still wearing her muffler.

Suddenly it all dawned on me that Temina's highwayman act might not be an act, and that she may really have been going out at night and robbing stagecoaches. It would all tie in, I thought, she would be gone for days, and sometimes she would turn up in the dead of night. At our original meeting, she had been trying to steal our horses. What she had told us by way of an explanation must have been a pack of lies. Also, she had taken to riding Bessy, that evil beast, who was one of the fasted horses I had even known. I licked my lips nervously and wondered what to do. Although there was, I admitted, no great love between me and Temina, I certainly didn't want to see her hung at a crossroads as a warning to others.

'If I could just ask the gentleman in the black scarf to reveal his face.'

Temina slowly moved her hand up to her muffler. I looked from her to the constable, wondering what was going to happen next. Apic looked equally confused.

'Temina!' cried the policeman, when he saw her face.

'Ok, ok, it's me.' she grunted.

'Incognito my lady?'

'Alright father, that's enough. Apic. Shiv. My father.'

The constable laughed.

'Gentlemen you are in bad company. I would advise you to rethink who your travelling companions are.'

The other road wardens laughed at this, making Temina blush bright red. Yarrow reached over to pat her on the hand,

'I'm sorry dear, I did not mean it. It was nice to see you again last month when you came to visit. I know I never had any time for you when you were young, but you are such a fine girl now, I am proud to have you as a daughter.'

Temina gritted her teeth, 'I have no time for this, old man. I visited you because Mallonax nagged me into doing it. I am going to be out of Glamis for a while, so I will say farewell to you now.'

Yarrow shrugged, but could not help but smile, 'You are like your old father, always on the go. Farewell Temina. Visit me again, when you return.'

Temina wheeled round black Bessy and without further comment cantered off down the road. Apic and I nodded and said farewell before trotting off after her.

'What did you make of all that?' I asked Apic, as we rode along.

'I knew she had a father here abouts but she never talked about him. I wouldn't pry too much, you know what she's like.'
'Don't worry!' I laughed, 'I've no desire to feel the rough side of her tongue!'

We reached Werfen two leisurely weeks later. As Adea had once predicted, the country around here were heavily cultivated, and fields of summer wheat stretched off as far as the eye could see in the lands surrounding the city. The city itself was beautiful, built on a series of hills and ridges from local granite, centring around the palace in the middle, which dominates the skyline as you approach, situated as it is, on a large volcanic outcrop of rock. It is far bigger than Tullis, and it took us long enough to travel through the outskirts, and for want of a better word, suburbs, to the city gates. These areas consisted of pleasant looking cottages and other low buildings. Their owners obviously took pride in their appearance, as many were decked in hanging baskets of flowers, and there wasn't one that didn't have a little garden at the front with gaily-coloured roses, asters or hollyhocks growing in it. When we reached the city gates, the guards motioned us through with a few stern warnings about drawing blades within the city limits. They were dressed in the blue and gold livery of Werfen. They almost didn't seem to be proper guards to me, they were so friendly and courteous, although they did seem a little preoccupied. I thought I might know why. For the last couple of days, the only thing that people had been talking about, in the taverns and inns that we had stayed in, were the rumours that abounded of the Lunarian army preparing to march into Enttland for purposes unknown. Whether there was any truth to these rumours I had no way of verifying, but it was all very strange. The Lunarians sounded like a very odd bunch of characters. They had started life as a nation as a rough alliance of savage tribes in the great forest south of the Askbakar Mountains. A terrible warlord united the tribes in the worship of the evil Lunar gods, and anyone not wishing to join the church was burned. Part of their doctrine was that they turn night into day. They slept all day, and did their work through the night. They now had a massive army, and were excellent cannon makers, for one thing they had a very worrying amount of artillery pieces in their arsenal. Much of the forest within their borders had been cut down to feed the Lunarian furnaces. They were also famed for their excellent horsemanship, and favoured as their steeds, their own Lunarian breed of stocky white ponies. We had seen little evidence of any military preparations by the Enttish, but it was said that the majority of the Enttish army was still in Hombard to the north, resupplying after a series of border battles with Eask.
Everyone was terrified of first hearing the thunder of the Lunar guns, then the white faced long haired savages attacking in mounted hordes and dragging people into the night to be murdered. Some of the old timers remembered when exactly that happened thirty years ago, when Lord Grampus met them on Flaid Field and pushed them back over the mountains.

We rode into the city.

From Adea's letters I knew that she inhabited a house called Rochen Manor, in the town's old quarter, and that she lived with her parents. Through her correspondence I had learned she had indeed been a lady at court of sorts, a chief maid to a royal princess of Enttland. Her parents had been terrified that they had seen the last of her after the attack on the royal party in the Great Forest, and they were overjoyed to finally have her delivered up to them in the capable hands of Carab.
Incidentally the royal party had reached Ferron without further molestation, apart from one of the royals being injured. The mouse like princess was married off to some insipid inbred princeling to cement the relationship between the two nations. I am quoting all this from Adea's letters.
Her father was a minor noble of some type, a royal cousin, although, apparently if you threw a stone in Werfen, the royal capital you would hit one, so it wasn't quite as auspicious as it sounded. Her mother was an artist of sorts and delighted in collecting 'eccentric characters', and was very anxious to meet me.

We decided to visit a tavern that Apic had discovered on the east quarter, the area of the city that most reminded him of Tullis, to clean the road dust off us and have a meal before going to visit Adea and her family. They were expecting us sometime this week or possibly the next, as Adea's coming of age birthday party was at this time, and although we could have easily turned up as we were, I thought that Adea might prefer it if we didn't look like complete vagabonds. Both Apic and Temina preferred to dress in black. Apic looked like a well-dressed clerk or possibly a favoured servant. He wore a richly embroidered black waistcoat, god only knows where he had got it from, and knee high riding boots. On his face, he wore a short goatee beard and I'm sure he thought he looked very dashing, but I always thought of him as the skinny corpse-like runaway galley slave. He had a rapier in a buckskin scabbard at his waist, and carried his belongings in a dark leather satchel. Temina, if anything was the ideal female counterpart to Apic. Again, all dressed in black, and wearing as always her three-cornered dandy-highwayman style hat. Usually she wore her hair up in a black scarf, but as it had been so warm today, it lay down on her shoulders like licks of flame. She wore baggy trousers done up with buckles at her knees where they met her riding boots, and an expensive looking travelling coat, over a dark blouse and doublet.
As for myself, I think I must have been unconsciously going for a pirate-gypsy look. At the time I had had my left ear pierced twice, a ritual that all apprentice mages had to undergo to mark there rank. One earring for each bach, a secret sign to other magic users. I wore my hair short, but preferred to tie a bandanna on my head to keep the road dust out of it. I wore a course woollen shirt, and a dark brown leather jerkin, and black leather bracers. Over this if it was cooler I wore I deep rich red blanket,

which I had found in a basket at the tower, and had fallen in love with. It was so red it was frightening, and I wore it with a broach at the neck and tied with a black studded leather belt at the waist. On my legs I wore thin trousers and black suede leather chaps, and my feet were shod in hobnailed boots. I had taken to sporting a large moustache that grew all the way to the base of my chin, and I usually only shaved about once a week.

So, to sum up, we looked like a real set of rogues, and part of the reason I wanted to stop was to change into something more suitable. I wondered what sort of reaction I might get from Temina if I asked her to put on a dress. But first things first, we all agreed to wash the dust from our throats with a few ales before we even thought of sending for a tailor. Mallonax had provided us with plenty of gold, so we ordered up ale and a bottle of the fine local spirits.

As we took our first mouthfuls we were treated to a floorshow, as the landlord argued with a servant. We only made out the occasional word in the heated debate, it seemed to revolve around money, and at last the servant cried, 'My master will here of this!' and stormed out of the inn, leaving the landlord to shrug his shoulders.

My friends and I looked at each other and exchanged amused winks, and reapplied ourselves to our drinks. I thought it might be an idea to let Temina have a few softeners before the dress subject was brought up.

Later that evening, about nine or ten, we were all pretty drunk, and arguing. Well, more like Apic and I were teasing Temina about her dress sense.

'Come on Temmy,' I nagged. 'It's going to be Adea's birthday party, you can't expect to go dressed like that!'

Apic snickered.

'I'll, I'll, not...' Temina stumbled over her words, then burped, making us insensitive men laugh uproariously.

'I'll not be dictated to by the likes of you!' she cried.

'Something in blue taffeta I thought...' laughed Apic

'Yeah with a nice big pink ribbon at the bust!' I joined in.

Temina pouted and folded her arms, 'And what about you two? The king of the gypsies and his evil henchman!'

'Ah now,' I interrupted. 'That's King Eric the Flat, and the Lord High Keeper of the Royal Pantaloons to you!'

This piece of nonsense forced a smile onto Temina's lips.

Just then a female figure dressed in a rich purple velvet cloak entered the tavern, silencing those close by as they turned to look. She approached the busy landlord and engaged him in conversation. This went on right at my shoulder so I could hear every word.

'I assure you I have not been paid my lady,' the landlord protested. 'You'll not get the wine until I get the money. And you'll not get any Ferronish wine anywhere else in Ent at this time of year.'

'My servant has paid you! If my husband were here, he would soon sort you out!'

The landlord shrugged, I turned to look up at him, he looked shifty and nervous.

'Perhaps you should talk to your servant about what he thinks happened to the payment.'

The lady gasped at this affront and stepped forward to shake her finger under his nose, but the landlord was jostled at the back by a drunkard or someone, and pushed forward into the lady. She lost her footing and fell directly into my lap and for the first time her hood fell back and I saw her face. She was a good-looking woman in her forties, or would have been considered good looking if her features were not twisted in outrage.

The beer in me made me laugh at the confounded expression on her face.

'Unhand me at once you villain!' she cried.

'My lady!' I cried back and laughed. 'I thought you had come to pay me a visit!'

'Well,' she gasped and stood up. The whole inn began to laugh at her, and suddenly seeing the compromising and ridiculous situation she was in, she made to run from the room. I grabbed her by the arm.

'My gods sir! Unhand me at once!'

'Just wait one moment my lady, as you have pushed yourself into my company, I will get to the bottom of this.' I gave her a hard look and she stopped struggling.

'Now, this man, you accuse of not handing over goods that you have paid for, is this correct?'

'Well, yes, twelve bottles of Ferronish Wine.'

'And you declare that you have received no such payment?' I said, addressing the landlord, who shifted his gaze nervously to the floor.

'Yes, ten silver for each bottle, sir. But this is a matter between me and the lady, I will thank you not to interfere.'

'Too late for that. And my lady,' I continued. 'What did you give your servant, and when did you send him?'

'I gave him six gold coins, if it's any of your business, and he was sent this morning,' she said, and wrenched her arm away from my grasp, but she didn't try to run away.

'Well now,' I said, examining the landlord. He was tall and thin, with very little in the way of hair, except for that which poked out from underneath his collar. It was hot, but he seemed to be sweating more than was necessary. I suddenly felt sure of his guilt. He was wearing a white apron and a loose cotton shirt. At his belt was a large leather pouch.

'Ahem, well now, six gold is a lot of money. If you would be as good as to show me the contents of your purse sir.'

'I will not!' cried the landlord.

Someone in the room cried out, 'For shame!' then another further back shouted, 'Get it out, Varset, you old thief!'

'Curse you!' hissed the landlord looking me directly in the eye, 'Very well, I'm robbing myself, you can have the thrice damned wine, and much good I hope it does you!'

He signalled over a potboy and yelled at him, 'Don't just stand there you idiot, go and get the Ferronish crate!' and threw his dishcloth at the child.

As the boy brought up the crate, the lady turned to me, and said, 'Why thank you sir... ah, thank you... oh this way boy.'

She left the inn obviously flustered, the potboy struggling with the heavy crate behind her. Apic laughed and slapped me on the shoulder.

I raised my arm and knocked on the dark wooden gates. It was situated in a tall red brick wall that was over grown with moss and ivy. Fully opened the gate would admit a decent sized carriage. An elderly servant in a powdered wig and dusty red jacket opened the portal and said ponderously, 'Ah. Shiv and his party, you are expected.'

As we followed the venerable ancient up the driveway to the house, I muttered to Apic, 'Where did they dig that one up?'

'By the look of him, they probably made him up from spare parts and old dog bones about three hundred years ago.'

As we rounded the tree lined drive and got a good look at the house, Temina whistled and said, 'Nice place. Needs a bit of repair though.'

Apic and I nodded in mute agreement. Rochen House was obviously as old, if not older than the servant who lead us to it, and although it looked cared for and loved, it spoke of there maybe not being enough money to, for instance, repair a collapsing gable on the upper floor, or fix some of the guttering that was working loose.

We were all slightly hungover after last night's revelry, but I had had the forethought to send a card on ahead. We had agreed to wear our own clothes for the time being, but tided up a bit, and made as respectable as possible. I removed my blanket, as the mere sight of it was giving the other two a headache, and my bracers to give myself a less martial air. We would send for a tailor and get clothes made for Adea's birthday party next week.

The interior of the house was as large and impressive as the outside, although, again, I detected a slightly dilapidated feeling about it. We were ushered into the large entrance hall, and invited to scrape the mud from our boots.

'The master is currently engaged in town, but I will inform the ladies of the house,' said the servant formally and bowed.

A door opened and another younger servant said, 'Please come through to the sitting room gentlemen', then 'Ah... and lady,' as he spotted that Temina wasn't a man.

'Don't worry, you're not the first to make that mistake,' I commented to him as I made my way into the room, which earned me an elbow in the ribs from the lady in question.

We sat down and waited. I glanced around the room. It was well furnished, obviously by a woman of taste. There was also a lot of memorabilia around, like an old cavalry sabre, and an ancient looking suit of armour. Although just a guestroom of some sort, it seemed that it was used by the family. There were a few samplers on a nearby table, and someone had been decorating a wooden box with shells. Underneath a desk in the far corner was an animal cage, and by the window amongst other clutter was a large arrangement of flowers.

Presently there was a clattering and Adea entered the room, followed by a huge wolfhound.

'Shiv! Apic and Temina!' she cried and embraced us, the dog trying to nose into the action.

'Hello Adea, where is Carab?'

'He's out of town but will be back in time for my party, but mother is upstairs, and will be down presently. Ah here is Meg.'

A girl of about thirteen rushed into the room from another door, then froze as she got a look at us.

'Say hello Meg, these are my friends from Glamis.'

Meg was dressed prettily in a red dress, covered in a white pinafore, which was just as well as it was quite grubby. She had her hair done up in pigtails and looked every inch the tomboy. I wondered if Adea had looked like this when she was young.

'Hello,' she murmured which made us laugh.

'I have heard a lot about you, young Meg,' I said, which was true, Adea had talked of her a lot in her letters. With a nod from Adea, I approached her younger sister.

'I have something for you,' I said as I knelt down beside her. 'Please observe, nothing up my sleeves', and indeed there couldn't have been, as I had no sleeves, my shirt terminated at the elbow.

'And with the magic words…Abra Cadabra!'

With a fine flourish I produced a white rabbit from thin air, and the little girl clapped her hands in joy. I handed the rabbit over to Meggan who accepted it gingerly.

I stood up and Apic whispered to me through his smile, 'Just don't tell her what usually happens to them.'

I nodded.

A woman entered the room and began a sentence,

'Get that hound out of here, it's like a menagerie…' and stopped midway through.

It was the lady from last night.

I stood there in amazement, and wondered what she was going to do next, whether she was going to blow her top or not, but then her face broke into a dazzling smile and rushed to embrace and kiss me on both cheeks.

'Well, you must be Shiv, I must say, you were a godsend last night in the Feathers.'

Adea broke in, in confusion,

'You were in the Feathers last night mother?'

Her mother gave her a look which meant - don't inquire to deeply dear, it is connected with your birthday.

'And this must be Apic and Temina. I have heard so much about you all from Adea and Carab,' she sighed and clapped her hands. 'Now what will you take? Wine? A little fruit cordial?'

I smiled and said, 'If you can bring me some boiling water, some milk and honey, I have something you might like to try. A leaf I have been growing on my little plantation in Glamis. I call it *tea*, it is a most excellent drink to take in the afternoon.'

And thus it was that I introduced tea into Werfen, probably the singular most important thing I did during my adventures, and a new culture was born. And we were still taking tea when Lady Wellven's husband, Lord Wellven arrived home from his day at court.

'Yes, you must have been quite a god send for poor dear Agatha,' joked Lord Wellven, 'I would have gone myself had I known, and not been delayed at court. Going to a tavern in town all by yourself, Agatha, for all love!'

'Yes, alright Demmy, there is no need to go on about it.'

Lord Wellven was a tall man, although in his middle age he seemed to have put on quite a lot of weight. There was certainly a lot of him. He wore a tight jacket and a stiff collar that held up his slightly saggy chin. He wore no beard, and was no longer blessed with much head hair. Lady Wellven was dressed in a pleasant dark blue frock, and wore her hair in curls, she had obviously dressed to meet us. At first I thought that, the evening might turn out to be like an awkward visit to your posh auntie, but it soon turned out not to be the case.

The evening revolved around the conversations we were having. There was no standing on ceremony. Wine and more hot water were brought up as required, and food turned up at seemingly irregular intervals. Animals and children ran through the house, much to the consternation of the parents, but you could see on their faces how much they loved their full house hold. We were shown around the house and grounds, and ended the night down on the terrace by the pond, taking wine and eating pastries. I am afraid that Lady Wellven and I began to monopolise the conversation. She had an insatiable thirst for tales of my lands, and how I had learned to use magic. In the pleasant darkness, lit only by the taper that had been lit by the servants, I could see that Adea was asleep in her fathers lap, and I suspected that he slept as well. Apic and Temina had gone down to the pond and were engaged in a conversation of their own.

We had already talked about a great many things. Magic, travelling, the many strange things in my world, and we had drifted onto art.

'Yes, from what you have shown me in the house, in your splendid gallery, I would say Enttland is currently in the period that we would have called the Renaissance. A harping back to older art styles, but with a touch of the Baroque, you have many great paintings in your collection. You can see the imagery is being taken from the ancient motifs. The voluptuous ladies, the dramatic poses.'

'Yes, but what I want to know is what will come after that.'

'Well,' I continued. 'After that, if you follow the same line that we did you will eventually get to Rococo, Romanticism, Impressionism,'

'What is Impressionism?'

'You'd love it. The one you did of the picnic table is so like something by Van Gogh. The bold, but simple strokes, the dynamic use of light and shade. You are ahead of your time, Lady Wellven.'

At this she blushed, then said, 'And after that?'

'Um.. well, after that, I mean, Impressionism was a reaction. Each new artists period or movement is a reaction to the last. Cubism challenged Impressionism, but it was born out of the first terrible war in my lands, and the disillusioned returning soldiers who started Dadaism and Surrealism.'

'Cubism?'

'Thus,' I said, taking a quill and a piece of parchment from the table, and sketching a simple cubist portrait, 'See how the face is broken down into facets. It no longer tries to offer a realistic picture of the subject, but breaks it down into components to show it in its essence.'

'And the other two?'

'Put simply, the representation of dreams.'

'Stranger and stranger,' the lady mused.

'Haha!' I laughed. 'You haven't heard the last of it. Wait until I tell you about Fauvism, Pop art, Abstract Expressionism, and the thing that, to my mind killed off expression in any modern sense, Conceptual Art, fuelled only by the desire to shock and make money.'

I am sorry, but I so enjoyed the looks of horror that came over Lady Wellven's face as I described to her all the modern art monstrosities that I could remember from my past. Sharks pickled in vast tanks. Exhibitions of someone's unmade bed. Painting using elephants dung. Tins of an artist's excrement, sold for twenty thousand dollars a time. An exhibition that consisted of a nutty American artist under a blanket, sharing a cage with a coyote. She was so upset that I had to console her with remembrances of modern art that I did like. The wonderful paintings of Rene Magritte, and the seminal work of the surrealist Max Ernst.

We continued talking well after everyone else had gone to bed, and Lady Wellven resolved to attempt her very first surrealist painting the very next day.

We stayed with the Wellven's for a week and a half, and as the days progressed towards Adea's birthday, the house became more and more hectic. It was Adea's twenty-second birthday, which was celebrated here as we would the twenty-first. For a lady at court it was especially significant as it meant you were now of marriageable age. There was to be a big ball, and marquees in the garden, no expense was being spared. All this was taking place in semi-secret while Adea was at court.

The first guests started arriving at about nine o'clock. Apic and I were already positioned by the drinks table, consummate party animals that we were. I had presented Adea with my gift earlier that morning, a jewelled brooch that I had enchanted, and then stayed well out her way, as she had clearly gone insane with party nerves. The spell I had cast on the brooch was pretty pointless, as it was meant for enchanting weapons, but Adea liked the way that it made it sparkle, and had immediately pinned it to her gown.

Before the evening truly got under way, there were some speeches. I was in the garden, with the main body of the guests. I had temporarily lost Apic. I glanced around for him, but he wasn't in evidence. He would have been easy to spot if he was around, dressed as he was in a dark bottle green waistcoat, and a white ruffled shirt. He was also wearing a long bledlow coat with ridiculously large cuffs. I myself was much more stylish, in a navy coat, with gold buckles and piping all the way down the front, and a quiet splendid pair of blue pantaloon style trousers tucked into my knee-high boots.

'Thank you ladies and gentlemen!' cried Lord Wellven holding up his arms for silence, as everyone cheered. I gave up looking for Apic and looked on at Adea's father.

'Today is one of the proudest days of my life. My eldest daughter's coming of age!'

Cheers and laughter.

'Now, all I need is a young man to take her off my hands now she is of marriageable age!'

More laughter, Adea blushed by her father's side. I smiled as I went off to the bar to see if anyone was around. Lord Wellven continued to crack jokes and embarrass his daughter as I left the garden.

I took a path that lead to the dining room, hoping to find some more of the fine pate that I had been eating and happened to pass Temina coming the other way with a plate full of cakes.

I gave her a knowing smile as she looked at the plate guiltily.

'These are not all for me, Shiv,' she said by way of explanation.

I laughed and stood back to look at her. She was dressed elegantly in a dark blue satin dress with an empire waste line. Her hair was piled up on her head in red curls and she wore long white gloves. She was very pretty.

'I must say, you look lovely Temina.'

Automatically assuming I was teasing her she replied, 'I feel like a Tullis tart in this get up.'

I grabbed a cake off her plate and shoved it in my mouth. Temina laughed and made to pass me on the path, 'Right then, I am off to listen to the speeches Shiv, get your own cakes!'

I met one of the many people I had been introduced to in the previous few weeks, in the dining room as I was helping myself to more food.
'Hello again, Shiv,' said the polite young man. He was much more lavishly dressed than I was, and I felt like a peacock in my party get-up. Wearing a tall powdered wig, a light peach coloured long coat and an enormous ruffled shirt, with large billowing cuffs, he was enough to make me choke on the chicken leg I had been chewing.
'Hello Boris,' I said as I remembered his name. I also remembered he was one of Adea's cousins.
'What a lovely party, isn't it? Adea was at my parents last week. She told me all about her adventures with you in the Great Forest. I was enthralled. So much more exciting than the life my father has planned out for me.'
'Oh really?' I replied politely.
'Yes, two more years at the academy, three years in court, then I am to become the personal companion of the Prince of Plumlow.'
'Sounds dreadful.'
'Indeed. The Prince is an insipid idiot, a milk sop, with no more idea of manly pastimes such as hunting and drinking, than his mothers lap dog.'
I was slightly surprised at the venom in that last statement, then composing myself, I said, 'You hunt?'
'When my father lets me. I wish. I wish I could be like you Shiv, always travelling, doing the things that you want to do. My life is all planned out.'
'Well,' I shrugged, not really wanting to become his agony aunt, but regardless I said, 'You don't have to do everything your father says, I'm sure.'
'I know,' sighed the young man, 'But he controls my money supply.'
I laughed, 'In that case, you are your own worst enemy. Don't look for excuses for not doing something! Never mind, you aren't missing anything, I seem to have spent most of the last few years either being chased by nasty people, or being thrown in jail. A life of adventure isn't all it's cracked up to be.'
With that pearl of wisdom I left Boris, as I spotted Apic and went over to get him.

Later that night, Apic and I were heavily engaged in conversation with two young ladies that had been anxious to be introduced to us, as the exciting new friends of Adea and Carab. The one I was talking to was a dizzy young thing, with a lovely round face, framed in a mass of blonde curls. I liked her a lot as she was a little drunk, and probably not used to wearing the large flouncy dress she was in. She giggled and clutched at my arm alternatively in horror, then joy, as I told her of my adventures in Foona. I wish I could remember her name. Apic's companion was perhaps more intelligent, but not as much fun, in my opinion. She was taller, and had red hair done up in a bun, and wore a long flowing green gown. They were engaged in a slightly more serious conversation about horses. I hadn't seen much of Adea, as she had so many people to go around and meet, but I was a bit concerned that Carab hadn't arrived yet. I think it was some time after midnight. Just as I was thinking that, the man himself turned up. We were in the garden, and I saw him come through the house and head towards the group that Adea and her family were in. I gave him a wave and he nodded curtly at me, and stoically continued on.

'Oh aye,' I said to my companions, and started to walk over to the birthday girls group, 'This might be interesting.'

I was almost jogging by the time I got there and started elbowing my way through the crowd.

Carab stood with his large hands holding Adea's. Something had obviously been said, as everyone was silent as I got to the front and said, 'Hey, what's going on....', then quickly shut up. Carab had obviously just dropped a bombshell.

Lord Wellven cleared his throat and said, 'Well sir, I expect it is no surprise to you that this is no great surprise to me. I know you are a good and honest boy, from an excellent family, although maybe a little bit further north than I would have liked. Ahem, sorry, yes, I am sure that I speak for my wife as well, when I say that I am delighted, and that you may certainly take my daughters hand, if she is willing...'

The lord stopped talking as his voice was beginning to break a little. Lady Wellven clapped her hands together gleefully and rushed to embrace her daughter and new future son-in-law. Everyone began to offer their congratulations.

There was a very loud explosion in the distance, followed by a series of smaller reports. I thought it might be fireworks.

A few minutes later, there was a commotion at the front gate, then a town guard ran into the garden and shouted, 'The city is under attack!' which caused instant confusion. Suddenly the party erupted into chaos, as everyone ran around looking for whomever they had come with, and finding servants to shout orders at. The men stalked around in agitation and most of the women were in tears.

Carab and Lord Wellven organised things as best they could, getting the guests away in their coaches as quickly as possible. More reports came in, and what I had thought were fireworks got louder and louder. I climbed a tree to look out over the garden walls.

The bombing was picking up pace. The whole southern section of the city, luckily not where we were, was being pounded by the Lunarian guns, and in the distance, over the river I could see that some areas were already in flame.

Some time later we were still at the house, all the guests having left and a general debate of should we stay and defend the Wellven's home, or pack as much as possible and flee the city was going on. Several servants had been sent to the river to see how the battle was going. This was mainly family business, so Apic, Temina and I took another look around the house, to see how it could be defended. After a while we decided that the gates should be given up and any invaders coming to the house would be met by us at the door. I would use my magic to hold them off, or even scare them away, while the others attacked targets of opportunity. I would even give my gun to Apic if need be, which made him lick his lips nervously.

The consensus in the house was that although the family shouldn't leave until it was clear that the city was lost, that the coach and wagons should be hitched up, as much as was needed loaded onto them, and the rest of the house locked up and secured.

When the old servant, Limer, came back from the Jade Bridge and reported that the invaders had crossed the river and were storming the palace, Lord Wellven cried, 'I don't care what anyone else says. We leave. Right now!'

Everyone was very tired, and Adea was very tearful. I felt so sorry for her, something like this happening on her birthday. The house was in complete disarray. Crates, boxes, chests, valises, and bags were everywhere. Anything valuable that couldn't be taken was being locked up in the cellar. It all seemed to be happening so slowly, and although I was helping out as much as I could, I kept feeling I was more in the way. All my worldly possessions could fit into one pack.

I volunteered to go down the road on a quick scouting expedition with Apic, to see how the battle was going on.

We reached the main square, and looked at the burning palace across from us. It was a depressing sight. The city defences were putting up a brave fight, but they were heavily outnumbered by the Lunarians. A squadron of Lunar cavalry, mounted on their stocky white ponies crossed the square at a gallop.

'They have moved the guns up to the river,' I pointed out. 'The opera house is on fire.'

'Oh Shiv,' groaned Apic. 'This is worse than Che. We had better go back to Rochen before they come under the guns.'

A shell exploded right in the house we were standing beside, and sent bricks and mortar flying everywhere. We ran for cover along the street, and our feet decided to take us back to Rochen as fast as they could. A troop of mounted guards, in their bold blue and gold livery rode past us at a trot, towards the square. As we rushed on, I noticed that many buildings were on fire, and smoke was beginning to fill the air, reminding me uncomfortably of my brief visit to Usak. We rounded a street corner, and were hit by a wall of heat coming from the tall burning building on the opposite side. People milled around everywhere, and some were drawing up water from a well and throwing it on the flames but to little use. There was a shriek from someone in the crowd, and people started to point up to a fourth floor window. Just visible through the smoke billowing out, was the figure of a young girl, dressed as a servant.

Several people shouted, 'Jump!'

I looked at the height, and the hard cobbles. I doubted she would survive such a fall. She started to scream, which could be heard over the bustle of the crowd and the pounding of the guns. Apic looked at me.

'Yes, yes. Alright, I'll do something,' I said.

I ran towards the building crossing the street, then suddenly leapt into the air. My cloak billowed around me like a crow's wings, as I took off into the smoky breeze. There were gasps from the crowd. Soon I was at the window, coughing and spluttering, as the wall of smoke streamed out at me. The girl looked at me in terror.

'Come here,' I shouted, gesturing her towards me.

Her face was a mask of fear, and she shouted back to me, 'You're not standing on anything.'

'I know!' I cried back, to be heard over the roar of the burning building. 'Trust me!'

She was covered in soot, her black face streaked with tears. I drifted closer to her, trying to get in underneath the smoke.

'No, no, no!' she screamed as I grabbed her hand.

I suddenly snatched her into my arms, sweeping her from the window in one fluid motion. I then realised that she was a thicker set girl than I had first thought, and I had a brief 'wily coyote on the wrong edge of a precipice' moment before we both plummeted to the ground. Luckily, the flying spell acted as a parachute and broke our fall a bit. She landed on my stomach, totally winding me, as we landed on the cobbles.

Apic helped me up, and prised the plump wench from around my neck.

'Enough playing around,' shouted Apic, 'Let's get back to the house!'

I could only wheeze in reply.

As soon as we had reported what was happening in the city, the family immediately stopped everything, all the packing and storing had to be forgotten insisted Lord Wellven, we had to leave right now. We rode through town to the north gate, an area that was as yet untouched by warfare. Half the population of the city seemed to be packing up items into carts and fleeing, or barricading up their doors to await developments. We joined the throng of people pushing out of the city, jostling, cursing and bustling along for many miles and in the early hours of the morning we had finally reached one of the northern hills that overlooked Werfen. My friends and I were mounted. The Wellven family were in the large family coach, laden down with supplies and their most prized possessions, what little they could get onboard before they had left.

As we crested the brow of the last hill I turned round on Chestnut to look at the flames below. The others carried on ahead, and wagonloads of wounded soldiers plodded slowly past me. I reflected on the violence I had witnessed over the years, and that it probably wasn't going to get any better.

There were fires all over the city, but no guns were being used. The capital had fallen.

Yarn put his head into his hands and sighed. Dr. Lock could see that he was obviously upset about recalling the destruction of such a beautiful city. 'Where did everyone go?'

'Hombard mainly, or the surrounding countryside. Don't worry though, the future wasn't so bleak for the rest of Enttland.'

Dr. Lock nodded and said nothing. She looked out over Edinburgh. As Yarn had told the story she had imagined, in her minds eye, this city as the target of invasion. She had imagined the castle coming under bombardment, and soldiers fighting on the Royal Mile. She wondered idly if Yarn's idea of Werfen was based on what he saw in front of him as he also looked out over the balcony.

'Well, gosh, it's after ten, it's just as well I brought something to eat with me this time!' said Dr. Lock.

This raised a smile to Yarns lips, 'Yes, I'm sorry, I've really gone on and on tonight.'

'That's ok, if I were at home, I would only be watching the television. Ever since the cat died, the house has been so cold and empty.'

Yarn considered this, 'So you live all alone?'

'Yes,' shrugged the good doctor.

'Not married?'

'No,' she said and nearly blushed.

'Really? You must be knocking on a bit though, I would hurry things up if I were you.'

'You cheeky swine!' she cried and punched Yarn playfully on the arm. 'I'm only twenty-nine.'

Yarn grabbed her other arm as it came round, and they wrestled for a moment, nearly toppling over the chairs they were sitting on.

'That's ancient, what does your mother think? She must be in despair!'

'That's none of your business!' gasped Heather. 'You're being very forward tonight!'

'I just felt like cheering myself up. It is nice to see you laughing, I mean...' said Yarn, then flushed bright red.

'What about you, do you remember? Any girlfriends, a wife before? Or did you meet anyone on your adventures? Temina perhaps or your little blonde girl?' mocked Heather.

Yarn suddenly realised he was holding Heather's hands, and he let them go. Running his hands through his hair, he smiled and said, 'No. And no.'

'Oh well. It sounds like neither of us has been very lucky in love.'

'So it would seem.'

The next morning, Dr. Lock popped into the ECNO to sit on Sara's desk and have a quick chat.
'So how's your boy?' asked Sara, as she put down the phone and looked up at Heather.
'Well enough in himself, he was quite cheerful last night.'
'Oh really,' teased Sara. 'And what time did you get home last night?'
'Hmm, about eleven.'
'Hardly worth going home at all!'
'I know. How's Keith?'
'Better. He's at home now. The stitches come out next week.'
Keith was Sara's husband, who had been in hospital with a ruptured appendix.
'What a business,' continued Sara, moving onto another bit of gossip from last week. 'Down on Ward Seven. The liquid nitrogen. What a way to go. Frozen. Do you know who it was?'
'God. No, although Terry knew him. He wasn't frozen though. It was the fumes. The canister ruptured and filled the room with fumes. It was that that killed him. There are still two more in intensive care.'
'I know,' Sara continued to gossip. 'Terrible, do you know who they were?'
'Not personally, but you know Yvonne, one of them was her husband.'
'No!' gasped Sara. 'She's pregnant isn't she?'
Heather nodded.
'I was talking to her just last week,' said Sara. 'She was telling me about one of her patients on Ward Ten. You remember? The coma?'
Heather shrugged.
'He's just come out of it, after, what? something like two months. They think he's Polish or something, but he can speak English with a very thick accent.'
'Poor Yvonne.' sighed Heather.
'I know.'

Chapter Fourteen - Hombard

How can I begin to describe the chaos that ensued as everyone at once tried to flee the city? The long line of refugees snaked its way from the city's north gates. Those that could rode on carts or carriages or mounted on horses. It wasn't long before we crested the ridge of the northern hills, and the city was lost to view from us. It was something like seven in the morning. No one had had any sleep. From the shouting of the guards on the road we knew that a counter attack was being organised, and soldiers were being rounded up and formed into battalions. It was like trying to fight through a river torrent, with the refugees going one way, and the guards another. Everywhere was panic.

The next few days were a chaotic flight from terror, but on the third day we passed a detachment of Enttland soldiers on the road, and Lord Wellven rode up to their commander to talk to him. The commander seemed to recognise him and they had a long discussion. It appeared that this was the vanguard of the main Enttish army, which had just left Hombard and was making its way as quickly as possible to Werfen to retake the city. We all nodded sombrely at each other and wishing each other luck, rode on our separate ways.

On the fourth night we had the misfortune to encounter a band of Lunarian skirmishers, which had pushed far forward in advance of the main force. There was quite a selection of us, which included me, Apic and Temina, Adea and all her family, and not forgetting Carab. Besides the people that I knew, that night we were camped with a wide cross-section of the populace of Werfen. There was a family of tinkers, a chandler and his wife, two well-to-do looking noblemen separated from their families and looking slightly bemused, and a coach load of assorted scribes and clerks from a lawyers' office who had escaped together en masse.
As was usual, Carab, Apic and I were grouped around the campfire bemoaning our lot.
'How come every city we visit ends up in flames?' I asked the world.
'You're a fucking jinx,' answered Apic miserably.
'These are violent times,' said Carab to the fire.
Boris came over and handed each of us a sausage.
'That's the last of the meat,' he stated and sat down beside me to eat his ration. He was dressed a lot simpler tonight, in plain brown travelling clothes. His long blonde hair was tied back in a tail.
'Tullis,' I said. 'Tullis is still intact as far as I know.'
'Don't even think of such things!' cursed Apic. 'You will destroy my town with such rash words.'
Carab grunted, 'Stop it will you, both of you, this is no time for your childish bickering. The Enttish army is still strong enough to push the invaders back

over the mountains. In two weeks time, we will be back, and repairing the city.'

'I hope you're right,' said someone I didn't know on the other side of the fire.

Suddenly there was a scream, then another voice shouted, 'We are attacked!'

Then just as quickly five figures rushed into the circle of the fire. They were caked in mud from head to foot and carried long dangerous looking spears. The white mud made then look like mad ghosts, with their hair done up in dirty top knots. I didn't have much time to reflect on their personal hygiene before one was rushing towards me. I leapt to my feet to meet him, and shot him squarely in the chest. This startled everyone around me long enough for Apic to run one through with his rapier and Carab the opportunity to kick another into the fire.

As the wretch screamed and writhed, more of his companions attacked us. It all got a bit confusing, but the battle for me was a simple task of shooting any Lunarian that came near, and they soon learnt to stay out of my way.

In a brief moment of calm around me I cast a simple spell of protection that would ward off arrows. I had never tested this particular magic, as I had never wanted an arrow fired at me, even in the name of research. I had no idea if it would work against spears.

Just then, one Lunarian did throw a spear at me, but missed by a few scant inches, leaving my theory as yet untested.

Right beside me, one of the lawyer's clerks fell to the ground with a throwing axe lodged in his chest, aimed from somewhere in the dark.

Seeing he was beyond help, I rushed over to where Adea and her family had been camped. Lord Wellven was holding several of them off with his sabre, but had sustained an injury to his left arm. As I rushed them, I used the last three bullets in my gun to kill his attackers. One of them I only winged, and he ran off screaming into the night, leaving a trail of blood.

'Thank you, Shiv,' then, 'Lookout!' he cried as a spear flew directly at me, and bounced off.

He gasped, 'How?'

'Magic,' I said and smiled. 'Everyone get behind me. It's time to break out the big stuff.'

The Lunarian skirmishers formed up into a larger group for another attack, which was just the opportunity I had been waiting for. As they advanced on us, I got a clear view from one of the campfires, and I let fly with a volley of fireballs that burst right into their ranks.

Now a single fireball looks a lot more dangerous than it is. It will give someone a very nasty burn, and it can easily kill if the victim catches fire, but in essence they are just a long trail of flame and smoke, terminating in a large flash and a bang. However, the dozen or so I fired into their group was enough to scatter them into the trees and leave two of them smouldering on the ground. A cheer went up from our circle of defenders.

'I take it all back,' said Apic in amazement. 'Shiv whatever I said, I take it all back!'

It was a good victory, and I think only about six people were killed and including Lord Wellven about ten injured, but nothing very serious. I knew one fairly weak healing spell, and I used up the last of my power casting it on the wounded.

The victory was slightly marred by one of the Lunarians who had crawled into the woods to die, and he proceeded to scream and scream all night.

'Can't you do something?' asked Apic, as we settled back down again.

'I have no magic left for tonight, or tomorrow for that matter. Do you fancy going out there to get him?'

'No chance.'

I shrugged and said, 'Try and get some sleep then, we'll probably need it.'

I will skirt over Hombard briefly. We arrived there about a week and a half later, after an exhausting journey. The city was swollen with refugees, but luckily Lord Wellven had family here, who were only too glad to make room for us at their house. On the road we had passed the main Enttish army, en route to Werfen, and we all gave them a hearty cheer, as they passed us in their thousands. There were mounted, armoured knights, uniformed soldiers and simply dressed pikemen. There were armoured dragoons, splendid in their red uniforms and many other types of soldier such as scouts and skirmishers. They all had the same steely look of grim determination on their face. Hombard was a pleasant enough city, on the border of Lodz, situated on the south bank of the Omdz River. It was nowhere near as splendid as Werfen was, or had been, and the people were a lot less cosmopolitan. This was very much a border town and much used to warfare. The walls were thick, and still used, and the guards here seemed a lot surlier.

As soon as I could arrange things, I made preparations to leave. We had spent a week in the city, and news had arrived of Werfens recapture the day before. Spontaneous celebrations broke out in every quarter of the border town. Adea's family were already making preparations to return home. I had made my announcement about making an overland journey to Vegas, and had invited those that wanted to, to join me. The seas were getting far too dangerous these days, and I counted on my newly acquired magical skills to handle any danger I might encounter in the Norob Forest. We rode out of Hombard like a scene from a cowboy film.

There was me, on Chestnut, and Apic on Old Bones' Daughter. He said he would follow me to make sure I wasn't responsible for ruining any more cities in my capacity as harbinger of doom. Obviously where Apic went, Temina followed, on that evil tempered hellspawn masquerading as a horse, Bessy. Carab, had his own reasons for wanting to go to Vegas of course. He had not yet been to see his father and wished to introduce him to Adea, who was coming along as well.

The farewell had been as you might expect, Lord and Lady Wellven had implored me and Carab to look after their daughter, and to take care of ourselves as well. The world was getting dangerous for everyone though, and we all wished them luck for when they returned to Werfen. Adea and Meggan cried a lot, and I was almost getting impatient by the time we managed to tear her away from her family.

'And good luck getting home!' called Lady Wellven to me, as we left, and she followed us out onto the street.

'Thank you my lady. I hope life gets quiet enough for you to start painting again!'

'Good bye mother!' called Adea one last time, not wanting to take her eyes from her family.

'Good bye my love, take care!'

The situation between Adea and Carab was this, although permission had been given by Adea's family for the two to be wed, Carab wanted to get his father's consent before the marriage took place. I thought he was perhaps being a little bit too 'by the book', but he wouldn't be teased out of it.

Carab rode a huge charger who had had no name until Meggan had christened him Bunny, which we all agreed, suited him. Adea rode her father's horse, a well behaved mare called Tulip, whom always appeared, to me anyway, to have the same expression you might expect to see on the face of a lady of breeding forced to slum it, especially when she got close to Chestnut who would talk to anyone. There was also Boris, Adea's cousin, who still struck me as a slightly dandified fop, but who was after adventure, and looked that he might be quite handy with the rapier that hung from his side. He rode a piebald gelding called Poppy. How a male horse came to have a name like Poppy, Boris could never be prevailed on to indulge.

On our first day out I asked him,

'Does your father approve of this then?'

'Not really, but he had to admit that things probably won't be the same in Werfen for a while. And besides, I have to take care of my cousin,' he replied and smiled.

'Good. Although, maybe by the time you have hung around with us for a while, you will start to miss your idiot prince!'

'I hope not!'

I had a very good reason for going to Vegas, my research demanded five days of darkness, only attainable north of the Arctic Circle. The spell that I wished to cast was once used many years ago, when the wizards were so powerful they could blot out the sun, but I used my knowledge of geography. I would wait for the arctic winter to arrive, and then cast the spell to open a portal to my world. That was the theory anyway.

It was quite a long journey that we had planned, and it would mean we would have to go through the Western Norob Forest, through which there is no road, as all trade used to go by sea. According to folk lore and legend, the Norob Forest is a nasty place full of ghosts and spirits. There were also three kingdoms to get through, Julgia, Joppa and Luxor, and local knowledge of these places was a bit shaky. Even Carab admitted he knew little about Julgia and Joppa. Wet, was about all he knew. Wet and Cold. He knew a lot about Luxor, most of it very derogatory. Vegas and Luxor shared a border, so I supposed there was probably some enmity between the two nations.

The first week of travel was uneventful as the road from Hombard to Bydgoszcz was well patrolled by the Lodz army, a set of stocky men dressed in grey uniforms and all armed with long pikes. Lodz sits on the south coast of the Frost Sea, possibly about where Germany or Poland would lie in Europe, although it is considerably smaller than either. The people here were mainly short and pragmatic in appearance. Most of the forests in this region had long since been chopped down to make room for farms. The soil was fertile, and if it had not been for the constant wars, the nation would have flourished. As it was, the place had a very martial air, and we were never very far away from a stern faced guard or soldier. From Bydgoszcz, the largest city in Lodz and a major port on the Frost Coast, we travelled to Tyngz, a small border town, the last frontier before entering the Norob Forest. As we passed the border guards, they issued us with dire warnings and notified us of their belief that no one would ever see us again.

The western Norob forest was a bit of a let down to be honest. We saw precious little of any ghouls or ghosts the entire month we spent travelling through it. There was no shortage of signs of goblins in the area though, we found totems and traps on a daily basis, but we stayed out of their way, and they stayed out of ours. There was no sign of human habitation anywhere, not even a woodcutters hut, or the home of some recluse, which I found so odd, this close to civilisation. There was no trail for us to follow, but the trees were large and widely enough spaced for us to ride through. Each night we camped in a convenient spot and set up a large fire and a rota for the watch. The forests were very spooky at night, totally different in character from the Great Forest to the south. We had been well aware of the dangers then, but at least we had known what they were. Here it was different. The oppressive silence, the tall dominating trees, everything about the forest seemed to make us feel supremely unwelcome. As the days progressed into weeks, the oppression became greater, and I often found that we were talking in whispers when we camped or stopped for a break, as if we subconsciously sensed the evil that watched us from the darkness. There was plenty of game around, although we always hunted sparingly. Whenever we killed a buck or a hare, it felt like we were poaching.

Horses are funny animals. They often have a very complicated social order, and will rebel against any human attempt to interfere with it. As we travelled through the forest, slowly and in single file, the order we went in was chosen by the horses and not the humans, as we felt it was much better to keep them happy, and hence, quiet.

Bessy, always had to be at the front. If she wasn't she would complain and toss her head, and try and bite the nearest creature, and if nothing was immediately at hand, she would reach her neck round and try to bite her rider's leg. As a consequence, Temina was almost always on point, whether she liked it or not. Old Bones' Daughter was the strongest horse in our group, but quite timid, and had formed a subservient bond with Bessy. She liked to be behind Bessy if possible, and would grow quite anxious if she didn't have her bullying friend within sight. As a result, Apic usually rode behind Temina. Piebald Poppy was reasonably well behaved when being ridden by Boris, but he was quite clearly insane. The big shock of mane on his head that obscured his dark mad eyes, lent even more to his crazed appearance. He was quite capable of doing anything, and would take great pleasure in tormenting and teasing the other horses and riders. He had a habit of sneaking up on the other horses and drooling on their rumps, if not carefully attended to, and Old Bones' Daughter was probably the most tolerant of this behaviour. Because of this Boris usually rode behind Apic. Poppy generally got the blame for everything, if a disturbance was heard at night from the horses while we were camped, someone would always say, 'What is Poppy doing now?'

Adea's mount, Tulip, was very well behaved, and could be placed anywhere. Chestnut had the heart of an angel, but she was a little bit of a tart. Currently her best friend was Tulip, although Tulip tended to look down her long nose at her. Like Tulip she was so good natured that she could be placed anywhere, so Adea and my place were interchangeable. Carab's horse, Bunny, was a long legged ex-cavalry charger, who had seen more than one battle. He was the strong silent type, and although he never caused anyone any problems, he wouldn't take any liberties from anyone, not even Bessy. Bessy bullied all the others at every opportunity, but she never went near Bunny. Not after the first time anyway. It was funny, that even us humans treated him with more respect than your average horse. The others I would just push around like regular horses, for instance I might well kick Bessy back if she kicked at me, and if Chestnut came to rub me while I was busy lighting the fire or something I would push her out the way and shout 'Who let my horse loose?' It was different with Bunny though, he was never tied up at night, and if he joined us at the camp fire of an evening, the others, us humans, would practically budge up to make space for him. I always thought of him as a retired army general, and treated him with the utmost respect lest I earned one of his famous long disdainful looks. Bunny always liked to be at the back, to keep an eye on the others and round up stragglers, so this was where Carab rode. To mess with this set up, once it was established would put our equine friends noses out of joint, and cause consternation and moodiness, so we generally didn't rearrange them unless we had to.

So far we had not encountered a single thing to give us reason for our uneasiness. I began to feel that it may just have been because we were being lucky. Then one day our luck ran out.
It was a hazy summer day in the brooding forest, the same as any other. Adea and I were whispering together.
'I feel as if the trees are watching me. Every day it is the same. The sooner we are out of this forest the better,' she shivered.
'I know,' I said, as we rode on. Underneath the trees, the air was cool, cold almost. 'It's as if we are trespassers, and the game keeper is waiting for the right moment to catch us.'
'How much longer do you think we will be here?'
'Three more weeks, a month? This forest is vast.'
'Hellfire and...' Adea's curse was cut short when Temina called back to us, 'A house!'
Indeed it was, I saw, as I caught up with the others in the clearing ahead. A quaint looking, ramshackle cottage, with a twisted stone chimney, bathed in the summer sun, situated as it was, in the centre of the clearing.
We rode up to it, and in a group examined the dwelling. No one as yet had dismounted. It had an unreal quality about it. It seemed so odd to see such a small and innocent looking dwelling in such a grim and forbidding forest. The thing in my head began to itch.
I looked at Carab who shrugged.
'Hello?' I called out.
Nothing happened. Eventually I called out again, 'Anyone at home?'
Suddenly there was a sound from inside, like something being knocked over, then a rattling at the decrepit door. One of the horses whinnied loudly and nervously stamped its foot. I didn't know which one it was, all eyes were glued on the door.
It slowly opened, and a wizened old crone stepped into the light. She was hunched over, probably by the amount of dusty old clothing she was wearing. I couldn't see much of her face, as she wore a large black hat, but she certainly had enough warts and whiskers on her chin.
She didn't look at us, but instead locked her gaze on the ground to her left, and wrung her hands.
'Yes?' she inquired.
'Oh right,' I said and coughed. 'We're just passing through really. We were surprised to see a house so far out in the woods.'
'Oh really?' she replied.
Apic slumped in his saddle, and nearly fell off, before Carab caught a hold of him. I looked around in alarm, then looked back at the crone.
'Did you? I mean..?'
Then Boris started coughing like he was going to bring up a lung. Again I looked round at her, and shouted over Boris's hacking.

'Right, I know magic when I see it, listen here old lady...'
Suddenly it was night time. In one split second it had gone from a bright summer's day, to the dead of night. The horses all panicked and Chestnut galloped off into the trees, with me frantically trying to get my feet back into the stirrups. In the inky darkness underneath the trees, I could see nothing, then I was suddenly swept to the ground as a low branch struck my head and I was flung from the saddle.
I stood up, in a daze, but quickly collected myself.
'Lumtinh Tymnhbg Trumpdt,' I said, and the area around me lit up like someone was holding a torch beside me. In the distance through the trees, I could see the cottage. I could also see the glowing white figures that were gathering around it. I drew out my revolver.
As I jogged nearer, I could see Carab, waving his sword around to fend off the strange white creatures, while holding Apic up. There was no one else around, and no horses. I rushed over to them. These glowing white apparitions closed in around us affording me a little time to study then closer. They looked like the tortured souls of the long dead. Glowing white and rattling chains they flitted between the trees, leaving trails of cold vapour. I had no idea back then what these creatures were, assuming them to be ghosts or ghouls. However, the undead of Norob are many and varied, and after reading a text on the subject much later found them to be classified as wraiths.
Suddenly a ghostly hand reached out from behind a tree and tried to grab me. I ducked out of the way of its grasp, and took a few steps back. The wraith slowly drifted towards me. It looked like the shade of an old man, dressed in ghostly rags and chains, his mouth open in an eternal scream. A pale white aura surrounded him similar to the others, and he emitted a low keening wail as he came towards me. I swept at him with my staff, but it had no more effect than on a cloud of smoke. The wraith lashed at me with one of its claws and I barely stepped back in time to avoid its blow.
'Pinmhgy Yta Peng,' I said, and a fireball struck the ghostly apparition, shattering it into a million shards of smoke, which rushed off onto the tree branches with a whistling intake of air. Magic harmed them at least.
Fighting back my terror, I glanced around for more danger then ran on towards the cottage.
Carab was frantically fending off a crowd of wraiths as they tried to close in on him. I think I made it to him just in time, and destroyed two more with fireballs, which pushed the others back for a moment or two.
'They have taken Temina and Boris into the house. My blows have no effect, my sword passes though them.'
I let one of the ghostly figures get too close and its hand passed through my arm. Suddenly I felt a chill run through me, and I was almost sick.
'Don't let them touch you,' warned Carab. I could hear the terror in his voice. Apic groaned, he seemed to be coming round. An idea hit me and I quickly drew the sword from Apic's belt, while Carab defended us. I then touched Carab's sword and the one I held enchanting them, and they

slowly started to glow a dull red, but this wasn't the only magic I was thinking of using.

One of the last spells I had learned from Mallonax before I had left his tower was for the magical animation of weapons. If the spell was successful, it would make the sword dance around as if it was wielded by an expert swordsman. I had never cast the spell before, but terror is a wonderful focus, and I began to concentrate. Apic watched me in bleary-eyed wonder as I gathered blue light around his sword, at first a little, but building up into an intense ball of mana around my hands. Then with a sudden cry I hurled it at our enemies.

I had almost had time to let out a sigh of disappointment as the sword arched towards the ground, but then it suddenly lifted off with a shower of sparks and a metallic shriek, directly at the nearest group of ghostly wraiths.

'That should help!' I cried, and the next blow destroyed a wraith in a silent explosion of mist and vapour. We battled our way to nearer the door of the cottage and had nearly finished off all our enemies, when the door was flung open and the old woman threw out a handful of small bones. Apic was nearly fully conscious now, he watched in amazement as his sword fended off the last of the wraiths. I looked at the tree line of the clearing, there were many more white figures forming in the darkness, and just as I was taking that in, skeletons began to rise out of the ground around us where the bones had fallen. We began to edge careful away from the door. Apic drew a dagger from his belt. The skeletons wore rusty bits of ancient armour, clattering and throwing off grave dust and soil. They carried various old style weapons, such as gladius and piliums, and waved them around in front of themselves as they slowly advance towards us.

Suddenly in a group they charged, and I let fly with a salvo of fireballs, using up the last of my magical energy, and dropping the front rank. This dismayed the rest of the skeletons not one little bit, and they fell on us like hounds. Carab swung his long sword and felled the first one that came near him in one mighty blow. Then I stopped watching the others and concentrated on my own battle, as two of them advanced towards me and Apic. We edged further backwards.

'Use your magic!' hissed Apic.

'I have none left!'

'Let me at least get my sword back then.'

It was now lying on the ground in a pile of skeletal bones, its magic spent, but its duty done.

On a nod from me, we charged at the skeletons, and I got one a fortunate blow, knocking it over. Luckily for us, they were quite slow in their movement and so made fairly easy opponents to fight, but they had strength of numbers, so it was difficult to give any telling blows and not leave myself open to attack from one of the others. Apic had kicked down one however, and I had clubbed two more to the ground when I heard Carab cry, 'To the house!' and I looked up to see him step over another fallen enemy and rush towards the cottage. His neck was running with blood. We ran after him, dodging the weapons of the skeletons, and piled in behind him as he booted in the door.

'Apic, watch the door,' I said, and gave him my staff to fend off the remaining skeletons, his sword still being unrecovered. Carab and I stepped into the main room, and I gulped back a gasp of horror, as I saw the bodies of Temina and Boris in heaps on the floor. The old crone turned to us and cackled, but was cut short from any other actions when I shot her with my revolver and was propelled backwards hitting the wall with a dusty thump. My ears were ringing from the gunshot, but I still heard Apic shout, 'Help!' as he was pushed back by the crush of the undead at the door. I looked around at him.

'She's getting up Shiv!' yelled Carab making me look round again.

The witch was slowly getting to her feet, and seemed to be readying a spell. I knew then, that whatever she was going to cast I had better put a stop to it. I pointed the gun at her and pulled the trigger. It went click. 'Damn!' I cursed, either it had jammed or the witch had done something to it. Carab charged at her with his sword raised, but she swatted him back with one sweep of her hand, knocking him from his feet with an invisible blow. Next Apic was at my back and the room was beginning to get pretty crowded. Undead were at the windows and at the door. I began to panic, thinking that I was going to die here, pulled apart by the dead. I was beginning to struggle for breath as wave after wave of terror hit me. I took in the clock on the mantle piece, the log basket and the bones scattered on the table, thinking these were the last things I was ever going to see.

Carab was getting slowly to his feet, and Apic was pressing me backwards. Any minute now, I thought, this room is going to be full of the undead, and the rest of my life experience is going to consist of biting teeth and cold fingers on my gizzard.

Then I heard the distant sound of hooves, of a horse charging, that got louder and louder. Suddenly Bunny was in the doorway, being ridden by Adea, and he reared up and trampled the bones of two of the skeletons under his hooves. There was a terrible commotion, as the horse went almost into an equine battle frenzy. I took the opportunity to leap over at the old woman and stab her in the heart with my belt knife. We struggled on the floor for a minute, as the noisy battle raged around us, and I pinned down her arms with the weight of my body, and pressed the knife into her chest. We were practically nose to nose when she let out her final rattling cough and she cursed me with her last foetid breath. Suddenly all the skeletons dropped lifelessly to the floor, and the remaining wraiths disappeared. Summer sun streamed in through the window.

It took us a while to round up all the horses, and attend to the wounded. Carab had a nasty cut on his shoulder, but nothing life threatening. Boris was concussed but otherwise unharmed. Temina took quite a long time to come round, but eventually she woke up, and demanded to know what had happened after the wraith had touched her and she had lost consciousness.

'A necromancer of some kind, I think, Temina,' I said, as I kneeled down beside her blanket covered body. Everyone else was attending to other matters, but as they saw her awaken they gathered round.

'I had the most awful dreams,' she said, and shuddered.

'Don't worry, it's all over.'

'Is everyone else ok? Is everyone here?' she worried, looking around at us all.

'Yes,' I replied. 'We're going to rest up tonight, then put some distance between us and that house tomorrow.'

'Good. And next time, if I see a cottage, I think I'll ride right past it.'

We had learned the hard way, how the Norob Forest had gotten its fearsome reputation, but the real fun didn't begin until we reached Julgia. However that can wait until next time.

Dr. Lock let out a big sigh. Realising that she hadn't moved from the position she had been sitting in for quite a while, she stretched out her arms and legs, reaching above her head and yawning. As she stretched out her legs, she kicked over Yarn's half full mug of tea.

'Shit!' she exclaimed and sat up straight with a jolt. The tea sloshed over the tar flooring and over the edge of the balcony. Yarn looked over the railing with an exaggerated look of concern on his face.

'Don't worry, I don't think you hit anyone.'

'I was totally wrapped up in your story. Did you figure out who that old woman was?'

'Just a random nutter. There are lots of strange things in that forest. The undead are crawling all over it, and undead tend to attract necromancers.'

'Necromancers, like Lord of the Rings.'

'I suppose so. We had other encounters with the undead before we left the forest, especially at night, but nothing as scary as that first time in the cottage.'

'It sounds like a nasty place anyway.'

Yarn stood up and began stretching his legs.

'What's up? Cramp?' asked Heather.

'No. My arse has gone to sleep though,' replied Yarn and laughed. 'Ow!'

Heather laughed as well, 'Your arse has gone to sleep?'

'It's not funny! I must have been sat down for too long.'

Yarn stretched out his left leg, and his knee let out an alarming crack. 'Ow!'

Heather now had a fit of the giggles, and tried to say, 'That sounded sore!'

'That's it, have a laugh at my expense! Oops!'

'Ow!' cried Heather, as Yarn trod on her foot. 'You did that deliberately!'

Yarn raised his leg up and looked around in confusion, looking for somewhere to put his foot in amongst all the plant pots, tea trays and dirty cups. He trod on a tray, and it whooshed up and hit him on the shin. 'Bugger!' he said and tried to clutch his leg, then fell over, smashing something, and knocking over cups.

Heather shrieked with laughter.

Yarn laughed as well, sat as he was on the floor, 'My bum is wet! Tea is soaking into my trousers. What clumsy oafs we are today.'

Heather stood, and put her hand out to help Yarn up. He accepted her hand and stumbled to his feet. Suddenly their faces were very close together.

'Turn round,' said Heather quietly.

'Huh?' replied Yarn.

'Turn around, let me look at your arse,' she said and giggled.

'Oh right,' Yarn said, and obeyed her command.

'Your soaked!' she said and laughed, covering her mouth with her hands.

'Och!' sighed Yarn, trying to stretch round to look at his rear, 'Well, at least these aren't mine. These jeans belonged to some dead guy. Stop laughing at me!'

Yarn suddenly grabbed Heather and began to tickle her.

Heather shrieked again, and cried, 'Get off me you nut!'

'Watch, you'll knock over the kettle.'

'Ok, ok, enough, unhand me!'

Yarn sighed and sat down again. Heather sat down and whipped the tears from her eyes.

'Well, that was fun.'

'Ew yuck, ' Yarn squirmed in his seat. 'I'm going to have to go and get changed now!'

Chapter Fifteen - Julgia

Julgia is a very wet country. It rained and rained, endlessly. Although I could cast a spell to keep the rain off, it only lasted for an hour or so, so I usually used my big trusty black and white golfing umbrella. The others coveted my umbrella, and were constantly trying to steal it. Everyday, I had to grab it from some thief.

'Give it back right now, Apic!'

'No.'

'Don't make me come over there!' I called from my position in the riding line.

'You had it all day yesterday, fair is fair.'

I sighed, then said, 'Wastgy Ytrwqh,' and cast my rain retardant spell.

'You've got it until this spell runs out,' I called to him.

'What about me, I haven't had my turn yet!' cried Adea.

It was a mountainous region, but still the first real country north of the Norob Forest, other than small collections of villages on its northern fringes. Evergreen forests crept up the mountain sides to the snow capped peaks. The towns and villages of this country clung to the steep slopes like black slugs. It seemed to be permanently raining, and in the distance, trapped in a valley somewhere, you could always hear the sound of a thunderstorm. The locals said that the region made its own weather. The first few villages we travelled through were made up of strong sturdy mountain folk, with a pioneer's attitude, cutting a living from the wild forests. As we travelled further north, the atmosphere grew more oppressive, the citizens seemed tired and broken. Guards dressed in black, and wearing full-faced helms strutted around like lords. The guards were the strangest I had ever seen, they never revealed their faces, and were all very tall and muscular, and wore enough armour to put an Enttish knight to shame. They were arrogant and loud, and tormented the country's populace endlessly, like playground bullies. I almost longed for the trackless wilderness again.

It was difficult terrain to travel on as well, the roads wound their way up to a high mountain pass, then back down the other side into the next valley. As the crow flies we might travel just five miles on bad days. The horses were not used to such steep paths either, and even the malcontent Bessy seemed to prefer to keep her head down and not bite at the others, as if she also sensed the desolation in the area.

Each deep v-shaped valley had a village, and each village had a castle nearby brooding over it like a vast stone vulture.

After over a week of this, we had all pretty much had enough, the conversation and banter had dried up, and each night we arrived at a village, soaking wet from the rain, and entered usually the only inn, invariably a cheerless place with just a few stony-faced patrons, looking into their tankards and mumbling. It was quite common to see runes and pentagrams carved into the wall to ward off evil spirits. The people in all of the villages we travelled through, had the same white, and drawn composures, as if they were not getting enough vitamins in their diet. They looked worn out and shabby, and almost to a man, they had the same plodding way of walking, as if they had the weight of the world on their shoulders.

The inn we entered in the village of Graz was the same as all the others we had been in. There had been two guards, dressed in their black breastplates and anonymous full-face helmets, in the square, harassing a tinker and throwing stuff from his cart. This was such a common sight for us by now, that we just ignored it. I walked into the common room, shaking the rain from my cloak, while the others took the horses round to the stables. The landlord, a tall thin man, with very little in the way of head hair, greeted me with a grunt.

'How many?' in Julgian.

I had picked up a little of the language, enough not to need magic to help me.

'Six, with horses.'

'I only have one room, you will have to share.'

'Fine. To drink?'

'Wine only, last years.'

'Fine.'

Eventually we were all seated in the common room, steam rising from our shoulders and our cloaks by the fire. The landlord's fat wife brought us some bread and stewed vegetables. I noticed that she only had one leg. Well, in reality she had two, one of flesh and the other carved out of mountain pine, but that would have been quibbling.

'Keep it coming, I'm starving!' said Apic.

'Hmm... ' grunted the woman, 'Foreigners, we don't get many of you lot through here.'

'I am amazed,' jibed Apic. 'I felt such a pleasant climate must surely have visitors flocking here.'

'Funny man,' she growled and walked off to the kitchen, her wooden leg clicking on the floorboards.

'I don't think you will have much of an audience again tonight Shiv,' mentioned Boris, looking around the room. There was only one other man in the room, an elderly gent drinking quietly in a dark corner, presumably the village drunk.

'I know, I don't really have the heart for it since we left, where was it? That village on the border. They really liked the story about the secret diamond mines.'

'You steal all these stories don't you?' asked Boris smiling.

'Well, stealing is maybe a bit...'

'Aye aye, here we go,' said Apic as the old man got out of his chair and lurched towards us.

He stumbled up to our table and leant both hands on it, then burped.

'Hey!' I cried, the person nearest to him, 'Don't come up to us when you're stinking of piss.'

'Foreigners! There is no place for you here!'

Apic laughed. Carab stood up, and Adea shifted away from the smell.

'Yeah, yeah, don't go out on the moor, and all that. Do you know we meet someone exactly like you in every village we go to?' I said.

'You'd best not stray from your room tonight,' the old man warned, gazing up to look out the window.

'You don't scare me you old fart. If I go out tonight, the most dangerous thing in the dark will be me,' I took a coin from my belt pouch. 'Here, take this and leave us alone.'

The old mans eyes lit up, and he snatched the coin from me, calling the landlord, 'Basil! More wine!'

Later that evening the landlady came to show as to our room.

'Thank you for your kindness to old Zed. He lost his daughter recently and hasn't been the same since.'

'What happened?'

The woman looked at me in a peculiar way, and eventually said, 'She fell to something that is all too common in these parts…'

The thin landlord, who had been listening suddenly snarled, 'Silence woman! They are strangers, they cannot understand our ways!'

She turned to him and said, 'What of it? Why not speak? Why? Zed's daughter. Before that Yerris, before that Irene and Glemy. Perrin last summer, and Abitha in spring? What of it?'

'Silence woman,' hissed the landlord, his face going red with rage.

'Well,' she muttered. 'I will say no more, but thank you for your kindness none the less.'

I nodded, a little too drunk to be bothered about what she was saying, and reached to get my cloak. I started to put it on.

'You are surely not going out now?' asked the landlady in amazement. Her rat faced husband looked up from the bar.

'Certainly I am, the rain is off, and I fancy taking a turn in the fresh night air.'

'Now, sir, don't be so foolish. You are drunk'

Everyone had turned to look at me, I noted Apic's smile, and Adea's concerned look.

'Oh really? What is so scary out there? Demons, vampires, werewolves?'

The landlady sighed and said, 'Well, on your own head be it, but don't say I didn't warn you.'

'That's that settled then. Who else is coming?'

Everyone looked at everyone else.

'Aw come on, at least you two.' I said motioning at Apic and Carab, 'After all that we've been through?'

'There is no need to go looking for trouble, Shiv,' said Carab.

'He's right,' joined in Adea.

'I'll come with you,' said Temina, and unsteadily got to her feet.

'Temina! Don't encourage him!' cried Adea.

'That's the girl!' I laughed and slapped her on the back.

It took about another half hour to figure out what was going on. In the end, me, Apic and Temina decided to go out and take the air, while the others waited for us, and were to pile out if they heard any trouble. It didn't help that most of us were drunk.

'Nice night,' I remarked to Apic, who was cowering within his large riding cloak.

'Yes,' he stuttered, his teeth chattering. It was cold enough for us to see our breath.

Temina stalked along, her hand resting on the pommel of her rapier, full of alcohol induced courage. I smiled at her, and she nodded back.

'OK Shiv, we've proved out point, let's go back,' said Apic, putting his hand on my shoulder.

'You agreed to go to the gates with me.'

He sighed, then nudged me in the ribs with his elbow.

'Huh?' I said and looked at him. He motioned above us to a window in the third floor of a nearby house. A young woman was at the window, dressed in a night gown.

'Oh aye,' I said and smiled.

'Honestly, you two,' said Temina.

I was captivated by the young woman, she seemed to be so fair and pure, with milk white skin and dark blonde hair. She gazed out of the open window, with a faraway look on her face.

'She's nice,' I said, as we all looked at her from the shadows.

Just then, there was a fluttering from somewhere just above our heads, and a large black shape blotted out the moon for a second, then seemed to land on the roof of the house that the girl inhabited.

The black shape flowed down the wall and crept to the window. I caught a glimpse of an arm as it reached out towards her. The figure pushed back the hood of its cloak to reveal a pure white face, shining in the moonlight, topped with slicked back jet-black hair. We stood and looked up at this in open mouthed wonder. The male figure crept closer to the girl, clinging to the side of the house like a human fly. He let out a low hiss.

Things began to dawn on me, and I began to sober up a little, as I realised just what exactly was going on.

'Hey you!' I bellowed up at the window.

The man whipped his head round at me and hissed in surprise, revealing large yellow fangs.

'Yes you! Leave that wench alone!'

'What are you doing?' whispered Apic to me loudly in terror. I heard a shing of metal on metal, as Temina drew her sword behind me.

'I'm talking to you bat boy!' I continued to shout. 'Don't make me come up there!'

Suddenly the spell on the girl seemed to break, and taking in the deadly situation she was in, all in one terrible instant, she screamed and fainted, disappearing from view behind the windowsill with a thump.

The vampire floated down to the ground, and walked towards us. I felt Apic grip my arm in fear behind me and I heard Temina let out a small gasp.

He walked purposefully towards me, his black cloak flowing behind him like vast wings. His young face was very handsome, and he wore stylish black clothes, and carried a thin rapier by his side. In my drunken state, I thought that, despite being obviously undead, he looked like a very friendly, affable young man. His cheeks were a little bit too round, and his smile a little bit too warm to be considered in any way evil or threatening.

'Hello,' I said.

'Well, well,' he replied. 'It is always nice to see new faces in town. But you shouldn't really walk around at night you know. The guards don't like that sort of thing.'

'Sorry, we are a little drunk.'

'Speak for yourself.' muttered the trembling, and obviously suddenly very sober Apic behind me.

The vampire seemed to sniff at the air, and then said, 'Ah, a wizard, I sense your power.' then he pointed to my ear, and with a smile said, 'And the second bach. Your bravado becomes clear.'

I smiled back at him.

He suddenly executed a very precise bow, and said, 'Lord Rutven of Graz, at your service sir.'

'Shiv von Scotland, at yours,' I replied, and bowed, not losing his gaze for a second.

'Well, I cannot tarry I am afraid, I have business to attend to, but I would be delighted to see you up at the castle, at any time that is convenient for yourselves of course. We get fewer visitors than we used to these days, but someone with your... ah... sense of humour, would certainly... brighten the place up.'

I was left in little doubt about how I might brighten the place up. Big red splatters on the wall for starters.

'That would be delightful,' I replied. 'Look forward to seeing us soon.'

He bowed again, then looked up at the sky and sniffed. With a small leap, he was in the air, and flying swiftly off above the roofs of the houses. Our eyes followed him, as he formed a black silhouette against the moon, and then in one final swoop, was gone.

'Take care now,' I said to myself.

Needless to say we didn't get much sleep that night. I wracked my brains to remember all my vampire lore. The others seemed to have some confused views as to what and what did not affect vampires, and what they could and couldn't do. I wondered how much was fact and how much fantasy, and how much of the stuff that I knew would be relevant. All my knowledge was based on horror films I had seen. I cursed myself for never reading any Ann Rice.

We eventually got some sleep in the early morning, awaking around midday, and discussed what to do gathered around the fire in our room, all still in our night shirts.

'Well, at least we are all agreed that we can't just walk away from this,' I said.

The others nodded, Apic said, 'Yes, but there is no need to get ourselves killed... or worse.'

'Listen, we'll load up on garlic, rowan stakes, blessed water, silver, sunflower seeds, what else? Yeah, rose petals, mint and white mice.'

I turned to Carab, 'Are you absolutely sure about the white mice?'

Carab shrugged, 'It was a story my grandmother used to tell.'

I sighed and rubbed my eyes with my right hand, 'Ok, all that. And plus a few nasty spells that I think might help. I say, we go up there and kick his undead ass.'

Apic then said, 'There may well be more than one of them though.'

We all considered this. A lot of discussion later, we divided up the shopping list, and went into the village separately to see what we could find.

Later I returned to our room, with a bag full of garlic bulbs and sunflower seeds from the grocers shop on the market square. I had also stolen a handful of mint I had spotted growing in someone's garden, in case no one else found any. White mice wouldn't be a problem, I could pull them out of my sleeve as and when required.

Temina was already back, sat on her bed sorting out bottles and putting them into a satchel.

'Ah, holy water I take it,' I said as I entered the room.

'Yes. I got some mint as well, in case no one else did,' she said, and looked up at me. 'Listen Shiv, I know I don't often - well, I don't often say anything very nice to you.'

'Oh, right,' I said and smiled.

'But I thought you were very brave last night. I know me and Apic were terrified.'

'Oh, it was just the drink.'

'No, I mean it. I saw you in a different light last night. And you were brave too when you killed the necromancer.'

'Thanks Temmy,' I said not knowing what else to say.

'That was all really,' she said, then suddenly blushed, and smiled.

I laughed and clapped her on the shoulder.

'Well, don't stop being nasty to me, we don't want the others to suspect!'
She looked down at the bed, smiling and shrugging, obviously very embarrassed.
'I'm sorry Shiv, for so long I've harboured a grudge against you, that you became Mal's apprentice and not me. For so long I've, well, found reasons to dislike you.'
This wasn't exactly news to me, but I was surprised by her depth of feeling.
'Then last night, I realised that that vampire had more respect for you than I did. It made me think.'
'Hey!' I said, and put my arm around her. 'We're friends aren't we?'
She smiled and put her head on my shoulder, then said, 'It's been a long journey.'
'You can say that again.'
Just then, Apic arrived, holding a large bundle and opening the door unannounced with his foot. When he saw Temina and I in an embrace, he flushed bright red, and seemed to flounder for something to say. Temina quickly got up, and seemed to be at a loss for words as well. I resolved to have a word with Apic as soon as I could.
'Did you get them?' I asked him innocently.
'Yes', he said, and unwrapped the bundle, revealing a faggot of sharpened rowan stakes.
'Excellent,'
'I got some mint as well, just in case no one else did,' he said, and pulled a bunch from his pocket.

Later Carab arrived with some silver holy charms and symbols. He also had some mint. Adea was five minutes behind him, with a large bag of rose petals. She also had a bag of mint. Finally Boris returned, looking slightly sheepish, and he admitted that he had had no luck finding anything on the list, although he had grabbed some mint on the way back to the inn.
I laughed as something dawned on me,
'Do you realise we have all walked past the same garden, seen the same mint and taken some? The poor people that live there are going to think some very selective herb thieves have robbed them!'
I hooted with mirth, but no one else seemed to find my joke all that funny.

We agreed to ride up to the castle that afternoon. I was nervous, but not as nervous as most of the others. Carab seemed calm and collected, but he did have a place within him that he could go to, and not feel fear. I think it was the same place he had lived in the entire time he was a galley slave. As a result, he was being very quiet. Boris was perhaps the most nervous looking out of all of us. He was deathly pale and looked like he might throw up at any minute. I tried to give him a smile, and the look he returned me was of abject misery. Much to Adea's disgust, Apic, Temina, Boris and I were passing round a bottle of the local rot gut whisky to steady our nerves, but as we got closer to the castle she reached over to me and said, 'Give me a swig of that.'

The castle from the outside was like an architect's nightmare, painted black. Or perhaps I should leave it up to your imagination, as everyone knows what a vampire's castle should look like. It wasn't far away from the cliché, with a tall, square keep-like structure, held on all sides by great sweeping flying buttresses, and with taller towers within its walls. From the foot of the drawbridge, it put a strain on the neck to look up at it. Valley mist drifted between the tallest of the towers, and a low keening wind echoed through the battlements. The moat was very deep. I shuddered looking down at the water far below us as we crossed the drawbridge into the courtyard. Cautiously we dismounted and crossed the yard on foot, towards the tall gothic style entrance doors at the rear. There were lights on in some of the upper rooms, although the curtains were drawn.

Hesitantly I stepped up the stone stairs to the entrance and raised my hand to knock at the door. It swung open before I touched it.

'Typical,' I muttered.

'Listen Shiv,' gabbled Apic behind me. 'Maybe this isn't such a good idea. I mean, who are we to interfere in a set up that has probably been going for hundreds of years.'

I turned to him and gave him a withering look, which successfully silenced him. He him look at his feet in shame.

I walked slowly into the large entrance hall, and the others followed me as quietly as they could.

I must admit I was pleasantly surprised by the interior. There were no cobwebs, or rusty suits of armour in evidence. Instead the decor looked quite tasteful. There was a large marble fireplace on the left side of the hall, where a low fire smouldered. There were tapestries on the walls, that looked innocent enough, and an expensive looking desk sat across from the fire, with papers scattered across it, as if someone had been doing their accounting. The ceiling was incredibly high up. I looked up at the second story balcony, and further up in the gloom I could just make out the rafters.

There was light coming from a room across the hall, and I slowly approached it. The door was slightly ajar, and with a quick look behind me to make sure I wasn't on my own, I stepped into the room. It was a long dining hall, and sat at the far end of the table, eating by himself was Lord Rutven. It was a very elegant room, and brightly lit by the man-high candle stands that were strategically placed along its length. There must have been big bay windows on one side, but they were covered by curtains. The floor was wooden parquet, polished to a high sheen, and the vast dark mahogany table had a lovely centrepiece of local wild flowers and grasses.

'Ah, welcome, come in,' he said. 'I trust you are here for some sort of encounter, no? Laden down with stakes, holy water, and what not I, presume?'

I suddenly felt a little foolish and looked back at the others as they crowded into the room, who nodded at me to say something. I turned back to look at him, and said, 'Well, yes.'

'That's great Shiv,' hissed Adea behind me. 'That's really telling him.'

I waved my hand behind my back to try and make her shut up.

'Wouldn't you rather have something to eat?' he said, and gestured at the table. 'I can have Forbin set some extra places.'

'We already ate,' I replied, although the food did smell nice. I walked up the length of the table towards him, my booted footsteps echoing down the hall, so that we didn't have to raise our voices to talk.

'So, is it just yourself up here then?' I asked.

'Just me and father, although he doesn't get out of bed much these days, the poor old fellow.'

The others spread out a little in the room. I saw Carab flick the leather catch off the scabbard of his sword with his thumb. Lord Rutven noticed as well.

'Listen, there really is no need for this you know. I am not a violent man.'

'You're not a man, full stop,' I replied, as I got closer to him, 'We're human, you're undead. This is the way it has to be.'

'Very well,' he sighed, and started to undo his shirt. He then bared his chest to me. 'At least make it quick.'

'It's a trick!' cried Adea, the only one of my companions who had found her tongue. 'Don't touch him!'

'Listen,' I said. 'This is stupid. If your going to be like that about it...'

He was suddenly on his feet, and standing too close to me for comfort.

'Not that easy is it? You. You.... Foreigners,' he hissed as if this was the greatest insult known to man, suddenly seething with fury, 'You come here, and you look down your noses at our ways and customs. This is the way it has been for a hundred generations. Every single member of the Julgia aristocracy is undead. Killing me won't solve anything, it will only bring the whole country down on you.'

He was stalking around now gesturing wildly, 'And you come here, with your ideas of mankind having their own monarchy. What a ridiculous notion. You cannot rule yourselves. I see your southern states, a mess of wars, petty power struggles, famine and disease. Fwah! A farthing for you all! I wouldn't want to suck on your rancid foreign blood if you offered me up your neck on a plate.'

'Ok mate!' I bellowed at him, stunning him into silence. 'That's enough. I just need to look out that window to see what state this country is in. You are nothing more than leaches sucking the blood of a weak and miserable people. Men are not like cattle, you have beaten everyone in this land into submission, with a thousand years of blood soaked tyranny. Don't try and call it by any other name. You are a parasite, and you know it, and if...'

There was a sudden shing of metal, and something silver flashed in front of me.

I looked down at Lord Rutven's rapier that was inexplicably buried in my chest with him at the other end of it, holding the hilt with an almost apologetic look on his face.

I gurgled for a second, in utter disbelief, 'Just because you know I'm right...', and slumped to the floor. Someone screamed.

Temina was suddenly there, and slashed her rapier right across the vampires cheek, bringing forth a wide splatter of blood. He clutched at the bloody wound and cursed.

I watched in amazement as Temina went toe to toe with him, and they fenced across the parquet floor, each blade a whirring flash of silver.

Doors burst open, and dark robed servants began to pour in. I heard Carab draw his sword, and sounds of a struggle behind me. I drew my revolver and shot a robed figure, as he was about to strike Temina from behind with a dagger. He crumpled to the floor in a heap.

'No cheating...' I gasped.

The next moment, Apic was by my side, trying to get me to my feet.

'Oh Shiv. No,' he cried.

'I'm ok, just get me up,' I lied.

I leant on the table and looked around. Temina continued to battle Lord Rutven, and they seemed evenly matched. Carab was fending off the hooded servants, grunting and cursing to himself. Boris was slightly further down the hall, doing a remarkably fine job of fencing with two of the servants, even as I watched he deftly ran one through with a perfectly executed lunge. Adea had even drawn her short sword, and was being forced to defend herself. There were many ornamental swords and pikes on the wall. I pointed at four of them in a line, one after the other, and recited some wheezy magical words.

One by one, they started to twitch, and then leap from the wall with sparks and shrieks, to attack the nearest enemies. Just in the nick of time by the look of it, as Carab had been getting overwhelmed.

Temina was loosing the fencing match, blood poured from several wounds on her sword arm and lead leg. Although she was obviously an expert, she was no match for the unnatural speed and agility of the undead.

I motioned to Apic to get the stuff from the satchel. He nodded and frantically started pulling items from it. He grabbed some mint, and hurled it at the vampire, which landed on his shoulders and head. Apart from making him look silly it achieved nothing, and he irritably brushed himself off. Temina was beginning to lose ground.

'Do something!' she pleaded.

'The holy water Apic,' I gasped.

He picked up a small bottle and threw it at Rutven. I watched in horror as it bounced off his chest and rolled right under Temina's foot, sending her flying backwards with a grunt of vexation. The vampire turned and started towards us.

'What have I done!' cried Apic, as he drew his sword and bravely stood up to defend me.

It only took Rutven one blow to sweep him aside like a rag doll.

'Now it is your turn,' he growled and advanced on me.

'White mouse?' I said, and held it up in front of him.

'Gah! Get that vermin away from me!' he said, sweeping it from my hand. It gave a little startled squeak as it was catapulted across the room.

He grabbed me by my shirt and held my limp body right up to his.

'I don't usually bite the necks of foreigners, but in your case I will make an exception,' he said and opened his mouth to reveal the long fangs inside. My heart fluttered in terror. I reached my arm forward to touch something behind him.

'Kynh Yu Pihjaj,' I said.

'What did you say?' he asked in sudden confusion.

'I just cast a very powerful and short duration enhancement spell on Temina's sword. She can now use it to kill undead.'

'Wait…' was all he could say before I saw the tip of Temina's rapier push though the front of his shirt, and I was dropped to the floor.

As is traditional upon leaving a vampire castle, we set fire to it before we went. Most of us were injured in some way, although Temina and I were the worst, so it was a bit of a lack lustre effort, involving no more than kicking over the candle holders. However, it was a rewarding sight to look back over the tops of the trees as we rode back down into the valley, and saw smoke billowing out of the upper windows. Despite our injuries we decided to forgo the pleasures of Graz village, and continued on our way. When it became too dark to travel any further we set up camp, and lit possibly the biggest fire we had yet kindled. I was very faint from blood loss, and I wasn't really fit to be moved. After I was bandaged up, I felt cold, but still alive. It had been a lucky blow, missing all of my vitals, and my heart just by a whisker. I cast a cure spell on myself, to speed the healing process. Temina was suffering from shock and blood loss. Although all her wounds were quite small, she had many of them, especially on her right arm. Adea bandaged her up, and I cast a cure spell on her. As the two walking wounded we were leant up beside a broad tree together and wrapped in blankets. Later we were brought something to eat. I leant with my head lolling back on the tree, I had no strength left.

'I can't believe it,' said Temina.

'What?'

'What just happened.'

'I know.'

She began to shiver.

'Hey, hey. Take it easy,' I said, although I had no strength to move and comfort her.

'I fought him. I actually fought him, he was so… fast. And strong. I was terrified.'

'Hey, but you killed him though.'

'Yes, a cowardly stab in the back.'

I tried to shrug, but started coughing. I could taste blood on my lips. Adea who had been half listening to us, rushed over to Temina as she started crying.

She made soothing noises and rubbed her hand, saying, 'You did so well. You were so brave.'

I began to slip into unconsciousness. I could hear Boris and Apic sat by the fire, recounting the day's adventures to each other over and over again. They whispered and giggled like school boys, neither willing to believe what they had been involved in, and that they had survived. The last thing I heard was Adea beside me saying,

'Someone should watch these two tonight.'

The next day I spent all my magical reserves repeatedly casting heal spells on Temina and myself until we were practically glowing. Although it is not the best way of recovering from wounds, we would not have been able to travel otherwise. As it was, well I don't know about Temmy, she had retreated into herself a little, but I was still in a lot of pain. Each step Chestnut took sent a little stab of pain right through me, but after a while the healing spells really began to kick in, and by the end of that days travel I was a smiling imbecile.

Joppa and Luxor both took about a week each to travel through, and eventually we arrived at Kolopa, in Lahtl, the southern most shire of Vegas. I will not go into great detail about these two countries at the moment. Joppa was a pleasant enough place, everything that Julgia should have been but was not. Our ride through their tall mountain kingdom was very pleasant. Luxor was a flatter land of misty marshes and strong walled towns. The people here were taking on a more northern look, with long blonde beards and their hair tied in braids. However Luxor still had a more civilised look and feel to it. In each town we passed through, there was a large imposing courthouse, and a sturdy looking jail.

Once we reached Kolopa, I got the feeling of real wilderness. The climate was totally different, it was late summer now, and the evenings were as clear and crisp as crystal. The people that we saw working in the fields beneath the incredibly tall mountains were all fair and very rugged in appearance. Lahtl was the southern most of the thraldom's, and the one that belonged to Carab's father, Carris.

Carab described the thrall system to me. Thralls were not slaves exactly, but bondsmen, who were bonded to their land. It was a mutually beneficial system, he assured me. The bondsmen certainly didn't have anywhere better to go, and the freemen had all the headaches of taxation, war payments, army service and a hundred other things. All the bondsmen had to do was work, and all their needs were taken care of.

Apic and I made short work of all that sort of stuff, needless to say, as it certainly sounded like slavery to us, just by another name. Carab may have continued to defend the status quo in his country, but Adea had a few choice comments to make as well, and soon he agreed that he had no liking for it himself, especially having experienced slavery first hand. He shrugged and said that it was the way that it had always been. It was a tough place to live, in winter particularly, and if you couldn't say anything else for this feudal system, then it did at least make sure everyone got fed. I pointed out that the bondsmen we could see working in the fields, although they seemed happy enough, were wearing metal collars to show their status, and Carab grumbled something about making changes when he succeeded his father. He also mentioned to me that I had better keep a low profile as far as being a wizard was concerned, they tended to burn magic users in Vegas.

Kolopa itself was a very fair town, with a strong wooden stockade wall all around it, and a sturdy looking stone castle in its centre. There were also a few more stone buildings around the market square. We got a very good view of it as we descended into the valley, our horses by now seasoned veterans of mountain travel. A guide had also met us at the border, not that we needed one, but it was customary for the thane to send one to meet members of his family. He and Carab discussed changes that had occurred during Carab's four year absence.

I listened to their conversation for a bit, but soon grew bored, as it was all about things of which I knew nothing. I did gather however, that the ruler of all Vegas was still alive, King Turku, who would be celebrating his fortieth year of rule this winter. It was him that had introduced the Luxorian judicial system, that although effective, in that in the last ten years it had more or less stamped out fighting between the aggressive thanes, it was still universally loathed. The mainly Luxorian lawyers were a hated class, but generally it was held that they were a necessary evil. The new courthouse, built last year, was situated right beside the castle.

Carab growled, 'They tore down the common hall to build a courthouse?'
'Well my lord!' laughed the guide. 'Better than the constant threat of war from your neighbours, I know old Turku is oft defamed for importing the Luxorian laws, but all these noble lords who were once constantly at loggerheads for lands and rights are now so tied up in red tape, there hasn't been a single dispute these five years past.'
Carab nodded, 'What about the ordinary man?'
'Well yes, my lord, the ordinary freeman, and the ordinary bondsman do suffer a little, I suppose, in that the freeman obviously pays more taxes, and is more likely to run afoul of the law. And the bondsman is worse off in that he is more likely to be punished for a wrong, but as I said, a necessary evil.'
'I seem to remember my father saying that Luxor would conquer Vegas, not by the sword, but by cunning,' commented Carab.

The guide shrugged and smiled, 'My lord, we are Vegans, and have no head for paper work. Let the Luxorians do what they love, I say. My wife is Luxorian truth be told...'

And the conversation moved onto families in the town, and who was doing what, and with whom. The road was wide enough for the usual rules about what horse went where to be relaxed a bit, and I drifted to the rear of the group, so that I could exchange witticisms with Apic and Boris.

Soon we were in the town, and Carab was being treated to a hero's welcome. It looked like everyone was on the street, cheering and waving, and throwing petals. Carab and Adea rode at the front, waving back, as if they were born to it. Boris and Temina next, and Apic and I brought up the rear. A burly man, with a vast amount of grey beard and braided hair rushed at Carab from the front of the crowd and wrestled him from his horse.

'My boy! My boy!' he bellowed.

The resemblance between him and Carab was uncanny. Carab was the image of his father. They were both tall and muscular, with similar chiselled features and broad jaw and forehead. His father was just older, although he appeared none the worse for it, and wore a beard while Carab did not. Others emerged from the throng to embrace and kiss Carab. Other members of his family I had no doubt. From what I knew of him he had a great many brothers and sisters, not to mention a barrel full of cousins. The shouting and cheering went on for so long, that both Chestnut and I eventually grew bored of it, and I rode up to the castle to find a stable to put her in. I shouted and waved to Carab over the throng, and pointed to my chest, indicating that my wound was giving me gyp, and then went to look for somewhere quiet to have a bit of a lie down.

That night there was a big feast in the castle to celebrate the eldest son's return. The hall for the feast was long, with many tables set in it. Light was provided by hundreds of candles set into sconces along the walls. The air was smoky with incense. There were rushes newly laid on the cobbles, and house dogs mooched about looking for food that had dropped to the floor. I was positioned beside Adea at the main table. We were both still wearing our travelling clothes, but no one seemed to mind. The feast was still in its infancy, although there was plenty of food around. None of our other friends were in evidence yet, and Carab and Carris had yet to make an appearance. Apic and I had been hungry though, so here we were. As we bit into chunks of roast oxen and braised duck I took the opportunity to talk to my friend.

'So Apic. While I remember,' and smiled at him. 'What is going on between you and Temina?'

'Ah. Now, Shiv.'

'Well, if a lady's honour is in question, then say no more about it.'

Apic laughed nervously, 'There is nothing really, and yet. Well, you know we get on really well, and I know she is … interested.'

'Oh yes!' I laughed, and slapped my thigh. 'Have you... you know?'

'Shiv, for shame!' he gasped, then admitted glumly. 'No. But there was one night, at Mallonax's tower, when we kissed.'

'You dog!' I was enjoying teasing him. 'But since then? What about at Werfen?'

'Well, there never seems to be any time, we are always on the move. Sometimes she ignores me, but I know oft times women will do that if they are interested in you.'

'Poor Apic. You've got it bad.'

'Do you blame me? She is beautiful. Like a flaming red rose. And so strong willed,' he said in misery.

'Stop it. You're making me sick,' I said, and made mock choking noises on a drumstick.

'Look,' said Apic, changing the subject. 'Here is Carab.'

I had a funny feeling that everything wasn't going to plan, when I saw him approach us with a grim expression on his face.

'Carab?' I asked, as he sat down beside us, and put his head in his hand. Here is another lovesick young swain, I thought to myself.

'I have talked to my father. It seems his delight in seeing me doesn't extend to changing his plans for my marriage.'

'Marriage?' I repeated dumbly.

'It seems I am to marry Gertine, my cousin, in Orebro, as was arranged at my birth.'

I was about to sat something, but I was interrupted by a commotion behind us and Carab's father stormed into the hall, 'Don't walk away from me boy, and don't defy me!' the large old man stopped when he saw how far forward the feast had come in the last few minutes, most of the guests were seated, and some were already eating. No standing on ceremony here.

He looked down at Adea who had entered the hall as well, and smiled, 'My dear, you must understand, you are a very pretty thing, but my son's marriage is arranged, to a good stout, and blonde Vegan girl.'

And with this he gave Adea a condescending look. She was short, slim and dark. Old racist I thought to myself. Adea didn't even pause to look at what might be on offer at the feast, and stormed off to her room.

'Father!' cried Carab. 'Adea. Come back!'

He stood up to follow her, but the grey haired old warrior grabbed him by the arm and said, 'Let her go son. It is best that she accepts it.'

'No father!' said Carab emotionally. 'She will not accept it, and neither shall I!'

Tendons began to stand out on their arms as their grip on each other tightened.

Carab forced his father away from him, and stalked over to the doorway Adea had fled through.

'Stop him!' cried the Thane, and the two guards at the door nervously stepped into Carab's path. Everyone in the hall was silent as this drama unfolded. I thought Carab might force the guards out of his way, but he turned back to his father, who then cried, 'I'll not have this! In my own house. Take him to his room and lock him in.'

The guards by the door, and the others near by took a step towards Carab, but he turned such a look on them that they stopped in their tracks.

'Don't just stand there,' bellowed Carris fevered with passion. 'Take him from my sight!'

The guards didn't touch Carab, but they did lead him away.

Later, as things began to settle down a bit, I tried to reason with the old man. I also noted that Temina and Boris had drifted into the hall to see what all the shouting had been about.

'What has the world come to, when a father must imprison his own son!' cried Carris.

The guests had begun to filter quietly from the hall, and Carris' strong warriors even had worried expressions on their faces.

'Your lordship,' I said to the thane, as I thoughtlessly grabbed him by the arm. 'Please your lordship, this isn't right!'

'Who are you?' he said angrily. Then, 'Ah, Shiv, his closest friend, perhaps you could speak some sense to him.'

'Your lordship, I know them both very well. They are in love, they are meant for each other.'

'Love? Pah!' he spat.

Suddenly a voice raised itself above the hubbub and cried, 'There he is, the sorcerer and demon worshipper! Seize him!'

A group of men dressed in black and wearing silver breastplates entered the hall. The warriors that formed the martial section of Carris' court tended to wear informal clothing when in the Thanes presence, although leather garments were favoured. These fellows had a much sterner appearance, and their clothing almost looked like a uniform.

'What is your business here, bailiffs of the court?' called the thane.

'We have a warrant for that man's arrest,' said one of them, pointing at me.

'Me?' I mouthed, pointing at my chest, then looking behind myself, in case they we looking at someone else.

'You indeed, Shiv, the demon summoner!' screeched a familiar voice. My heart sunk as Nadia stepped into view from behind one of the thickset bailiffs.

Temina began to draw her sword.

'No, no, put that away Tem,' then looking at Nadia I said, 'I'll go quietly.'

Dr. Lock finally broke the silence.

'Are you familiar with Swift, Yarn? Gulliver's Travels?'

'Oh yes, I seem to remember reading it when I was young. I also see what you're driving at.'

Heather smiled then said, 'You know then, about how his fantastical adventures were analogies for other things. The political situation at the time. Human nature. Value systems.'

'Oh yes. Don't worry. Your meaning is clear.'

Heather patted Yarn on the shoulder, 'Don't look so glum. We are friends aren't we? I'm not having a go at you. I'm just making conversation.'

Yarn looked up at her, and beamed a smile, 'I realise that. It's just. Oh, I know I shouldn't think for a second that you should have any reason to believe a word I say. It's just that I was having fun pretending that you did. Believe me, that is.'

'Oh, I'm sorry,' said Heather in concern, 'I didn't mean to…'

'No, no,' reassured Yarn. 'Not at all. I'm being silly. Your point is a valid one. I'm not so close minded that I don't think to myself from time to time, what if this is all just fantasy? What if all I am is a deluded fool? What if, the simple truth is, that all I am is a guy who is going to die of a brain tumour sometime soon, and who has these crazed loony-tunes memories, and that's all there is to it.'

The way Yarn had finished the last sentence had suggested a 'But', so Heather said,

'But?'

'But, there is something that lets me know, without a doubt, that this is all true.'

'Which is?'

Yarn pointed to the top of his forehead, where the tumour was. Heather sighed and leaned back, putting her hands behind her head.

Chapter Sixteen - Kolopa

I stood in the dock of the court of Kolopa, and surveyed the scene. There were four bailiffs at the main doors, two sat beside the lawyers, and two stood either side of Carris, who as always in trials that he took an interest in, was the presiding judge.

There were several lawyers below me, I wondered if any of them were for the defence, I certainly hadn't seen one yet.

Nadia sat deep in conversation with one of them, most likely plotting my untimely demise.

There didn't seem to be a witness box or anything else for that matter that resembled a courtroom, as I would imagine it. The dock itself was simply a barricade to prevent me from escaping into the room and running amok. I sighed, and continued to look round. I could see all my friends sat at a long table at the back that seemed to serve as a public gallery.

Eventually, after much conference with Nadia, and shuffling of papers, one of the lawyers, dressed in a ceremonial red robe and wearing a black skullcap, stood up and said,

'Shiv of Scotland, you stand accused of witchcraft and demonology. How do you plead?'

He was a short fellow, of unremarkable features, and he looked back at me with dull brown eyes, his expression unreadable.

I shrugged, 'Who cares?'

'Please answer, guilty or not guilty.'

'Well, in that I am a magician, I am guilty, I don't know how you define a witch. If that includes casting spells, then yes, guilty. I have never summoned a demon,' then thinking about it I said, 'I can summon rabbits though.'

'What are the extent of your dark and evil powers?' asked the lawyer.

'You had better believe I could fry you to a crisp right where you stand if I wanted to.'

The lawyer gulped and turned to Carris.

The thane looked over to his son in the public gallery and said, 'Is this true?'

'Yes father,' was the reply.

Carris lent forward on the desk he was sitting at and asked me, 'Could you use your powers to escape if you wished?'

'Yes.'

Again Carris looked at Carab, who nodded and said, 'Probably.'

'Well now,' said the thane and smiled. 'Could you give us a small demonstration?'

'Of course.'

'My lordship!' protested the short lawyer, 'A court of law is hardly the place...'

'Oh shut up Smisken, all the time you are chasing and bothering old ladies, with accusations of witchcraft. To my mind I have never once seen any of them cast a spell, or give any other kind of concrete proof, and here we have a sorcerer polite enough to offer us a demonstration? How could we possibly be so churlish as to refuse?'

I looked around for a suitable target. Smiling I spoke some mystical words and pointed at the paper knife on the desk beside Nadia. It jiggled then rose from the desk. There was a gasp from the gallery, as I made the knife whish round and round Nadia's head, before plunging back in to the desk, and imbedding itself with a loud twanging noise. For an encore I drew a white rabbit from my sleeve and handed it to a startled bailiff. I looked around, expecting a round of applause, but instead there was stunned silence.

The trial went on and on. They started speaking in lawyer-speak, and I began to loose interest. The courts in Vegas are almost exclusively run by Luxorians. It all had an odd Dickensian feeling to it. There were laws, and sub-laws, clauses and sub-clauses, rulings, findings and precedents. I heard Nadia mention the Monks of the Many Hammers, and I listened to him, while he described for the benefit of the court, how he had hooked up with them after I had abandoned him and had then made it his mission to track me down. He had picked up my trail in Werfen, and had sent many of his brethren on missions to gather evidence of my misdeeds. By then he had learned I was headed for Vegas, and he and a group of the monks decided to risk a sea crossing to Kolopa. They were almost immediately set upon by noggish pirates, and the ship was sunk. Nadia and some of the others had survived for three weeks on a raft, before being picked up by a Vegan longship. When he arrived in Kolopa, he wasted no time in contacting the Luxorian lawyers in town, whom, needless to say, he got on with like a house on fire, and plotted to take me into custody as soon as I arrived. The list of charges was quite extensive and included such corkers as regicide, being possessed by a demon, and defiling temples. I began to get a little worried, they were taking this all in, and Carris was looking at me in a much sterner manner. But then the red tape started being thrown about again, and I saw by the bored expression on Carris's face that I was more likely to die of old age before a sentence was likely to be passed. After what seemed forever, and not one decision being taken. Court was adjourned and I was lead back to my cell.

The next day I was beginning to get more and more worried that things were not going to go my way. Carris was still very angry at his son, and by the look on his stern old face I had the feeling that he was going to sentence me to death just for the pleasure of getting back at him. The lawyers were quickly coming to a conclusion. I was a witch, by my own admission, and for this I must be burned. Nadia looked on in obvious delight as the proceedings lead to the only conclusion that seemed possible. To make matters worse, Carab was nowhere in evidence and the public gallery had been cleared. All the better to stitch me up with no one around to support me. I looked around. Not a friend anywhere. Well, I thought to myself, I can always try and fight my way out.

Suddenly Carris addressed me in a loud authoritative voice that broke me away from my musings.

'Shiv of Scotland. Stand and accept your sentence!'

I gulped, stood up and turned to face him. Carris looked at me, then looked over my shoulder to the large double doors at the back of the room and made a hand motion to the guards there.

The doors opened and a large squad of guards stepped in, dressed in sturdy chainmail and iron helmets. In their midst I saw the unhappy faces of Apic and Adea. I sighed.

'Due to the nature of your powers,' intoned Carris. 'We have taken hostages to ensure your behaviour following the verdict.'

Carris shot the lawyers and Nadia an angry glance, then turned to me and said, 'I don't like to do this lad, but I need you to swear you will accept the verdict of the court and not try anything rash.'

I stuttered for a moment, in sudden alarm and panic and cried, 'But this isn't fair!'

Carris cleared his throat and replied, 'Swear to abide by the courts decision of sentence and no harm will come to them.'

'I need time to think!' I wailed.

But I could think of nothing. I had magic powers alright, but none that I could think of would whisk me, Apic and Adea from the courtroom without harming them, or the guards who, at the end of the day, were just doing their job.

Finally I groaned and said, 'I swear.'

Nadia cried, 'But you cannot trust him my lord!'

'Silence!' bellowed the thane. 'I like none of this one bit, hostage taking does not sit well with me!'

Carris composed himself and continued, 'Very well. Shiv, you are indeed a witch and although on reflection I may have been a little hasty in my anger and brought these proceedings further along than I would have had them, I have no other choice.'

Silence fell in the courtroom.

'I sentence you to be taken to the Hard Rock Tree and be burned to death at the earliest convenience of the court.'

I shuddered in sudden terror. Perhaps while these boring proceedings had been going on all of yesterday I should have been formulating a daring plan of escape and not just dozing off.

'Bailiffs take him down.'

I let myself be lead back to my cell.

A few hours later I was still lying back on my uncomfortable straw pallet, thinking desperately of how I could escape the cell and rescue the others, or how I could cheat death atop a pile of burning faggots, when the door opened and in stepped Carab.

'Oh hello,' I said and got up. 'I see he let you go then.'

'Yes Shiv. It is bad, the nogs are invading the west coast.'

'Oh God.'

'My father came to my room, and asked what he should do. This was unusual.'

'What did you say?' I asked.

'The first thing he should do was release me.'

'Then what?'

'The second thing he should do is release you.'

Suddenly a free man and all past sins seemingly instantly pardoned I was taken to Carris' war chamber. I was sat down with Carab at the central chamber and tried to gather what was going on from the war chiefs and the runners that came into the chamber, usually panting for breath.

The next few hours were a flurry of activity. Riders were sent out, and riders came in. As the evening wore on the situation became clearer. Spy ships out in the Frost Sea had reported a large noggish force making its way towards Loggarth and Gorgo, the two provinces that lay on the western most promontory of Vegas. These were wild barren areas of rocky ridges and swampy valleys. There were a few villages but not much else, because of this the areas had no thane, and fell under the jurisdiction of the thane of Lahtl, Carris.

Messengers were sent to Ixnay, the capital, and to Luxor, to warn of the invasion. Adea, seeming free of all hostage taking goings-on, even sent a messenger to Enttland via the ambassador. A force was mustered as quickly as possible to meet the threat, and at about two o'clock in the morning, we rode out of the city gates, at the head of the Lahtl army.

Despite our hurried start and desperate speed, it took us four days to reach the coast, four days of merciless marching, with precious little sleep. I pitied the foot soldiers, they would have been having a worse time than us. Nobody talked much, we were too tired. On the third day, another messenger from the coast arrived, and a quick meeting was called by Carris and his commanders. I don't know what was discussed, because I wasn't invited, but Carab told me later that the possible reasons for an invasion were discussed. They had agreed that it might well be the case that the north nogs were trying to establish a northern kingdom, as they feared the south nogs would wipe them out. As it turned out later, they were wrong.

We had a good vantage point on the landing area from a large grassy hill, south of the inlet. The spies' reports had been correct. We could see the fleet quite clearly as they approached their intended beachhead. I looked away from the sea and inland. I could just make out a forest of spears. This was the formation that was going to guard the archers. I gulped. It was going to be a big battle.

Yesterday all of us, bar Carab, had camped out a mile south of this hill, and gotten as much sleep as we could. Later, Carab and Carris had turned up and gone over the plans for the next day with us. We stayed out of the main briefing, as the other war chiefs didn't seem that chuffed about the presence of a convicted sorcerer and his lackeys. Carris had at his disposal, five thousand armed thralls, four thousand warriors, two thousand archers and about another thousand irregulars making a total of twelve thousand. There were many more warriors than this in the kingdom of Vegas, but they were all inland. Carris couldn't expect any more reinforcements for two or three days. Also at his disposal he had ten cannons from the royal arsenal at Ixnay, and a bombard manufactured in Bellavia which had been given as a gift for Carris's fiftieth birthday as thanks for his help against the constant pirate threat in the Diamond and Frost Seas. His troops had been busily making trenches and sharpening rows of spikes since they had arrived two days ago. The spy vessels had reported in excess of fifty galleys from Ertia, each filled with two hundred nog warriors, making a total of an estimated ten thousand. Not very good odds when fighting nogs, but they weren't expecting an opposed landing, and with our artillery pounding at their ships, we may stand a chance. They knew we were here by now, small pickets had been going forward of the main fleet. I imagined they would not be very happy about it though. That our spies had spotted them so early and a force mustered so quickly to meet them must have seemed like sheer fantasy. But we were here. Exhausted, but here.

I considered all this, as we stood there, the wind whistling in from the sea, waiting for the nog galleys to come within range of the archers and the guns. I had carefully chosen my position on the south flank of the bay, underneath the lee of one of the massive mountains, as a place I could rain down fireballs on any nogs that came within range. I estimated my range to encompass anyone who crossed over a small stream about a hundred yards out from me. I also had a possible escape route planned out, a gorge in the lower section of the mountain which I would cross by means of a magical bridge spell. It was no wonder the nogs had chosen here to land. This was the only patch of suitable beach in either direction on this rugged terrain that I could see. Otherwise it was all just wave shattered rocks and cliffs.

The galleys got closer, the sound of oars and sails, cries and shouts, drifting across to us on the wind. A knot formed in my stomach, partly from anticipation of the up coming battle, and partly because this was the first time I had seen a noggish ship since being a slave. I could see the anxiety on the faces of Apic and Boris as well. Much to Temina's annoyance, but not to Adea's Carris had strictly forbidden any women to be near the battle, they were with the baggage about half a mile to the rear. Apic and Boris were acting as self appointed wizard guards.

'This is going to be a busy day,' I said.

'You can say that again,' agreed Apic. 'Life is never dull around you, Shiv.'

'I warned you about this sort of thing didn't I Boris?'
'I know,' he shrugged and smiled wanly. 'I'm not dead yet though.'

The cutters and pinaces from the nearby ships were drawing up on the beach when all ten cannons went off with a mighty roar. They were firing from sheltered positions behind the dunes, so I couldn't see them. But I saw the effects the cannonballs had as they crashed into the waves around the ships. Only one hit a ship, crashing into its bows and sending deadly splinters flying everywhere, the others smashed into the waves, throwing up massive geysers of spume.

Then the bombard bellowed into life and a massive gunpowder filled shell exploded on the beach killing half a dozen nog marines as they charged across the sand. This was the signal for the archers to start firing off volleys of arrows, angled high in the air to rain down on the advancing nog warriors. Suddenly the sky was black with arrows, and almost all the nogs on the beach that had not thought to raise their shields were brought down. The guns continued to shake the earth and arrows fell on the rear formations of noggish marines. Apic, Boris and I stood on our mark, underneath the mountains in silence, as we watched the first wave of marines disintegrate. There were bodies everywhere. More landing craft were drawing up onto the beach, and another wave of warriors hit the shore, and then another, the steady attrition of the guns and archers was now not enough to hold them back. They were on the first dunes, and getting close to where we were standing, when the bass tone of a signalling horn blew two deep notes over the din of battle, and thousands of Vegan warriors and armoured thralls charged onto the beach from behind the dunes to meet the enemy head on, bristling with spears. I saw Carab leading the charge on a huge black horse, and his father close by wielding a large warhammer. I was distracted from watching the main battle by Apic tugging at my shirt and pointing to a company of nog marines advancing down their right flank towards us. I cast a spell that turned the ground they were on into quicksand, and they were suddenly bogged down. A group of archers nearby spotted the easy target, and moved up onto the dune ridge to pick them off individually. Yet another shipload of nogs disembarked nearby and I fired a volley of fireballs into their midst, killing several, and luckily setting the ship's sails on fire.

After that the battle moved away from us a little, but it seemed that the courageous Vegan warriors were winning and pushing the nog back towards the sea. But at a price, there were many slain, and many wounded being carried back to the marshalling point at the rear.

'What the hell is that?' shouted Apic again, this time pointing out a little further to sea.

Boris took small nervous steps from one foot to the other.

'Oh shit!' I cried. 'That is something with a head the size of a house.'

As I spoke these words, the monster behind the nog ships, stood up, waist height in the water, sending a mini tidal wave washing towards the shore. It must have been well over a hundred feet tall, its pale flesh covered in barnacles and seaweed. Its great flat head was covered in long lank tendrils of hair, and a set of vast green rubbery lips protruded out from underneath a pair of deep set malevolent eyes. The warriors on the beach were beginning to see this huge sea giant, and many were breaking and running for the cover of the dunes. The sea giant took a mighty ponderous step towards the beach, making the nog vessels around it lurch around like toy boats in a millpond.

'Bloody hell,' I said.

The guns halted for about ten minutes. By the time the giant set foot on the beach they had been repositioned and all fired at him in unison. All but three missed, barely visible streaks of metal flying past it like flies. One hit it in the chest and bounced off, and another in the knee. The last to hit was right in the forehead, which ricochet off with a crazy high pitched screeching sound. Apic stood there slack jawed. Boris seemed to be very pale. I didn't feel any better. I could see the Vegan army was breaking, almost half of them had fled the beach, despite Carab trying to rally them. I couldn't see his father anywhere. The giant reached down onto the beach and picked up a fleeing warrior and casually tossed him into its mouth. I started to run down to the beach, Apic and Boris doubtfully following me. The next few minutes were fairly hair raising, and the images I remember of them are burned into my memory. It was like trying to see a band at a busy open air concert. Everyone was either trying to get to the battle, or away from it. The noise and confusion was incredible. Ahead of me, looking up over the heads of the warriors around me I could see the giant from the waist up. I continued to push forward through the press, there were no nogs in evidence, I wasn't close enough to the front yet. I considered casting a fly spell to get closer, but then I had a horrible vision of what sort of target I would be presenting to every nog on the battlefield. Soon though, the crowd got thinner, and I could see the main line, where the bravest of the Vegan fighters were still engaging the noggish marines. The nog marines all wore bright red coats, with black britches and boots. They carried long naval cutlasses. I thought I had lost the giant, when suddenly a shadow fell over me, and I realised it was right overhead. A foot crashed down right beside me crushing three Vegan thralls who had been nearby, in a bloodcurdling crunching of bones and a splattering of blood. 'Right,' I muttered to myself, as the giant took a step backwards and looked down at where I was standing. For a moment I looked up, it looked down, and our eyes met. I stood there motionlessly, as the crowd around me dissipated and I was suddenly alone. I looked at the sand beneath my feet and prepared myself, I could see the shadow of its hand as it reached down towards me.

I raised my hands above my head, and spoke three magical words. A great bolt of lightning shot from my fingers in a long arch towards the giant's head. The bolt struck it squarely between the eyes, and I was jolted over and landed on my back as I channelled everything I had into the spell. Arks of light sizzled around the giant's head, and it raised its arms as if to swat away flies. The light grew brighter, then there was a sudden discharge, which set its hair on fire, and it began to fall over. As I watched, it was as if everyone else held their breath, and stopped fighting to watch this thing fall. In slow motion it began to topple over, as if pole axed, without bending its body. A great crashing sound interrupted the silence as it collapsed onto two of the nog ships, totally destroying them, and then screams as the nog sailors and the poor human galley slaves suddenly found they were in a very awkward position.

I decided that my job here was done, and turned to make my way back to the ridge, as a great cheer went up, and the Vegan army counter attacked. 'What happened to you?' I asked Apic, who had made his way back as well, a lot more dirty and blood caked than when I had last seen him. There was blood all over his face and his hair was all red and spiked up.

'Don't ask,' he grumbled, but told me anyway. 'I got swept up in a charge, there wasn't enough room to swing a sword. For about five seconds I had my face pressed up against a nog's breastplate.'

'Bloody hell, what did you do?'

'I drew my dagger and stabbed him in the thigh. Have you seen Boris?'

'Here he comes now,' I said and pointed, as a poor bedraggled young man jogged up towards us. He was drenched.

As he came I noticed that the stunned sea giant had picked itself up. My sudden terror was dissipated when I saw that it was turning to head back out to sea, groggily shaking its singed head.

'What happened?' asked Apic to Boris as he approached us.

'I went for a swim!' he said, and laughed in manic elation. 'I tried to follow you, but got lost in the fray. A group of us charged a boat as they were disembarking, but they were too strong. We had to flee for our lives in the surf! I killed one!'

'Good!' was all I could think to say.

'I watched as you knocked over that...thing. Incredible.'

'Just as well he was as vulnerable to lighting as I thought. Oh gods, what are they doing now?'

Down on the sand, the nog marines had opened up a small beachhead, and shaman were leading a selection of chained together slaves onto the beach. There seemed to be as many nog slaves as human. Those without a vantage point on the beach would not be able to see what was going on, but we could. I think some nog marines had out flanked the archers during the whole episode with the giant, as the only arrows being fired were at individual targets on the shore. The guns continued to fire, but sporadically. The shaman unloaded a large cauldron, and one by one they lead the struggling slaves to it, and slit their throats. The blood poured into the cauldron in great gurgling spurts. In a few minutes, the vessel was full, and the shaman began to chant. Smoke began to pour from the cauldron and started forming shapes in red clouds above the heads of those on the beach.

'Oh! Oh!' cried Apic. 'This doesn't look good.'

A jet of flame burst from the smoke, and then another. A great reptilian head emerged, then a body and two scaly limbs, and in an instant flipped over and flew back into the smoke. Everything was quiet for a moment, and then, in a great undulating charge, the dragon burst from the smoke, its massive black bat wings snapping above its head, and a jet of flame shooting from its mouth onto the battlefield below.

'Is that one of their gods?' asked Boris in wonder. I didn't know.

For the second time, the Vegan warriors began to break and run back to the dunes. Carab looked up at me from the battle, and I had to shrug my shoulders at him, palms up, trying to indicate that I had no magic that could fight something like that.

The dragon swept overhead like a living jet fighter, shrieking and belching flame in great deadly streaks on the unfortunates below.

So many warriors and thralls were running around in flames now that Carab signalled the call for a retreat to be given. Those on fire ran to the sea to douse the flames, only to be cut down by the advancing marines. As my hand went to my mouth in horror of their plight, I noticed a group of nog marines beginning to approach our position. The dragon flitted over head, strafing the poor warriors still left on the open beach.

'Shiv?' asked Apic nervously.

'Running away might be an option.'

We waited on a ridge above the gorge as the nog warily approached the bridge. They could see us from where they were, high above them and we gave then a little wave.

'Do you think they will go for it?' asked Apic.

'They will if I do this! All together now lads,' I said, and standing up, I began to undo my belt buckle.

Apic laughed as he realised what I was doing, and even Boris joined in, as together we all mooned them.

The leader of the noggish detachment growled in anger, and motioned his troops to follow him across the bridge. The bridge itself was about six feet wide, and had no sides. It appeared to be carved from one solid piece of rock. I waited until the leader was nearly at the other side and about ten other nogs were on the bridge. I snapped my fingers, and with a loud pop, the bridge disappeared and the nogs were left suspended in mid air for one brief 'wily coyote' moment, before plunging onto the deadly rocks below. The nogs still remaining on the other side shouted and shook their swords at us in fear and anger. We laughed and ran off.

There was something on his lapel. It may have been mayonnaise or salad cream, White anyway, and dried up. The old man tutted and scrapped at it with a fingernail. He then continued to look at the map of the hospital on the wall of the corridor. He was dressed in a tweed jacket, and wore a thick pair of glasses. What a nice old man, thought Heather, perhaps needs directions to the toilet or something.

She approached him and asked, 'Can I help you?'

'Oh yes,' he said 'I'm looking for the….wait one second,' he took a piece of paper from his top pocket and unfolded it. 'The Edinburgh Centre for Neuro Oncology,'

'Oh right, I'm just going there myself. Who are you looking for?'

The old man looked at the paper again, then said, 'Dr. Heather Lock?'

'Oh!' exclaimed Heather and laughed. 'That's me!'

The old man extended his hand, and as Heather shook it, he said, 'Detective Inspector Edward McEwen. You may call me Ted though dear!' As they walked along the corridor towards the office, he said, 'Yes, I was talking to Ian, Dr. Barage that is, in the pub last Saturday, we're old friends. He told me about a patient of yours, nicknamed Yarn. I asked him to describe him to me. I suppose as a policeman, I was merely curious. Then I started thinking about old missing person's cases, and checked through the records on Monday. Marvellous things computers aren't they? Well, the upshot is, that your man, Yarn, matches the description of my man, Patrick Fogle, an Edinburgh resident who disappeared from his home three years ago.'

'Three years!' cried Heather.

'Yes dear. The damnedest thing is that there isn't a single photo left in the file. Can't think what has happened to them. I remember him though. If it's possible could I see him? And possibly ask him where he's been for the last three years?'

Heather suddenly burst into laughter, and explained to the bemused policeman, 'If you ask him that, you may get more than you bargained for!'

Yarn accepted the folder from DI McEwen silently and gingerly flicked it open. He began to read it, but then suddenly threw it to the ground as if it were red hot.

'Yarn!' cried Heather.

'That's ok. I'm sorry I upset you Patrick,' said the policeman as he picked up the folder. Heather sat down beside Yarn, rubbing his hand she said, 'It's ok Yarn, just take it easy.'

She looked up at McEwan, who put the folder under his arm and said, 'Yes, perhaps I'll… If I could just see you later, Doctor. Once he's…yes.'

Ted McEwan and Heather Lock sat at a table in the canteen and sipped cups of coffee. It wasn't very busy. The lunchtime rush had been and gone.

'It's him alright,' stated the policeman, flicking through the folder.

'Incredible,' said the doctor. 'Three years.'

'All his family details are in here. I should contact them. I wonder if he is well enough to make a decision like that?'

'Oh,' said Heather, in a daze. 'Oh. You know he has a brain tumour? He has six months to live, probably less.'

'Ah,' he replied. 'Ah. That does put another complexion on things. His family have probably already accepted their loss. Probably moved on a long time ago. To find him after all that time, then to lose him again. Terrible. Tricky one that.'

Dr. Lock examined her coffee sadly.

'If you don't officially show me that folder, then I don't have to do anything about it,' she said. 'Oh, I don't know why I just said that!' she cried, and put her hands to her mouth.

'Yes, I mean, no,' replied the old man. 'Your quite right. I shall have to think about this. I will hold onto these documents for the time being then. At the end of the day, it's up to Patrick though.'

Chapter Seventeen - The battle of Kolopa

We made it back to Kolopa as fast as we could, and rode into the town three days later, utterly exhausted but none the worse for our recent adventures. Carab, and the main force had not arrived back yet, but I was able to tell Adea that as far as I knew he was still alive.

The next day he arrived, leading the remains of the opposition force. At about the same time, reinforcements from further north started arriving, lead by a warlord from Orebro, and many more thralls from the surrounding area were drafted. It was all go.

Kolopa took on a very martial air, as it swelled with troops. Spies from Loggarth reported that more noggish ships were landing, and skirmishing forces were being sent out to capture the surrounding villages. Carris had been injured at the beginning of the invasion, a very nasty blow to the arm at the first charge which explained why I hadn't seen much of him in the battle. He was still well enough to supervise the strengthening of the town's fortifications. The Luxorians seemed to have forgotten to re-arrest me. Nadia was not in evidence.

We waited for the siege that we felt sure was inevitable. News began to come in as well, from further afield, of nog invasions in Borland, Bellavia, and other countries. No one seemed to know if this meant a new alliance between the north and south nogs, or that the invasions were independent international adventures. The only topic of conversation obviously, on the ramparts during the day, and in the taverns at night was what exactly was going on? Apic and I, and those others that knew a little about the noggish situation were of the opinion that some sort of alliance had been formed. The northern nogs had advanced all the way to Foona, and had conquered all of southern Nillamandor except for poor beleaguered Ferron. We knew from traveller's gossip that the southern nog nations had split into two factions, one on each side of northern Fiarka, one run by the shaman and the other by the tribal chiefs. Perhaps the north nogs had allied with one of these factions. It appeared that the whole noggish empire was breaking up, and taking the rest of the world with it. Whole tribes were involved in vast land grabs.

When a captured nog noble came in, taken by a daring group of Vegan scouts, right from his tent on the beach, we got all the information we needed. Far from what we were imagining, the situation was a lot worse. I was invited by Carris to sit in on the integration, and lend a magical hand. The noble freely told us, once I had threatened to cast some nasty spells on him, that all of nog were reunited. The usurper was dead, and the shaman had seized all the secular power from the remaining tribal chiefs. One shaman had risen above the rest to become the supreme primate, a war hero of many years, who had made his name at Usak, and risen through the ranks by intrigue and assassination. The thing in my head began to pulsate as I remembered Zort. The master mind behind the invasions was his right hand man and ambassador, terribly injured, but fuelled by hatred of humankind, and a desire to see them all dead or in chains. With the alliance now formed, every nog, from the highest shaman to the lowest foot soldier felt sure that all of Nillamandor could be conquered. They had also formed an alliance with the Lunarians which explained their recent attack on Enttland. Foona would fall in a matter of weeks, Tyria would follow, then Bellavia. At the same time the huge force here was to sweep through Vegas and take the lowland countries to the south and meet the other nog forces coming from the south in one gigantic pincer movement. It was very chilling stuff. I questioned him further on the subject of Zort. It appeared that Zort was quite willing to give the conquering of all the nations of human kind over to his commanders, while he searched for a lost noggish god demon. All contact with this god had been lost around the time of the conquering of Che. It was an unheard of thing, there were ten demon gods of nog, and one had never gone missing before. Sometimes they would take on bestial forms, like at Che, and walk amongst mortals. What was the god's name I asked? The noble did not know, it was forbidden for anyone other than shaman to know a god's name. After he had told me this, I had to go and have a lie down. I was overcome with fatigue and sweat broke out all over my body. I could feel the thing in my head pushing against the side of my skull. What had been that things name? It had begun with an 'A'. Agog? Agot? I had a feeling that if I knew the god's name I could exert some power over it. Who was to know back then that I would make such powerful enemies? I was willing to bet Zort knew exactly where I was, and other paranoid thoughts began to enter my head. It looked like Tup was still alive and in a strong position. I imagined he was still likely to be bearing me a grudge, after all, I had shot him twice. I tried to put aside the idea that this whole war was just a way of them getting their hands on me. From about then on, I stopped getting much sleep.

Within a few days, the forward spies were coming in reporting that a large nog force was moving towards Kolopa, and next day after that, they were visible, just, camped further down the valley. They didn't seem willing to attack just yet. That night, bright flashes could be seen in their camp, we couldn't work out what they were.

I walked back to the castle where our lodgings were. Although the streets were choked with a great number of tents, it was quite late at night so there weren't many people moving about. I traversed the main square, avoiding a group of drunken soldiers. As I passed, a bright blue light began to shine behind them. I turned round and looked at it in puzzlement. The soldiers also turned around, and began to back away from it as it expanded. There was a sudden cackling from the light, then a great many cries and shouts. The light opened, a group of Lunarians burst out and immediately charged at the soldiers. There was a brief scuffle, and each side lost about three men. The other Lunarians ran off into the town, and the soldiers gave chase. As they did so, a blue light began to form on the other side of the square, underneath an awning. Then I saw another, then another. Soon, the town was in chaos, as hundreds of Lunarians were teleported into the town. They were being killed very quickly. As I ran around, helping as I could, I estimated that the average Lunarians life expectancy was about three minutes. But it had the desired effect of drawing the defenders from the gates, so that when the main attack came, the cry of, "Ware the gates!' nearly came too late.

Suddenly I was in high demand. Carris himself summoned me, and I went to the main hall to meet him, the sounds of the desperate battle all around ringing in his ears.

I entered the castle, and was directed to the central tower, the tallest in the castle, that offered an excellent view of the whole town, where Carris had had himself positioned to survey the battle.

'Well my boy, it is good to see you again,' he nodded up at me.

The old man was propped up on a well-cushioned chair, his wounded arm done up in bandages against his chest. He was very pale, I thought he may be fevered, but tonight his blood was up.

He smiled at me and said, 'I am thinking of getting a repeal for the laws on witchcraft. Your services have been invaluable.'

'Thank you, my lord.'

There was cursing and swearing as a man was dragged up the stairs and brought onto the battlements. A guard approached the thane and said, 'My lord, what shall we do with this one?'

Carris looked at Nadia and said, 'Find a deep dungeon and throw him in it, no, on second thoughts, give him a spear and put him on the ramparts, he might as well make himself useful.'

'My lord!' protested Nadia. 'This is contrary to every law in the ...'

'Oh shut up,' scalded the thane. 'Take a look around, by the gods, my kingdom's fate is hanging in the balance,' and he gestured at the huge panorama of torch lit destruction all around us. The main gates were coming under heavy attack, but holding well. Siege towers were being drawn up against the north wall, and the defenders were raining hot oil down on them. Burning bundles of hay were being fired into the town from ballistas out on the plain, and many buildings were aflame. Blue sparks shone here and there, still, as more unwelcome guests from Lunar showed up.

Nadia cursed, and was lead away.

Carris looked at me, 'What can you do?'

'Well, I can do something about the fires...'

With the battle raged on well into the morning, the first thing I did was start the ritual to summon a rain cloud. It was quite a tricky spell, and I had never attempted it before, but I was willing to give it a try. It took a while to get everything prepared, the pentagram and the necessary ingredients. I then began to chant and gesture, as Carris and his guards looked on nervously. Eventually my chanting was done, and I stepped out of the circle, 'Right, that's it.'

Carris looked around, 'Nothings happening.'

'Give it a moment,' I said, and even as I spoke, the sky began to darken. The air took on the feeling of an approaching storm, and I felt a droplet of water hit my hand.

'You may need this my lord,' I said, as I opened my umbrella and handed it to him.

'Thank you,' he said graciously.

The heavens opened and a sudden deluge of rain hit the town, stunning everyone, but having the desired effect of quenching the areas that had been aflame. The battle took on a slower, muddier turn. I used up the last of my magical energy firing lightning bolts from the battlements at noggish and Lunarian targets as they presented themselves. I barely spared a thought for the men I was killing. During the battle, I caught glimpses of Carab, stoutly defending the gates, and rallying his troops to the breech. In the early morning, Apic came up to see me. By this time the rain had slackened off, but he was still drenched.

'How goes it Apic?' I said.

'Well. I was with Boris all night on the north wall. It got pretty hair raising, but each time they came, we beat them back. The Vegans fight like men possessed.'

'Boris is ok?'

'Yes. He has done well tonight, but he got a wound on his chest were a thrown rock hit him. Temina is taking him to the spital hut. Adea is with him as well. '

'Oh my god, Temina has been in the battle?'

'Yes. She dressed as a man, I couldn't stop her. I take it the rain was your doing?' he said changing the subject.

'That was me. I think they are beginning to accept that they will not take the town this night,' I said slowly, as we stood and watched the last of the attackers begin to retreat in the misty morning light. Their heart had not been in it for the last hour, despite the rallying cries of their commanders, and the day seemed to be ours.

Most of us were too tired to celebrate. News came in that it would still be three weeks before reinforcements from Ixnay arrived by land. It would have taken less by sea, but the Frost Sea was far too dangerous now. The troops would have to cross the bitter Axeblade Mountains, a difficult enough task even in high summer. It didn't give us much cheer, as reports came back of thousands more nogs landing on Gorgo and Loggarth we wondered if we would last that long.

Then good luck came, when an exhausted messenger arrived, dodging through the siege the next night, and reported that a combined mission from Enttland, Bellavia and Lodz had arrived from Bydgoszcz and had landed in Luxor two days ago, braving the Frost Sea, in a large fleet, and was travelling over land to Kolopa.

Thus the scene was set for the final battle. The siege had lasted over two weeks, and there was still a goodly supply of food, although the large amount of troops within the walls were eating tons of it a day. The siegers had thrown themselves at the walls again and again, and each time we threw them back, but at a cost. It was also heartbreaking to see the nog invaders turning the surrounding countryside into smouldering ruin.

The final battle was to be fought in these blackened fields of Lahtl. At that time, after three more unsuccessful attempts by the nog to take the city in the last two days, the command council estimated that the nogs had about thirty thousand warriors, and that there were still about ten thousand Lunarians, mainly camped on the other side of the river. Despite heavy casualties, there were still twenty thousand good strong Vegan warriors in Kolopa, and the combined allied mission on its way consisted of twenty thousand Enttish yeomen, five thousand Bellavian foot soldiers, and two thousand mounted hussars from Lodz.

It all started on the morning of the seventeenth day of the siege, with the allied reinforcements arriving on the Lahtl plains. The nearest invader to them was the Lunarian army, and a portion of it was sent off to meet them, charging into battle on their white ponies. A minor battle occurred, and the Lunar cavalry were repulsed. We watch all this from the battlements on the south wall, cheering on the Lodz lancers as they chased the Lunarians from the field. Almost immediately Carris decided to send a large Vegas force to sally forth to meet them, and the gates were opened. A noggish force in turn attacked. Soon, more and more troops were committed to the battle, as the day progressed, which centred around three farms in the valley. Some of this I learned about after the battle, some of it I witnessed first hand. The allied advance met the main body of the Lunarian army on the southern side of the river, and the fighting centred around the farm and mill right by the water. The Lunarians were no good at large manoeuvres though, and around one in the afternoon were finished as a fighting force, and their place was taken by noggish reinforcements. Carab, Apic, Boris and I rode onto the field at about three, and we ended up at the farm of Tallmount, which we defended for three hours, until the whole army was pulled back onto higher ground.

The farm was large and had stout walls. We joined a battalion of Vegan warriors, and a mixed brigade of Enttish yeomen and Lodz infantry regulars. The fighting was desperate, as the nog infantry tried again and again to take the farm. Each time, I was involved in the desperate hand to hand fighting on the walls. I lost sight of the others, but later Boris came to fight by my side, and told me the other two were helping defend the gates which had been piled high with overturned carts and bales of hay.

I was utterly exhausted from the fighting. My supply of magical power had been used up, and I was forced to use my staff to defend myself. I freely admit I am no fighter, and more than once I had to draw my revolver, and use one of my dwindling supply of bullets to defeat my foe. As Boris and I stood on the wall, watching the nog soldiers mill around in the woods, in a brief lull, Carab came up to us, and said, 'We move now. To the higher ground. Follow me.'

It all seemed to be organised chaos to me. I had no idea what was going on at all, I just followed the others as we jogged up the hill above the farm. We seemed to be joining other elements of the army, and everyone was frantically running around, trying to form up, back into their regiments. Commanders and captains were shouting orders everywhere, seemingly at random. It was six in the evening. I saw Boris rush past me, and grabbed him.

'Hey!' I cried at him, over the din of thousands of shouting men. 'Have you any idea what's going on?'

'We are cut off from Kolopa,' he shouted back in reply. 'The army is forming up to meet another noggish charge. It looks like the Lunarians have regrouped, and we are expecting a cavalry charge any minute. You can see them in the woods.'

I looked to where he pointed, but didn't see anything.

'Come on!' he said, and dragged me off. 'I'm with Apic and the Vegan royal guard.'

We rushed further up the hill. Order seemed to be slowly returning to the thousands of men on the hill. They were forming up into squares. I saw Apic in one of them, dwarfed by the tall warriors he was stood amongst, holding a pike twice his size. He gave me a little nervous wave. We joined him in the tight ranks of the square.

The din was beginning to quiet down. We were right on the flat top of the hill, there were no trees here, but all we could see from where we stood, was a patch of grass, and about twenty steps away, the grim faces of the men that forming the square opposite. Boris put his sword back in his scabbard, and picked up a discarded pike. Minutes dragged by, and the hill was silent, but for the muttering of nervous men. More time went past. Suddenly the silence was broken by a cry from further down the hill.

'Here they come!'

The ground began to vibrate, with the hoof beats of thousands of horses. I gulped, and tightened my grip on the pike that I had just picked up from the battlefield. The sound of the cavalry grew louder and louder, until I thought it might go on forever, would they ever get here? Then cries went up, and I heard terrible crashes, as the Lunarian cavalry met the squares lower down the hill. I strained to look, but I couldn't see anything.

Then they were everywhere, crazed Lunarian horsemen were charging right into our closed ranks and the battle became a mad crushed melee. At one point I had my head pressed right up against the flank of a horse, and tall Vegan warriors pushing into my back. Then the crush broke and I fell to the ground groaning. I realised I had no time to lie around and leapt up and grabbed a pike. It was chaos, the squares had broken, and the battle had dissolved into individual combats. I looked around, and dodged a sabre as a Lunarian horseman charged past me. Another went flying past, and without thinking I swept him from the saddle with my pike, then stamping on his chest I drove it right through him. My system was flowing with adrenaline, and I looked around for another enemy. A call went up, and the cavalry began to disengage, and flee back to their lines. They had been utterly destroyed as a force, dead riders and horses were everywhere. Noticing the carnage for the first time I was suddenly sickened. In some places the bodies were piled in drifts. In one hollow of the hill, it was as if the cavalry had charged right into it, and filled it with their bodies, at least ten deep, and overflowing at the top.

'Back into your squares!' someone shouted. 'Back into your bloody squares!'

I could barely hear him, my ears were ringing.

I looked for the Royal Guard and rejoined them. Boris and Apic looked dazed, but alive at least. There were a lot less people in the square this time. One of the warriors, a tall bearded fellow, whose mouth was a bloody from loosing some teeth in the battle, patted me on the back and I looked up at him and gave him a stupid smile.

For the second time that evening we stood and waited. Minutes rolled by. We rested wearily on our pikes.

Finally from the front someone called, 'The nog infantry is forming up in the valley!' and we all looked up.

Someone at the rear shouted, 'How many?'

There was a pause, then the reply came, 'All of them!'

Everyone started muttering nervously. One of the warriors by my side said, 'There are still twenty thousand of them! We will never hold them back, not after the last attack.'

No one seemed to want to contradict him.

Down in the valley, drums began to bang, and I heard the noggish army stir into life. Twenty thousand booted feet all marched in unison, and if the first cavalry charge had sent vibrations up the hill, then this was like an earthquake.

Someone at the front shouted, 'Here they come, form into lines!' I think it may have been Carab.

Everyone started bustling around, but soon our battalion had formed into a long line. All the other squares had formed into lines as well, and all we could see were the backs of the men standing in front of us. I felt dangerously exposed and had a quick look round. I cursed, when I realised, that as yet, no one was running away. Apic shot me a glance that suggested he had been thinking the same thing.

The sound of marching feet grew louder and louder. Our line crept slowly forward to look over the crest of the hill. It was a truly awesome and terrifying sight. Rank after rank of red coated noggish soldiers advanced up the churned up, ruined hill towards our remaining ragged forces, seemingly as unstoppable as the tide of the sea. Drums beat out a marching rhythm, and slowly they got closer and closer, each step shuddering across the battlefield. It was a good tactic, and it was certainly making my knees tremble. For the first time that day, the Lunarian guns roared into life, and to add to our troubles, as if we hadn't enough to worry about, we came under artillery fire. At first I saw the plumes of smoke rise from the trees in the lower valley. It took a second to dawn on me what they were and suddenly cannonballs were landing in our ranks, sending up great clods of earth and men. People started screaming. I crouched down. It was awful, you could actually see the balls come hurtling overhead, like black streaks of death. I knew a little bit about warfare from watching things like the Discovery Channel, and I knew that if we stayed where we were, the guns would decimate our forces in minutes. That meant either retreating, or getting under the guns. I looked down the hill, I could just make out Carab's head and shoulders, right at the front. He glanced round, to check the army was still behind him. I began to think again, as more cannonballs began to explode into the earth around us. Now, to get under the guns we would have to…

'Charge!' cried Carab, and suddenly everyone was rushing down the hill, like a tremendous human tidal wave.

I glanced at the terrified Apic and said, 'Oh no!'

I grabbed Boris, who would have been off like a rabbit, straight at the enemy, otherwise.

'No,' I shouted frantically, utter coward that I was, 'For the sake of our mothers. Hang back a little.'

'Shiv!' cried Boris, as a ball whizzed right past us, cutting a warrior in two where he stood in a shower of blood and vitals. 'We are no safer here!'

That was true, I admitted, and screaming like a mad man, I raised up my pike and joined the charge.

There was a huge crush at the front, where the leading ranks were being pushed onto the enemy by those behind. It looked like butchery. Then I lost sight of the front line as we came down the hill, and all I could see were the backs of the men in front of me. I got that, 'at the back of the concert and can't see a thing', feeling again, and I was nearly growing tired of inaction, when the lines began to break, and as if a curtain had been drawn back, I saw the horde of the noggish army right in front of me. I screeched to a halt. They looked haggard and battle weary, but still stronger than us. Bodies of both forces lay everywhere. I looked around to see what was going on. To my surprise, everyone was retreating,

'Don't just stand there like an idiot!' cried Apic at me. 'That's it, it's all over!'

I turned on my heels, and joined the panicked rout. The nogs gave a massive cheer and rushed to follow us. I could here a group of them panting up the hill behind us, no more than ten strides away.

As we crested the hill again, I saw that our army had totally broken. Everywhere, men were running for their lives, in random directions. Panic and fear began to grip my heart. So it was all over. With the battle lost, Kolopa would fall, and what then? This was just another leather booted noggish step towards total domination of mankind by their evil tyranny. Seeing the futility of thinking about such things, I tried not to worry about anything other than saving my own skin, which might well prove to be difficult enough, I feared.

As we ran on, I caught a glimpse of a vast dark shape on the northern side of the valley.

'Look Apic! Look! What's that?'

I looked like a massive army was descending into the valley.

'Reinforcements,' he gasped. 'But ours or theirs?'

'It has to be ours! Has to be!'

And indeed it was, and just in the nick of time. As the noggish army was sweeping us from the field, the long awaited reinforcements from Ixnay had arrived. Many of the original army stopped in their mad flight, and joined the fresh army as it took to the field, just as the sun was beginning to set. I had seen enough for one day though, and Apic and Boris needed no great persuasion to find somewhere quiet to sit down and watch the rest of the battle. The nog were swept from the field like chaff. They had fought a hard battle all day, and had nothing left to give. Soon, they were the ones being routed. They had been so close to victory, and now the Vegans were chasing them back down the valley. By the time night had fallen, there was nothing left to see.

'They have probably chased them right back to the coast.' commented Boris.

I stood up and said, 'Well I don't know about you two, but I fancy a bed tonight. Let's get back to the town and report in.'

Wearily we joined the ranks of tired warriors and trudged back to the city gates. Coming the other way, auxiliary forces gathered to attend to the battle field. Through eyes glazed with utter exhaustion I watched as the grave diggers piled the noggish bodies into funeral pyres. The bodies of fallen humans were taken away by their own forces to be disposed of as was the custom of each force. Other camp followers gathered weapons together and other equipment, or rounded up stray horses. And yet other, less official people, beggars and starving mendicants went from body to body looting.

A few hours later, more rested, we gathered on the battlements of the city gates, to watch the huge pyres burning in the night. We drank hot mulled wine. I gave Apic a meaningful look, but he didn't say anything. Adea came up the stairs and put her arm around Carab who handed her a cup of wine. I don't remember falling asleep, on the cold stone firing step on the battlement, but I awoke the next day in my own warm bed.

As always, Heather had been absorbed by Yarn's story telling, and it took her a little while to land back in reality, and collect her thoughts.

She smiled at Yarn, and had a look on her face as if she was trying to say something.

'Out with it, Doctor,' he encouraged.

'You know what I'm going to say. About your past. And about your family.'

Yarn nodded, then seemed to ponder what he was going to say next.

'Listen,' he said finally. 'I can't. It's too dangerous. I have forgotten them, and they have forgotten me. Everything I know, the thing in my head knows, and if I remember them, I will put them in danger. Every time I catch myself remembering my past, I make myself stop. It's trying to catch me out. Trying to make me give myself away. Each day it takes more of my strength to hold it in check.'

Heather looked at him taken aback. I have to keep reminding myself of how deluded he really is, she thought to herself, he's only one step away from a dreadful psychotic episode.

Yarn sighed, and said, 'I know what you think. You think I'm off my rocker. I don't blame you. If I were in your situation, I would too.'

'Yarn, it's not that I don't...'

'That's ok,' he interrupted. 'Just do me one favour. One way or the other, my story is going to come to an end soon. Will you at least hear me out? After that I will do what ever you want.'

'Of course,' she replied, and took his hand reassuringly. 'Anyway, what a battle. You must have been terrified.'

'You're kidding?' he said and laughed, all too willing to change the subject. 'I was bricking it. The whole day was one long horror show. Like being stuck on a roller coaster for ten hours.'

'Were you injured?'

'Not a scratch. Amazing really, all day, in that mass of destruction, and not a single scratch. Apic had a bruise from a horse's kick, and Boris had a small sword wound. Carab was a mass of cuts and bruises. Nope, I got off lucky. Not like Julgia.'

Yarn suddenly pulled up his T-shirt, and pointed to a two inch scar just above his heart.

'Look what that git did to me!' he exclaimed.

Heather was too shocked to say anything, and even had to touch it, to make sure it was real.

'Still hurts sometimes,' said Yarn. 'When it's wet or cold. It went right into me you know. Lodged in a rib at the back.'

Heather was dumfounded as she examined the scar. In her medical opinion it looked exactly as Yarn described it. A wound from a sword thrust.

'Incredible,' she said. 'How did you get this?'

Yarn looked at her like she was stupid.

'Oh yes. I'm sorry,' she apologised sheepishly.

'Honestly,' said Yarn, and pulled his shirt back down.

Chapter Eighteen - Pechenga

We celebrated the victory, and the expulsion of the invaders from Vegan shores in a series of festivals and feasts. Kolopa took on an almost carnival atmosphere, and the task or rebuilding the town was delayed, I think no one had the courage to face it, such was the destruction. I've never known anything like it, the party went on for three nights solid. Everyone seemed so elated just to be alive. It wasn't long before our timely allies had to leave though, to defend their own lands, and a series of processions were given to offer them a fond farewell on their march back to Luxor and the boats that awaited them.

I think Carris was beginning to soften towards the idea of Carab and Adea's marriage as he gave him permission for them to travel to Ixnay and put their case before the king. As Carab had been a real hero in the battle of Kolopa, we didn't see how he could be refused.

Troops were moving, and great wheels were in motion. I wondered if this was what world war two had felt like to my grandparents. To be caught up in such vast events. To feel like a very small entity, caught up in an incomprehensible war between nations. The whole of Vegas took on a martial aspect. Everyone was geared up for the war. Everywhere troops were in movement, usually from east to west, to defend the coastlines. Others were being sent further afield, to help defend the southern nations. What can one man do amongst such turmoil, with hundreds of people fighting and dying on battlefields up and down the length and breadth of Nillamandor? Carab's father was in his war room every day planning with his commanders and sending and receiving reports from Ixnay. As we set off, he pressed a bundle of papers into Carab's hands to be presented to the king on our arrival.

We set off, Carab, Adea, Temina, Boris, Apic and I, as we always travelled, on horseback and as a unit. Over the last few months we had learned to live together quite happily, and each person had their own role to perform in the setting up of camp. Carris had provided us with clothing more suited to the northern climate, and warm sealskin tents.

We travelled north, across the fertile valleys of Lahtl and then spent three days crossing the inhospitable Axeblade Mountains. There were warm bothies every ten miles across the pass, so we always had somewhere to stay at night, although the chill wind ever seemed to find a way in. Summer was ending, so the pass was quiet. If this had been a normal year we would have quite possibly been the last to use the pass, but as it was, poor cold messengers would be back and forth over the icy mountains all winter. From there we entered the thraldom of Orebro, an area of cool forests and salty marshes, sparsely populated by stockade surrounded villages. The people here were even hardier than the people of Lahtl, and had lighter complexions. A week later we crossed the mighty Borat River on a low stone bridge, although we had to wait for a regiment of Ixnay warriors to cross first, coming in the other direction. Finally we crossed Malbro, a thraldom of low mountains and forested valleys, and populated by woodsmen and hunters. There were a great many forest villages in this region, and we always managed to find an inn to stay in. A week later we were in the capital of Vegas, Ixnay.

Ixnay was far, far larger than Kolopa, but not as big as Werfen. It was a winter city. There was no snow yet, but it wasn't far away. It lay on the surrounding mountains, like a sleeping serpent, waiting for the time, when it would hold the city once more in its frozen coils. It was a colourful city also, the onion domes of its towers were inlaid with brightly coloured stone, giving it an almost fairytale appearance. Against the backdrop of the white mountains it was quite charming. It lay on the banks of the Mu River, right on the coast. It was the largest port this far north, and it would be a while before the estuary froze over. Hundreds of sea vessels wintered here. We arrived in the afternoon and rode right up to the King's palace, a large many domed impressive structure, in the centre of a wide square. Carab did not delay in meeting with King Turku and presenting him with the papers he had been entrusted with. I caught a glimpse of the king from the back of the throne room. I had expected him to be a doddery old man, but he was tall and looked strong, although obviously in his sixties.

Several days passed, as Carab met with the King, and plans were made. I had no idea what was going on as I was never invited to any of the meeting and no one but Adea saw much of Carab. We were all given very pleasant accommodation within the palace grounds, a six bedroomed cottage behind the south wall. I quickly found a large library within the city, and I discovered to my delight that Ixnay was quite a centre of learning. I spent my time researching the spell I would have to cast when I got further north. Apic, Boris and Temina spend their time drinking in some of the city's taverns. I don't think any of them ever had to buy a drink themselves. Everyone wanted to know what had happened to the south, and as heroes of the battle of Kolopa they were in hot demand. Adea would help me in the library sometimes or drift off to explore the city. With her boyfriend busy she had to resort to my company, not wishing to join the drunken revelry of the others.

There were some lovely baths beside the palace, very close to our cottage and one night, the fourth since we had been in the city I went to visit them, as I had done every night since we had arrived.
After entering the round stone building and undressing, I let out a great sigh of relaxation, and eased my way into a steaming hot tub.
The stonewalled hall I was in was dark, but lit with lanterns. Steam drifted amongst the many water tubs, and pools. A small aqueduct ran the entire

length of the room, and warm water could be siphoned off from it, by copper pipes, straight to each of the tubs. Cold water could be drained out of the tubs into gutters cut into the stone floor. The large bath hall did have the look of some sort of plumber's nightmare, but it was an ingenious system and I was most impressed. The water was even treated with something to take away the smell of sulphur. To me it smelled of camomile.

I was leaning back with my eyes shut. I could her Vegan voices in the background, speaking that odd language of theirs, but I had chosen a quiet corner. After a while I was woken up by Carab's voice close to my ear.

'Be careful you don't fall asleep and drown,' he advised.

'Oh. Hello. How as it been going with the king?' I inquired.

'Well. The war goes as well as can be expected. The nog have taken many of the ports in west Nillamandor, but Tullis still stands. There is still a sizeable noggish force in Gorgo. With the help of the gods we will drive them out.'

'That's interesting, but I meant for you and Adea.'

'Oh. I mentioned it briefly. I think he will allow it, but he has a lot more important matters on his mind right now.'

'I suppose so. You may as well get married. There is a war on, and at times like these, who knows what tomorrow holds.'

Carab shrugged in agreement, and leaning on the rim of the tub, he splashed his hand idly in the water.

'That's nice and warm.'

'Get in if you like.'

Carab disrobed, and neatly folded his clothes and put them on a nearby bench. We were not alone long, when Adea showed up, wearing nothing but a towel.

'Oh, it looks like you fellows had the same idea,' she said as she spotted us. 'Boris is on his way.'

She nodded her head in appreciation at the bath house and said, 'I'm going to enjoy this.'

I was startled beyond words as she removed her towel and climbed the ladder and hopped into the tub beside us.

'Adea! You're naked!' I exclaimed.

'Oh do shut up, Shiv,' she said and splashed water at me. I supposed over the last few months, what with travelling together, her social inhibitions had been eroded a little. It didn't stop me feeling uneasy at the sight of her bare breasts though.

Moment's later Boris was there too, and he rushed up the ladder, laughed, and dive bombed into the centre of the tub, sending a great splash everywhere. Adea tussled her cousin's hair as he came up for air with a big grin on his face.

'Good evening everyone,' he said.

'Anyone know where Apic and Temmy are?' I asked the assembly.

'In their rooms I think,' replied Adea.

I sent a servant out to get them.

'Right. Now that the gang is all here,' I said to everyone. 'I wish to discuss something.'
Apic and Temina arrived fully clothed. I wasn't surprised by Apic throwing off his and joining us, there was room for twenty in this tub, but I was surprised by Temina getting undressed, completely unabashed, and hopping straight in as well. I supposed I was the only prude present.
'I want to get to Pik Sedova as soon as possible.'
The lands beyond Vegas to the north were mostly a wilderness called Pechenga. There was a ruined city on the north coast, right on the arctic circle, called Pik Sedova. From what information I had gathered over the last few weeks it was an ideal place for me to cast my spell of returning.
'It is probably best that I go myself, maybe with a guide. I don't know if maybe some of you want to come with me....'
The others exchanged knowing looks with each other.
'It's probably a fools errand anyway, and I know there is a war...'
'Oh do shut up Shiv,' said Adea for the second time that night. 'We are all coming with you. You wouldn't last five minutes on your own.'
'All of you?'
Everyone was nodding. Boris said, 'We've come this far.'
Carab said, 'You will need me. I travelled into Pechenga when I was young. It is a cold and hostile place.'
I looked at them all, and sized up their reasons for deciding to come with me. Apic and Carab for friendship. Adea, the desire to be in the same place as Carab. Boris for adventure. And Temina, for what? Probably simply because she didn't want to be left out.
I nodded and settled back in the water, 'That's settled then, I hope you guys know what you're letting yourselves in for, that's all.'

We stayed three more days in Ixnay, preparing for our arctic trek, then one chilly morning we set off. No one had anyone to say goodbye to. The king had equipped us well, with warm winter furs, a large six-man tent, and provisions for the journey, but I never met him in person to thank him. The city was more like a massive marshalling yard for the Vegan army. We travelled through the northernmost province of Vegas, the thraldom of Miruma. The road was quiet, and the land was cool, but peaceful. Each night we had a warm inn to sleep in until we reached the small town of Dyxnat, right on the border.
I asked the landlord about the road ahead, and what inns we might find.
'This is it my friend,' he replied. 'There isn't anything further north than this. Just savages and wolves.'
We had reached the edge of civilisation yet again.

And so it was then, that we finally, entered the wild lands of Pechenga and travelled further north into the arctic circle. The snows were coming, and it would only get colder the further north we travelled. I don't think the horses thought much of the terrain we were now entering. They had warm blankets for the night time though, and plenty to eat. We had six pack horses with us to carry food for us and the animals.

There were mountains far to our east, and each day we travelled, we must have gained a hundred feet in height, on the gently sloping terrain, and each day the air got cooler. There was a strong chill wind, and it always seemed to be against us. The land was flat, besides the steady incline, and utterly swept of life by the blighting wind. Even the rocks were flat and round, as if crouching from the wind and small brown grass grew in between them.

For the first two weeks, one day was much the same as any other, expect maybe a little shorter. There was no trail to follow, but Carab seemed to know where we were going. Each crisp morning, we would rise, and throwing off out thick fur blankets, would get dressed in the tent. The tent itself was of a most excellent design. It was made of waxed sealskin, so it was waterproof, and very light. It was high enough for someone to stand in the middle, but not so high I would have called it a tee-pee. It was domed in the middle like a yurt. There was a flap at the top that could be opened up to let smoke out, if we decided to light a fire in the middle, which we usually did. This meant that the tent would soon get very cosy and we could strip off some of our innumerable layers of clothes. Once we and all our gear were in the tent there wasn't much room for anything else, but no one considered the snugness of the tent a problem. After we had dressed, two of us would take down the tent, and pack it up onto one of the baggage horses. Two others would boil water for the tea, and prepare breakfast for everyone else, while the last two took off the horses' blankets, rubbed them down and got their saddles on for the ride ahead. Who did what was usually decided by bickering, along the lines of,

'I took the tent down yesterday, it's my turn to make tea.'

'You liar! You just want to sit by the fire. It's your turn to do the horses.'

'No, Boris and me did that the night before last, your trying to weasel out of taking your turn!'

At some point in the morning, Carab would gaze up at the surrounding mountains to get his bearings, and once he was satisfied, we would set off once more.

Then the days travelling would begin, which always felt like a slow uphill climb. Eventually the land did level out and we reached a plateau. But soon after that we were right in the mountains, and we hit the snow line. It really felt like we were on the roof of the world. Snow drifted in the valleys we crossed through, and we were right underneath the peaks of the mountains. We usually stopped for about an hour in the afternoon, to have something to eat, and let the horses breathe for a while, and then it was on until late evening, and the first of the stars were beginning to come out. Then the whole camping process would be reversed. The tent would be put up, the horses put to bed, and the evening meal was prepared. Supply wise, we were doing quite well. We had plenty of provisions, dried meat, dried fruit and herbs, tough traveller's bread, warm Vegan vodka, and hard honey biscuits. We were never short of fresh meat, as long as you only wanted rabbit or pigeon, as I could produce them on command. Once we had eaten our dinner we would talk for a while, just visible to each other as shadows, from the light of the small fire in the middle of the tent. Or sometimes we would play chess on the set that Dombaba had given me. Usually though we would just talk about the places we had been and the people we had met. This to me was the best part of the day. As the wind blew outside we sat in the warmth of the tent, and told stories and jokes, until one by one, we nestled into our furs and drifted off to sleep.

As we progressed northwards the days got shorter and shorter, causing problems for us if there was no moon. The first two weeks of the month we had no option but to camp early, as to ride on in darkness would be madness. But as the moon grew larger, Carab assured us it would give us enough light to travel by and he seemed to be proved right as we encountered no greater difficulty than travelling by day. As the brief day ended, the moon would loom in the sky and cast its eerie shadows across the blasted landscape. We cast long black shadows against the snow, and no sound could be heard other than the breathing of the horses and the crunch crunch crunch of their hooves on the snow. We may as well have been on the surface of the moon, it felt so airless and quiet when the wind died down.

Over glaciers and high mountain ranges we travelled, for weeks across the trackless wastes and tall forests of sturdy pine. As we headed for the ancient ruins of Pik Sedova, I sometimes thought of what may be waiting for us. Carab described it as a legendary and mystery shrouded place, once home to a proud race of northmen, but abandoned for hundreds of years. One of the things known about this place was that it was dark for one month in the winter. The more we travelled north, the uneasier everyone became. It started so softly that at first I didn't notice it, but after awhile, I realised everyone was a lot quieter, and what had started off as a jolly adventure up into the mountains had turned into something else. Perhaps it was because we were so far away from civilisation or perhaps it was because now we were getting no more than four hours daylight.

Or maybe because the sombre mountains made us feel insignificant in some way. The going was getting a lot harder, that was for sure. It would often snow, and the nights were getting much colder as well as longer. The amount of distance we covered each day had nearly halved as well, as the terrain got harder to traverse.

Sometimes the thing in my head, whatever it was, demon, god, goose egg, I know not, would start to throb for no real reason, and I got the strongest feeling that I was under observation. This went on for the entire journey, especially at night. The throbbing would begin, and I would be distracted from whatever I was doing, whether it was tightening a horse's harness, or serving out breakfast. If someone asked me what the matter was I would shake my head, as if to try and dislodge it, and then shrug my shoulders and smile.

One night we were camped as always in our sealskin waxed tent, a fire lit in the middle, with the smoke escaping through the flap in the top. I was beginning to nod off, although Apic and Carab were still in conversation, and as I drifted off to sleep, I felt the throbbing again, and like someone opening the page of a picture book, Zort appeared before me.

'Give back what is not yours,' he demanded quietly.

I was so confused and fearful, that I couldn't say anything.

'Give back what is not yours,' he repeated.

'I am afraid you will kill me,' I answered.

'I will follow you anywhere, you cannot hide. Give it to me, and I will spare your friends.'

I shook my head, trying to wake up.

'Go away Zort, this is pointless,' I said, getting my bearings, and beginning to get angry.

'Jelliar and Juste curse you, human, how much more trouble can you cause? I know more about you than you may think. I can tell you things. Things about how you come to be here.'

'No, Zort, I'm not interested, I'm going to do things my way, you should know that. How long have you been in my mind?'

'For a long time. You cannot hide. I know where you are, like I know where my right arm is.'

I almost felt a strange closeness to Zort then, he may have been a mad monstrous dictator, but he had a single-mindedness of purpose, and a deep loneliness that I could relate to.

With one strong mental heave, I pushed Zort from my mind.

'Goodbye,' I said, and woke up.

I discussed it with everyone first thing in the morning, naturally, and we agreed to carry on, what else could we do? Zort was in Pechenga somewhere. It was hard to imagine how many warriors he could have gotten onto the continent, after the defeat at Kolopa, but they were behind us somewhere.

'This is a concern,' said Carab as he pondered the situation.

'That's an understatement,' agreed Apic.

We were eating our breakfast, although we had all mostly stopped while this conversation went on.

'Can't you do something, you know...' Temina waved her fingers around in front of her '...magical, to stop him.'

'I don't think so. My magic doesn't work like that. I would have to know a specific spell.'

'What I don't understand is,' said Boris, joining the conversation. 'Why he is coming himself. With a huge war going on, you'd think he would have enough to do, without having to track us down as well.'

I nodded, 'I suppose it's a prestige thing. He is the head of the church after all. If they all think I've stolen one of their gods, then I guess it's up to the high primate to get it back.'

They all looked at me silently.

'What?' I cried. 'You're all looking at me like my head is about to explode! It's all nonsense, I haven't got a demon in my brain. I feel fine!'

'Easy now,' said Adea. 'We are all worried that's all.'

I couldn't help myself, but I was getting very anxious and angry.

'Yeah, worried about your own skins! How do you think I feel, it's me they're after!'

I stood up and was shaking so much, I was spilling my tea.

'I've been pushed from pillar to post for years. Everyone wants something from me! Oh, Shiv save us! Cast a spell to make it all better! It's all very well if you want something, but if I'm not needed I get slung in prison. Go here, go there....I ....I,' I suddenly realised I was making a spectacle of myself. Everyone looked down at their mugs. Even Carab was speechless.

'I'm sorry,' I said more softly. 'I'm a bit on edge. Listen, if anyone wants to turn back, then of course I won't stop them. If I manage to make it through the portal though, Zort will have nothing else to do but go home...'

Apic stood up and gripped my arm, 'We are all with you Shiv. Besides, we can't turn back with Zort right behind us, you idiot! Look at the mess you've got us all into now.'

I looked at him, but he was smiling. Carab was shaking with laughter and holding his face in his hands. This unusual sight was making the others smile.

'You're right,' I admitted. 'This is all my fault. I will do my best to get us out of it though. You all trust me don't you?'

Carab threw a biscuit at me.

As Zort and I began to tune into each other's wavelength, the spying became a two-way thing. He could see us, but I could see him. At one point I'm sure they were only a day or two behind us. One night, in a startling vision, I suddenly saw them, Zort and about two dozen nogs, too many for us to fight, but they were poorly equipped and on foot. They looked utterly dejected, their uniforms were little better than rags, and they had piles of blankets draped over their weary shoulders. The only one who looked to have any energy was Zort, who was right at the front of their line, with a look of insane zeal on his face. The nog were essentially a southern race, and this climate ill suited them. I think there may well have been a lot more of them when they had set off. I reported this all to the others, and they nodded in grim satisfaction. Carab rubbed his chin.

'They can't be enjoying it up here too much.'

Apic laughed grimly, 'With all that fur, you'd think they'd be ok.'

Later that night I saw that Apic was doing something a little way off from the tent, near a snow bank. I wandered over to him in the evening gloom.

'What are you doing?' I asked.

'Building a snowman.'
I looked at his construction. It was a very obscene representation of a nog.
'This should be a pleasant surprise for them when they come this way!'
I laughed, which drew Boris over, and together we made three noggish
snowmen, or snownog I suppose, each more obscenely deformed and
hilarious (to us), than the last. Our giggles drew everyone over eventually,
and before we went to our beds, we left quite a large group of snownog to
wait for Zort. The humour that night around the fire was very ribald.
'I can just picture his face when he sees them!' I laughed.
'I bet he kicks them all over,' put in Apic.
'Yeah, or maybe he'll think they are an ambush and attack them!'
commented Boris.
Carab lay back and laughed occasionally as we went on. Even Adea and
Temina joined in our childishness for a while, until Carab finally said,
'We should sleep though. It is late, and we want to keep as much distance
between us and them as possible.'

A few days after my vision, as we crossed over the saddle of a low
mountain ridge, we caught a glimpse of them, far off in the distance, tiny
black specks on a white snowfield.
We were getting more desperate in our flight away from them now, as the
moonlight started to fade, we soon would have no light at all by which to
travel, and would be faced with the unsavoury prospect of travelling in utter
darkness.
We descended into the wooded valley on the other side of the ridge, and
they were lost from sight. It was late in the afternoon, as we entered the
dense forest on the valley floor and the first mists began to settle. This lent
the cold, snow covered forest a very eerie appearance, as tendrils of fog
drifted between the low branches of the trees. Gradually the forest got
denser, until we were forced to dismount and lead the horses.
As we travelled onwards Carab suggested we gather branches to make
torches from to light our way if the necessity came to travel by a moonless
night, the next being two days hence, or so he assured us.
As always, Temina was in the lead, and I looked up as I heard her let out a
startled yelp.
There was a band of tall men right up ahead, and more were silently
moving between the trees around us. They wore wolf furs, and many wore
the dead wolf's head on top of their own. I watched nervously as they
surrounded us. They carried long hunting spears, and seemed to be all
taller than average men, there wasn't one under six feet. They all had
slightly piggish faces, and mouths full of spiky teeth. They stood well
enough away from us to be out of sword range, and there seemed to be
about fifty of them, male and female.
'They are gort,' said Carab beside me.
I tried to remember what a gort was, then it hit me, and I remembered
Carab telling me about them two years ago in the Great Forest. They were

a race of beings half man, and half nog. No wonder they looked so ugly and pissed off. They must have exiled themselves up here to get away from all the racial hatred further south. I couldn't imagine mankind or nogkind accepting these half casts.

I handed my horse to Carab, and went up to the front were Temina was. One of the gort, possibly a leader as he wore an eagle feather in his hair, was shouting in a strange language and shaking his spear at her. I cast the spell that allows me to understand and speak another's language.

'….step away from being boiled alive and eaten. If the chief was here, your heads would be on spikes by now, and another thing…'

'Excuse me?' I asked, waving to get his attention. This surprised him and shut him up for a few seconds.

He then tentatively said, 'You speak the language of the Pechenga-Gort, how is this so?'

'I am a mighty sorcerer,' I admitted.

He nodded at this sagely. The others began to mutter between themselves, until one of them shoved their spokesman forward with a push, eagle-feather snorted at his ill-mannered companions, then turned to me and asked, 'Why are you in our forest?'

'We didn't know it was yours. We are just passing through.'

'This is gort land. You are not welcome.'

I looked behind me at the others, to them this was all 'Wabba-wabba-wabba'.

'I'm very sorry, we don't want a fight, we just want to pass through.'

The spokesman considered this, then said, 'What can you give us?'

I looked around at Apic, and said, 'Get my pack, quickly!' and he ran off to get it.

In a moment I was rummaging through me pack.

'Let me see…aha!'

I took out a Swiss army knife and handed it to him. He snatched it from my hand, and took it over to the others to look at it. There was much muttering and gasps. Eventually he came back over and said,

'This is good. We take this and that,' he said pointing. '… and you may go.'

I looked at where he was pointing.

'The pack itself?' I said. 'Ok then. Not the stuff in it?'

He shook is head, 'Our chief will be happy.'

'Ok,' I said, and started taking my stuff out of the pack, and putting it into a bag.

After that we were all great friends, and they even escorted us to the other side of the forest, and waved us on our way. As we set off I said to eagle-feather, 'Some nog warriors will be here within a day or so.'

He nodded, 'Thank you for the warning.'

I hoped they prepared a nice warm reception for Zort. I doubted that he would deal with them as diplomatically as I had.

From there we had several more weeks of travel still ahead of us. But I never once had a vision concerning Zort, and I hoped that he and all his travelling companions had met their end at the point of a gort spear. I doubted my luck was that good though. If the going had been bad before, it doubled in adversity now. The weather got worse, the days got shorter still, and the temperature dropped by ten degrees. Increasingly we travelled in darkness, lit only by our meagre torches, but if the wind got up we would have no option but to draw camp earlier than desired, then cower in the tent and wonder how far away the nogs were and how much advantage they were gaining. Eventually though, the moon started to return and there was no longer a need for torches.

Chestnut, despite being the most molly coddled horse in our group, had gotten a bad chest infection, and if the journey had been any longer I think she would have died. Two of the packhorses had already died, which was a great loss, as the load had to be redistributed. Pragmatically we cut the meat from their bodies and dried it by the fire for rations. Adea and Temina were absolute troopers. At the beginning they had done nothing but bitch and moan, but when the daunting scale and seriousness of the situation dawned on them, they knuckled down to it, and were invaluable in the camp as menders and darners. Apic was the worst effected by the cold I think. I had warned him over and over again about frost bite, but he had still managed to lose three toes on the journey. He was having a dreadful time, and I felt so guilty because the only reason he was here was out of loyalty to me. Carab the true north man, was faring very well, in fact I think if everyone else wasn't so miserable, he would have admitted that he was having a great time. This was just the sort of adventure he used to get up to with his cousins when he was a lad. Boris, well, Boris had retreated into himself, out of everything, he only really talked to Adea. I don't think he was enjoying himself much anymore.

Just when I was beginning to imagine that all life held for me now was endless trekking across an arctic landscape, we sighted Pik Sedova, and not before time as well. I slapped Carab on his broad back, and cried, 'You got us here in the end!'

'Did you ever doubt it?' he replied.

Pik Sedova had once been a northern seaport, the harbour wasn't fully iced over yet. The town was in a natural shelter, with mountains all around the bay. We descended into town by an ancient road that cut a pass through the mountain ridge, just as it approached evening, the day not lasting much more than two hours.

We looked around at the broken snow crowded streets, I don't think anyone could conceive that we were out of the white wilderness and back in something like civilisation again. An ancient, ruined civilisation, but this was the first thing we had seen that had been touched by man in months. It was getting dark, so we spent the last remaining hour of light making a quick reconnaissance of the city.

Most of the remaining buildings were nothing but piles of rubble, but part of what had once been a castle still stood, all of a wing, and there were many rooms that were still inhabitable. One of the amazing features of the castle was the hundreds of rusty suits of armour, that lay collapsed in the corridors, or still stood, stiffly rusted together in a four hundred year pose. There was one room in particular that looked like a storeroom for them, it had a creepy air, like a terra-cotta army, waiting to be summoned into life. I found a warm room and lit a fire. The others began to bring in gear, no one was speaking, I think they were all looking forward to their first warm night in weeks, Adea muttered about boiling some water for a bath. I sat down by the fire and opened one of my many spell books.

When I next looked up, I had to smile at the domestic scene that was in front of me. I had not noticed, but there had been the steady hum of friendly conversation for quite some time. The room was almost unbearably warm. I loosened my shirt. There was Adea, dressed in nothing but a towel, Temina drying her hair for her. Carab was washing himself in a decrepit wash tub, as I watched he took out a sock, rung it out, and laid it on the side of the bath to dry. Behind him was a line with a display of washing on it. Apic was all but naked, right by the fire in front of me, examining his feet with a frown on his face. Boris lay on an ancient chez-lounge, with his boots off and his head tilted back, blissfully smoking a cigar.
'What are you laughing at?' said Apic as he smiled and looked up at me.
'You guys,' I said with a twinkle in my eye. 'Gods, I'm going to miss you guys.'

'Sorry I'm late guys, clinic dragged on and on this afternoon … oh.', Dr Barage said, as he entered Mr. Hood's office.
Unlike his own, this one was immaculately tidy, with papers sorted neatly into folders and stacked on shelves. Dr. Lock and Mr. Hood sat at either side of the small conference table glaring at each other. He could tell by the look on Heather's face that they had been having words. There was a Dictaphone beside Heather's elbow.
Mr. Hood leapt up from his chair, so that Dr. Barage could get past and drop a bundle of patient's notes on the table.
'No need to ask who you two have been discussing then,' he asked innocently.
'Ah yes…Ian.. I'm sorry, that man needs an operation. Having listened to his last, instalment, shall we say, has just confirmed what I believe.'
Heather said nothing, and just glared at Hood. Dr. Barage sat down and clasped his hands thoughtfully.
'I don't necessarily need your permission to operate either,' continued Hood. 'I think, Heather, you have let your personal regard for the patient

sway you away from what is best for him. Ian, I believe you haven't managed to get a single word out of him, is that right?'

'Well, no, Terry,' Barage agreed grudgingly. 'But with Heather we had been making progress. He is definitely leading up to something with this story of his.'

'What nonsense!' snorted Hood. 'He will just string it along indefinitely. The simple fact of the matter is that without a major debulking of the tumour he will die in less than six months. The fact that he is suffering from these fantasies is clear indication that he has lost the ability to reason for himself.'

'There is such a thing as patient consent, Terry,' said Ian.

'Which we can bypass given the circumstances. I know I won't get Heather's consent, but I would at least like to get yours Ian. As I said, I don't actually need it...'

'Listen to this, Ian, this is the best bit,' interrupted Heather.

'...actually need it,' continued Hood. 'I have gone to the Directors with this, they have agreed to back me a hundred percent.'

'Oh Terry,' sighed Ian, who could smell another scandal. 'After last time? You really want to get your name in the papers again that badly?'

'Now, Ian, that was a completely different case. Mrs. Opal had a daughter, and it was her that caused all the fuss. As far as I know, this Yarn character has no family at all.'

'But he does,' interrupted Heather again.

'None that realise he is alive. I only know what you have told me Heather, that policeman has decided to sit on the files hasn't he?'

'Nothing has been decided yet,' muttered Heather.

'Be that as it may,' continued Hood. 'The time for decisive action is now. Are you going to back me on this Ian?'

'Well...' said Dr. Barage, glancing at Heather nervously.

Heather stood up and said, 'I can't stand this anymore. Ian you side with him, and I'll never talk to you again, and if you,' she shot an acidic glance at Hood, 'operate on Yarn, I'll go to the papers myself. Goodbye.'

With that, she left the room. The men sat in silence for a second, then Mr. Hood eventually said, 'As I understand it, Heather hasn't had a, ahem... partner for quite a few years now.'

'Oh Terry, don't try and read things into it,' said Dr. Barage, and sighed in resignation. 'You know she is a complete professional.'

'Still,' shrugged Hood. 'I've never seen her like that before over a patient.'

Chapter Nineteen - Pik Sedova

On the afternoon of the second day of our stay in Pik Sedova, Carab and I had a look round the ruins, to see how the land lay and to see if there were any possible dangers. Adea and Boris were back at the castle sorting through our supplies, and Apic and Temina had decided to take a ride round the surrounding forests for similar reasons to ours. Most of the remains were just low walls and piles of rubble, but towards the centre of the town, where the larger civic buildings had been, there were still some intact structures. Most of the west side and all the edges of the town had been overgrown by the surrounding forests and snow lay in drifts against any vertical object. As we walked around the silent square, where the most impressive of the buildings had been, we began to appreciate what a pleasant city it once was.

'Look over their Carab,' I said, and pointed out a row of tall pillars on the other side of the square. 'That must have been a court house or senate.'

Carab nodded, then pointed out a ruin nearby, 'And that was possibly the baths.'

The outlines of sunken pools could just be made out in the snowdrifts, and the occasional low broken pillar protruded from the ground.

We walked across the whole square, leaving a twin trail of footprints over the otherwise pure white blanket of snow. As we reached the other side, we approached the low remains of a building that still had a few rooms standing, and had a dark doorway in front of us. I slowly stepped up to the doorway, and stopped just at the lintel.

'What's that smell?' I asked Carab as I turned to look at him.

Carab sniffed and said, 'Bear.'

'Oh,' I replied. 'Best not go in then.'

We continued on our way, and followed an ancient street down to where the docks had once been. There wasn't much left standing, although the large stone bollards still stood in neat rows where ships had once tied up. The edge of the forest was quite close by, and I got a quick glimpse of something diving off into the snow when it spotted us.

'This is a real nature ramble,' I said. 'I think that was a mountain lion.'

Carab nodded wisely and said, 'We should head back now.'

I agreed, and we circled back to the castle, which was easy to spot, on the other side of town, as it was by far the tallest structure left standing.

The very next day, Boris, Carab and I went out on a very successful hunting trip and as we walked back to town, the three of us discussed many things, and soon the conversation turned to something close to all our minds. Noggish politics.

'I remember the name, Clak, who was he again?' I asked Carab.

Carab was the recognised authority on noggish affairs. He had made it his particular hobby while I was studying in Glamis.

'He was the clan lord of all the northern nogs.'

'And what happened to him?'

'Killed by Tup in the uprisings. Tup became known as Narf, during that time, or *crippled one*, after you had shot him.'

'Oh right, well, I'm all for equal opportunities in the work place. What about Jube? I remember Tup once saying that Zort was Jubes man.'

'Ah yes,' recalled Carab. 'There wasn't much love lost between Zort and Tup before the battle of Usak. Jube was the leader of the north nog Shaman, a really black hearted demon worshipper. It was him that was responsible for the renewed nog interest in blood rituals, and demon summoning. The giant and the dragon we saw at Loggarth are the direct results of his policies. He was assassinated last year, and Zort took his place.'

'Ok, that all makes sense. Mallonax's sources tie in with that. What about Chow?'

Carab nodded. 'The usurper.'

'Good,' joined in Boris. 'I don't understand all this at all, tell me about the usurper.'

'He was the leader of the southern nogs for a while. Originally it was thought that he controlled all of Fiarka, but it later seemed that he only controlled the east, while the west was controlled by supporters of the old, assassinated shah. The shah had controlled all of Fiarka, and after his death, several areas split off. There are vast areas of Fiarka further south that no one knows anything about, except that they are inhabited by even mightier noggish nations.'

'Blimey.'

'As far as I can see though, the nogs that once followed the usurper are now allied to the north nogs, under the joint control of Tup, who is now a national hero and head of all the clans, and Zort, more black hearted than Jube, is head of the shaman. They control both church and state now, and have mobilised every able bodied nog into a full on expansionist adventure. From the last reports I had heard, Foona was totally under their yoke. Tyra was putting up a spirited resistance, but was expected to fall. Obviously Bellavia is next in line. The mighty nog Diamond Sea fleet has been attacking and landing troops on Loggarth, obviously, and Borland, Eask, Tomsk, and Ferron.'

'It is terrible.' stated Boris.

'Maybe not though.' disagreed Carab. 'Kolopa was a mighty victory, especially in that it shows the nogs are not invincible. Zort and most likely Tup are here in Pechenga. If it has anything to do with me, they may well meet with a sticky end, eh Shiv?'

I laughed and agreed, 'They are a long way from home, and accidents happen.'

We returned from hunting with cheers and shouts of hurrah from the girls. I was glad to see Boris so happy again as well, he was a born nobleman hunter. The cold wasn't so bothersome in the lee of the bay either, and although snow lay thick on the surrounding forests, there was no wind. Between the three of us, we had bagged a deer, some sort of elk creature, and a brace of seals. They were being carried in by the packhorses. There was going to be a real meat feast tonight. According to Carabs best guess, the gort didn't come this far north maybe because this area was sacred to them, which was the reason for there being so much game.

In the days that followed we made haste to gather as much food and supplies as we could before the night descended for a whole month.

About three days after we had first arrived, all the preparations for the casting of my spell were in place. I had carved out a pentagram on the south-facing slope of a small hill in the middle of town. I had my candles ready, and we had erected a stone doorway in front of the pentagram out of fallen masonry. There was plenty of fuel for fires from the forest, which had grown over half of the city, which was just as well, as we were getting less and less daylight now. Soon we would get the five days of darkness that I required. I felt so sad at the idea at leaving everyone behind, but I was almost doing somersaults with excitement at the idea of going home. The others would all have to winter here as well, there was nothing to do about that. The return journey would be utterly impossible until next spring. As Apic helped me gather wood for the last of the large pyres around the site, I considered what it would be like for me when, or if, I got back. Would I be able to remember who I was, and whether I had had a family or not? Would I be able to fit back into normal society again, or would I just be too insane? After all, I thought, with everything I had seen and done, there must be part of me that was seriously unhinged. I supposed I would be like a disillusioned Vietnam veteran returning from the war. Another thing that interested me was whether or not I would retain my magic abilities. It made me smile to think of all the things I could get up to if I did.

'What is amusing you?' asked Apic, as he dragged a large piece of wood up the hill and put it down beside me.

'Just thinking,' I replied. 'You know we have no magic in my world.'

'No magic? But the aeroplanes, and televisions and toasters?'

'I've explained this to you before Apic. That is technology, not magic.'

'Ah, yes yes,' agreed Apic and smiled. 'What will the be the first thing that you do when you get back?'

I sighed and stretched, looking up at the darkening sky, 'Smoke a cigarette. Eat a burger. No, go to a supermarket, and get some decent food! Although that's a total fallacy to be honest. Up here we have been eating so well on free range meat, organic vegetables, everything natural and pure, and all I can think about is Diet Coke and pork pies.'

Apic smiled at me dumbly, following little of what I was talking about. I continued, 'It's funny how much of it I don't miss anymore. Sometimes I wonder why it is I want to go back at all. How long has it been now? Three years? Nearly three years. I wonder how much things have changed in that time. If I have friends and family back there, they will all think I am dead. I can go and visit my grave.'

Apic nodded, and stood with his hands on his hips, considering the large pile of wood before us. He looked up and winced at the sky.

'Here comes the snow again,' he said.

'Yeah, come on then, lets go back in, that's enough for one day.'

As we trudged back towards the castle, Apic said, 'I will miss you, Shiv.'

I clapped him on the shoulder and said, 'Well, I can't wait to see the back of your ugly face! No, that's what I mean. All my friends are here now. What have I really go to go back for?'

'I don't know, ' stated Apic sagely. 'But I know Tullis is my home, no matter how far I travel, I will always go back. You can't fight it.'

'I guess not.'

Then I ran out of excuses to stay. It was the fifth night of darkness, and the ritual was ready to be performed.

So I said goodbye to the horses, and by torch light we went up to the hill in a sombre procession. I lit the candles and opened my spell book, and began to read the long magical passages that would cleanse the pentagram of evil spirits, and prepare it for the ritual.

The others settled down to sit on some of the bigger logs by the large fire, and passed round some of yesterday's soup.

The first stages of the ritual took several hours, and I was beginning to get very cold from standing around in the permanent night. Out to sea, we could hear a storm beginning to brew, and far, far off in the distance, tiny flashes, as lightning moved through the clouds.

I also noticed my audience was beginning to get a trifle bored, but eventually it got to the most interesting bit. With a flourish I waved at the makeshift gate we had erected from ancient masonry and a flat log for the lintel, and a wavering flowing light illuminated it. The portal suddenly dazzled our eyes as it was created, in shining blues and yellows, like an old-fashioned tele blinking into life.

Everyone went, 'Ahh...'.

Thunder rolled high over the sea.

'Cosmic,' I said.

I glanced back at the others. This is it, I thought, the portal is open, all I have to do is step into it. It will close behind me, and I will be catapulted back to my world. Suddenly I just didn't have the heart to do it. Again, I looked back at the others as they all gazed at me expectantly.

Then I noticed something move in the background. I strained to see what it was and then, sending a bolt of ice down my spine, came a deep rumbling voice from the shadows behind a ruin.

'Ah, but don't go just yet!'

Two incredibly tall figures stepped forward and from the shimmering pale light of the portal I made them out as Zort and Tup. Zort was wearing a black robe, crusted with blood and ripped at the seams. Tup had a streak of white in his hair, and one of his arms was obviously useless. He didn't look like he'd had a good day recently either.

Other figures began to emerge from the ruins, stumbling and walking in a disjointed manner.

'My army,' stated Zort, smiling. 'If you can call it that. The gods have granted me certain powers, to help me regain their brother. One of them is the ability to reanimate the dead.'

The figures shambled forward, dead nogs and gorts, in terrible states of decay. We all flinched backwards, edging towards the castle. There seemed to be hundreds of them, some of them looked like they had died very recently, but some looked like they had been exhumed from icy graves that they had been in for centuries.

'This is it, human. This night, the ten shall be reunited.'

'Ok, Zort, now listen for just a second, I have one thing to say,' I said, holding my finger up, making him stop.

'Run for it!' I cried, then cursed as I realised I had no more magical energies left, it had all been spent on opening the portal. I joined my companions in a mad dash back to the castle.

'What do you intend to do?' panted Apic as he ran along beside me.

'How should I know? Why does everyone always think I have the answer?' I rushed into the main hallway and Carab and Boris barred our makeshift door just as the zombies started to hammer on it.

'Bloody night of the living dead,' I gasped, as we ran down the corridor. It didn't look like the door would hold them for long, arms were already beginning to break through the ancient rotten wood.

'We should get to the horses,' I said, as we gathered up some of our stuff from the living room in the rear of the castle. 'If they get to them, we've had it.'

I took up my sword, and went to the door to check that the coast was clear. I could hear groans and moans from down the corridor, but it was still empty.

Carab barged past me, and said, 'I will hold them here for a little while.'

I nodded at him, and ran off in the direction of the stables. I could hear the others following behind me. Over the sound of my panting breath and my thumping heart, I also heard the sound of groaning up ahead at the bend in the corridor. Suddenly a large group of zombies came cascading round the corner towards us. In desperation I tried the nearest door, and leapt into the dark room that lay behind it.

The room was waist deep in snow, and I waded desperately through it to get to the other side, where there was a large hole in the wall, exposing the room to the elements. I charged through the snow as fast as I could, and I could feel Adea's hands on my back as she stumbled against me. Then something gave way under my next step, and I slipped down about a foot, landing with my face in the snow. Adea landed right on top of me, and I felt something else give way, and together we fell into the darkness in a shower of icy snow.

I could hear Adea's voice, it sounded a long way off. I felt as if I was being gently rocked. She seemed to be upset about something.
'Please wake up Shiv! I'm sorry I landed on your head. Please wake up!'
My ears popped and sound rushed in. I then realised Adea's shouting was unbearably loud, and that she was shaking me. I gathered up the stray strands of my consciousness, and said, 'Ok, ok, I'm here. What happened?'
'We fell through the floor.'
'Where are the others?'
'I know not,' Adea seemed utterly terrified.
I looked around, it was very dark, but I could just make out the chamber we were in. I got a shock as I realised the room was full of silent, motionless figures. Then my pounding heart subsided a little as I saw we were in another chamber for storing the old suits of armour.
I tried to look up, but my neck exploded in pain, and I groaned and nearly passed out again.
Adea grabbed my arm and said, 'We have to get out of here.'
I could hear the sounds of violence in the distance. Groans, cries, crashes and smashes. A symphony of destruction I had heard too many times before.
'Yes,' I agreed, and clutching my head I stumbled off in a random direction. My eyes began to adjust a little to the light, there were several holes in the ceiling, and faint starlight illuminated this large chamber. There seemed to be hundreds of suits of old rusty armour down here. The people of Pik Sedova were really big on their armour I decided. Maybe this castle had been an arsenal or something.
We stumbled on in the gloom, Adea clutched tightly to my arm. Soon we reached a wall, and I chose a direction to follow it in. It rounded a corner, and I saw a set of steps leading up out of the cold stone chamber. There was even a light at the top, illuminating the top of the stairs. I tried to fit where we were into the map of the castle in my head. Somewhere near the old kitchens I thought. What was that light then?
Cautiously we went up the steps, Adea still digging her nails into my arm. We entered a small stone, windowless chamber that was lit by some seemingly magical source. The only feature of the room was a raised dais with a single suit of armour positioned on top of it. The orange light in the room made it glow a rich gold colour. For the first time I noticed there were runes carved on the walls, so I went over to have a look.
'What does it say?' whispered Adea behind me.
'I don't know. I recognise the runes, but they are... it's like trying to read Chaucer's English.'

After about five minutes, Adea was slightly less terrified, and she became more like herself again as she said, 'Shiv, we can't just hang around down here, while everyone else is in trouble.'

'Shh...' I waved at her, not taking my eyes off the runes. 'Listen, these aren't suits of armour at all.'

'What are they?' she asked, stepping closer to me and looking at the runes.

I turned to her and said, 'They are golems.'

'Oh,' she gasped, then realising she didn't know what I meant, she said, 'Which are?'

'Golems. Automatons like Dombaba. Animated metal shells. We are in the animation chamber.'

'Very good Shiv, but... oh!' she exclaimed, as realisation dawned on her, 'Can you make them come alive?'

'That's what I'm reading about.'

Another five minutes passed and Adea was sitting on the dais when I next looked up.

'Listen to this... to bring life to the grand armee, stryke the plate of the soldier in the animation chamber. Blah..blah..blah..Stryke with the key. If the key is destroyed, stryke with the token.... Blah..blah...blah, the token, is any item imbued with mystical powers.'

'What?'

'We need an enchanted item. And we don't. Shit.'

Some sort of item with a magical field of energy was require for the activation, if only I had some of my mystical resources remaining, but it had all been used on the gate and I would have no more until the next day. I cursed, realising that I had just been wasting my time down here, 'Come on, we better get out of here.'

I grabbed Adea, and started to drag her back to the stairs, then she screamed right in my ear,

'My broach!'

'Ach,' I cried. 'You nearly burst my eardrum!'

'My brooch? You made it magical on my birthday remember?' gasped Adea, as she undid it from her tunic. 'Will that do?'

'God yes!' I cried, as I took it from her, and went over to the armour on the podium.

'I'd totally forgotten about that.' I looked at the breastplate of the armour. There was a small indentation, about the size of a silver coin above the heart. Without any more thought I pressed the small broach to the hole. The hole took it and held it in place.

Nothing happened.

I looked at Adea and gave her a little shrug.

Adea said, 'Is it getting lighter in here?'

I glanced around. It was, the light was getting brighter and less orange. Suddenly the ground shook, and it felt like the room was moving. There was a grinding sound below us. A portcullis slammed down by the entrance to the stairs, sealing us in.

'Oh,' I said.

Stones began to fall from the walls, and it seemed as if the whole room was disintegrating. There was another shudder, and it felt as if we were moving upwards. Adea's fear returned, and she clutched at me again. I was no less terrified. The plaster of the ceiling came down in one large lump and broke around us as we cowered by the dais. It felt as if the room was being pushed right up and out of the castle. Suddenly, the whole thing lurched to a halt, and we were almost knocked from our feet, as more stonework fell away around us. Through the masonry dust I could see the stars, and I could feel the night breeze on my face. Gradually the grinding sounds below stopped, and the last of the rear wall fell over into the night behind us. I doubted if the original designers had intended the room to fall to bits every time it was elevated, but here we were regardless, alive if not necessarily well. I looked at Adea and wondered if I was as dusty looking as she was. Slowly we stood up.

'Well done, Shiv,' grumbled Adea, brushing dust from her clothes.

'I wasn't expecting that to happen!' I cried.

We were right at the top of the castle, on the last remains of an observation tower of some kind. Below us, in the ruins of the town I could see the portal and the big fires around it. I could just make out two shadowy figures that I presumed were Zort and Tup. Everywhere else I could see the undead army wandering about. There was a set of ancient stone steps leading down from the tower top to the courtyard here. Just as I was considering this as a way of getting down, there was a grinding metallic sound behind us and I looked around to see, to my amazement, the suit of armour step down from the dais. We stepped back in wonder, as it ponderously walked past us, and started to go down the stairs.

As we watched in utter disbelief, more golems began to come out of the castle, and with their rusty swords and axes engage the zombie army in battle.

I tried to take as little part in the battle as possible as I looked around the castle for the others.

The golems were all covered in rust, and each movement drew out a strangled metallic shriek that cried out for an oil can.

Everywhere, the golems and the zombies were fighting, but the undead didn't stand a chance. The golems that still carried weapons cut off limbs and heads with a slow surgical precision, while unarmed ones simply battered away with their fists. The zombies' only tactic was to rush a single golem and try to claw it to the ground and then pull it to bits. I watched many a combat like this, waiting for it to end before I could move on. Sometimes the golem would be pulled to pieces and then the spark of life that was in it would be lost. More often than not, however, the golem would batter them back, and continue to fight, even if it was missing an arm or a leg.

Adea was with me at all times, as we rushed from one hiding place in the dark to the next.

I spotted Carab and Apic over by the portal, I had no idea how they had ended up back up there, but I decided it would be best if we tried to make our way over to them. Breaking from cover I made for a nearby ruined wall, and followed it into town. Crouched down in the dark Adea following close in behind me.

There seemed to be hundreds of animated bodies moving around in the dark. The battle was strange, as it was so silent. Neither the corpses nor the golems made a cry as they knocked pieces off each other.

Eventually I joined the others by the portal.

'Let me guess,' said Apic. 'The suits of armour were your work.'

'Me and Adea,' then seeing his confusion I said, 'I'll explain later.'

I looked around in the dark, I think everyone was here. There seemed to be a lot of zombies around. We all had our swords drawn to fend back the ones that got too close.

'Oh no,' I groaned as I spotted Zort at the base of the hill. Each time he pointed his staff at a golem, a bolt of lightning charged from it, and struck it, sending its component parts flying in all directions with a terrible crash. He and Tup strode further up the hill and everywhere Zort saw a fallen zombie, he pointed his staff at it, and it would rise up wearily to do his bidding again. If it was missing a leg it would hobble along behind him, and if it had no legs it would simply pull itself along, its entrails dragging behind.

As they got closer, Zort shouted at us, 'Don't think I am stupid enough to cast a spell in your direction, pestilential human!'

He motioned his army forward, 'Kill them all!'

The next few minutes were a very confused and desperate melee. I tried to draw my gun, to get a shot off at either of the nogs, but I was far too busy defending myself. I couldn't see what the others were up to, as I hacked and slashed at the advancing zombies all around us. It was a total confusion of sword blows, snarls and claws. Luckily they were not the greatest fighters in the world, but they had strength of numbers and a dogged determination. Zombies that had been struck to the floor still tried to bite at my legs. I cut at them as they advanced and pushed us back to the portal, a great wave of undead flesh. Things were beginning to look a little desperate.

I could see Zort and Tup in the background, looks of grim satisfaction on their faces because they thought they had won. In a short break in the combat I had a chance to have a quick look round at the others. I had no idea were Boris was, Apic was unconscious and covered in blood, oh my god I thought, so much blood. I could hear and feel the thing in my head screaming to be let out. Carab was still at my side, battered and bloody. Adea seemed to be in a state of shock, I think one of the things had bitten her leg. Temina still held her rapier, but didn't have much energy left to wield it. We were ringed in, with out backs to the portal. Another group of zombies rushed at us, and Carab stepped forward to meet them, and started to chop them down in a business like fashion. I could no longer count on spell casting, so I gripped my sword, and once more leapt into the fray. I could see Zort was preparing a spell, a summoning spell I thought, judging from his hand gestures. Behind them I could still see golems battling the undead army. I hoped they would get to us in time.

The zombies began to fall to the ground as Zort drew in magical energy for his spell, and not a second too soon for me, as I had had three zombies clawing me to the ground.

I quickly tried to draw my gun, but I couldn't get a clear shot as a great cloud of sulphurous smoke puffed up in front of Zort, and suddenly there was a huge ten-foot demon, with horns three feet long charging towards us roaring. It seemed to be crying 'I come for you brother!' as it pushed the undead around it aside to get to us, although it was a little difficult to make out as it tried to articulate around all the teeth that were in its mouth.

'Right, that's it! Into the portal everyone!' I cried and picking up Apic I bodily hurled him into the light. I started to push Temina and Adea towards it too.

'Go!' shouted Carab, 'I will hold this thing off!'

Adea was sucked into the portal, I saw her screaming as she went. Where was Temina?

A huge claw flashed out, and raked across Carab's body, spraying me with blood. Carab was flung backwards, and his body crashed into me, violently throwing us both into the portal.

After that it all went dark.

Chapter Twenty - The Weston General

Dr. Lock stormed down the ramp from DCN and into the ECNO office. Every one glanced around at her. Sara, who had been working at her desk, looked up and said, 'Heather, what is it?'

'They are going to operate on Yarn.'

'When?'

'Tonight, at ten past midnight.'

'Oh shit,' exclaimed Sara.

Mark looked up from his paper work and said, 'How on earth did they get permission?'

'They didn't. Hood is quoting some sort of emergency surgery laws. I think he just made them up.'

'But Heather,' Sara said, trying to calm her friend. 'Perhaps it is for the best, you know…'

'It's after five,' interrupted Dr. Lock. 'You shouldn't even be here. Come with me and I'll show you something.'

Sara saw that she wasn't going to win any arguments with Heather tonight, so she got out of her chair and started to put on her coat. Mark, who had been checking the West Ham fixture list on the internet, stood up and said, 'Can I come?'

Heather led then out of the office, and up the stairs to Ward 10. She strode over to the nurse's station on the long central corridor of the ward and rapped on the glass to get the attention of those inside. As the woman on the desk looked up, Sara and Mark arrived, jogging to keep up.

'Well, where is he?' said Dr. Lock to the ward sister.

'Who?' said the sister looking up from her paper work.

'The man in room seven.'

'If you mean the young polish gentleman, he discharged himself last night. A young lady came to pick him up.'

'Shit,' cried Heather, turning to the others. 'I need to get to the Royal, you've got a car haven't you Mark?'

'Sure. Who are we looking for?' he asked as they walked quickly back down from the ward to the out patients exit.

'The guy in a coma, the polish guy. I talked to Susan, apparently quite short, had a goatee beard.'

Mark smiled and clicked his fingers, 'You think that was Apic!'

Heather paused and looked at him, 'You seem to know an awful lot about this.'

Mark shrugged, 'Sorry Heather, it's been right round the office.'

'Well, I know you all think I've gone insane, but being insane is far better than the alternative, believe me.'

It took about fifteen tense minutes for Mark to drive the two women across town to the Royal Infirmary. At the Surgical entrance Heather leapt out of the car, and was off down the corridor to the ward were the young man with the claw wounds had been. Mark shrugged and abandoned his car at the door, then he and Sara followed after the doctor.

'You can't go in there, it's the recovery room!' declared the chubby ward sister as they all barged past her. The patient had not been in his room, but a kind nurse had directed them to him. They entered the small dimly lit recovery room.

A large well-muscled man lay on the bed, bare at the waist except for bandages.

Mark hustled the sister out of the room and Heather approached the bed, and trying to calm down a little said,

'How are you feeling?'

'Not too bad, Doctor,' replied the young man in a strong Scandinavian accent.

'This is crazy,' said Sara, tugging at Heather's coat. 'You've put this all together in your own head.'

'It all fits Sara! Just let me talk to him,' she replied, then addressed the young man.

'Do you remember your name?'

'Of course, my name is Carab, son of Carris.'

Sara took a step back, and said, 'You have got to be joking!'

About an hour later Sara found herself sitting in Adea's flat in the Grassmarket listening to Adea speak. She looked at Mark, he seemed to be in a state of shock, which wasn't far away from how Sara felt herself. Apic was here too, and Carab, although pale, was standing by the window drinking a glass of water. He had a black shirt on over his bandages, but he moved very slowly as he put his glass down on the windowsill. Adea said her flat mates were out for the night.

'It was weird at first, especially for me, as I never really learned English properly, I am sorry, I always associated it with dirtiness.'

Apic laughed and Carab smiled.

'But Shiv had talked and talked at such great length about his home, that it was almost as if I had been here before. The attention to details he had been... you know. I had a flat in a week. I have a job in a shop on Cockburn Street.'

'Incredible,' said Heather.

'Crazy,' said Mark. 'It took me three months to get a flat in Edinburgh!'

Adea shrugged, 'I told a lot of lies, you require so much paper work in this land! But I had a few Jews that I sold which helped me get started.'

'Jewels, not Jews,' smiled Carab. 'This land is as I imagined it, full of fat merchants. Anyone can make their way here. That there are beggars on Princess Street I cannot understand.'

Sara seemed to be convinced she was in a dream. Or perhaps this was all some sort of elaborate hoax? Perhaps Jeremy Beadle was about to jump out and stick a microphone in her face.

'It took me a small time to be finding Carab.' continued Adea. 'And more to find Apic, I knew they were injured, so I was to be looking in the hospitals. I could not find Shiv.'

'He is at the Weston. Listen,' said Heather. 'If a surgeon operates on him to remove the thing in his head, what will happen?'

'I have no idea, what do you think will happen?' asked Adea.

'Shit, lets go.'

As they all got into Mark's car, a tight fit for a Peugeot 205, Sara broke out of the daze she had been in and addressed Heather,

'What are you going to do?'

'Stop the operation. By force if need be.'

'You really can't all come in here!' said an orderly, as they invaded the operating theatre en masse. 'There is an operation taking place right now!'

'I was told it wouldn't be until after midnight, it's only ten, what's going on?'

'I really don't know... oof!' the orderly said, as Carab shouldered him out the way.

Operating theatres usually have four or more main areas, divided into two sections, the outer section, which has changing rooms for the male and female staff, to change into their theatre blues and white clogs, prior to entering the inner section, where the scrub up area and the operating theatre itself are. To enter the inner area in your outdoor cloths is an act tantamount to sacrilege. The theatres were always kept immaculately clean.

Despite this, Heather walked purposefully up the short corridor to the operating theatre and threw aside the set of swing doors at its top. She entered the operating theatre, the others close behind her.

On the table, a body lay, almost entirely covered in blue sheets, with a small square opening over the top of the head. Sat on a chrome stool beside the opening, with a bloody scalpel in his hand was Hood, dressed in the hospitals blue theatre pyjamas, and wearing a cap and facemask. A large multi-bulbed theatre light was angled right in at the incision. Besides the patient and the surgeon, there was an anaesthetist and two nurses.

Mr. Hood looked up from Yarn's open head.

'What the hell are you doing in here?' demanded the surgeon as he stood up.

The two nurses and the anaesthetist looked at them in stunned silence.

'Stop that right now Terry.'

'For god's sake Heather, this is an operating theatre, who are all these people?'

Suddenly one of the nurses shrieked, 'Doctor!'

'What? Bloody hell!' Dr. Hood gasped as he looked back down at Yarn's open skull. There was something wriggling in it. Something sloppy flopped out onto the floor and scuttled off under a table.

Carab picked up a mop and slowly advanced toward it. Dr. Hood sat down on the floor. One nurse screamed and the other fled for a door.

Dr. Lock went over to the operating table and picked up the piece of skull in the kidney dish beside Yarns head. With little ceremony she pressed it back into place like the last piece of a jigsaw, and removing the clamps around his head, folded the bits of shaved flesh back into place over it. She quickly bandaged the whole thing up, and then turning to Apic said, 'Let's get him out of here.'

Something slithered out from the table and Carab nearly got it with one of his boots. It shot into the air and exploded on a wall, where it started to smoulder and sizzle.

'By the prophet's fiery beard! I don't like that at all!' cried Apic as they all hurriedly left the theatre.

Mr. Hood knelt in front of the sizzling wall, in utter disbelief. Everyone else had wisely vacated the theatre, but he continued to look up at the wall, his light breathing barely enough to make his surgical mask flutter. The sizzling green gloop grew larger and larger until it all flopped to the floor in one big splat, a few droplets of which landed on Hoods forehead making him blink. The blob grew larger and larger, and went darker, until it was a deep rich red colour.

Bubbling and spitting this mass started to pile up on top of itself, like lava flowing backwards, until it was towering right up to the ceiling.

Distinguishable limbs started to form, and other features began to be defined as the substance ran and bubbled into itself.

Then there was a demon standing there, smoke rising from its shoulders. It looked exactly how Yarn had described it weeks ago. Over ten-foot tall, with broad shaggy arms and the last of the gloop running down its bare muscle bound chest. It stamped on the floor with a cloven hoof, as if trying to get rid of a cramp and turned to examine its surroundings. As it slowly turned around, Hood got a good look at its horse skull head which had two huge horns, each at least four feet long, curved out from the front of its face, both of which looked as if they could gore a man in half with one toss of the beast's head. Its skin was a deep dark red colour, and shaggy hair covered most of its lower body and forearms. The room was filling with a nasty sulphurous smoke, which rose from the demon, and made Hood give a little startled cough. This caused the demon to notice him for the first time, and it looked down at him curiously.

Hood returned its look, but flinched as the demon suddenly lowered its head right down to his for a closer inspection.

'Thank you,' said the demon, its voice sounded like a composite of a hundred heavy smokers all talking in unison, while being tortured in the lowest pits of hell. Played backwards. At low speed.

If Mr. Hood hadn't been driven totally insane already, then the sound of the beast's voice would have been enough.

'For what?' replied Hood in a whisper.

'For releasing me.'

Hood whimpered slightly as a great clawed hand came towards him.

Heather and some of the others got Yarn to the ECNO, and she injected something into him, which she hoped would wake him up. Just as she was doing that, there was an almighty crash from DCN further up the corridor, and the sound of breaking glass. Somewhere an alarm went off. A head popped around the door and shouted, 'What the fuck was that?' and then disappeared again.

'Get him on the table,' said Heather. Mark and Apic lifted the limp body onto one of the computer operator's desks. 'Where is Sara?'

'I dunno, halfway to Glasgow probably. When we came in here, she kept on running down the corridor,' muttered Mark, who had a crazed look on his face.

Suddenly there was a terrific boom, making the room shudder and then a series of long drawn out screams.

Mark picked up a phone from the secretary's desk and dialled.

'Police please,' he said, glancing round the main door and up the ramp corridor. He saw the huge red demon, crashing though the fire doors, knocking them off their hinges.

It had a white sleeved bloody arm in one hand and the remains of a wheelchair in the other, which it hurled down the corridor. Once it had done that, it suddenly bounded into a loping run, its hooves cutting great gouges out of the vinyl with each mighty stride, and its knife sized claws carving lines in the walls and windows.

Mark shut the door and locked it.

'Fuck. In. Hell.' he said and dropped the phone.

Meanwhile, the others were trying to rouse Yarn.

'Come on Shiv wake up!' cried Adea.

Apic decided now would be a good time to try and shake him.

'Wake up Shiv, you motherless son of a…!'

'Are you crazy? Stop that!' cried Heather, grabbing Apic off Yarn's limp body. 'He's got a bit of his head loose for Christ's sake!'

Yarn groaned and his eyes popped open. Everyone started to babble at him all at once.

'Yarn, there is a demon running around in the hospital! It came out your head! What can you do!? Shiv, do something!' everyone seemed to be saying, all at once.

Yarn tried to roll over, and said, 'I'm going back to sleep.'

'No! No! Wake up!' screamed Heather.

Yarn tried to crawl across the desk and hide behind a monitor. Outside the office, the demon crashed down the corridor, obviously finding another victim outside the canteen if the screams were anything to go by.

'Wake up Yarn dam you, it's eating the catering staff!'

'God, all right then,' said Yarn sliding off the desk and standing up. He put his hand to his temple, and nearly collapsed on the floor, 'Jesus, my head.'

'Please be ok, please get up,' pleaded Heather.

Yarn tried to stand fully erect, then shambled over to the door and unlocked it. Opening the door, he looked down the South Corridor at the trail of destruction left by the demon. There were huge racking marks in the walls from its claws and in the ceiling from its horns. There was a decapitated body of a woman wearing a blue tabard on the floor. There was a lot of noise and blood was everywhere, as if the demon had been indulging in some gruesome finger painting.
Yarn stumbled off down the corridor in a lurching run.

From the south corridor, the demon crashed through the doors and up the steps to the staff canteen. It took down most of the wall as it entered the single wooden door. There were a few people in here, all alerted by the noise, and terrified to almost insanity. The demon bellowed a laugh and hurled the severed arm it held at the nearest person. It picked up a table and threw it out a window, before exploding through the till area and into the kitchens sending food flying everywhere. Someone bolted past it, and in a flash the demon cut him in two with one of its mighty claws. Bloody gushed everywhere, and swept across the floor, making the women cowering behind one of the work benches scream. The demon slipped on the blood slick it had created, and in a manner that would have been comedic in any other being, crashed through the kitchen. Shouldering right into a wall, it pushed it over into the porter's office and brought down a large chunk of Ward 10 from above. A bed started to fall from the ward and a stunned patient fell near to the demon, who picked him up and hurled him out the window. As the demon left the kitchen, it kicked over an oven that caused a large explosion once the gas from the ruptured gas main hit a pilot light. From there it headed through the porters office and into the link corridor. It picked up a large steel food trolley and hurled it at someone who dodged out of the way and into a lift just in time. Cursing in a good-humoured sort of way, and chortling to itself, a sound like a gurgling drain, the demon continued down the south corridor towards main oncology. Down the hill it strode, clawing at anyone who was foolish enough to step in its way. An elderly and apparently very deaf WRVS woman was closing the shutter to the small shop at the bottom of the corridor, and as she turned around and caught a glance of the demon, she dropped dead of a heart attack.
The demon contented itself with hurling furniture through windows for a while, and then spotting some doctors making a break for it down the corridor, it ran straight through the oncology doors, breaking them off their hinges and sending masonry falling everywhere. It swept a fleeing doctor off his feet and smeared him against the wall. Another dove round the bend in the corridor but fell over an abandoned notes trolley. Desperately he got up, just as his friends corpse was flung at him. The last thing he saw was a cloven hoof descending towards his head.
Seeing no more immediate victims the demon knocked down a wall to get through to a small conference room, then battered straight through the

glass of the wall to wall windows and jumped down into the car park. It landed on the roof of a Range Rover, then leapt to the ground and scooped up a BMW that had a frantic doctor in it. The demon lifted the car above its head and flung it over the roof of the hospital. The BMW landed somewhere around Ward 7.

Yarn and those others who were brave enough to follow him, followed the trail of destruction down to the main oncology department. Cautiously they stepped into the waiting room and looked out of the automatic doors at the demon. It was continuing its game of throwing cars through the second story ward windows. There had already been some loud explosions, and fires were beginning to do serious damage to the hospital.
Yarn leant in the doorway and caught his breath.
'Hey!' he called at the demon.
The demon had a car poised over its head, but it slowly put it down and turned towards Yarn. The others cowered behind the seats in the waiting room.
'Yes?' said the demon. It's voice sounded like a hundred records being played simultaneously backwards at too slow a speed.
'What do you think your doing?'
The demon seemed to be puzzled by the question, 'I have been stuck inside your cursed head for two years,' it grumbled. 'I am having fun.'
'Not here you don't.'
The demon laughed, like the scream of a thousand lost souls, 'And what do you propose to do about that?'
'As you said. You were with me for two years; don't you think I haven't learned a little about you? We have been closer than brothers for all that time. I probably know more about you than my own father. You see,' said Yarn. 'I have remembered your name.'

'Oh,' sighed the demon in resignation, kicking at the crushed car beside its feet like a discarded toy. Maybe it couldn't make up its mind whether to run for it, or to attack Yarn, as it stood motionlessly. To do one, seemed to go against its destructive urges and to do the other would risk going back to wherever it had been after the first time it had attacked Yarn, or Shiv rather, way back in Che.
Yarn raised his arms and light started to gather around him. Deep shadows began to form around him as more and more sparkling light formed over his head and arms. Everyone else cowered lower behind the waiting room chairs, as a high wind started to whip around him and he channelled more and more magical energy towards himself. He started to chant in a low monotone at first, but as the shrieking of the wind grew louder and louder, he needed to shout to be heard. The demon stood motionlessly in apprehension as Yarn completed his bellowed chant and finally shouted, 'Be gone Agotahl!'

The demon shrieked as dark tendrils began to form around its feet. They crept up his legs, and held it firmly to the spot, rendering it immobile. The demon cursed and spat as it tried to break free, first trying to lift one leg, then the other, like a man trying to struggle out of a mire. Gradually the tendrils began to work their way up to its waste, and the enraged bellows of the demon grew louder. It ripped at the tendrils with its claws, but only succeeded in pinning down its left arm. It suddenly stopped struggling, as if resigned to its fate.

Then it started laughing.

'Maybe I will take some company with me!' and it reached out its right arm. Yarn's feet lifted off the ground and he was drawn slowly through the air towards the demon.

Behind him Heather cried, 'No!' and rushed over to grab him.

'No Heather, don't touch me!'

There was a blinding flash and for a moment it was as if the world stood still. Carab, despite his injuries was rushing towards Yarn and Heather, to try and help, although he knew not how. Apic and Adea were crouched behind a row of seats in the waiting room, sheltering from the in-rushing light and energy. Mark had been blown flat on his back by the magical forces at work and dazed, all he could do was watch the unfolding drama. As white light filled the area, seeing became very difficult and everyone was suddenly alone in silence, even the screams from elsewhere in the hospital were no longer heard.

If there had been anyone to witness what happened next they would have seen the intense light suddenly revealing the car park and waiting room again. Air rushed in, in a sudden gust and sound returned. The cries of the terrified and injured mingled with the sounds of fire and destruction. The demon and many of the people who had tried to defeat it had vanished.

When Mark woke up, he could hear police sirens in the distance. He sat up and shook the broken window glass off himself. There was no sign of anyone else. A paramedic with a first aid bag rushed over to him and started bandaging his bleeding arm. Mark hadn't even noticed.

'Where is everyone else?' he asked.

The paramedic was speaking, but Mark couldn't hear him. There was a sudden pop in his ears and an inrush of air, and then the sound of sirens was suddenly deafening.

'... no fucking idea what happened here, mate. It's like fucking Hannibal Lector has been through the place. There must have been an explosion in the car park, there are cars everywhere!'

'Sorry,' interrupted Mark. 'I was with some people, a tall guy, a short guy and two women?'

'Just you mate. It always happens in the Weston, but this takes the fucking biscuit. We're going to have to move you now, we can't stay here, the whole place is on fire.'

The paramedic moved a stretcher into position beside him and said, 'Ready?'

Mark lay back and closed his eyes.

Heather woke up. She was warm, it felt like she was outside in the sun. Wincing, she rolled over onto her back, and propped herself up on her elbows. She had sand in her hair. Her eyes began to adjust to the bright light, she could hardly see a thing it was that dazzling.

She felt like she should say something like, 'Oh My God', as she realised she surely must be lying on the same tropical beach that Yarn had been marooned on all those years ago, but she suddenly didn't have the energy to do anything. She lay her head back down and groaned.

A little later she heard a voice beside her,

'Hey, you ok?'

She raised herself up again, and shielding her eyes from the sun with her hand, looked up at Yarn.

'I don't know. Your head?'

'Fine,' he said. He was just a silhouette, but she could see he was looking around, and scanning the shoreline, 'I cast a few healing spells on my head. I'm as high as a kite now.'

He paused for a moment, then offered her his hand, 'Want to get up?'

Reluctantly she took his hand and allowed herself to be hauled up to her feet.

For the first time she began to take in her surroundings. The beach was as Yarn had described it, weeks ago in the hospital. A pure white sandy strand, with the deep azure blue of the ocean and sky on one side, and the dark green depths of the jungle on the other.

The desire to say 'Oh My God' welled up in her again but for some reason she found it hard to say anything.

Yarn gave her a small smile, 'Feeling a bit weird?'

'You could say that,' she replied.

Yarn took her hand, and together they started to walk down the beach. Presently she took off her shoes, to let her bare feet enjoy the sensation of the warm sand.

THE END

Printed in Great Britain
by Amazon